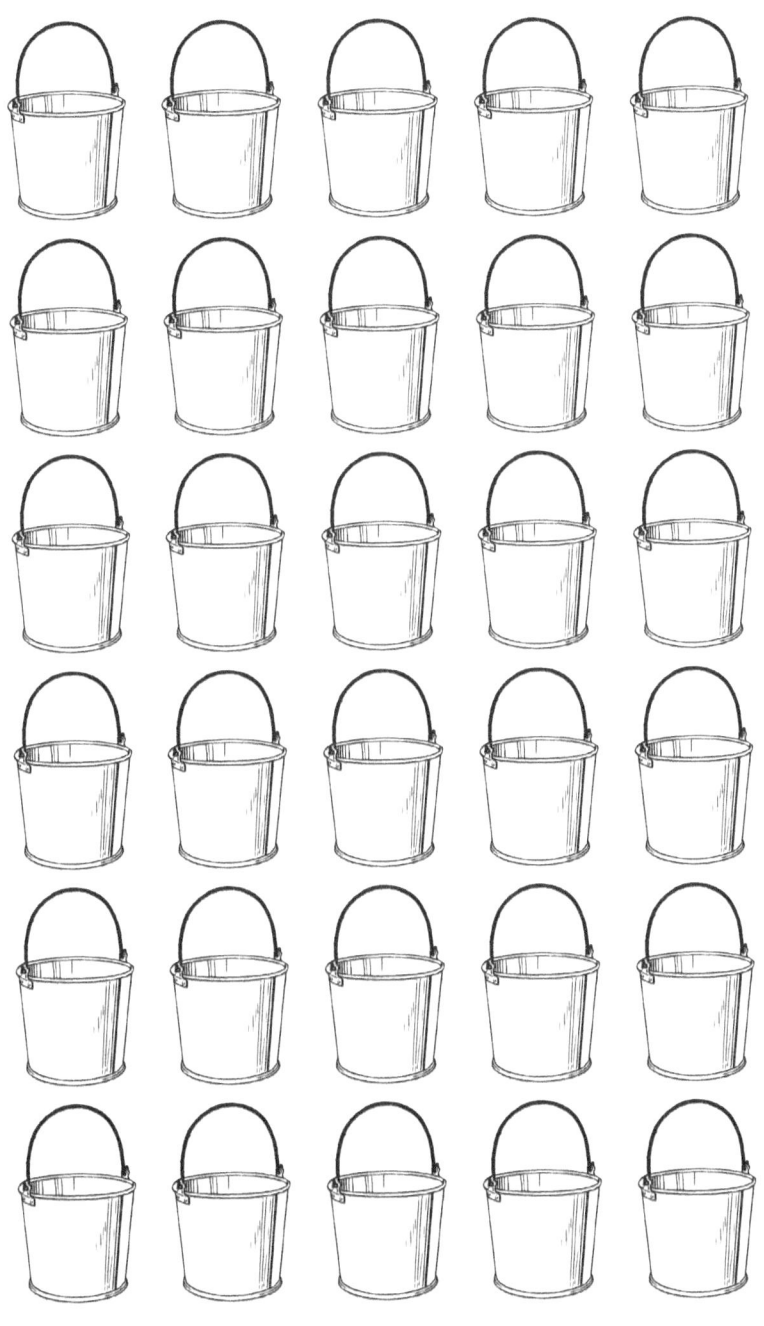

Pure Slush Books

January
February
March

2014

a Pure Slush compendium

First published December 2014
Edited by Matt Potter

Pure Slush Books
4 Warburton Street
Magill SA 5072
Australia
Email: edpureslush@live.com.au
Website: http://pureslush.webs.com
Visit the Pure Slush Store: http://pureslush.webs.com/store.htm

Front cover photograph copyright © Jonathan Hillis

ISBN: 978-1-925101-33-1

Pure Slush proudly features (both online and in print) writers from all over the English-speaking world. Some speak and write English as their first language, while for others, it's their second or third or even fourth language. Naturally, across all versions of English, there are differences in punctuation and spelling, and even in meaning. These differences are reflected in the stories *Pure Slush* publishes, and it accounts for any differences in punctuation, spelling and meaning found within these pages.

stories by

Guilie Castillo Oriard

Townsend Walker

Derek Osborne

Gloria Garfunkel

John Wentworth Chapin

Lynn Beighley

Andrew Stancek

Rachel Ambrose

Gill Hoffs

Susan Tepper

Jessica McHugh

Shane Simmons

Michelle Elvy

Len Kuntz

Michael Webb

James Claffey

Gwendolyn Joyce Mintz

Stephen V. Ramey

Gay Degani

Sally—Anne Macomber

Mandy Nicol

Margaret Bingel

Darryl Price

Teresa Burns Gunther

Matt Potter

Gary Percesepe

Nathaniel Tower

Kimberlee Smith

Vanessa Weibler Paris

Joanne Jagoda

h. l. nelson

January

Wednesday, 1ˢᵗ January 2014

The Miracle of Small Things

by Guilie Castillo Oriard

There's no stillness like the stillness of Curaçao on New Year's Day. Pointless tropical sun on deserted asphalt, every business shuttered, everything forlorn. Not even trash stirs: the wind is on furlough too. There's also no New Year's Eve like Curaçao's, which might explain the stillness. But to Luis Villalobos it feels like the cold shoulder of the world.

Luis has just ruined his life.

He brakes for a red light even though his black Wrangler Rubicon is the only vehicle in sight. He's seen no one, not even on foot, since pulling out of Milena's carport. Feels surreal, a desolate dimension he's crossed into by accident. In a sense it is: utterly different from Mexico City, London, Hong Kong, anywhere else he's lived. But he isn't here by accident.

He was lured, away from the plum at the legendary Cabrera y Machado of Mexico City, to this tiny speck of land no one in the civilized world can or wants to find on a map, by the one−in−a−million carrot of replacing Milena as MD next year. Would've been just the start; Luis's ambitions know no limits. Apparently, his intelligence does.

He could've had his pick of sexy inebriated females last night; they all seemed to find him irresistible. Stepan told him to enjoy it, that new−kid−on−the−office−block popularity. "You single? Go for it, bicho. Won't last forever." Wearing his new colleague's permission like a groupie brandishing a backstage pass, Luis went for it. With the Managing Director of Ehrlich Fiduciary's Curaçao branch.

The boss.

Luis taps his forehead against the steering wheel – softly; a headache is already barreling down the helpless conduits between neurons. Even with the car's A/C at full blast, he catches whiffs of Milena's Carolina Herrera.

In a world where profit justifies not just means but everything else, there is only one taboo: sex with a colleague. That's the sleaze line. Sex with the boss – well. Professional hara–kiri, just not quite so swift.

Luis runs his tongue over his teeth and checks the light. Still red. He craves a toothbrush. A shower, with a Karcher high–pressure cleaner. Then he'll scour the internet for plane tickets, make some quiet inquiries. Perhaps Cabrera y Machado hasn't yet replaced him.

Luis tries to pick details out of the cotton in his head. The dancing – salsa. Jesus. No other woman came close after that spectacle. Then, at the beach bar, Milena on the sand rolling up his pants. They walked under the moon and the fireworks until she stumbled, they both fell into the surf, came up drenched and sandy and laughing and – kissing. "We can dry off at my place," she said.

He knew, even through the haze of all that beer.

The traffic light blinks, turns orange. Did he miss the green? He steps on the clutch, the gearshift grates – anyone might think he's never driven a stick before. The Jeep lurches, catches, finally moves across the empty intersection.

Last night was a test, and he failed. Milena's found a weakness; she'll never trust him. No way he can work with her now, much less take over for her next year.

Something's off. Feels too simple.

In the three weeks he's known Milena (not counting the afternoon she interviewed him in Mexico five months ago), he's never seen her do anything, no matter how spontaneous it might seem, without calculating to the decimal every consequence, advantage, risk.

The self−pitying mini−him argues he's being paranoid. The Mexican gentleman in him is aghast at blaming the girl. But his gut feels the spot−on pang of truth. Last night wasn't just a test, wasn't just premeditated. It was blueprinted.

Luis marks a right turn, then a left. The *tck−tck−tck* sounds like his father's tongue clicking. You've been had, chamaco.

He pokes at the remote on the sun visor. The Warawara Resort gate swings open with a silent faltering, second−guessing itself. He shoves the gearshift into first, burns rubber shamelessly on the climb into the parking lot.

On the walkway to his condo, he fishes in a pocket for his keys with a chuckle of grudging respect. Ah, Milena. She owns him now. No wonder she looked so smug standing in her kitchen this morning, wearing his shirt. And he was so flustered, couldn't even find the words to ask for the shirt back. He fell for it, all of it. Well, she better enjoy her moment. He's taking the first flight out, cutting those puppet strings.

Where the hell are his keys? He clearly remembers them in his hand − when? Not today. Last night? Oh. At Milena's. He thought he was following her to *his* place, tried them on her front door until she giggled and handed him a Montblanc keyring. "Maybe this one?" It worked, and he pondered that for what felt like an instant but must've been longer because then he was falling on a wide bed and Milena was straddling him, undoing the remaining buttons of his shirt and whispering, "Luigi, I've been looking forward to this."

Luigi. And he felt like Rudolph Valentino while his self−esteem − and his keys − fell to the carpet, unnoticed.

There's a spare of the patio doors hidden in the bougainvillea by his pool. He cuts through the white−pebbled alley between his condo and the neighbor's, giant−steps up to the deck with knee creaking − and stops short.

There's a monster in the patio. Black, gigantic, sinister –
although this last tones down when the monster wags its tail.
Thump–thumm–thumm–thump.

Luis falls back to the pebbles. "Fuera. Shoo."

The monster opens its maw, rolls out a too–pink tongue.
Panting. Like a smile the Big Bad Wolf might give ol' Red
Riding Hood.

"Shoo. Go on." Luis claps loudly, but the only effect is a
speeding up of the tail. *Thumpathumpathumpa.*

He picks up a handful of pebbles. Damned if he's going to
let a dog manipulate him, too. But the monster's tail plunges
between his legs and he skits away with a very un–monster–ish
whimper before Luis lets fly the first stone. Black eyes, frightened
but also hurt, pine at Luis from across the pool. In the sun the
monster has become a skeleton: protruding hip bones, ribs so
marked Luis can count them – and the vertebrae above them.

Luis steps up to the deck. "Sorry, guy. I wouldn't've –"

The dog cowers, backs away, never takes his eyes off Luis.

"Look." Luis raises the hand with the pebbles, slowly, and
with a chalky clatter releases them to join their kin. "See? No
more rocks."

Is that a twitch at the tip of the tail?

"Forgive and forget, okay? I don't need a guilt trip."

The twitch this time is unmistakable.

Steps crunch in the alley. Vikram, Luis's Indian neighbor,
ducks into view from under the palm trees bordering his yard
and hollers, "Marjan, that dog is back!" Then he sees Luis. "Oh.
Hey, is that dog yours?"

Luis will never know what he would've said because Marjan,
Vikram's Dutch wife, calls out in her nasal whine from their
porch, "I'm calling Animal Control again."

"Wait."

Vikram looks Luis up and down. "It's yours then?"

Luis glances at the dog. He'll tell himself later the eyes did it.
In them he sees – imagines he sees – a plea. "That's right."

Vikram purses his mouth and studies the moment. "You need to take better care of him."

Great. Now he's a dog abuser.

But Vikram smiles before disappearing back into the palm trees. "I know a good vet," he says with a wave. "I'll get you the number."

Luis turns to the dog. "I just bought you some time, bud. Now scat."

The dog sits up and cocks an ear.

"You want to end up in the pound?" The dog shakes its head and Luis laughs. "Get outta here then."

But the dog stretches instead. The gesture looks ingratiating, almost flirtatious.

He's never owned a dog. Ma's allergies meant no pets. Later, living alone, he never had time. Not that he does now. Besides, he's leaving. Like, tomorrow.

Going back home, his own tail between his legs. Begging for his old job back. Giving Pa the satisfaction of another *I told you so*. They say decisions are choices between consequences. Compared to Pa, Milena is a beast he can tame. She might be surprised to find out how much he knows about puppeteering himself.

"You realize you'll need a bath, bud."

Tail wagging.

"Shots, too."

More tail wagging.

"Don't even know what you're agreeing to, do you?"

That panting wolf-smile.

"All right, then. Here, bud. Come on. You got to let me touch you."

La Ronde / Madge and Gina

by Townsend Walker

That was it, that was it, it was all over for him, he hit me for the last time yesterday after his team lost the Orange Bowl in overtime and I'd said, honey, relax, chill out, it's only a game. Only a game he said, only a game, what the fuck do you know it's only a game. I don't know why I married such a dumb ass low-class broad. I must have been crazy thinking that you could ever learn anything and that snide remark you made to my mother on New Year's Eve about how the children never see me because I always come home after midnight, if I do come home. How do you think that makes me look in front of my own mother and father who never liked me anyway? You know what I'm going to do, I'm gonna shut you up good, you losing no good bitch. Take that you stupid slut, and that, and that. As long as you're into telling stories, I'll give you some to tell. You're going to tell everyone you slipped down the stairs New Year's Eve because you drank too much; you were too soused to walk. That's what you're going to tell people. You got that story? Good. Hasta la vista, baby.

Gina and Madge are sitting in the Rose Club at the Plaza today.

"I lay on the floor for what must have been hours."

"Have you seen a doctor, Madge? You were always good at make−up, but you're hiding nothing from me. Your face is not good at all."

"I'll be okay, nothing broken and I didn't let him kick me in the stomach or back. Plus, I gave him a bloody nose, that's something."

"Waiter, two double martinis, Hendricks, please."

"Where were the kids while you were being Frank's punching bag?"

"Overnighting with school friends in the Village."

The women had been friends at Convent of the Sacred Heart in high school, two scholarship girls bonded against the snobs from the upper East Side; Gina was part of the tunnel crowd and Madge was from down on Avenue B. Scholarships to Barnard, majored in journalism, worked together on the *Post* and married well. Economically, if not otherwise for Madge. She'd bagged her blue blood, but it came with bruises. Gina married her second cousin Leo, a teddy bear and good father. His company had some luck and he got into doing construction for the state.

Other than the contrast afforded by hair and face − Madge, pale and blonde; Gina, olive and dark − they are sheathed by Herrera, shod by Blahnik and coated by mink. They shopped together, went to the matinees together and were working on a book, tentatively titled *If Only He Knew*. But never got their families together. Frank only associated with people who had blue eyes.

There is a couple in the corner they hadn't noticed earlier − older man, younger, much younger, woman sitting on a small plush sofa, holding hands. Brassy hair, lips much too red for her wan complexion, dress shiny and tight. She doesn't belong. He, on the other hand: silvery smooth hair, a recent tan (salon or tube), well−cut grey suit and solid pale blue tie. He looks uneasy. Like she insisted on coming to the Plaza to the point of no nookie and he's afraid of seeing someone he knows.

21

"See that tramp over there," Madge says. "That's the type Frank's been shacking up with."

"How do you know?"

"Dumb fuck had a photo on his phone."

"I think I've mentioned this before, like maybe 500 times, but why don't you divorce the bastard?"

"With all his money and friends, he'd make it hell for at least two years. And then I'd have to deal with him over the kids for another dozen. And there's those little you−know−whats his lawyer might uncover that would play havoc with the pre−nup. Plus little Olly, if he ever got around to a DNA sample."

"You mean the chastity belt clause? Why didn't you get one from him?"

"Marriage with Frank looked so good at the time, who was gonna quibble? Besides, he was the virgin when we met. Go figure."

Madge scoots her chair close to Gina's.

"Only way out is to put this guy away, for good. Way I figure is with Frank out of the way I'd have all of the money, not somewhere way south of half. He's a partner at Goldman, has a couple mil in stocks, plus a five million dollar life insurance policy. I could be a lot pickier next time around."

Gina crinkles her face. She's puzzled.

"You're gonna do what?"

"Not me, somebody. I need your help."

"This is a little out of my league."

"I thought you might know someone."

"Why do you think I'd know someone?"

"You're Italian, you're from Jersey, you'd know someone."

Gina sits back, twirls the liquor around her glass, sniffs it, holds it up to the light to see the yellowish color, sniffs it again and takes a long sip. She purses her lips as if she is about to say something, decides against it and looks over at the mismatched couple.

Madge is unsure what's going through her mind.

"Gina?"

"That was a stupid ass racist statement you made about Italians."

Madge lowers her head and turns bright red.

"Been with Frank too long. You're right about that remark, but I'm desperate."

"This is pretty serious stuff, you've thought about it? I mean, what would Sister Agnes say?"

They laugh.

"I'm thinking of the kids."

"Huh? Oh, if they had to spend time with Frank?"

"He is a total disaster as a father. Must be his upbringing, of which he had none. He takes them to the park, he loses them. One time we found Olly at the edge of the pond trying to pet the ducks."

"Well, I might know someone. My brother Joey."

Madge nods: she dated Joey when she was a sophomore.

"He sometimes runs with my uncle's crowd, who runs with, you know, those kind of people."

Madge jumps up and throws her arms around Gina to a symphony of clashing gold bracelets and dangling earrings.

"God, how I love you Gina."

"So what does Mr. Wonderful look like after all these years?"

"Not much changed from when you saw him ten years ago: six foot three, 200 pounds (going to chubby, he says it's Pilates' muscle), perpetually tanned (some gel he uses), curly black hair (going to gray, he says silver), still has that beak, Brooks Brother's dresser, loafers, always loafers with tassels. And those Hermes ties, you know, the silly patterned ones everyone on Wall Street wears. Outside, he's always got his Prada Aviators on, blue tint, all seasons."

"Waiter, a couple more please."

"Hey, you want to stay with me for a while 'til this cools off? Bring the kids; Leo will understand."

Friday, 3rd January 2014

The Meet Cute

by Derek Osborne

It has been quite a week. Usually the boat is down in the islands this time of year but a series of contracts is keeping them up in Miami. They're shooting two feature films and a *Miami Blue* episode. The *Miami Blue* crew, in particular, knows how to party. They are mostly young and single and ended up hanging out for the holidays.

Because New Year's Eve fell on a Tuesday the union people are having a field day. They've only been able to shoot a total of five days over the past fourteen. It's good for Max as well. Contractually, CBS has to hold the boat no matter what the reason. They had a good shoot the day before, going from 5AM right through sunset (the director wanted that wonderful pink light you only find in south Florida), so Max volunteered the boat for a little party this last evening by way of saying thanks. He figures a nice little gathering of twenty or so (most of the *Miami Blue* talent and senior staff have already flown out), some burgers and beer, a few guitars – a nice way to end the gig.

"Pam," he says into his SAT phone, it's his sister again, she's always calling at the worst possible times, "Pam, I'm in the middle of docking the boat."

"I don't care," she shoots back, "It's always something. Stop the engines and talk to me."

"I can't."

"Did you make the appointment?"

He hates these calls. Just when life is going well someone throws a glass of reality in his face.

"Yes," he says.

"When?"

"Later this month."

"What day?"

"I don't know, the 26th I think."

Eddie, his first mate, is up by the bow giving hand signals. It's a big boat.

"Pam, I *really* have to pay attention to what I'm doing here."

"At Sloan−Kettering?"

"No," Max says, raising his voice, "Bob's fucking Cancer and Hot−Dog Emporium."

"Please don't yell." He can hear it, the tears coming. "I'm trying to help," his sister says.

He's trying to line things up so he doesn't take out the other guy's boat. He spins the big mahogany wheel, reverses the port engine and moves the joystick controlling the thruster. *Gadabout*, Max's boat, is a classic wooden sailing yacht, over ninety feet long including the bow sprit and mizzen brace. He and the crew are trying to squeeze in between two Italian Mega yachts there on the marina's main pier.

"I know you're trying to help," he says back into the phone.

"It's just bringing it all up again. I hate it."

"Pam, I'm fine."

The family is no stranger to cancer, if that is what's going on. His wife passed nearly six years before from ductal carcinoma, a three−year battle before that, a double mastectomy − the chemo − the waiting. Pam has a right to be worried, there's history on both sides of the family. Maybe it's been part of his own dance these past few months, maybe not. He's been feeling off, then fine, then off again for no reason. One thing they all learned from Maggie's death, early detection is key, and he's been avoiding.

"Hey, something to cheer you up," Max says, letting the boat slow to a stop, hovering there off the pier, "I'm falling in love with Rebecca Vasquez."

"Pia?" Pam says. Max can feel the shift; *Miami Blue* is her favorite show. "Is that who you're shooting with?"

"That's one of them."

"Why didn't you tell me? You met her? What's she like? What's Thaddeus like?"

"Pam, I'm docking the god damn boat. I'll tell you when I come for the tests."

He can see Eddie with a *what−the−fuck* look on his face. Eddie came with the boat. He's Jamaican and has all their easy ways but he's also a serious waterman. Over the years he's become a good friend.

"Get their autographs?" Max can hear Pam saying over the phone.

"Goodbye, Pam."

"Please?"

"Love you ..."

"Don't blow this off ..." she starts, but he's already shut it down. He's promised them all he'll go for the tests. His sister's no dummy, she got his daughters involved. He's had calls from all three.

Moving the thruster again, he and Eddie start slipping the yacht toward the pier. No words are needed; they've done it a thousand times. Eddie stands ready to throw the lines.

Max is doing his best not to look at the gathering crowd. It's not that he can't dock the boat and talk on the phone at the same time, that's a piece of cake; it's the other thing, the rumor that Rebecca Vasquez, the actress who plays Pia on *Miami Blue*, intends on joining the party. Seems she has family in Miami and has been staying there during the shoot. Seems her personal assistant, Anja, has hit it off with Eddie. Seems Anja and Rebecca like to hang out together. He's ignoring the other thing, what Anja told Eddie, that her boss thinks Max is "interesting." Max has been in the business long enough to know the flirting that often goes on is just a part of the show. Everyone flirts; everyone's *on*, it's in their blood. It reminds him of what Katharine Hepburn once told a reporter when asked what made her a star. "I don't know," she said, "but whatever it is, I've got it." They all have it to some degree, some more than others; Rebecca, a lot more than others. There's no denying Max is attracted, who wouldn't be, but there's also a pragmatic side that allows him to skipper a big boat across oceans, run a successful business, deal with producers whose sole job is to get the most bang for the studio's buck. Life holds fewer illusions these days, especially since his wife's passing.

But Max has been letting himself fall more and more into the fantasy. It's fun. They haven't actually spoken; just the stolen glances and study–hall notes from Anja to Eddie. He's feeling it though, that tingle, that mutual vibration, slipping past her there on the boat, both of them consummate professionals, avoiding eye contact, and yet. Her wanting to come to the party doesn't prove anything, no more than she enjoys her co–workers and likes the boat, and everyone loves *Gadabout*, so much he always assumes it's the boat and not its skipper they want to be with. *She's half your age*, he reminds himself, working the thrusters while minding the stern. Once upon a time he might have laid siege to her doorstep. In truth, he's feeling more like fifteen than fifty–five, replaying each moment, dissecting every nuance, especially after what Anja said the night before, study–hall be damned.

"That's not all she's going to miss."

The conversation had been about the boat, or so he thought. He'd gone out for a bite to eat with her and Eddie.

"Becky wanted to come out with us tonight but, you know, appearances and all that."

"Of course," Max said.

"Don't misunderstand," Anja went on, "Beck could care less. But there's paparazzo down here." And then she had leaned in, and this is what had him looped in the loops of her hair, "I think she'd really like a tour of the boat."

Standing now at the helm, working the thruster, he steals a moment to look at the dock. There have to be fifty people bunched up like kids on a class trip, but there near the center, a bit off right, as if they've framed and lit the scene to bring out her eyes and that wild hair she prefers off camera, the V−neck tee, her pirate's smile, Rebecca has indeed shown up. He knows that smile; right about then a fait accompli, no use trying to hide anymore. It went like that, right then, right there, from doubt to surrender. The very best, Max thinks − the very best − he'll have a nice memory of a divine two−week flirtation, the rising star and the middle−aged sea captain, another day in the life.

"Calm down," he says beneath the engine's monotone, drinking in that look aimed right at him.

"Max!"

It's Eddie again; he's shouting and pointing, their bowsprit ready to spear the other boat's canopy. Max reverses just in time. Eddie raises his hands in the air, again. Max works the lever and the boat backs out a few meters. He steals another look at the dock. The crowd seems oblivious but she hasn't missed a thing. It both embarrasses and makes him like her all the more, every inch of her laughing now, a good−natured, sly little grin spreading fast across her face.

Gotcha, her eyes are saying.

Max throws a line to one of the marina's attendants and shuts down the engines. The men on the pier start hauling the yacht alongside.

Yes, he's thinking, returning her smile, *you have indeed.* He lets his own smile fade, holding her there. *You're not the only one who's got it,* he's telling her. She blushes − looks down − comes back radiant as ever. He's feeling quite proud of himself when a return line thrown from the dock smacks him right in the face. The crowd doubles over. He grabs the line using every ounce of self–restraint. Even Eddie is holding onto himself, doing his best to look the other way. But Rebecca isn't laughing, far from it. He sees her there, the crowd fading and laughter blending out into the evening – her smile – the one he was sure he would never see again.

Sweet Jesus, he's thinking, *what do I do now?*

Saturday, 4th January 2014

Ralph Rudinsky here …

by Gloria Garfunkel

Ralph Rudinsky here Chief of Quality Assurance for a large diversified corporation Orwellian Industries a big important job that's hard to keep up with so it's already January 4 and I still haven't made my New Year's Resolutions because I have so much to do I even take work home so I feel it's OK for me to take these few minutes out of my hectic work for resolutions now which include being perfect at all times not let my bipolar disorder interfere with my work though I am in a manic episode now and hypergraphic writing and and hyperverbal and do not want to obsess about my boss Stan Stealth cat fur grain moths my manipulative Borderline Personality secretary Serena or my passive–aggressive assistant Jake or my sociopathic boss did I mention him and be nice to everyone especially people I hate as mentioned above and just yes Stan to death and get a lot of work done which is easy in a manic episode because I never sleep and can make up for the depressive crashes when I can live on Ritalin–Sudafed and caffeine and still cannot stay awake and never tell anyone outside my family and girlfriend Chloe that I'm bipolar or they'll hold it against me like they did at my last job when I was fired.

Sunday, 5th January 2014

Carmine

by John Wentworth Chapin

Pinks and oranges plume outward in a gaudy riot, each burgundy- or lavender-accented petal evoking Mardi Gras or day-glo psychedelia. It overshadows the carefully crafted competition: pure creamy yellow, black and white bull's eye, Kermit's head. It's supposed to be a flower, but it's more like Barbie's Malibu Dream House: Tornado Aftermath. Nothing holds a candle to this most glorious of cupcakes. Charles tells the woman behind the counter that he wants the pink and orange flower, and she nods, carefully boxing it for him.

"It's for a celebration," he prompts. She doesn't respond, and he wonders if she slams closed all doors to conversation at home or just at work.

Charles has always been a celebrator of anniversaries, milestones, rites of passage. ♡JUSTIN♡ *Happy three months of dating! Thank you so much, Mrs. Blaisdell: I have simply loved the first half of ninth grade. DARRELL — Congratulations on 27 months of sobriety, Mister Straight Arrow!!!!* There were made-to-order t-shirts, celebratory emails strewn with clip art, baked goods. There was champagne (though not for Darrell).

As he reaches into one pocket to pay for the cupcake, another pocket vibrates, followed by the opening notes of *Everything's Coming Up Roses*. The bakery woman seems deaf to the music, as though classic showtunes regularly leap from her customers' persons.

"It's my mother," he explains. "Everyone deserves a custom ringtone."

He wishes she would say something arch, like *Your mother? I thought Ethel Merman was in your pants.* She doesn't, however. The witty repartee in Charles's life comes from his own mouth, frequently in hindsight.

He answers his phone with an apologetic grin to the bakery woman. His mother launches into a story about rubbery shrimp scampi. He listens a moment, and the bakery woman hands him his change. If he takes the change, she will disappear into bowls of frosting or *mille–feuilles.* He's not ready to give up on her yet.

Charles interrupts. "Did you call to celebrate?"

She and the bakery woman are both silent.

Charles says, "It's been one whole month since December 5."

The bakery woman rattles out her change–holding hand; his mother at least has the social skills to ask for clarification.

"That was the day of the *accident,*" he says. The bakery woman leaves the change resting on the glass counter, tapping it and nodding at him. "I'm trying not to remember all the blood," he says loudly. "I'm celebrating that I am alive!" The bakery woman retreats to a tray of cookies.

Charles's mother makes a few unsatisfactory noises; she doesn't want him dwelling on the macabre, but she does want him dwelling on the shrimp scampi. He begs off with an excuse that he is at the register at a bakery, as though his attention were required. He promises to call her later, which he will remember tomorrow that he did not do.

He collects his change and the cupcake and calls his thanks to the woman across the store. He wishes she'd tell him a story about when her sister got diagnosed with Stage II cervical cancer but last November they celebrated her victory of five years of remission.

She doesn't.

At home, he sets the cupcake on a plate. Outrageous colors. He's even more delighted by it now than he was earlier. He doesn't want to eat it and ruin it; it will be dry, because it's way too beautiful to taste good. He lets it be and tries to find a distraction.

He flips open his laptop, but he just doesn't feel like working this afternoon. He steals a glance at the cupcake. One month! He calls his friend Stephanie, but she doesn't answer. He texts his friend Jeff, but Jeff doesn't answer. That his pool of friends is so shallow worries Charles.

He has an epiphany: no one is answering because he's dead. He's not alive – he died in the accident, and now he's a wandering ghost.

This unnerves him, and he seeks solace in the cupcake, a candied bonfire in his slate–colored kitchen. Wandering ghosts don't have day–glo cupcakes. Just to be sure, he cuts a wedge and pops a bite into his mouth. It's surprisingly moist and tasty, and the riotous frosting is softer than he expected. Orange, with a hint of pomegranate.

"You are alive, and that is one damn good cupcake, Charles," he announces to his empty apartment. It's meant to be jovial and nerve–settling, but his voice bounces off the walls.

He abandons his cupcake, and the apartment door slams behind him.

Charles climbed out of his car, sidestepping a city lamppost, then jerked his head toward a loud, awful crash of metal and glass. A runaway Volkswagen tore into the sides of two cars and continued at full speed down the sidewalk toward him. It hit a woman. She flew onto the windshield in a spray of blood. Two boys turned to see the gray Volkswagen; Charles couldn't see their faces but he saw them both killed, one tossed onto the hood, the other crumpled under the tires. The car continued straight at Charles and rammed into his car, the lamppost, and a mailbox, all at once. The woman and the boy on the hood flew forward onto Charles as the car came to a complete, hissing stop. Five seconds of mayhem ended with three people dead and Charles standing on a city sidewalk covered in crimson gore, shocked into a stupor but otherwise entirely unharmed.

He looked around him; a heavyset woman stepped out of a sandwich shop, her mouth open, looking straight at Charles.

"That car was headed right for you. If ..." she mouthed, before she started screaming.

If his car door hadn't been open. If the lamppost hadn't been right there. If if if. Charles saw death coming at him and he didn't even get out of the way: death just stopped.

Charles is entirely a−religious. It makes no sense to him that he was spared for a reason. Charles doesn't feel guilty.

"I feel lucky," he tells the group of four guys clustered at the bar. Charles has bought everyone in this group a round, and they have twice returned the favor. They are a familiar bunch, but he knows none of them before tonight. One guy − Charles thinks his name is Tony, but that seems wrong − asks what's changed since the accident.

"I feel like I got a new start," he says.

"Doing what?" Maybe−Tony asks.

Charles doesn't have an answer. Something about the guy unsettles him. In a good way. "I usually have a bunch of New Year's resolutions," he says. "Not this year."

"Do you love your job?" Maybe–Tony asks. Charles does PR for a printing company; it's all old guys who complain about Twitter and the death of print and they think it's a riot that Charles is gay and drill him with inappropriate questions.

Charles shakes his head.

"Did you think about quitting, chasing a passion?"

Charles smiles. "I almost got killed. I didn't win the lottery."

Maybe–Tony says, "Sounds like maybe you got a wake–up call and went back to sleep."

Now that's some witty repartee, Charles thinks.

"That is one out–of–control confection," Maybe–Tony says when Charles ushers him into his kitchen. They were making out in the front hall a moment ago, vodka and lust.

Charles offers him a bite.

"Are you asking me to split your cupcake?" Maybe–Tony snickers.

"You told me to chase a passion," Charles says.

They set the cupcake between them on the couch and nibble at it. The conversation rapidly abandons flirtation.

Maybe–Tony says, "Most people would get very religious right about now, thanking God and carrying on." Charles confesses disinterest in religion and confides to Maybe–Tony his weird moment earlier when he thought he was a ghost.

"Not that I believe in ghosts," Charles says quickly, and then he resumes his story.

While Maybe–Tony listens, he haphazardly traces a bright pink scar on his jaw, as though he's tickling himself or reassuring himself that his scar is still there. It's oddly compelling, making Charles want to touch it. The longer Charles talks with Maybe–Tony, the less he wants to get naked. His desire is to stay up all night talking.

So Charles does something entirely unexpected for Charles: he tells Maybe–Tony his desire.

Maybe–Tony breaks apart the final piece of cupcake and tells about the time he fell off a chairlift. Charles licks the last of the bright orange frosting from his fingers.

Monday, 6th January 2014

First Impression

by Lynn Beighley

"Jenn, you'll sit here," Bill says, putting his hand on the back of the chair next to his. Because I don't know these people very well yet, I obey. If this wasn't my second week at my new job, and my first time out for lunch with my new coworkers, I still would have obeyed, because I'm like that. My seat is in a corner. To my left is Bill, to my right is a dusty windowsill where two flies are having sex. I've never seen copulating flies before, but there's no mistaking it.

I've learned that Bill has a big announcement to make, and apparently any excuse to go out to lunch is generally a good one. Bill has escorted a group of seven of us to Kontry Jed's All U Kin Et Buffet. We're waiting for the waitress to take our drink orders. "I bring my grandmother here almost every Sunday. They know me," he says. "I'm a regular, and they treat me well because they know they'll get a ten percent tip from me, every time."

I look around at the other customers, clearly also regulars. Ten percent sounds cheap to me, but I suspect that at this particular establishment it's on the high end of the tipping spectrum.

None of us has ever been to Kontry Jed's. Bill stands up, as though he's going to give a speech. Which he does. "Since it's all you can eat," Bill explains to the table, "you should be strategic. Start with the expensive foods, like the meats, not the cheap starches. Don't fill up on the bread." His intensity embarrasses me. I see a few people snickering.

I hear one of my new coworkers, I don't remember his name, whispering to his neighbor in his best Bill voice, "No, don't fill up on the bread! No bread, it's not strategic." I don't think Bill heard, he's paying rapt attention to the drink orders being taken by a dead-eyed waitress in a stained, wrinkled white shirt. But I heard, and Noname has earned a place on my asshole list.

The buffet is, well, let's just say that I hate buffets, and this place epitomizes why. I think the horny flies' offspring will find a welcoming home in the macaroni and cheese. I stick to the salad bar. Figuratively, although if I touched the gloppy counter, it might be literally.

"Of course he wants to sit next to you. Our Bulldozer likes redheads," my new coworker Alan whispers to me as we fill our plates. I've already learned that Bill Plover has a nickname he doesn't know about, Bulldozer, or more often shortened to Bull when his coworkers are joking about him. It's partly because he's a little on the short side, with a thick frame. You wouldn't call him fat, just very bulky. Bulky Bull Plover.

Bill plods as he cases the food stations. He moves like a stegosaurus on his stocky legs, which doesn't lessen his resemblance to construction equipment.

"But it's not just how he looks," my boss Jonathan told me in an unguarded moment in his office. "It's not only the way Bulldozer moves. It's also that he's so on and off. Black and white. Hit or miss. He has no low gears. He plows through things as if they aren't there. If a bulldozer was a human, he'd be our Bully boy." He pauses and adds, urgently, "Hot and cold. That's it." I didn't know how to respond to such frank talk about a coworker. Was this some kind of test to see if I gossip? I just nodded and the conversation shifted to more appropriate, but less interesting topics, like ordering office supplies and reserving conference rooms.

We're all finally back at the table, me with my wilted iceberg salad and iced tea. The flies are gone. Bill stands and starts tapping his water glass with his knife. I watch it nearly topple, and grab it before it does, getting a sharp rap to my knuckles from Bill's knife.

"Here's my news," Bill says, glancing at everyone, but mostly gazing at me, "I've been selected to be on a reality television show." He sits down as everyone starts asking questions. We're sitting close enough together that I can feel his body heat.

Bulldozer on *Survivor*? Surely not. *Amazing Race*? *Biggest Loser*? No, none of the current crop of reality TV shows I can think of makes sense for him. But he's going to be on television, and that impresses me, even though I hate that it does.

"It's a new show called *You Tell Me*," he explains. "It's about crowdsourcing. About the hive mind. For the next year or so, social media will tell me what to do. Little things like what I should wear, but also bigger things, like dating decisions."

Everyone looks at me, I'm not imagining this.

Wingy

by Andrew Stancek

I fly.

That is the blunt truth with which it all begins. It is as good an opening as *In the beginning was the Word and the Word was with God and the Word was God.*

I have no motor. I have no Atlas−like musculature, special body parts or contraption of any sort. I don't chant incantations, turn keys, push buttons. I don't have an IQ of 200 or more. I am as ordinary as most of the six billion inhabitants of this planet and I have, for the first time in the history of mankind, figured out what birds do instinctively.

I fly.

I am not imagining it. No reason to lock me up. Experts of a thousand kinds have seen and tested and the whole Internet world has oohed and aahed and it cannot be explained away.

I fly.

My name is Adam. In retrospect it's funny, prescient, ironic. It's a name given to me by my parents who meant nothing by it. They were not harking back to the first man, formed out of clay by the Almighty's hand. They chose a name they were familiar and comfortable with, one in my father's family for generations.

Zajac, my last name, well, all the hilarity you can have with that. I've heard it throughout my childhood, my normal childhood before The Event, and since the millions of words written about me, I've heard a lot more. My parents are Slovak and the name means rabbit, or more precisely hare. Yes, the headlines made it into Bunny, told me to hear, hear, to come here and there and everywhere. Adam Zajac, A to Z, is significant as well; I am of course the alpha and the omega. The first ever and after me, perhaps, the deluge. In North America the name came to be pronounced the English way, so in my teenage years the wits called out "Hey, Jack." Enormously clever.

What else needs to be said? I already said I am unexceptional. Or was, anyway. I am not, truly am not, comparing myself in any way to Einstein but I've always liked that line of his, "I have no special talent. I am only passionately curious." That describes me as well. In addition to the curiosity, I had the great fortune to be ill and bed-ridden for almost two years. During that time I was able to read, to think, to observe, to truly observe. I have imagination, curiosity, observational talent, and I was given leisure. I could indulge in ways of thinking that in an adult would be laughed at. Professors of aerodynamics, engineers of all sorts, they have prestige to think of, deadlines, adult preoccupations, but to me those did not apply. Leonardo was of course the greatest of all time, but his mind took him all over the place. He was not ordinary; he was a genius, and that is what prevented him from pursuing one idea to its fruition — he had thousands. I was ordinary and only had one. And I did it.

I fly.

I've grown to accept the name they hung on me: Wingy. It sounds like loopy, dingbatty, wacky. They didn't really mean that. If you pushed them, they would chuckle and say I am nuts, of course. I am one of a kind. No one has ever done what I do every day, routinely. I've shown it hundreds of times and they cannot prove I am a fake or a charlatan. So they admire me but resent me as well. Wingy is descriptive. A headline writer used it first and it stuck. My feats, including the name, have gone viral.

And as I said, I am fine with it. Wingy. If you want, you can hear other words in there, too: king, ring, sing, longing.

I've decided to write my story, my side. So much has been written about me that you might think another word isn't needed. Of course I cooperated at the beginning, with everyone: the scientists, the doctors, the engineers, the writers and the hyenas. I got sick of it, and I became less open. I'm no fool. I know many would prefer I was never born, never came to the world's attention. But they cannot undo me.

Maybe no one will ever read this. I'm not writing for a learned journal or for the popular press, only for me. Maybe it'll be read next week and maybe a hundred years from now. So I'll pour out the me whom no one knows, my feelings, my way. If you know the story, move on, skip a part or two. But I just may surprise you. Even if you think you know, something may startle. Hold onto your seats and enjoy the ride.

Isa

by Rachel Ambrose

Isa, my roommate, is a great snack buyer, so I almost never go hungry even though I hate the grocery store. Maybe if my apartment wasn't so comfortable, I would feel the need to leave it unprompted once in a while. But that day is not today.

I do leave my apartment to go to work for an elderly lawyer named Mrs. Hatfield who smells like lavender soap and lilies. I tidy her desk, empty the trash, answer her phone and schedule her calendar. Every so often someone comes in to see her and I escort them to her office, where she greets them with a powdery kiss on the cheek and an offer of gumdrops. I have a little plaque on my desk with 'Claire Worthington, Administrative Assistant' written on it. My pay could be called meager at best. I pay my bills, but paying for anything else is pretty impossible. But then Saturday mornings hit, and isn't that the best, logging on to your bank account page and seeing two or three hundred more dollars in there, like the money fairies have visited during the night? I pay off my bills straightaway and then look at the double−digit amount that's left, and I think about buying truffled fries or imported tea from England or an eggplant−colored cape. I always talk myself out of it, but Saturday mornings are precious, dream−laced things nonetheless.

I would like to burrow into my little yellow pool of shag rug and stay there, like a little mouse, sometimes poking my nose out for bits of cheese and fruit. The sun shines on it every day and I think it would be a lovely way to spend my time, all huddled up in warmth and gold.

Worryingly, these days, it seems like my hermitting issues are moving to take over, well, my entire life. Or rather, they're making me avoid actually existing. Well, I'm alive. Of course I am. I eat and breathe. But getting out there with people, interacting, behaving like a real adult of twenty—six years, that's been much harder these days. My therapist, a softspoken Irish lady named Ruthie, has suggested I keep a journal. "Being accountable, if only to yourself for your own experiences, will light a fire under your ass," she told me at our last session. Ruthie has a gift for the well—placed curse. In this case, it surprises me so much that I immediately go out, buy a composition notebook, and start writing down words with which to further berate myself. Somehow I don't think that this is what Ruthie had in mind.

But, see, somewhere after college, or maybe right before it ended, the fire under my ass just went out. The constant striving to be the best, to hand in papers well before deadline, to rewrite those papers three or four times the night before they were due, all that passion, just left in a big hurry. "Graduate college!" your parents tell you. "Go get a job and live your life!" Well, plonk, here I am. I've graduated college. I've got a job. What do you want me to do now, authority figures? Give me a map, because without all those demanding voices in my head, I'm a little bit lost. "Be more ambitious!" my parents tell me now. "Ask that old dingbat for a raise! Ask for more responsibilities! Freshen up your resumé." But I don't HAVE to do that. I'm feeding myself. I'm paying my little portion of the rent. My cell phone is still connected. So it's a shift from things I felt I was bound to do, to things I feel I might or could do. I could, if my little heart so chose, ask Mrs. Hatfield for a raise. I could ask for more responsibilities. I might even be able to get a new job if I tried hard enough. But the thing is, I'm utterly satisfied with the modicum of responsibilities I have. I see Isa bring home these stacks of papers from her office every day, and granted, it pays more than mine, but I might just like sitting on my couch with my laptop and Netflix and takeout Chinese. Or at least I think I like it. How do you know if you like something new if it isn't shoved in your face? If no parent or teacher is putting it on a spoon and making airplane noises until it gets close enough to your mouth that you have to open up your lips and try it? What, you mean you people just go out there and give it a shot? Who are you? How did you get that way? Tell me.

You know that if you switch around the letters in 'tried', you get 'tired'? Maybe you get tired after you've tried too hard. I think that's what happened to me. Not even tired as in "I'm tired, I need a nap." I mean tired like that old faded blue sofa in your den that's slowly become covered with stuff, so much stuff that you can't even see it anymore, and it's not a proper sofa. But even though it's tired, and not really serving its purpose in life, it's still sitting there in your den, and you're used to seeing it there, and the familiarity of it soothes you enough that you don't want to go get a new one.

So it's a bit of a shock when Isa comes home one night with a nip on her face and a cloud over her head. She gets angry easily, she's constantly blaming it on her Mexican and Spanish heritage, but tonight she's really pissed. I corner her after she's taken a shower and is wrapping her hair up in a topknot on her head. "Hey, what's going on with you? Bee in your bonnet?"

"More like a nest of wasps," she says, tossing her head. "You remember how my little brother Paulo slipped on the ice a month ago and hit his head? I guess he has to have someone move in full time to take care of him and drive him to doctors' appointments, so my parents picked me to be the nursemaid."

"Why can't they do it?" I ask, irritated for her.

"You know my mom and dad," she says. "She's always off on some hippie retreat, he's busy with his engineering firm. How dare I expect my parents to parent, eh?"

"Well ..." I say. "Is it going to be for long? How many doctors' appointments can he go to?"

"They don't know how long it's going to take," says Isa. "If I were you, I'd try and find a new roommate. I don't want you having to pay all the rent all the time, I know you can't afford it. Want me to put an ad on Craigslist and see if I can find anyone who's not a crazy axe murderer before I go?"

"Sure, thanks," I say, relieved that she's taking point on this; what in the world would I say? 'Part Time Hermit Seeks Someone Who Will Buy Potato Chips and Pay Rent'? 'Part Time Hermit Wants Someone Silent to Live with Her'? Right.

"Maybe I can come see you on weekends," I say. "We can work out a rota or something if you need help. How many doctor's appointments can one person possibly have?"

"Yeah," says Isa. "They want me over there in a few days, though, so I've gotta start packing now. Wanna come help?"

I snort. "Please. Let me just sit here in my misery and mope for a while about your untimely departure from our hitherto blissful living situation. You don't know, I might get someone who doesn't wash and uses his dirty boxers as dish rags."

"Sweetie, you know me better than that," soothes Isa. "I'll find you someone nice. Nachos for supper later?"

Nachos sound good, but I would have traded all the queso in the world for her to never grab her suitcase from the closet.

Carpet Muncher

by Gill Hoffs

I have a double–bed at home, and I have a side I like to sleep on, but what the latter is depends on who is paying for my company that night. I wake up on the left today in a rented bed, next to Robin, whose wife understands him well enough but doesn't have the figure or temperament to stand beside him at a business do and impress the other suits with Robin's good taste, or the stamina to help him blow off steam with a half–hour blowjob afterwards. Apparently it makes her jaw ache and her cheeks sore, and he has a tendency to get some in her eye. Now I've known him a while, I'm sure his aim was deliberate.

When he was interviewing me at the agency, he said, "I'm wondering about your oral endurance," as he drummed his fingertips on the arm of the chair, eying my lips with an air of scepticism.

I raised an eyebrow at him, plucked the office boy's vanilla thickshake from his desk, and sucked the cup dry, holding my potential client's gaze all the while. I prefer to avoid super–sweet icecream drinks – I'm a coffee girl, myself – but it was worth the calories to snag Robin. I could smell the top–notes of his aftershave and knew it cost more than Cristal.

Once we'd agreed on our first 'date', and I'd kissed both cheeks goodbye in the London way, which seemed posh for Manchester and no doubt impressed him with my professionalism, we fell into a routine of coffee and catchup, dinner with colleagues from overseas, then the blowjob before bed. He likes to wake up with me in the morning. I don't feel I'm really earning my overnight fee by just spooning with him, tucking the duvet around his feet when it's cold, and serving him espresso in my special way before he returns to work ... but I can live with it.

This morning it's dark when he finally murmurs "Fuck" and knocks his Blackberry to the floor, silencing the beeeeeep of the alarm. I've already laid out his shirt and tie the way he likes them, smooth and flat and formal on my side of the bed, with his trousers hanging off the chair nearby, and fresh socks on my pillow. Years of working early shifts in a supermarket, stacking tins on shelves and indulging my OCD through 'facing' the labels just so, means I rarely sleep past 5.30 anyway. I've had plenty of time to shower then prep his hotel room using just the streetlight reflecting up from the city streets below and call down to room service, as well as email my gran thanks for the Christmas present of potpourri and plan Friday and the working weekend that lies ahead.

Robin rolls onto his back, angles his arms in triangles as he tucks his hands behind his head, and waits for the knock at the door. The threads of blood lacing the whites of his eyes make his blue eyes seem all the more vivid, and I can see from the tepee over his crotch where the rest of the spare blood in his body has gone. I smile at him, and make a show of stretching across the table by the window to tweak the curtains back, then saunter across the thick red carpet to flick the little brass knob beside the doorframe, turning the side lights on, and, from the groan in the bed, Robin too.

We're several floors up, twenty maybe, and the top floor of an office is opposite our room. Its windows glow yellow and I can see some poor wretch on the phone there already as the cleaners drag a vacuum around by the hose like a reluctant child. Robin, for all his tasteful clothes and business–like exterior, loves me to put on a show. I sometimes think he should have been a film director.

The knock comes, and I raise an eyebrow at Robin, who licks his lips, nodding for me to open it, and I do. Naked.

The guy holding the coffee must be used to it by now. I half expect him to comment on the winter weight I gained from too many (working) Christmas dinners, or the too−long pubes I had my stylist wax into the silhouette of a Christmas tree (I even wore a crystal stick−on star for the man I had dinner with on Christmas Eve, but it's long gone now, tucked into his wallet as a reminder of services rendered) which reminds me, I need to go get that seen to before tonight's appointment with Tony the Tongue. But no. Just a smirk, then theatrically raised eyebrows and a gasp of morning breath. He pauses, tray in hand, letting his eyes wander to my tits.

I step back into the room, allowing him to step forward, and without a word, I take the little white cup of coffee from the tray. And stumble, on purpose, so the rich black fluid slops a few drops over the side. They hit the carpet, not my foot − when Robin first told me what he wanted, I practised at home until I could spill it just right − and the waiter finally speaks.

"Well, that was careless. Don't expect me to clean it up."

Not quite the script we'd worked through earlier, but close enough. I wink at him, and put the coffee down on the little table at the end of the bed, where Robin watches from the pillow, pupils like LPs blacking out the blue.

Now the icky bit.

Bending over, I place my hands on the plush red carpet, wiggling my arse a little at the coffee guy, then get down on my knees, lower my head, and make Robin think I'm sucking the stain out. I make slurping noises with my mouth, like when I suck his cock, and make sure my legs are just far enough apart for the floor show. My hair is long enough to hide my face, and by biting my lips a bit and sucking them in through my teeth a few times, I can make them swell and redden enough to give

Robin the impression I've delivered the show he's looking for. When I hear Robin's breathing quicken I discreetly tap my toes. As I moan and wriggle my arse a little faster, the room service guy takes his cue.

"Have you cleaned my carpet?"

I sit up, nod, and as I slo—o—o—owly lick my lips and sigh, and he squints at the wet patch on the floor, we hear the nnngh from my client on the bed. Ignoring the mess now dampening the sheets, the coffee guy purses his lips, and leaves.

The door closes and, getting up off my knees, I take Robin the rest of his espresso in bed. He tosses it back in one gulp, and hands me the empty cup with a stubble—cheeked smile before crumpling the sheets to the side. Swinging his hairy legs off the bed, he stands up with his cock bobbing like a nodding dog in the back of a minicab, and pads through to the shower.

I step into my day outfit of green knitted dress and warm—but—still—sexy boots, smear cherry balm across my lips, pick up my bag from the table by the bed and close the door behind me as I step into the hall.

The lift doors open, and I walk into the wood—panelled elevator and press L, daydreaming about the hours ahead. Time for a browse round the sales before I take the tram home, and feed the cat before I meet tonight's client.

And a wax.

Tony might not mind a mouthful of bush, but I'm pretty sure he'd gag at a Christmas tree.

Snakes and Snails

by Susan Tepper

They keep the schoolyard under lock and key. It's silly. Teachers all over the place and those aides who don't know nothing but stand around, anyhow, like guards.

I move my car from spot to spot. It's better that way. Today being Friday is the last day I get to see the kids. Weekends are dull. I'm parked under a big leafless tree across from the chain link fence they put up to protect the kids. The kids, squealing and screaming, are such little darlings. I call them *my little darlings*. They can't hear me saying this, of course, being that I'm in the car and they're in the school yard.

Each week I pick my two favorites. Two favorite little darlings. On Monday I first picked the red head boy who I would guess to be about seven years old, based on the sizes of the other kids, tho' my red head boy is taller and thinner than most of them. He has spirit! I love a kid with spirit.

I had spirit growing up until my da beat the crap of it. Beat it with a belt. Not a good thing to do to a boy. You turn off a boy's natural spirit, you get a crouching, fearful bag o' bones. That's what you turn your boy into from the beatings. They said I failed in school because I was *slow*. They didn't get it that I had to move slow, always slow, to avoid pissing off the old man. You pissed that bastard off, the belt came out faster than a boy can stick out his tongue.

My car has a fair amount of acorn dings from sitting under these big trees during the fall. I would hear those acorns smacking the hood and the roof and there wasn't a thing I could do. If I moved the car, chances were pretty good I wouldn't be able to find another parking spot. It's crowded around here from the apartment houses. Too many cars and not enough good spots from where I can watch the kids.

Last week a cop car drove real slow past me and went around the loop and drove past me again. I took out the newspaper I save for emergencies. I put it against the steering wheel and read an article about the rise and fall of cholesterol among Chinese peasants. I read every word so carefully I can still practically recite it by heart. Goes to show.

The red head boy is very good on the jungle gym. These days they cover the ground with thick black rubber to protect the kids who fall. The read head kid never falls and he pulls some pretty tricky stunts. He can twist into a pretzel then swing to another bar.

Not to leave out my other favorite for the week: a small kid with blond hair. Towheads they call them. He's a fearful little tyke, the kind you want to cradle on your lap and rock. Back and forth, back and forth, back and forth. Whispering in his little ear that there is nothing in the world to be afraid of in my arms on my lap.

I want to get out of the car and stretch my legs but this is impossible. My one leg aches from being snarled under the steering wheel. This piece of shit car is older than dirt. I really need to buy a new one, something in a good color that will blend. A taupe color or a dark tan. Those cars people never remember. They get into accidents, hit and runs, and no witness can quite finger them. For the time being I'm stuck with this old Dodge Dart. A blue, much too bright. I'm sure it's what caught that cop's attention. But, cops being cops, he did his round and probably went off to do a drug deal or visit a prostitute. Those cops don't fool anyone who grew up in a neighborhood like this one.

My little blondie boy is playing in the dirt with a pail. He's kneeling and digging. One of the teacher aides is talking to him (I can only imagine) and now he's getting to his feet, dragging his little self toward the swings. She must've told him to be more physical. My da used to throw that shit at us kids: be more physical. "OK, Da, right."

Somehow that gets me to laughing. I was in Desert Storm when he shut his eyes for the last time. Now that was a trip. Desert Storm *and* the old man's sudden ending. *If I have to go make it quick,* he used to say.

"Well bless you, Da, bless you." What would make him think he was different from the rest of us? "We all gotta go, Da." It busts me up laughing again saying this stuff.

Now my little red head boy is chucking handfuls of shit at some other kids. Everything they do just drives me up a wall! I want to grab them and spin them around and tickle them until they fall down on the ground the spittle dripping off their chins from so much fun and laughter! *Snakes and snails and puppy dog tails, that's what little boys are made of.*

Father Eleanor

by Jessica McHugh

Father Edward McKenzie powders his nose, pretending the Almay in the vintage Duska tin is authentic. His grandmother's old phonograph sits quiet in the corner, but as he sways to Kay Starr crooning from his laptop, he imagines her song floats from the player instead. It's a harder stretch than the makeup, but it's easier to believe than the delusions about his wardrobe. As much as he imagines his body hugged by mocha lace and fur trim, the mirror betrays his fantasies. His 'gown' is no more than an ill-fitting bathrobe torn to the thigh. But he has time before he's forced to face reality. Tossing a blanket over the mirror, Edward feels beautiful again.

He pictures gloved hands beckoning him into a waltz. There's no chance he'll refuse. Even when secondhand heels constrict his feet, crushing his toes to a feminine taper, he is more beautiful for the pain. In the muscular arms of his waltzing partner, he is as dainty as the January snow grazing his window. He doesn't care who his partner is, only that he has someone who won't shrink back from his powdered stubble or slapdash gowns, someone who sees through to the innocent soul like Grandma Eleanor always could.

Then again, she'd never seen him quite like this. When he'd worn her clothes, she'd viewed it as playtime, not knowing her grandson never wanted playtime to end. Lord, how he longs to walk the world in painful pumps, the breeze of freedom dancing through his long blonde hair and laying silky kisses on his cheeks. The best he does now is a ceiling fan and the wiry slaps of a wig he stole from a dumpster behind JC Penney's.

Stole. He, Father McKenzie, stole from the garbage to feed his sins.

His stomach lurches at the truth, and he pulls the blanket from the mirror. His face powder is splotchy. Patches are soft and white as a young bride, but the rough and ruddy skin between can't be mistaken for anything but a man's. The waltzing fantasy ends, and his partner disappears. But Kay Starr sings on, her *Wheel of Fortune* spinning, spinning, spinning. Leaning into the mirror, Edward sighs. Like Kay, he no longer dreams of winning.

With fifteen minutes before Saturday mass, Eleanor stands behind him, her hands on his shoulders. *Put on some lipstick, dear. Doll yourself up and greet the new day with joy. We'll walk together like we used to – proud and lovely.*

Edward shakes his head. As much as he wants it, he could never embody Eleanor like that. She looked most beautiful on Sunday strolls to St. Peter's, at the threshold between the world and worship. With sunlight on her back and God's light on her face, she was one of his angels. How could a man stuffed into women's clothing compare to an angel?

No one cares what garments a soldier of Christ wears – just that he's true to his lord and congregation. I promise people will accept you, Edward. Don't you trust me?

He nods, but his trust in her doesn't change the world around him, and the battle ends the way it always does. He pinches the false lashes from his eyes before splashing water on his face. Mascara runs through the ravines to his chin – trails of black tears that freckle the sink after falling. His wig removed and makeup gurgling down the drain, Edward dons his lovely lies again. It's hard to imagine anything more constricting than a corset, but the grief he wears with his vestments makes breathing difficult. He shuts his grandmother's Duska tin and snaps his collar closed, searching for the man of God in his reflection. With Eleanor's crucifix around his neck, God shines in silver, but Edward sees no man in the mirror.

You Can't Choose Your Friends

by Shane Simmons

Sandra had some sort of 'breakdown' before the festive season. What with Stephen abandoning her just weeks before Christmas in favour of "that slut of a bastarding bitch," I've been lumbered with her for Christmas Day, Boxing Day, New Year's Eve, New Year's Day, oh, and most of the other days in between. We're almost halfway through the bloody month and I'm still tending to her histrionics.

"You're my 'life coach'. I need coaching back into life." From the glossy white floorboards she picks up the oversized wine glass I'd bought her for Christmas and downs its contents whole.

Me? She's selected *me* as her 'life coach'? Ha. Sandra makes me laugh, even with her panda eyes and random tears followed by outbursts of swearing. If age grants wisdom, then surely Sandra should have five years of foresight to explain why I'm not long twenty–two, and still I find myself with no one bar this scorned woman for adult company.

"I hate her. And I hate him. I HATE EVERYTHING!"

On a daily basis she screams, texts or finds some other way to relay her resentment to me. I'd suggest she hire one of those planes that writes fluffy messages in the sky to spell out the word

"CUNTS" over their love nest, but she'd kill me for resorting to any form of humour so early on in her heartbreak.

Heartbreak?

She pours a quarter glass of wine for me before snatching the bottle away to her vase–sized vessel. "Do you think they're happy? Do you? DO YOU?!"

I push out a sigh and crumple down into my shoulders, but as per, Sandra doesn't notice.

"They can't be happy because they're bastards! How could she do that to her own sister? Could you do that to your sister? COULD YOU?!"

Sandra's more than aware that my sister's husband is a putrid example of the male form. An oversized, balding figure who keeps the last precious strands of his hair in a halo that encircles his ball–shaped head. The idea of his greasy self makes me gag without too much effort. As Sandra stumbles out of the room, I rustle a bottle from the bag at my feet. I pour myself some rosé and swig it down. I had planned well: I'd bought one with a screw top. I only just slip it back in the bag before Sandra reappears with yet another box of tissues.

"Aren't you drinking?" She eyes up my empty glass and glances down at the two barren bottles by her feet. Of which I'd only tasted a few drops. "How could he? Just, how could he? Do you know how long they were shagging for, behind my back? DO YOU?!" She punctuates each word with a finger, jabbing in my direction, her face plumped and purplish, as if Satan himself will burst forth from under her skin.

"NO! NO I DON'T! And *you* need to stop screaming at *me* about all this!"

She stops jabbing the air and stares. Her finger curls up into her fist.

"Oh, it's like that is it?" she whispers, slurring. "I need some company after my man has left me, for my BLOODY SISTER, and you can't be arsed?" She topples around, grabbing hold of the mantel but maintaining her glare.

"Seeing as you told me how you shagged his cousin in the toilets at some wedding reception months before the two of you split up, I think you're being a bit of a hypocrite!"

"Get out." Swivelling on the spot, she points in the vague direction of the door. "Just go!"

I pick up my bag and coat from the sofa.

"Fuck off. Fuck off!! Fuck off!!! FUCK OFF!!!!" she yells, and drops to the floor.

"You mad drunken cow." I step over her and walk out. As the door slams behind me I hear her shrieks wither into sobs and I pause on the landing. Should I go back in and get her up and off to bed? Tomorrow she won't even remember what's happened.

I descend the stairs and her whimpers disappear behind me. I step through the hall she shares with her neighbours and head out the front door into the crispest January night. I'm only two minutes around the corner from home, but I take the long way just to draw in lungful after deep lungful of biting London air.

Monday, 13th January 2014

Cornfield

by Michelle Elvy

When a story begins with a blowjob in the back seat of a stolen car, you can bet on how it will end. There will be a high–speed chase scene, profanity, cops, *those fuckers*, trying to fuck things up, and a broken heart, or at least one sore dick. But this is not that kind of story. This is a story not about the stolen car or the guy driving it or the boyfriend of the girl in the backseat, or the boy who gets the blowjob (who's not the boyfriend). This story's more about the boy sitting in the backseat who simply unlocked the car so his friends could speed away on a joyride. This is the story about the boy who's not even sure why he's there with them. This is the story about the boy who goes along for the ride and sits in the back seat while one friend drives like a maniac and the other sits with feet on the dash and lights up a joint and the third eventually ends up with that blow job, when the boyfriend of the girl, the one in the front seat, is too stoned to care. This is the story of the boy who sits in the car racing down the highway, who dreams of something so far away and so incongruous and far–fetched he's never mentioned it. This is the story of the boy who sits in the backseat of a stolen car speeding down a Maryland highway on a cold January morning who dreams of Cape Horn.

§

"Shit. It doesn't fit."

"Try from another angle."

"C'mon, Stevie, you gotta apply more pressure."

Stevie is trying to tune out the trio behind him. They have plenty of advice as always, but it's only Stevie who knows how to break into a car in record time. It's not that hard, but none of his pals has the patience or skill to maneuver the Slim Jim just so, especially in the stone grey pre–dawn of a winter morning. He knows which cars to choose – better if they're from the 90s, even earlier if possible. The newer models are no good, too much electronic fancywork, GPS tracking and all that shit. He likes old–fashioned cars, the kind his dad used to drive, big and metallic and not all plasticy. He learned with a coathanger on cars with big windows and locking mechanisms with obvious knobs, but he can crack into the smaller Japanese models too. Anyone could, really. Except his friends.

He's used to their background noise, but on this day they are just standing around, hands in pockets and lips flapping while he freezes his fingers off.

"Shut the fuck up, guys!"

"Yeah, let the master work!" chides Lucky, who's been called that ever since he got nabbed by the cops for selling drugs a few years back when it's his older brother who is the real criminal of the family. Lucky's no criminal. Lucky just likes weed a little too much.

Stevie shoots Lucky a look: "Dick."

Lucky comes back with the best – and, if you're Lucky, *only* – comeback for *Dick*: "Pussy."

Stevie ends the conversation: *Click.*

"Who's calling my boy a pussy now?" says Manny as he pushes past Stevie and hops in the driver's seat. At eighteen,

Manny is all bravado and bulging biceps, and imagines himself the leader of this unlikely group of bandits. Manny always drives.

The others climb into the car and are soon heading down Route 2, out of town and rolling on long straight roads through the old tobacco country of South County. "Where to, boys?" asks Manny. "All the way!" comes the answer, always the same.

Sometimes *all the way* is as far as the Safeway parking lot, because Rick has to get to work by 7am and can't afford to lose this job, even though he plays bad–ass but really is the biggest pussy of all. Rick is a twin and can't seem to shake the idea that he's the smaller and weaker of the two brothers. Rick is what Mannie calls 'soft'. Rick is afraid much of the time. But Rick is probably the meanest of the lot.

Sometimes *all the way* is as far as the Galesville Market, where they stop for ham and cheese subs and Old Harry, the owner, gives them each a gumball because their enthusiasm is something he doesn't see much of these days and he always thinks them younger than they really are – never mind the fact that they show up in a different car each time. Old Harry likes the way they giggle: boys being irrepressible boys and slapping each other on the back. He does not see them as delinquents. He does not even consider that it's a Monday morning and they should be in school. He just sees boys who are hungry on a bitter January morning.

Today they stop by Ellie's and she nestles into the back seat between Rick and Stevie. She leans to the right onto Rick's shoulder and yawns, but Stevie is sure he feels her thigh press against his. Manny keeps driving, faster than usual, as corn and sorghum speed by. Lucky rolls a joint but only he and Rick take part, passing it back and forth, front to back and front again. Lucky turns around and grins at his girl and at Stevie but can't see Rick so passes the joint up over his head again. A half–hour goes by and Lucky falls asleep and Manny drives faster and Stevie squishes himself into his own corner of the backseat when he sees Ellie reach her hand down Rick's pants.

"Seriously, Manny, where're we goin'?" says Rick from the back seat, just making conversation all cool while Lucky's girl gets busy in his pants, but just then there's more to worry about than an errant handjob as blue and red lights come flashing behind.

"Shit."

"Hang on," says Manny, and veers off down a side road. A sharp turn comes up too quickly and the car swerves. Ellie squeals and is thrown right but when the car straightens out and Manny resumes driving fast along another short straightaway, she doesn't come up for air.

Stevie is now struggling to keep his eyes forward. He's used to all the fuck−ups but this is not his kind of game. He thinks he might be sick. He's not sure whether it's Manny swerving again or the idea of Rick getting blown at 9am in the seat beside him. He rolls his window down and leans his head out into the freezing wind. His ears feel like they'll fall off but he dares not come back in. Lucky's passed out up front, and next to him they aren't even trying to be quiet anymore; Rick's making little sobbing noises and Ellie's head's bobbing more exuberantly.

Even worse, Stevie's about to look despite his best intentions.

But he's saved from his own depravity when the car lurches hard to the right and the next thing he knows he's airborne, tossed like a ragdoll and soaring across acres of a desolate winter cornfield.

The dreams are always like this. He's lifted on a blanket of warmth, surrounded by a frozen January sky. Great Grandpa Gus, the one who worked on whaling ships, floats by but is too far away to hear Stevie's call. Stevie is cushioned on clouds like cotton candy and Gus is rioting along in heavy seas below. Stevie reaches out a hand to grab the ship's rigging but as he extends his arm the canvas tears with a screeching sound and he watches helplessly as first the topsail flutters away in the wind and then the ship turns inside out, halyards howling and rigging wrenching angrily from the decks and flying up with the sails. The great heavy hull is the last to go – lifted from the dark ocean and rising up, up, up, set twirling in the tornado–black air. Stevie tries to call for Great Grandpa Gus but panic rises in his gut because his voice won't reach from southern Anne Arundel County, on January 13, 2014, to Cape Horn where a great sailing ship is tearing apart at the seams nearly a century before.

The world slows and both ship and clouds disappear and all that is left is the cornfield now rising at an alarming speed upward toward him. In one instant Stevie thinks he sees fire off to the side and he may even hear music – *Nothing lasts forever but the earth and sky* – underneath the screeching tires and burning rubber and crunching metal. But he's not sure because he closes his eyes, only for a moment, and things go black.

When Stevie wakes in the hospital near midnight and his father says, "Where've you been, son?" and his mother covers him in kisses saying, "My darling child!" his mind first flashes to Manny and Lucky and Rick and Ellie and then he reaches once more for Gus. He tries to recall the cornfield over Maryland – or was it Kansas? – and he wants to say something about dust or wind but instead he replies, "Cape Horn".

Storm Lake

by Len Kuntz

The storm hit without warning, and now snowdrifts as tall as four feet are blocking the front door.

I try to call my wife but there's no cell service. Today's our anniversary: seven years. She's in Baltimore for a convention. When she returns we're supposed to make a decision about whether we're too broken to mend, her having had an affair with her boss, me being too scared to leave her.

Snow continues to drop, thick as mud, plates of the stuff. Outside tree branches break every half hour or so, the wreckage sounding like thunder and gunfire.

The power's been out since evening. Rotten food odors fill the kitchen. The refrigerator leaks dirty water. The silence in the house is so still it's unnerving, and now I can see my breath.

The dog stares at me, her head cocked, as if she senses doom. When I let her piss in the house, then mop up the floor, she scampers to a corner and begins mewling.

Outside, the lake is a white shelf, an ivory island. Ducks — looking more like decoys than the real things — cluster in the northeastern corner. Part of me wishes I owned a gun.

Our house in the woods is set a mile back from any road, and I know no one will be coming soon. Power outages in these parts can take days to be repaired.

The dog starts to moan, as if it's sick or injured or possessed. When I toss a sock at her, she shreds the thing in an instant.

The marriage counselor my wife and I tried always seemed to take my wife's side. He said my wife's motivations for the affair could be numerous. He suggested I was, in many ways, more than responsible. He said men who ignore their spouses are asking for trouble.

When I look over at the dog, she's chewing the leg of a stuffed chair and staring at me, growling as she rips off splinters. "Have at it," I say.

I ball up old newspapers and my wife's *Vogue* magazines and start a fire in the sink. I go to the bedroom and rummage through her dresser drawers, returning with lacy bras and thongs, most with the price tags still on. They're slow to catch flame, smoldering a ghostlike smoke.

When I was a kid, my brother and I used to walk across the lake when it froze over. He'd go out the farthest, mocking my cowardice. I told him I'd heard another boy had fallen through the ice, but that only caused my brother to titter and call me chicken shit.

The homes across the shore all have their lights on. It's a half mile trek. I get my coat and hat and boots. I walk through mattresses of snow, down a slope to the frozen waterfront. I look back at the house, hooded with drifts of gleaming white. I tell it goodbye and I think I mean it.

Wednesday, 15th January 2014

First Inning

by Michael Webb

I awaken in the middle of a dream, pursued by wolves in a lonely, arctic forest, emerging from the phantasmagoria of dream life into my bedroom full of polished wood, the black empty flatscreen TV, and a forlorn action figure on its side on the floor. Usually I don't sleep heavy enough to miss out on a kid invasion, but apparently I did today. I sit up, shaking my head to clear it.

Stretching out my throwing arm without thinking about it, pinwheeling it around in a big arc, I work the sleep out of the muscles. I play with it constantly. All pitchers do. You listen for pops or cracks, sore spots, adhesions, anything that might impede throwing a ball at high speed. We have to do everything perfectly, repeating the same series of motions thousands of times in a year. Making your living with your body, you are on a knife—edge, ready for the imperfection that would head you towards your final pitch.

I pull a red Diamondbacks shirt on from a couple of springs ago, thinking about how much looser it used to fit, and stumble downstairs. I hear the familiar buzz of voices, inane chatter from my daughter, more coherent speech from my son, my wife's voice with the edge of authority in it, keeping them on task. It sounds foreign to my ears, even after all these years – spending 7 or 8 months a year mostly away from them makes me a stranger in my own life.

Around the corner and into the kitchen, all gleaming metal and burnished wood, I see them all, buzzing through the morning with practiced precision. Angela has a very short tennis skirt on, her legs still hard and toned like the cheerleader she was.

"I'm playing tennis with Marissa today. I figured we wouldn't wake you," she says. Marissa Adler is married to Steven Adler, a fellow Arizona State alum, a part time outfielder who took me deep in extra innings in Baltimore the last time I faced him. We are still friends, although he seldom lets me forget about how he beat me.

"Thanks, dear," I say.

Coffee is still warm in the pot, and I pour myself a cup. The kids eye me up and down. The younger one, Maddie, is almost scowling. It's still unclear to her what I do, and she still finds my presence strange. She is never entirely ready to trust me. Not yet.

"You have APC today?" Angela asks. Athletic Performance Center: the scientists, nutritionists, physical therapists, and sadistic personal trainers whose job it is to prepare my body, and specifically my shoulder, elbow, and wrist, for the months of work they have in front of them.

"Yeah," I say. "11 to 1."

"So you can pick them up? I need to go to Macy's to look for a dress for that event on Saturday." In the favor–trading world of professional sports, I had agreed to attend a charity dinner for the Phoenix Suns' foundation in exchange for some NBA tickets. I don't want to go, but fair is fair, plus Angela loves getting dressed up.

"Sure, hon. No problem."

"Did you hear that, Madison? Daddy will pick you up today, not Mommy."

My daughter looks uncertain, her tiny face forming around a frown. "But Mommy! Miss Rose say ..." Madison hates surprises. You have to lay out a schedule for her every day, so she knows what to expect. Our son Dylan, on the other hand, couldn't care less, taking bumps in the road with a surfer's easy calm.

Angela cuts her off. "Miss Rose knows your father, Maddie. It's fine. Trust me. He's allowed to do pickups."

"OK," she says, unconvinced.

I see a stray lace on Madison's tiny pink sneaker. I bend low to tie it.

Angela continues bustling, preparing lunches and school bags, wiping noses and taming cowlicks. I watch the house function as it must while I am away. Dylan is concentrating on his cereal, taking enormous bites and chewing them slowly, a small smile on his lips. I have never seen anyone enjoy food as much as he does.

"Would you get Dylan's inhaler, hun? It's in the −" Angela begins.

"I got it, Mom," Dylan says between slurps of milk, pointing to a silver case next to his school bag.

"Oh," she says, surprised. "Good boy, Dyl. Thanks."

Then Madison jerks her foot away with a snarl. "Noooooo," she insists. "Mommy do it!" I feel a tiny pang of fear and hurt at her sharp tone. I understood intellectually that it is hard for her, that Ange does things one way, and they're used to that. But the rejection stings. Angela stops on her way through, stooping so she shows me a flash of her upper thigh, her polished short fingernails darting as she ties the wayward lace without a word.

They are ready a few minutes later, lining up as I put the milk back into the refrigerator and wash the kids' dishes. Ange always tells me I don't have to do that, because she spends all of my money, but I feel like I have to do something.

"Say goodbye to Daddy," Angela says as she herds them out the door.

"Bye, Dad!" Dylan says brightly.

"Bye," Madison says, and they leave. I listen to their footsteps crunch down the drive, their voices loud and bright again. I wonder about how I have become the interloper, even while I do bring home the large checks that pay for the house and the cars and the food and the private schools and the trips to Disney. The house echoes with silence, and I shrug and go upstairs to change into exercise wear.

Another year of large numbers beckons.

Making Music

by James Claffey

The Bird wakes with the sound of the dawn chorus, birds chattering on the telephone wires outside his window. On the floor, the Holy Water bottle; the events of the previous night return to his memory in full, terrible Technicolor. He makes a promise to go straight up to the Parish Priest's house that very morning and see what Father O'Hehir will make of his troubled night.

The town is clad in a cloak of dust and boredom as he moseys up Main Street towards the small stone church on the corner of Market Street. A brindled bitch lies in the shadow of the Bank of Ireland, nursing three scrawny pups, and the Bird thinks for a moment that the one who fights the other two off the teat mightn't make a decent fighting dog. The dog's persistence is exactly the quality needed in a good fighter. But training them to inflict harm on other dogs is an awful amount of work he thinks, and gives his head a shake.

His beard itches, and when he runs a dry tongue across his lips, the salty–sweet taste of day–old beans reminds him of how little money he has in the biscuit jar on the kitchen dresser. Never mind, he thinks, as he moseys through the church gates and into the dark entryway where the white marble font he's dipped his fingers into all his life sits. He pushes the double doors open and enters the echoing church as Father O'Hehir limps across the altar, genuflecting half–way, and continuing towards the sacristy entrance. Four silent confession boxes flank the back of the church, the dark chocolate wood stained with the absorbed sins of so many years. The Bird coughs. The echo stops the priest in mid–step.

"How's the Bird?" Father O'Hehir asks, walking through the gilded altar gates and up the aisle towards his visitor.

"Grand, thanks be to God," the Bird replies. "Though, I wanted to have a word with you about the Mammy." The Bird stumbles on the words. He fingers the collar of his shirt. "Well, it's a ... it's ... it's a bit delicate, Father," he says. "But, since the funerals I've been having nightmares, and I'm certain the Mammy is visiting the house at night."

"By the Hokey, that's a powerful tale altogether," the priest says, his eyebrows aquiver. "Are you sure it's not the rats in the attic you're after hearing?"

"Now, Father, I'm after seeing my own Mammy these past nights. Didn't she only appear to me as if she was an angel from Heaven?"

"Was it a dream you were having?" the priest asks.

"Father, as God's my witness, she fluttered her wings and shook her tail feathers at me from the bedstead."

The priest scratches his chin, raises and lowers his eyebrows twice and beckons to the Bird to follow. From a recess in the holy water font he takes a plastic bottle in the shape of the Blessed Virgin Mary and fills it with water. "There now, sprinkle this across the windows and the threshold of the door to the bedroom and you'll be game ball."

"What if that doesn't work, Father?" the Bird asks, sliding the bottle into his pocket.

"We'll cross that bridge when we come to it, won't we," the priest says, with a knowing wink.

The Bird runs a hand through his sandy hair and heads off toward his house, the distant rainclouds unloading their burden on the green hills to the south. He passes along by the large façade of McKettrick's Public House and thinks he might have a jar, but frets that if he doesn't take care of the holy water, he'll have another restless night.

Inside the house once more, he creeps upstairs, the opened bottle held in front of him like a burning stake. The bedroom is dim and on the bed his mother's nightgown lies crushed in a ball. Kneeling, the Bird recites a decade of the Holy Rosary and takes the bottle of Holy Water and scatters it in the closet. Small trails of vapor rise from the wooden boards. "Oh, Mammy, are you trapped in there?" he asks. Not a sound, only the rapid beating of his own heart. "Hail Holy Queen, Mother of Mercy, Hail our life, our sweetness, and our hope," he intones, spraying the water on the windowsill and then across the foot of the door. His duty done, he shakes out the nightdress and folds it neatly, placing it under the pillow.

Maybe later, he thinks, he will take a bicycle ride over to Clara for the *seisiún* in Hogan's Bar. Thursdays, local fiddlers, bodhrán players, and tin whistlers get together in the main bar around the fire and play until closing time. More often than not there are some of the town's young girls gathered in bunches, like spring flowers at the Saturday market in Mullingar. He holds out hopes of meeting a husky young one with wide hips and a straight smile, who might overlook his under–bite and pay him a little attention.

As a boy, he'd had no luck with the girls. Partly because his father was the town undertaker, and most of the town's children were afraid of "catching death" if they touched the Bird, or even came close. When he told his mother that he hated what his father did for a living she only hugged him tight and said he'd had no choice in the matter since his father's family had been burying the local population for over 150 years.

At the local dances, hops, and other social occasions he finds himself alone at the side of the room, wallflowering it, and sucking his drink through a straw. The Bird prefers the outskirts of the crowd, staying to himself, nursing his pint and sneaking looks at the pretty girls from under his cap; even though he's had Murtagh the Solicitor sell the business after the parents' funerals, he knows the locals will always associate him with the burying of the dead.

Hogan's is hopping when the Bird arrives. Punters at the bar are three deep and he elbows his way into the throng and waves a fiver about for an age before Breda, the owner's wife, gives him a smile and tilts a pint glass under the tap.

"Busy night, Breda," he says. "Is the *seisiún* about to start?"

"It is, Bird, it is. We're waiting for the lass on the tin whistle to arrive. French she is."

"By God, is that a fact? French, and playing the *feadóg*?" the Bird replies. He's learned a tune or two on the old brass pipe, but hasn't much aptitude for music. Still, he enjoyed the traditional music, grew up with it on the radio, and wasn't his daddy a great one for the *seisiúns.*

"Aye. She's a Breton, I hear they're descendants of the Celts, down there," Breda says, and rushes to the other end of the bar where another customer waves a note in the air.

With his pint in his hand, the Bird makes his way to the wall adjacent to the toilets, where he can enjoy the music and slip out the emergency exit should he want to get off home early. The distance home is a good five miles, and on the bicycle in the dark will be a treacherous one. As he settles into his corner, the musicians tune their instruments, and he admires the way the fiddle player pings the strings with his little fingernail. A sparrow−like woman with grey hair winds her way through the crowd and sits on a short stool with the other musicians. She undoes the clasps of a small, narrow box and pulls out a shiny tin whistle.

"Good of you to put in an appearance, Melody, even if you are a bit on the late side," one of the players ribs her.

"My name is not Melody," she says, under her breath.

"Ah, lighten up on her, doesn't she come farther than all of us? Go on, Noreen, get her a glass of Guinness and blackcurrant would you?" the bodhrán player orders his wife.

A bucketful of reels and airs later the Bird goes to the toilet and relieves himself standing at the porcelain urinal where he reads the sports pages of the newspaper behind a Perspex cover. When he returns to the bar the woman with the long gray hair is just outside the exit on a steel Guinness barrel smoking a cigarette. The Bird sucks in his gut and sticks out his chest, intent on making a good impression, and after coughing so as not to startle her, he says, "You've quite a pair of lips on you, if you don't mind me saying so."

"Thank you. Though I don't know if you're talking about my playing, or whether you want to kiss me down below!" the woman replies, in a slight foreign accent.

"Oh, no! I m ... mea ... meant your music. I apologize," the Bird says, stuttering.

"Now I should be disappointed, no?" she says. "My name is Elodie." She holds a hand out for him to shake.

"Pleased to meet you, I'm sure. I'm called the Bird. The Bird Mahony," he says, and takes her small hand in his and shakes it once. He blushes, not quite knowing what to say next.

"What a curious name, Bird? Why are you called Bird?"

"Oh, my mammy said when I was born I looked just like a baby chicken, so they called me Bird, and never anything else."

"I think it's a lovely name, Bird." She smiles again. "You have traveled far to hear the music, Bird?"

"The next town over. Sure, it's only five miles." The Bird runs a finger inside his collar and feels the sweat around his neck. "Well, I must be going now, it's a long cycle back home." He puts a thumb and forefinger to the peak of his cap and nods at her.

"Well, I do hope you come to hear us again," she says, smiling at him. She stubs the cigarette butt with the toe of her boot and wanders back to the other musicians. The Bird looks into the space she's occupied, for a full minute, until the strains of Cooley's reel wafts out on the night air. Whistling softly, he slips out to his bicycle, clips the trousers about his ankles and mounts with a grunt. As he pedals the narrow road home a light rain falls and he whistles all the louder.

The Suicide Club

by Gwendolyn Joyce Mintz

You'd think Mora's smoking something other than a cigarette by the way she jumps when she hears me behind her.

"Damn, Aaron," she says, shaking her head from side to side. "You scared me."

"Sorry." I push the gate to the fencing that surrounds the dumpster open and heave the garbage-filled bag into the metal container.

Mora has one arm tight around her waist for warmth, the hand of the other, balancing a cigarette before her face.

"Why're you over here?"

"Scott said we can't smoke by the back door anymore; it doesn't look good for customers." She rolls her eyes and takes another drag.

"I thought you gave up smoking this year."

"My New Year's resolutions last about a day, two if I'm lucky."

I chuckle, close the gate and replace the chain.

"What about you?" Mora asks. "You make any resolutions you can't keep?"

"Nope. I made one and so far, I'm good."

"That's why you've advanced here and I'm still just above minimum wage." She takes a last puff, drops the butt on the ground and squashes it with the toe of her shoe. "So what is it?

I'm curious."

I hesitate. Then taking care with my words, I say, "I, uhm, I'm not planning on being here another year. I've resolved to get things in order so I can go."

"Lucky you. I wish I could leave this place. Where're you headed – another job in town or you're leaving altogether?"

I glance up at the sky.

"I won't tell Scott. Hell, he deserves to lose a good worker like you."

I take a breath. I can trust Mora. I know I can.

"I'm going ... Mora, I'm going ..."

She raises a brow.

"I'm going to kill myself. I'm getting things in order so I won't be here, alive, after this year."

She examines my face. A whispered "wow" escapes her lips.

I think, in the minutes that pass, that I should go back in but my feet have frozen in place.

Mora fumbles with the cigarette carton in her pocket. She takes another and lights it. After a few drags, she says, "Sometimes I wish ..." She glances at me. "When I got out after the second time, I really believed that things would get better, that I could make them better." She shakes her head and looks away.

"I know. I don't know how to change things either, to get them to change. I've tried but I'm done."

She faces me. "Would you have said goodbye?"

"I was planning to, yes."

"Do you know when?"

"Nah. Just when some things are in order."

"You are so much braver than me." Mora flicks the half–smoked cigarette to the ground. She stomps it out and walks away.

§

My shift's done before Mora's and she stops me at the time clock. Asks what I'm doing now that I'm off.

Going home.

"Let's go get a drink at Kelly's."

I stare at her and maybe she can read me because she says, "Yes, I want to talk about it but I'm not going to try and talk you out of it. I'm off in half an hour. Meet me, okay?"

She's up to something but I agree to meet.

"One?" the hostess asks, her hand hovering over the stacked menus on the podium.

"I'm meeting someone. But we won't be eating, probably just drinks." I eat free at work – I'm not paying for another meal. This is one thing noted on my list of 'THINGS I WILL MISS'. Although I know I won't even be aware, but that's beside the point.

"Sit at the bar or do you want a table?"

I take the table. I need the space between me and Mora so I won't feel so vulnerable.

"Your server will be right with you."

"Thanks," I say as I'm stripping my jacket off. Before I place it on the back of the chair, I watch the hostess walk away and note that great asses will be another thing missed.

I'm still sipping at my draft beer when Mora bustles in. She glances around, finally zooms in on my raised arm flagging her. It's not until she's at the table that I realize she's not alone.

Alarm must flood my face because suddenly Mora is

apologizing and reassuring.

"This is Diane," she says. "I met her at the psychiatric hospital."

I don't know if she was a patient or a worker. "You tried to kill yourself too?"

Diane nods.

I turn to Mora.

She avoids my eyes, peels off her coat. She and Diane pull out chairs. They sit on either side of me.

I raise the mug to my lips. I give Mora time to explain. But before she does, the server pops up. Mora orders a Bloody Mary and Diane, a soft drink.

When the three of us are alone again, Mora says, "Diane needs someone to talk to."

I turn to Diane. She's fiddling with her hands.

I'm pissed at Mora, though I'm not sure why. I grunt then spit out, "She needs to talk but you're talking for her?"

Mora jerks back a bit. She turns to Diane. Back to me. "Damn, Aaron."

"No, damn you, Mora," I tell her. "I'm not a freaking counse –"

"I want to die," Diane interjects. "Or not live the way I'm living. Either way, I, I just want someone I can share that with. Someone who's not going to try and talk me out of it."

"I just thought maybe the three of us could talk about it sometimes," Mora says. "I haven't decided completely that that isn't the road for me, but it'd be easier to talk to someone who understands because they want the same thing."

The server returns with the drinks.

We drink in silence.

Putting down my mug, I mutter, "A suicide club."

Mora chuckles. "Yeah, I guess."

I turn the empty mug in circles. Watch the water drops it leaves behind.

The irritation I felt is replaced with some kind of calm. I feel close to these two simply because we're tired of fighting alone.

"Fine," I say.

"Then we'll meet again? Let's say in a month? See where we're at?" Mora suggests.

I bite the inside of my lip for a moment, then bob my head up and down.

"Although," Diane adds, "it would make me happy if I couldn't make it."

Compassion

by Stephen V. Ramey

Anne closed the curtains at precisely 10:30 this morning. She's only trying to slow the heat leaking from these old wooden window frames, but sometimes I think she thinks she can control entropy. The downside is that it leaves me in a dim room with twelve–foot–high ceilings. I haven't even bothered to push the lever that opens the recliner.

My father died November 11, 2002, but he was diagnosed on January 18, 2000. To me, that day – today, January 18 – is the meaningful one, the day his death took root.

Footsteps sound upstairs. Anne must be done reading her email. I imagine boards denting and rebounding as her steps continue onto the staircase. Panic shoots through me. My eyes seek the tablet in sleep mode on my lap. How long have I been sitting here? Fifteen minutes? An hour? Anne will want to see progress.

I touch the touchpad, and work through the memorized motions of making the computer aware of me. The word processor page takes form. I feel a moment of hope. Maybe I started writing before ... but, no, it's blank.

A stair tread cries out. Anne's hand appears on the railing. *Type something!*

I ... But it's so trite, to open with "I". I press Backspace, and the page is blank again.

Anne stops at the threshold between rooms. We recently removed carpet from the dining room, and were pleased to find the original wood flooring in good shape. I wish I could say the same for the living room. We took up this carpet last year. The pine boards were dinged and scraped, warped in a few places. We covered the worst with an inexpensive area rug.

"Well?" she says.

"It's starting to come together," I say. I'm supposed to write a letter to the editor about the city's plans to demolish another building. In the five years we've lived here, three buildings have come down in the downtown district, leaving gaps in the Victorian era façade like extracted teeth. If this continues we'll have no smile, nothing left to connect us to our glorious past. Once, New Castle rivaled Pittsburgh in industry, and boasted the largest tin mill in the world.

"Read what you have so far," Anne says. Her voice is flat. She knows.

"I ..." I stare at the floor.

Anne takes down our coats from the rack beside the door, and tosses mine across the room. It lands in a heap. "We're going for a walk."

"Okay." I set the tablet aside. My stomach mimics a clenching fist. I love my wife, but it's so easy to despise her too.

"Why are you having problems this time?" Anne says. She digs gloves from her coat pocket and pulls them on.

A shiver comes over me. It's cold enough out here to make me realize how warm it was inside. I ball my hands into my pockets as we pass the Pizza Hut and start across Grant Street toward the more historic sections of downtown. The sky is a continuous layer of cloud, but bright despite it. Probably because I've been indoors all morning.

"I can't find an interesting way into the piece," I say. I've never been close to my muse. Lately it's been a struggle just to glimpse her wing dust.

"It's just a letter to the editor," Anne says. Her gaze is dull as pewter. I remember when her eyes used to shine, or was that my imagination? A bus growls past, water splashing from its tires. An advertisement shows a happy family. *Refresh Dental brings out your best smile.*

"You're supposed to be a writer," Anne says. "Half the letters they publish wouldn't pass a third grade grammar test."

"It has to be good," I say. I watch my black sneaker step up onto the crumbling sidewalk. We have slate by our house. It's cracked too, but that took a hundred years of wear. This concrete was poured since we moved here. "What's the point of writing something just to write it?"

"The point is that you agreed to do this for the Historic District Board," Anne says. "That's the point."

I blow a warm, moist breath into my hands. *Did she forget my gloves on purpose?* "All the more reason it should be good," I say.

"What it should be," Anne says, "is *finished.* The meeting is tonight. You were supposed to send it in last week."

"I know, I know." I hang my head. I'm wearing sneakers with Velcro instead of laces. How lazy is that? My toes are cold. I look up.

A half-block ahead, the traffic signal turns red, and the red cascades block after block after block. This part of New Castle isn't much different from most small cities: a funeral home, a 1960's office complex, traffic lights. Even here, though, there are signs. The church across the way, with its turrets and crenellated roofline, brings to mind Conquistadors. The next block features a towering Catholic church with stained glass windows that recall Renaissance artwork. Victorian houses–turned businesses dot the neighborhood, the stiff formality of their construction offset by complex steeple rooflines and gingerbread trim painted in primary colors.

"You'll finish when we get back," Anne says. "I thought it might be helpful to walk past the building."

"I'm not sure anything will help," I mumble.

We pass the Humburg Insurance building, a low slung seventies design with angled plate glass and wood shingle siding. Snow speckled with black cinders is piled within the shadow of its eaves. I wonder if New Castle isn't like that, stained with the past and slow to melt. Maybe that's why I'm having problems.

"Hey!" A woman waves from across the street.

"Rose," Anne says.

A smile overtakes me. I wave back. Rose is Italian and finds more reasons to laugh than to frown. I like her. She's also a witch.

"I wish you would smile like that for me," Anne says.

"I wish I could," I say. She winces and I want to take it back. I don't mean to be passive–aggressive, it just slips out sometimes.

We watch Rose bustle across four lanes, bundled in winter boots, coat, gloves, and a floppy knitted hat that hides her gender. Nothing, however, can mask her energy.

"How are you guys doing?" she says. She stomps slush from her boots, then dips past my guard to give me a hug. There's an intoxicating aspect to Rose's spontaneous hugs. No manipulation, no ulterior motive, just the bliss that comes from being momentarily aware of a compassionate universe. I squeeze back, but that adds nothing.

Rose steps back. "Jimmy and I danced beneath the full moon on Thursday."

"Naked?" I say.

She laughs. "Do I look stupid?" She rubs her gloved hands together, then slaps them. "Are you guys coming to Jimmy's gig tonight?"

"Where?" Anne says.

"Cracker Barrel, seven–ish."

"I didn't know Cracker Barrel did live comedy," I say. *Especially Jimmy's irreverent satire.*

Rose gives us a Mona Lisa smile. "They don't know it either. It's part of his Stealth Comedy Tour where he goes into a business and does a routine. We're going to record it for his webcast. I'm in charge of that."

"Sounds interesting," I say. "Count me in." The Cracker Barrel is about fifteen minutes east, near WalMart, Lowes, Staples and other capitalist vampires.

"You're not going anywhere until you finish your work," Anne says. She nods to Rose. "He's grounded."

My whole body tenses. "I'm not a child, Anne."

"Prove it," she says.

"Ouch," Rose chimes in. "There's a spell for writer's block, you know." She bites the end of a gloved finger, pulls off the glove with her teeth, and produces a Smartphone from her pocket.

"You have it on your phone?" I say.

"You've never heard of Google? Some writer you are." She swipes and types, then extends the phone toward me. There's a list of ingredients, and more than a page of instruction.

"Looks complicated."

"If this stuff was easy, anyone would do it."

I push the phone away. "It's not actually writer's block. Fourteen years ago today, Dad got his cancer diagnosis."

Anne frowns. "Why didn't you tell me?"

"I shouldn't have to. I told you last year, and the year before that, probably."

"I'm sorry," Rose says. She puts the phone away. "Is he, did he ... pass?"

"Two days before his seventieth birthday," Anne says. She doesn't like to be caught without the facts of a situation.

"That's so sad," Rose says.

"It's been twelve years," Anne says. "And they weren't even close. Mostly, I think it's an excuse not to write."

"She wants me to demolish my father's memory," I say, "but insists I write letters when the city plans to tear down one lousy building. Doesn't that seem hypocritical to you?"

"A building dies with its destruction, and deserves our protection," Rose says. "Your father isn't gone, Stephen. You shouldn't let grief block out the light." She glances to the sky. "If you want, I can help you let go."

"Seriously?" Anne says. "That's what he needs."

"Gee, thanks," I say. "It's nice to have supportive friends and family."

Rose grabs my hand. "You have to ask yourself," she says, "whether a person does a blind man any favors by polishing his cane."

"I don't know what that means."

She shrugs. "We can either pay lip service to what you believe is important, or we can try to open our eyes to what *is* important. People who cling to ghosts are avoiding something in their reality."

"He's afraid of something," Anne says. "Failure, maybe?"

"Oh, it's more than that," Rose says. She presses my hand to her cheek. I feel my fingers unclench, cup her warm flesh.

Anne's expression dissolves into a stunned stare. Her eyes cast at me, cling, repel. Her lips push together. *She's jealous*, I think. *Afraid.*

The Storm

by Gay Degani

If a stranger stands, say, on the top of the creek bank in wooly darkness, he might wonder about the cabins, so oddly placed on this residential street. Vacation rentals built a hundred years back, five of them, plainly shingled, form a U around a weedy courtyard. On the other side of a thick border of Eugenia trees, a Mediterranean mansion sits on a knoll. Other homes along the road belong to a middle world, neither imposing nor humble, built in the thirties when the nearness of Riolito Creek seemed a special place to live until a dam and flood channel changed the natural swell and ebb of the creek and stole much of its natural beauty. On the edge of the city, far from schools, homes mismatched and unkempt, the neighborhood has become less and less desirable.

This stranger, unmindful of the growing wind, might notice Jamie in the front cabin, holding aside the curtain, hair clipped back from her neck, the yellow light from behind turning her to silhouette. It's too dark for the stranger to see the crease between her brows, the grim set of her mouth, but what tells him everything, is the sliding slope of her shoulders.

Leaves skitter along the Old Road. A gust rustles through sycamore and oak. Jamie turns away. The abandoned curtain sways.

Lily and Collin watch "Sesame Street" on the VCR Sean brought back from one of his trips, "Property of Lincoln Motel" scratched into the back. What will he bring this time? Ice bucket? Shower curtain? Those little soaps and shampoos and plastic–wrapped cups that make the kids squeal when he empties his pockets?

"I'm hungry," says Lily from her spot on the carpet.

Jamie says, "Okay, sweetie," but before heading into the kitchen, she checks the window again. Only blackness. A whoosh of wind rattles the windows; a door slams across the courtyard at Mr. German's, a light pops on.

"Mom." Impatience from Lily. "Hungry."

Jamie puts the kids to bed and checks her cell. Nothing from Sean.

He said he'd be home tonight, but maybe not tonight, "maybe" meaning go to bed and don't think about it. Not this time. She's sick of being let down. She tiptoes into the kids' room, slides open drawers, and quietly pulls out underwear, t–shirts, jeans, sweatshirts.

A groggy "Mom?" comes from Lily's bed.

Jamie says, "Go to sleep."

Flicking off the living room light with her elbow, Jamie remembers shoes for the kids. Decides to get them tomorrow and heads into her own room, dumps the clothes on the bed, and drags her big blue Samsonite from the closet. She has no relatives except for an aunt in Oregon, but she hesitates to go there. If she leaves Sean, she doesn't want to be found. At least not until she clears her head. She told Lily if Daddy didn't come by tomorrow, they'd get in the car and join him for a mini–vacation. Swimming at a motel, maybe. She only half–lied.

§

She's asleep when a thundering crack, a ferocious shudder, sends her hurtling from bed. Earthquake? The kids are crying in their room. She yells, "Get on the floor by the dresser. I'm coming," as she flies into the living room and trips, falling headfirst into something that shouldn't be here, something sharp scraping her face, something sharper stabbing her ribs. The smell of dust and dirt fill her nose. Then, the house isn't shaking at all. Cold air sweeps through her, and looking beyond the giant branches of a tree – a tree? – she sees a spray of stars. How did the night sky get inside her house?

The answer hits her. The oak from out front fell through the roof.

Collin wails, and Jamie, tangled up, can't get to her feet. She tears at her sweatpants caught on a broken branch. Grabs and yanks and yanks, but the fabric holds. Panic clogs her chest as she struggles to break free.

"Mama!" cries Collin.

"We can't get out," hollers Lily.

"I'm coming." Scratching, thrashing, cursing, Jamie drags off her pants, and leaving them dangling on a stem, she tries to climb into the living room, but a limb cracks under her weight. And where the hell is Sean? The fucker.

She struggles out of the jumble of wood and prickly leaves, and crawls into her bedroom, spies Sean's baseball bat and uses it to smash the window. Jumps back as glass shatters, and then, carelessly knocking away the shards, scrambles onto the dresser and tumbles into the chill. The wind stings her legs, waters her eyes. A man rounds the corner of the cabin. Sean! But it's not Sean. Stumbling to her feet, she shoves the man toward the window of the second bedroom. "My kids! Help me get them out."

§

When Jamie and the man carry Lily and Collin around to the front of the house, the neighbors, the persistent wind whipping hair and bathrobes, rush to greet them. Jamie gapes at the giant oak on its side, her cabin sheared down the middle, with chaos and debris on one side, her own personal still–life on the other.

A short while later, lit by candles and a kerosene lamp, tenants from the other cabins crowd the landlady's living room like flickering ghosts. The man who helped Jamie rescue the kids clears a space on the sofa, hands her a blanket to cover her legs. She lets her children settle on her lap, wincing from her cuts and scratches, feeling out of body, out of time. The blustering wind howls.

She turns to the man, "Who *are* you?"

Mr. German puts his hand on the man's shoulder. "This is my boy, Mars. Just came down from Frisco." To his dad, this middle–aged man is still a kid.

"Thanks for getting my little guys out, Mars. How – how bad is it?"

"Wind up to 90 miles an hour," says Sybil, wrapped in one of her Hawaiian print housecoats, bringing over a tray of instant coffees. She hands one to Jamie. Mars and his dad take cups and nodding, move away to join the other cabin tenants hovering around the windows.

"I guess you couldn't wait for me to put in a skylight in your cabin," says Sybil to Jamie. "Glad you're all right. Your husband's not home, I take it?"

"No, he's roofing in Fresno."

"A roofer who no longer has a roof! You have your phone, honey?"

Jamie shakes her head. The landlady hands her a cell. "How about some hot chocolate for the kids? Might as well drink the milk before it spoils. We may not have electric for hours."

"Thank you. They'd like that." She watches Sybil thread her way through the clutch of neighbors, then punches numbers into the cell, thinking Sean should be here instead of gone. Always gone. She wants him here now. She sputters into his voice mail, "Come home. A tree – we – just come home."

After Lily and Collin fall asleep on their mother's lap, Mars helps her carry them into Sybil's second bedroom.

"How old are these two?" he asks.

"Almost three and five."

"Nice kids."

"They are. Thanks again, Mars. We're lucky you were around."

As he leaves, Sybil tiptoes in with jeans for Jamie to put on. "Everybody's outside. Go on to sleep, honey."

But sleep is the last thing Jamie can do.

As the sun creeps up, the wind turns quiet. The ravaged neighborhood is littered with broken limbs, twisted Eugenias, piles of leaves. A splintered electric pole, its wires strewn about, the corner stop sign bent at 45 degrees, sirens in the distance announce apocalypse. Neighbors from up and down the Old Road mutter about the mess, the noise, and the miracle that no one's seriously hurt.

Exhausted, Jamie gapes at her own disaster. Mars moves next to her, startling her, says, "It's not so bad," but she shakes her head and picks her way around the ruined cabin to her bedroom window, Mars ambling behind. "Kids sleeping?"

"Sybil's feeding them Cheerios. I need my phone. Sean probably left me a message."

"I can climb in and get it for you."

"Thanks, but just give me a boost. I want to look around."

"So your husband," he says. "He's not here?"

"He'll be here."

Once inside, Jamie searches the bedroom floor for her cell.

"Got it?" Mars peers in the window.

"Yeah." She holds it up. She moves closer to the door to the living room.

"Any message?"

"Yes," she lies.

The old oak sprawls like some kind of fallen dragon. Light sifts through branches, dust motes laze on air, her suitcase, the Samsonite, squashed by the foliage.

Monday, 20th January 2014

Indignation

by Sally—Anne Macomber

To: Milton Flaxmill, Red Cow Publishing
From: Trudy Polaris
Date: January 20, 2014 1:21 p.m.
Re: My Book

Milton,

I was dismayed to see that once again, on the latest version of my new book *Nuclear Fission in the Pyrénées*, emailed to me only this morning, that the title does not include the two accents in *Pyrénées*.

I have lived with this project for three years and the two accents are integral to the book.

I can only conclude their non—inclusion is a sign that you do not take me or my work as a writer seriously.

I will not be publishing my book with you or Red Cow Publishing, and will be taking it elsewhere.

Trudy Polaris

Tuesday, 21st January 2014

Thorns

by Mandy Nicol

The screen door twangs shut behind me and a dozen flies. I heave the shopping bags into the kitchen. Put the milk, meat and marge in the fridge and leave the rest on the bench, including the fourteen cans of dog food for Peregrine. Mum watches from the dining room. I flick the switch on the kettle.

"Cuppa?" I ask.

"Oh yes, I'm parched."

I look out the window. Peregrine is lying under the thorny acacia. Dead to the world. Didn't welcome me home, doesn't notice the rabbits nibbling along the dam paddock fence. I stare at him until the kettle boils. He doesn't move. *Shit, maybe he is dead.* I glance at all the dog food I bought then knock on the window. Loudly.

"What is it?" asks Mum. "Is something there? What's the matter Nadia?" Her voice rises to that shrill pitch she's fond of.

Peregrine has his head up, ears cocked towards the house.

"It's all right," I say, "Just rabbits getting too close to the roses."

I wonder what Mum will call her next dog. She'll have to work hard to beat Peregrine. I pour boiling water into the teapot. Can't use teabags when she's watching, even though I've proved she can't tell the difference.

"Any mail?" she asks.

"I got an invite to Tom and Ellie's wedding."

"Nothing else? Nothing for me?"

"Err, no Mum, nothing else."

She slumps, but only for a moment, and I wait for it. I count in my head and get to four.

"Well it's perfectly understandable. That job has him moving around like a movie star and now he's in New York. Hong Kong, Dubai, and now New York. New York! Can you believe it?"

She smiles at the photos on the mantelpiece before trundling along. "Of course he's probably still settling in and getting to know his way around, meeting people, going to dinner parties, you know how popular he is. Well, he always was popular, even as a little tacker. Remember his twenty–first? I think everyone in town was here. I bet they have him doing those, what do they call it now, meet and greets? Yes he'd be doing a lot of that, he'd be very good at it … I'm sure he just, well, he probably hasn't had a minute to himself …"

I keep my mouth shut, pour out the tea and get the last of her birthday cake out of the fridge.

A New Ned

by Margaret Bingel

Wednesdays are the worst. Ned wrote this in bold, angry letters across his new calendar, barely used, just opened three weeks ago when he remembered that January is technically a brand−new month, and with it, you open your brand−new calendar and hang it on the wall.

The calendar, a standard 12−month with holidays and weekdays measured out, pictures droopy−eyed beagles wearing monocles and top hats nestled between their floppy ears. Ned thinks beagles are the most unfortunate dogs, and now forced to wear these distasteful props … He stares at the January picture of a puppy yawning in bed, wearing a red bow−tie. Why does my mother insist on getting me these sad−looking calendars, he wonders. Does she really think this makes life bearable in any serious kind of way? She needs to get a dog. Ned sighs, and, looking at the January page repeats his angry words in his head.

Wednesdays are just the stupidest, most wasteful days of the week, especially when your Tuesdays are really your Mondays, on the first three−day weekend you get right after Christmas. He raises his hand and tracing the letters with his index finger, pretends to write it all over again. Of course, this is why I just took the whole damn week off, he thinks, fingernails dragging across the week where he wrote, VACATION, in neat red letters.

It isn't that he doesn't like the calendars his mother gives him, he thinks, as he sits down at the table to his coffee, newspaper, and cooling toast, but Ned Billingsly is not excited about growing old. Today, he thinks, as he sips his coffee and pushes aside his newspaper, is the day I'll make time stop.

He drinks the last of his coffee and eats the last of his toast. He lives alone, but loves to sit by his window and watch the buzzing people scuttling off to their appointments, schools, jobs, lovers, restaurants, and football and basketball and hiking and bird−watching. His favorites are the cyclists (they move so fast, like they're cheating death) and children. Children are special because they haven't figured out time yet, still living with the idea that the Now That Is Going On is What Will Always Be. He believes in children, even if he doesn't believe in himself anymore.

Ned looks out his window, and sees a chatty woman herding a group of yellow−jacketed, glassy−eyed, cold, breathing dragon's breath in the chilly January air automatons. Most likely a new group of outreach youth, Ned thinks. Or teachers. Probably teachers, he shrugs while standing up and moving his dishes to the sink. He turns the hot water on. Rubbing a soapy washcloth over his plate, he thinks about what it's like to be happy. As long as I get my gun, I'll be happy, Ned thinks, placing his dripping plate into the dish rack.

My gun, and my bullets.

Done with the dishes, he looks outside the window one more time. It's January, but the snow on the ground isn't so much light, fluffy stuff but deceiving ice piles and slicks on the sidewalks. The last thing Ned needs is to trip and hurt himself with his gun in his hand. He slips his coat on, and, feeling for his wallet and keys in his coat pockets, and looking down to check he has both shoes on his feet, he steps out into the cold, locks the door behind him, and walks towards the bus stop.

He walks past many beautiful things, things he's seeing for the first time: trees with snow−covered branches; prismatic icicles; two women in love, strolling and laughing, their mittened hands clasped together. While watching the beautiful women, he doesn't see the patch of black ice on the sidewalk. Stepping on it, his leather soles slip out from under him, and he falls backwards, his head smacking pavement.

One of the women breaks her clasp and rushes towards him.

Ned doesn't respond. With his eyes half–closed, he looks like he's dreaming. Blood leaks from his ears, and falls in droplets on the ice.

Thursday, 23rd January 2014

I was a fool yesterday

by Darryl Price

I was a fool yesterday. I'm still a fool today. I can feel it in my bones. Sleep did nothing to dampen this sensation in me. Does this feel good? I'm not really so sure. Yesterday it felt like I had discovered something so right that it just might change the world as we know it. Today I only know I am still in the full grip of this thing that renders me useless to myself as a trained to take a bullet for the King bodyguard. I have become a second–class citizen in my own country of self. How is this even possible you ask? Well, let me start by saying that sometimes we are very simply confronted out of the blue with someone so beautiful that we become instantly obsolete ourselves from the brush of experience. It wipes us out, and when we do discover we may still have say certain rudimentary motor skills such as walking and talking they become a wonder to us, as if newly procured. That's what I'm trying to tell you. This has happened to me. And today I mean to act upon it – if I can get out of bed and showered in time to again meet my destiny face to face and ask her out. But I'm not done telling you about this phenomenon yet. Here, let me start it all over again for you. It's fun. Or crazy. And. I want to. It's that fantastic! Just like in the movies you feel like making a kooky song out of anything that moves, anything mundane. The sun through the stupid blue curtains. All of a sudden like a stage full of soft ballerinas dancing in unison to a low slow moon song. The way your slippers feel sliding onto your feet first thing. An excited bird tattling on a bad cat outside the still drying off from the clouds of night early morning window. The click of the same lamp switch becomes a bittersweet call to arm. A car going by and fading into another lost silence. All incredible. I mean it. Anything becomes everything. You can't help but make that connection from now on. It's impossible and happening and you feel hungry and full at the same time. The water coming out of the faucet is nothing short of an actual bona fide miracle. Do you get the picture? The man in the mirror is for real. Dude. It's all too much. And you can never get enough. Never never never.

Friday, 24th January 2014

People Skills

by Teresa Burns Gunther

I can hear Stella halfway down the block. As soon as my key's in the lock she's at the door. Stella's long legged and sleek. All I want to do is rip off my suit and dive into a cold drink – it's been a shitty day. I didn't get my raise; my boss says I need to work on my people skills. He'll find any excuse. Last time it was presentation skills. What next? Better Post–it note placement?

"All right Stella. Hold your horses." She's all over me, slobbering love, then sniffing my heels after I kick them off. I'm so happy to see her. She goes bat shit as I slip on clogs and grab her leash. She drags me out of the house barking at anything that moves. I pull my coat closed against the wind. Joyce and Larry are out front. Stella jerks her leash from my hand and races up their walk, growling. Joyce double–times it up her stairs.

"Stella! No!" I hurry to grab her leash.

"She's a ticking toim bomb," Joyce says in her hard–edged Australian. She glares down on us from her top step, arms crossed on her massive breasts. "You should muzzle that beast." You'd guess she's a dyke by her buzz cut and baggy clothes, but she's married. To Larry, a software engineer complete with long, pale ponytail, thick glasses and teeth so crooked it hurts to look at them. Larry stands like a string bean wall between Joyce and Stella, his arms spread wide for protection.

"She wouldn't hurt a flea," I say, coiling Stella's leash and holding her close. "You just don't know her."

Joyce's shoulders are up in her ears like she expects Stella to shred her porcine body. Stella's a beauty; a mix of Akita, Shepherd and Ridgeback; at least that's what the vet and I figure. She's the sweetest dog in the world, a little territorial, but as a single woman in San Francisco I like that she's watching my back. People these days … if they aren't crazy, they're just plain nuts. I get that some people are afraid of dogs; they say they have good reasons, but in my opinion they're missing an important chromosome in their DNA. Stella's the only person I can count on.

"She's just wound up," I tell Larry. "She needs her walk. TGIF."

"Hey," Larry calls after us. "We're having friends round later if you'd like to come by." Joyce looks like she might bite him. I say thanks, but no, I have a hot date.

I do have a date, through an internet service. I always thought dating services were for losers, but it's not something I'm good at. Because, I'm not a phony. I hate pretending to like someone or fake interest when I don't feel it.

When my doorbell rings I lock Stella in the kitchen. I'm disappointed when I open the door. Another fool who lies about his height. Do guys really think I won't notice?

"Hi, Rachel?"

I nod.

"I'm Bart."

I sigh. "Clearly, you're a creative writer."

"Pardon," he says, his shaggy head tilted.

"You said you were 5'11"." I open the door. "Come in."

He hesitates, looks back at the street, then steps inside. "Nice place," he says.

"Thank you." I close the door. "Want a drink. I sure could use one." I remember I'm working on my people skills. "Do you like wine, beer, or tequila?" I smile.

"A beer sounds good." His voice is loud and Stella starts barking. Bart eyes the kitchen door, shaking as she fights to get out.

"I hope you like dogs."

"Oh, yeah," he says, weakly. The five o'clock shadow on his round face is not a good look.

I grab Stella by the collar and bring her out. "Stella, this is Bart." I laugh at the way the fur rises up along her spine. She's so cute. "Meet my bodyguard."

"Jesus," Bart says, inching away. "She looks like she's out for blood."

I put Stella in my bedroom and tell her Bart's a scaredy-cat but no way will he try any funny business. She barks when I close the door. "Quiet Stella." She sniffs and I hear her jump up on my bed.

"Hey," Bart says, standing by the door, "Wanna go out? I saw a place down the street."

Outside, it's a clear night, though cold without a fog blanket. I'm relieved to see Mrs. Franklin has finally taken down her Christmas decorations. All that fake joy irritates me.

"How about pizza and beer?" Bart says. "I'm starved."

I want to say that it wouldn't hurt him to miss a meal, but stop myself, because I *do* have people skills. We go to Firavanti's, a mediocre place I'm tired of. But the flats I put on for Bart pinch my feet and clearly this guy isn't springing for a taxi.

We order, then do the *where are you froms?* and family histories, though mine is short. It's just me now, if you don't count a cousin always looking for a handout and a theatrical father who lives for a stage unless it's a family home. He exited stage left from ours when I was six.

"Has your dog ever bitten anyone?" he asks.

"You're afraid?"

"Hell ya. He looks hungry." He grins.

"Stella's a she."

His smile drops, but picks back up a little when the beer arrives.

"So what do you do?" he asks. I see him check his watch.

"I take money from dead people."

"Come again?" he asks.

"I work for the IRS. Probate." He starts to say something, but I hold up my hand. "Believe me, I've heard every IRS sob story there is." He purses his lips. That's when the pizza arrives.

We eat for a few minutes. Things are going pretty well. I ask him about his work. He smiles. "I teach political science at the university."

"That must be hard," I say.

"Sometimes." He nods. "I like it," he says. "It's a great job. The kids are pretty smart. It's exciting to see young people get involved in the world, developing their own opinions now that they're out from under the dominance of their parents' ideas." He smiles. "It's my opinion that −"

"You know what they say about opinions? They're like assholes, everybody has one." It cracks me up. I slap the table. Someone told me that once. Hysterical. But I'm laughing alone. "Don't you think that's funny?"

"What? Calling me an asshole?"

"It's a *joke*. Wow, you're sensitive."

He watches me while he eats, then asks, "Have you been on many dates − with lovematch.com?"

"Yeah. They've all been pretty bad. How about you?"

He raises his eyebrows. "Some," he says, "are better than others. Much better."

"Isn't that the truth?" I say. "And my boss thinks I need to work on my people skills." I shake my head. "Can you believe that?"

He nods like the professor he claims to be and says, "Sage advice." Then he signals the waiter and asks her to split the bill.

Morgana Malone and the Case of the Mysterious Flood

by Matt Potter

"You have no idea what you're talking about, do you?"

He's at it again. With five minutes of the gallery tour left, his voice still sounds from the rear of the twenty–plus group: soft enough for the old ladies in front not to hear, but insistent enough that I wait for his intake of breath before he speaks, and wince.

And I was hoping my new orange bob made me unrecognisable.

"You can see by the way the colours *pop* out at your eyes," I say, hand shaking at the picture throbbing on the wall, my apricot broderie Anglaise shoulder ruffle flapping against my upper arm. "It's a really eye–popping painting." I turn my head from the blue and yellow and green and purple and other ugly colour swirls and step towards the doorway.

"Nobody has any idea what she's saying," he says – to someone, anyone, no one, everyone, who knows: the old ladies have all turned away from him as far as I can tell. "She's talking into the ether and it sounds like Sanskrit. And that hair colour?" he snorts. "She looks like a carrot."

My heels clack on the parquet floor as I walk, through the large doorway and into the next gallery. I'd challenge him, if this wasn't my first day on the job. *Carrots used to be your favourite vegetable*, I'd say. And wait for him to deny it.

Perhaps becoming a volunteer gallery guide to meet men was not such a good idea.

(I'm so sick of bogus profiles on the internet! They all look great on the screen – *Me: down to earth, like people to be themselves, good sense of humour* – but then you meet them! Men worth millions still living with their mothers. Men who are 'single' betrayed by their wedding ring tan lines. Men who say, "I'm paying so much in child support I need to know how fertile you are," even before I buy them a drink.)

I clasp my hands in front of me as I turn on my high heels to face the group. Two old ladies stare, giving me their brightest attention.

"As you can see by the brilliant bas–reliefs above us on the ceiling, we're now in the original part of the Gallery." I clasp my hands tighter, to stop myself from gesturing towards the ceiling with shaky fingers, to keep my balance on my high heels.

Old ladies muster around me.

A guffaw sounds from the back of the group.

The bastard knows I've always hated my brown hair.

"This part of the Gallery first opened in 1882," I say, "and was built with a generous bequest from Sir Farquhar McPherson, whose brother Sir Darymple McPherson made an equally generous bequest three years later, to match the original."

"What media were used to create the bas–reliefs?" He's standing off to the side now.

I look at him and see there's something different about his eyes: whitened, and flattened, like the wrinkles have been blasted off.

"They look incredibly unique," he adds, "or maybe even uniquely incredible, so I'm fascinated to know what they're made of." He smiles. "Can you inform us?"

I look at another older woman who stands, head cocked, waiting for my answer. A gold tooth glints inside her puckering mouth.

"Plaster of Paris, creek water and old egg cartons," I say, "all mooshed together in a big cauldron and slapped up there with large paintbrushes made of virgin horsehair." I smile, holding back a scream. "Thanks for joining me on this tour this afternoon. Please enjoy the rest of the Gallery."

I turn. My heels are brisk on the marble floor and as I pass him I smell his cologne, woodsy in that Eastern Bloc way I remember so well. "Don't follow me, Grigor," I say, "or I'll call Security."

Other voices disappear behind me. I walk through the next doorway, head down, heels clacking, and then through another door and then another door marked 'Staff Only' and down the stairs, clack–clacking my way to the toilets marked 'DANGER – subject to flooding'.

As soon as I hear the restroom door pushing open, my eyes flash to the latch. Unless he climbs over or under the cubicle walls or over or under the door or has a screwdriver to unscrew the lock or a gun to shoot the lock off, I'm safe sitting on the toilet lid.

The restroom door wheezes closed behind him. Knuckles rap hard on the cubicle door.

I hold my breath.

"What are you doing, Morgana? Why are you pretending to be someone you're not? As soon as I walked into the gallery and saw you standing by the *Guided Tours here* sign with your shoulders slouched and hugging your elbows like a street waif, I knew it was you. You can't hide behind that orange hair colour."

My eyes are wild in my head. "You have no right to come here, Grigor. This is for staff only." I answer with what I hope is strength and confidence.

But you're not staff, you're only a volunteer, I expect him to say.

"Your voice sounds weak and unconfident," he says instead. His signature Spanish sandals poke under the door and his voice sounds skewed, as if he's talking into the painted wood and his chest. "You need to come back to intensive therapy."

I look down at my shoes. Open—toed and two—tone peach and tangerine to match my hair, they're a mere school ruler—length away from touching the toes of Grigor's sandals and perfect for a January summer day except the closed heels rub raw under my ankle bones and they're so high any degree of nerves makes the balancing act —

"I have a free appointment at 9.30 on Monday," he says. "I can get Zebadie to block the time out in my schedule for you. I can call her now and get her to keep it free. I can do that if you want, Morgana." He shifts his weight and his sandals squeak on the marble floor. "I can do that for you right now. I can call her up and tell her it's an emergency and have you booked in for 9.30 Monday morning. It's as easy as that." I hear the rustling of fabric. "I'm getting my mobile out of my pocket now and calling Zebadie to make the appointment, even though it's a Saturday now. And you won't have to do anything but turn up at 9.30 on Monday. That's only two days away."

I clear my throat. "I won't marry you to get discount therapy, Grigor."

"You won't have to this time," he sighs.

I shake my head.

His voice softens. "Things will be different this time."

I fold my hands in my lap. I have another thirty minutes before my next tour and after fifteen years in therapy with poor timekeepers, am pretty good at waiting.

"Please," he says.

I twiddle my thumbs, then breathe out, relaxing my spine and slouching against the cistern, my apricot broderie Anglaise shoulder ruffle now reaching down to my navel.

"I promise," he whispers.

I can't believe I say it, but I do. "What did you do to your eyes, Grigor?"

I hear a sharp intake of breath against the door. I wince.

"Just some light freshening up," he says. "They help me see better into people's psyches now the excess skinfolds are gone, so I have a much clearer vision and I'm really pleased with the result. Now my eyes look the way they were always meant to look."

I remember the mirror he kept behind the couch in his consulting room. He would watch his reflection while counselling patients about their body image problems.

Grigor's voice deepens again. "But that's really not important now, Morgana. It hasn't escaped my notice that you've dyed your hair the colour of my favourite vegetable."

I cross my ankles, but leaning back perched on the toilet lid with crossed ankles doesn't work (unless I want to stretch out and touch toe–to–toe with Grigor) so put my hands by my side, wrapping my fingers around the edge of the seat to steady myself. But the cold of the white porcelain is a shock to my fingertips so I sit up again. The toilet seat creaks.

"Are you constipated, Morgana?"

Standing up, I press the button. The sound of water splashing out of the cistern and into the bowl fills the cubicle. And then I feel wet washing past my toes, and looking down see water rushing from behind the bowl and flooding across the marble. "Oh," I say.

Grigor's Spanish sandals step backward and I hear wet splotching across the floor. "I'll get Security," he says, and the door opens and wheezes closed.

Pressing the button again, I watch more water flood across the floor. "Call Emergency Services too!" I shout, hoping he hears. Cistern half full and I press it again.

I bought a *Men of Emergency Services* calendar last week and a lot of those guys look definitely single.

Breakable

by Gary Percesepe

Yesterday morning I moved my just–divorced self into a new house. In the afternoon I went to the dentist.

A root canal tooth was acting up. I need a new crown. $500 after insurance. My ex is a teacher, with excellent insurance and small co–pays. The day we signed divorce papers, barely a month ago, I lost my health care coverage and had to COBRA.

This morning I woke in the old house and realized I had no clothes. I did have the dog of the family. Dylan spent the night with me at the old house. My ex is spending the summer with her new boyfriend in another state. I think it is Arkansas, but it might be Missouri. I get those two confused. She asked me, could I watch the dog while she is gone? I said sure.

But I had taken my summer clothes over to the new house. So, no clothes. Also, no shoes. They were in a Hefty trash bag, my shorts and tops in another. I moved them in the fourteen foot U–Haul truck that a friend rented for me. I threw the two Hefty bags on the floor of the closet in the guest room at the new house.

The landlord at the new house says no dogs. So I spent the night at the old house with the dog, but without clean underwear or a change of clothes. Also missing were some books I've been reading, books that I keep stacked on the end table next to my bed, along with my writer's journal, in which I scribble story ideas, bits of poems, memories from childhood, impressions from the day. Movie scenes with notes: *Kate Beckinsale running, tight T, face pinched, write story from mood.* The bed and the books are at the new house, three miles across town. Along with the journal. The dog of the family looks at me and yawns.

I put on yesterday's clothes and go to the new house.

On the drive over I think about a woman I know in New York. Pari is getting a divorce. She is a writer, too. A damn good one. I would say she's "in the middle of a divorce" but it's hard to know if she's in the middle, since it feels like this will go on forever, and what's half of forever? Her ex is a Wall Street guy who moved his girlfriend into the country house in Connecticut that Pari decorated, even as Pari was having to move into her mother's basement in Jersey.

The other day, Pari took her two kids by taxi to Penn Station. She texted me to say that they were headed to the Hamptons to stay with a friend for a few days. Eliot is twenty months, her brother Sawyer is five. The three of them got on the train and Pari texted me again. Elie was singing the ABC song, but all she knew was, *"Now I know my."* Just that much, *"Now I know my,"* over and over in her baby voice. "She calls Sawyer *Waya* and herself *It*," P texted. "My two kids, Waya and It."

I'm a native New Yorker, living in exile in Ohio for many years but returning about once a month to see family, visit with friends, and occasionally give readings from my novel. I'm considerably older than Pari. We met on an online dating service. At the start, we agreed to take romance off the table.

That worked for a while. We said: friends, sure. We lived in different states.

Soon enough we were talking on the phone. Texts and emails. Things speeded up. We shared comical stories of dates gone bad, of how unfit we were for human relationship.

Then one night, walking back to her place in Tribeca after a reading, she gave me a sidelong glance. A sly smile, and then she jumped at me. Mid air, I caught her, and we stumbled back off the sidewalk of West 4th Street to the side of the Hebrew Union. She is Jewish. We laughed at that, and collapsed in a heap against the cold brick wall, pulling at each other's clothes.

A month later we were in a hotel room. It wasn't so much that we fooled around. It was that we'd laughed and cried together. We told each other things we'd told no one in this world. Beating her small fists into the hotel pillow, she curled into a fetal position and asked me to hold her. These are things difficult to forget.

Sometimes I feel like a barometer. I register every feeling in the forest. I would like to feel less.

When I am with women other than Pari, however, I feel nothing. Even when having sex. OK, when having lots of sex. Nothing.

One morning, before we had met face to face, she sent me an email from her BlackBerry. "I've a half gallon of whole milk in my arm like a baguette. Such is life with two wee adorable mongrels. Milk and strawberries and goldfish crackers. Three meals a day of this. Better than tying cooking twine around roasts for a grumpy banker who says too salty or worse I'm not hungry. I'm sad, Gary. Angry often but deeper, sad."

Sometimes I wonder if Pari is a place holder for me, holding the place I have reserved for love once I am able to feel again. Love is so easy to mimic, especially for writers. Sometimes I worry that, having met her, and felt the deep connection we have felt, having cried together, with the memory of her runner's body quivering in my arms, her tiny starfish hands, her size five feet that I bought shoes for in Italy and handed to her in the lobby of her building in New York, to cries of delight – oh, we're not in love. We are divorce friends, fellow travelers. But I *could* have loved her. I wonder if I will ever be able to love anyone ever again in the way that I have loved Pari. She is impossible for me, an impossible love, but by loving her I keep at a distance all possible loves. She is safe and unsafe at the same time. She holds the place where I hope to show up again, missing less.

We both feel something, maybe even something like love, but there's nothing to be done about it.

The furniture I moved to the new house looks comical in its new setting. The old house is an Italianate beauty, over 5,000 square feet, with twenty rooms. A winding mahogany staircase built in 1860 that looks like it was borrowed from the set of *Gone With the Wind*. Large paintings that had been hung with care on walls twelve foot high.

The new place is an 800 square foot box. Two small bedrooms. The master bedroom is barely large enough to contain my king-sized bed and dresser. If Gulliver had furniture it would have looked something like this.

I go to the guest room to retrieve the two Hefty bags. Then I go out to the garage and locate the box that holds my bed books. I sort through the box until I locate the books I need: three books by James Salter, a novel by Meg Wolitzer, the new translation of Proust by Lydia Davis, and two memoirs by Dani Shapiro that I have been re-reading as I prepare to interview her.

It's Sunday. I look at my watch. A day to kill. Kill the days. My new vocation. I decide to drive to Yellow Springs to see a movie. Something about sitting alone in a dark room appeals to me. A way to escape, sure, though I'm perfectly aware that it is me I am trying to escape. Stories help. Anyone's story. Anyone but me. A place to give myself the slip. Isn't this the purpose of movies? But looking for a parking space in town, I find myself thinking about my visit to the dentist yesterday. And the girl who worked on me.

Open wider, she'd said. We've got to get this old glue off.

She held her silver instrument tight in her gloved hand. Into the maw of me, this pink cavity, past my confused tongue, the family voice thick in my throat, she probed deeper.

I wondered if she was pissed because she had to come in to work on a Saturday, but didn't have much time for that thought. I flinched.

It's a root canal tooth so you shouldn't feel any pain. Except when I get below the gum.

I squirmed. Gripped the arm of the chair tighter.

Are you OK? We can get you some Novocain.

I'm fine.

I told you to watch what you eat. What did you eat for breakfast this morning?

Granola, I said.

Uh huh, she said. In her goggles and her 1980s Stevie Nicks hair she looked like bad MTV.

Sorry. What should I be eating?

Soup. Yogurt. Soft stuff. It's on the paper I gave you.

I threw it away by mistake.

It's OK, Stevie said. The other option is, you can keep coming in here every day for a new cap.

Thanks.

She told me the dentist waived the $500. Somehow he must have gotten the news about me. Is it that obvious? In the same way that a friend paid for the U–Haul yesterday, and four of my friends spent a half–day moving me. Jeff and Richele disassembled my bed. I couldn't bear to watch. They re–assembled it at the new house. I shut the door. Later, I hugged them.

Most of the time I feel like a rambling wreck, but there are occasional grace notes. The way that Pari cares about me, and that I care about her, even though we cannot use the L word, even though we are not "in love", even though we both know it's not us. But we can still accompany each other. Even when it appears we walk in circles in the dark, we're together, somehow, through this. That's grace, too.

The assistant discarded her goggles and turned off the bright light she'd trained on me. She looked less like a space alien this way.

Look at it this way, she said. You've got a thin piece of plastic in your mouth. It's a temporary plastic crown. You have to be careful, OK? It's breakable.

The village is crowded. Dinner, movies. Couples. Shapes, sizes, colors, genders. Some holding hands. Some not.

Miraculously, a space opens in front of Mr. Fub's Party. Where I'd purchased so many toys for my kids when they were small. Grown now. No more toys.

I back into the space, thinking of Stevie. Breakable, she'd said. I know what she means.

Waking Up Samford

by Nathaniel Tower

Samford McGee wakes in a sweat. "What day is it?" he asks the naked woman at his side. He has no idea what her name is or where she came from or if she is even a woman at all. It might be a waxed man with long hair. Or perhaps a mannequin. Or maybe even an alien life form.

The body turns to look at him and smiles. It's a living thing, that's for sure. Definitely a woman. Look at those cheek bones. No man could look like that.

"It's Monday, silly," she coos as she cranes in for a kiss. Her breath reeks of cheap booze.

"No, what's the date," he says.

"January 27th," she says, her breath more foul than before, as if the second opening of her cavern has released the full power of the stench.

"No, I don't think that's right," another voice says, and Samford suddenly realizes there's someone else in bed with them. He props himself up on his elbows and peers over the woman's body, scanning her for hideous flaws in the process. He finds none and relaxes momentarily until he notices the body on the other side is not another woman.

"It's definitely the 27th," the woman says, her finger sliding across her phone. "See? Says it right here."

Samford wonders how she managed to conjure the phone. He scans her body for a secret compartment, but the only openings he sees don't look big enough. As she pulverizes the phone screen with her fingertips using impossible rapidity, Samford peeks at the creature on her other side. The man is hideous, but Samford can't stop looking. He knows this man from somewhere, he's certain of it. The idea that they have slept together, in the carnal sense that is, creeps into Samford's mind and he turns his eyes back to the woman. Her flawless body tells him he would have done anything she had told him.

Samford drops flat on the mattress, the impact rippling under the other bodies. Both stir, but neither looks at him. A rickety coil springs into Samford's back, and he shifts to find some comfort.

When the woman takes a break from her all−important phone messaging, he taps her shoulder and, leaning in close, whispers, "Who is that?" He even points, as if the question itself isn't obvious enough.

She laughs but says nothing.

"What the hell's so funny?" He's still close to her ear, and she recoils at the boom of his yell. The other man props himself up and glares at Samford.

Shaking her head free of the ringing, she laughs again. "You really don't know who this is?" She looks over at the man and they share a laugh. The man slaps her thigh and Samford watches the skin and tissue jiggle up and down her leg.

"No, I don't. Look, I don't know what spell you have used on me, but I want answers!" Samford roars. She must be some type of witch. He sits up fully, tugging the sheet to cover his shriveled member. His eyes drift down for comparison, and he sees the other man's member is just as shriveled.

"Relax," she says as she brushes her fingertips along the sheets covering his thigh, eliciting instant erection. Samford is unsure why, but the other man is suddenly erect as well.

"Tell me the truth!" he yells. He's staring at the other man this time, and the answer starts to make itself clear to him. The woman confirms it.

"Why, he's you, silly." She laughs again, as does the man.

Samford doesn't quite understand, but he doesn't need to ask. The woman hands him a brochure. Again, he is unsure how she summoned this item.

Samford scans the brochure and it all makes sense.

"So you cloned me?"

"Something like that."

How does he know if he is the real Samford? Perhaps the woman brought the other man home, engaged in raging intercourse with him, then created the body that the man who currently believes is the real Samford is currently residing in. He doesn't know for sure that any raging intercourse has been had. He just assumes that any man naked with her must have done something. The clouds in his mind make him almost certain that he isn't the real Samford. The real Samford would remember a night like that.

Samford, or the man who believes he might not be the real Samford anymore, leaps out of bed, his erect member bouncing like a jack-in-the-box. Pointing a finger, he shouts, "I want him out of my house." As he stares at the man, he decides that *he* isn't the real Samford either.

"It's my house," the man says.

Samford looks around and does not recognize a single thing here. For a moment, he stares at the couple, naked on the bed that isn't his. His body begins shaking and he points his finger at the giggling pair. "I refuse to stand idly by and be a clone of an ugly man!" he roars at them before bolting from the room, tears flooding his eyes. He hears erupting laughter and the sudden sounds of spontaneous lovemaking. Covering his ears, doors banging behind him, he sprints down the street. Even with his hands above his head, the smacking of his feet on the pavement and the slapping of his erection against his legs is deafening. He will run until he's home, but then … he has no idea if he has any real home at all.

Tuesday, 28th January 2014

Twelve Days Old

by Kimberlee Smith

Etheline Margaret Pritchett, my baby, latches onto the handmade rattle dangling from her daddy Dean's fingertips with a purity of instinct and fervor as if she's reaching out to my breast for the first time. She wraps her sweet, plump fist around the circle of cloudy yellow ribbed spires, each nub as long as a dog's fang. Her bare feet pump in the air and her arms flail with the spontaneous reaction to thousands of nerves awakening. She looks up to Dean and my mum Maybell's faces glowing down upon her. I'm glowing on her, too.

You'd never reckon they've just come home from the funeral except that Dean is wearing a brand-new black suit and Maybell is in her Sunday church dress, thick black hose, and some fancy black shoes that maybe even came from that posh department store David Jones.

They stopped on the way home from the cemetery at Doyle's for fish and chips and watched the blinding white cruise ships docked at Circular Quay, seeing that Dean's parents had never been there and this is a special day. They'd driven up from Jervis Bay for the service and lunch, but are tear-assing right back down, not even staying long enough to pay a visit to our new house. I feel like its mine, still.

Today Etheline is twelve days old. I'm her mum, Melodie Margaret Pritchett, and I'm twelve days dead. Today was my funeral.

I watch, as I have since the day I was bitten by that coral snake, but as time passes the urge to remain so close to them weakens. Now, that transition might seem selfish or insensitive, but unless you've died you can't imagine how things tweak and your mind isn't your same mind, seeing things differently than when I was in my body, alive. Bear with me now, because I am new to this whole death thing. And not that I knew what to expect; in truth, I never gave it a thought, my own death. But here it is.

Before I get into what's going on today, January 28 (one of the hottest days of the summer, it seems, with water restrictions and panting dogs and nothing much moving at all) I'll let you know that it's pissing me off how everyone's sitting around the table during tea discussing my own personal afterlife.

Maybell's mewing like a newborn kitten that can't latch on to a teat. She's certain I found everlasting peace and that God's hanging around making sure every wish I ever had is coming true. Dean and his parents sit there mute, nodding like those hard plastic bobble—headed figurines. I try to box his mum Doreen's ears – I know she never cared for me back then or even now – but my damn hands passed right through her head like a vapour and my arms just wrapped around myself and passed through me as well.

The theory that I'm in *Heaven,* like it's a place you fly up to in First Class or something, is what they're comforting each other with in conversation. But it's just an abstract something that people conjure up when a loved one dies. A fable for the living so they don't have to think about what might be the truth, and I'll tell you, it is. That when you die, you're just *gone.*

124

As of yet, I've not travelled through a tunnel of light and butterflies, passed through pearly gates, danced on a moonbeam, or floated on a cloud. No harps, no angels. No nothing. All that romantic, gooey stuff is supposed to happen right away, from what I was led to believe as a child. No reuniting with long-gone relatives or old beloved pets. What a fucking downer.

I think I'm still here in their world, somewhere. I feel lost. What my family considers the passing of time is a measure of distance; time has no purpose here. Everything happens in what could be a second or even an eternity. I am afraid I'm slipping fluidly away. I don't have a supernatural skill set that I can use to flap the feathery white wings I'm kind of waiting for – would be nice; a gift upon arrival – to say where or how I go anywhere from here, wherever here is.

I find my *self* (the abstract part, not the body part) in this limbo land and the sensation is like I'm looking in a rearview mirror. Some distance, some hindsight, and a heap of uselessness. Retrospection and hindsight are gifts that deliver wisdom to the living. But since the dead don't grow, I haven't figured out how to put them to any practical use. Other than to tell you about Etheline in a way no one else can, the way I'm experiencing it. So stay with me.

Only two months have passed since we moved into our house at Kookaburra Springs outside of Homebush. On the way home from Doyle's, Maybell and Dean lament that it would have been much kinder on all of us if they didn't have to wait so long to get my body into the ground. *Tests* had to be run. They didn't argue, probably out of guilt. I should hope so, anyway, on account of the accident mainly because they keep the serpents *in the house*. But I'll get into that later. I've got nowhere to go, and you might as well be patient and hang on. It's a mindblower of an accident, my death. I'm not quite comfortable explaining the circumstances of it, not quite yet. I can barely believe it, myself.

My family watched the cemetery workers (maybe they were the gravediggers, too, but they must've tidied themselves up a bit) lower my good old wooden casket – my physical *forever home* – two meters deep in a hole dug out of the dirt especially for yours truly this morning just as the scorching fireball that is our closest star hauled itself up from the western horizon into the sky. Flies were droning drunkenly, aimlessly. Thousands of despondent jacaranda blossoms surrendered to the brutality of the day ... it's important to note that jacaranda trees have always been my favourite, and oh, oh, especially at that magic hour when the sun needs to be dragged to bed and the floral perfume just about screams out to you.

For Christmas, just a month and three days ago, as a gift to me and to celebrate our new home, Dean planted a half dozen baby jacaranda trees in the front garden of our house. It was a really great surprise. He told me he got up as soon as I had fallen asleep that Christmas Eve and was digging, planting, and watering the infantile trees until sunrise. Man oh man, was he proud of himself for keeping such a secret. Maybell didn't even know. He said he was nervous as a bug they were going to die, since he had them hidden for two days in our shed. Kept checking on them and making sure they didn't dry out, their tiny root balls wrapped in burlap sacks. He tended to them every day. He would sing quietly as he cared for them, but I teased him he wasn't singing to himself, he was singing to the jacarandas. Now he tends to them with an obsession as if I myself had reincarnated those saplings. And I know when he sings, he's singing to me.

§

When he and Maybell brought our baby home from hospital, he stood in the front garden for what must have been an hour, crying his eyes out. It hit him right then that I would never get to enjoy those trees, but in a strange and kind of beautiful twist of fate, Etheline Margaret would be able do so with him. He promised her and himself (and even Maybell, who lives with us) through choked sobs and a broken bird voice that he would tell her the story of Melodie's Christmas trees to our baby girl as a tradition, every Christmas Eve. It's a sweet thought, but maybe a wee bit depressing when the baby starts to grow into a little girl and gets crazy excited about Father Christmas coming but all her daddy wants to talk about is dead mum's trees. I hope that's a temporary, stage–of–grieving type of thing.

So back at the cemetery, poor Dean soaked through his suit, but holy smokes did he look handsome as the day I met him ten years ago, and Mum's armpits had sweat rings the size of melons staining them. I bet she would have plucked out her own eyeball to take off those rubbery black hose. Even in that atrocious 38°C heat, Dean cupped his hand around Mum's shoulder to steady her, taking care not to squeeze her into him too hard, but I know he needed it, too.

My corpse was like a puckered old balloon that lost its helium, gussied up in one of Maybell's formalish dinner dresses – the only thing that fit on account of my abdomen is still stretched out from the baby. The man at the funeral home says my regular clothes won't fit right (I don't know if he meant he couldn't squeeze me into them, or for some insane reason they might appear uncomfortable at the viewing?) even though the baby was born nearly two weeks ago. Reason being it takes a while for the maternal swelling to go down, even though they drained out the bodily fluids that pooled on account of gravity. I'm a postmortem paperweight, if you need help visualizing this nightmare. Maybell has them dress me up just like her, though I'm sixteen years younger. So the mortician made me look half-whore, half-marionette. I don't wear makeup, never have. What a travesty.

They had some help from the hospital trying to locate my father to let him know a granddaughter was born and also that at that same time his own daughter passed away. He was long gone, on a traveling revival, spreading the word of his precious Bible, and he could not be found. It's just as well.

On this twelfth day, Etheline's wrist twitches and a jagged rattle spire grazes her cheek. Her mouth flies wide open and her eyes clench shut like there's fire in them and she howls one prolonged, plaintive wail that fades like a dying spark. A thin trickle of blood dribbles down her face from the duct of her left eye to the crease at her left nostril, then down the peachy little slope that reaches her top lip. Her eyes are amber slits. Like a serpent's. She slips a few of the rattle spires between her lips and suckles and the blood from the tear of her skin makes her lips the color of cherry cordial.

"Well *GOD* damn! She scratched herself up pretty good, but it don't seem to faze her. Smiling, she is, even! Tough as nails, just like her mum," Dean says.

Maybell speed walks from the family room where they keep the Moses basket that Etheline sleeps in over to the kitchen sink, wets a bleached rag with cold water from the tap and just about runs back to the baby, daubs the track of blood that trails down Etheline's face, then presses the rag tenderly against the wound to stop the blood from coming.

"Oh, shut up with that nonsense. And don't take the Lord's name in vain, will you not, *please!*" Maybell says all squinty-eyed and sour-pussy. "That there is just gas looking like a smile. And the baby did not scratch herself up, your toy did. It's dangerous as the snake itself. Reminds me in a bad way of Melodie. A real bad one."

She'll be scarred for life, I'm certain. But the weird thing is, instead of losing color from the trauma, her face flushes like a porcelain doll with dollops of rouge on her cheeks. The cut triggers something that makes her even more vibrant and alive. I am not entirely surprised. Our family has a long history with incidents of unusual sorts.

By now Dean's out on the front porch smoking a cigarette he just rolled for himself. He likes the tobacco that smells like cloves. He sucks in hard and exhales deep to keep breathing steady and stifling the complicated thoughts swirling around in his head like a tornado, else he might find himself saying something that'll bite him in the ass.

"Do you mind? That smoke is blowing back through the screen and stinking up the whole house," Maybell says. "Terrible for the baby, second-hand smoke. You know I been trying to quit. A little consideration wouldn't hurt." I have to agree.

Dean crushes the sweet and pungent butt out in a ceramic ashtray shaped like a saltwater crocodile. Gold script across its scales spells out 'February 14, 2012 Dean + Melodie 4 ∞'. We had the inscription done custom. It was a souvenir from our wedding up on the Sunshine Coast. I think that's all we got in terms of keepsakes.

So, I wonder now. *Infinity.* ∞.

Wednesday, 29th January 2014

Slim Jim

by Vanessa Weibler Paris

I always wanted to go by Jamie, but by the time I was old enough to say so, there was no escaping it: I was Slim Jim.

In reality, it doesn't matter what I'd been named: The kids – and later, the adults – would find a way to make it work. Vincent would've been Skinny Vinny; Anthony stretched into Bony Tony; Richard made into Rick the Stick; Dean turned into Lean Dean or Lean Cuisine Dean or String Bean Dean or maybe, when someone was looking for a big laugh to impress an eye–rolling high school girl, String Bean Dean the Fat–Burning Machine.

The waiting room is empty, save for me and a woman across from me who is deep in a magazine. She's about my age, with shoulder–length light brown hair and dark eyes behind glasses. The cover shakes as she jiggles crossed legs. I try to focus, to see what she's reading, but all I can see are digitally darkened flesh, splashes of purple and yellow, oversized type promising things that are hot! and sexy! and summer–ready!

"It's only January," I say, without meaning to.

The jiggling stops, and she looks at me. I can read the cover now that it's immobilized: *Summer Fashion: Sexy Ensembles You'll Want to Slip on Stat.* It's only January; why are they talking about summer already? It's too soon for summer, too soon to be stripping off stiff safe denim and loose wool sweaters and protective parkas. Why, in January, must anyone be thinking about bare legs and exposed arms and –

"What?" she says, looking up.

Is she shocked by me? Disgusted? Will she text a friend later to say, *OMG I've never seen anything like it he was like a SKELETON you wouldn't even believe it OMG*?

"Um, never mind," I mumble. The shaking resumes, naked glossy woman on the cover bouncing like she's on a mini–trampoline.

"Carla?" a white–smocked nurse calls out, and the woman tosses a pen on the table and springs off through swinging doors.

I pick up the magazine and flip to the table of contents. This issue promises to bare celebrity baby bumps, share low–calorie summer cocktails, and reveal the weirdest places readers have had sex.

I wonder if those places include a pet cemetery, or a country club golf course, or the stacks of a public library. I think of Bobby's bachelor party last month, where he and Andy and Dougie tried to outdo one another as we sipped smooth whiskey and smoked slow cigars in a five–star hotel suite. The four of us have been best friends since grade school, and Bobby's the first to get married.

"No no no," Bobby's brother Larry had barked, lips wet with warm chocolate from a $5 minibar Snickers, "I did it in an airplane bathroom with – wait for it! – a stewardess. And I plowed her – wait for it! – from behind. Yes, boys: I am a card–carrying member of the mile–high club, so I beat all you assholes."

"You're a pig," Bobby said.

"You're just jealous," Larry informed him. "Hey, Slim Jim, what about you? Want to try and one–up that? What's the wildest place you ever done it? Skinny little guy like you, you coulda nailed two–three stewardesses in the airplane john! All of ya shoved in there at once. Ha!"

There had been a long moment of silence, then I'd set down my crystal tumbler too hard and laughed. "Oh, no; you're right. You win. No one can beat that."

"Watch you don't break that glass," Barry had said, burping and weaving off toward the bathroom. "If you can't hold it with your skinny girly wrists, we'll call down and see about getting you a sippy cup."

I stared at my arms, at my hands, and felt Bobby and Andy and Dougie not looking at me.

"Sorry, Jim," Bobby had finally said.

"That's okay," I said, but what was he sorry for, really? It isn't his fault I'm still virgin at age 28.

It's 10 minutes past my appointment time. There are occasional bursts of laughter behind the glass windows at check–in, but no one calls me back. I'm still alone in the waiting room, except for an aquarium full of quizzical looking fish. I flip further into the magazine, where I find the monthly quiz. It challenges readers to ask *Are You Confident?* The boxes are marked off already, big swishing Xs in bright purple pen, and at the bottom, '1–10 Points: Doubtful Dater' is circled several times.

"You're never sure you're pretty enough, exciting enough, or sexy enough for a guy," the magazine explains. "Your insecurity is holding you back. Take a risk and you might be pleasantly surprised."

I look at the purple pen on the table and picture the woman from the waiting room. Carla. Her bangs were a little long. Maybe she's overdue for a cut, or maybe she likes to hide behind them a bit. Her jeans were loose and she'd hiked them up when she stood; maybe, unlike the woman on the magazine cover, she isn't the type to flaunt her body. Maybe she's not sure she even likes it.

Maybe she takes off her clothes when she's home alone, and forces herself to stare in the mirror with all the lights on. Maybe she turns off the lights when she can't look any longer, then wraps herself up in towels and cries in the dark.

I remember the way she said, "What?" to me. Was there a quaver in her voice? A falter?

I remember the glasses, not contacts, with thick dark frames. How they swallowed so much of her face. How they made her eyes look far away.

"Jim?" a gravelly voice calls out. "I can take you back now."

I drop the magazine and rise to follow the nurse. Carla comes through the other door and walks toward me.

She's walking toward me, right toward me. "Carla," I say hoarsely, and she stops and looks up at me with a jolt. "Carla," I say again, with nothing after.

Her eyes widen. She leans down to grab the magazine and the purple pen, begins backing away slowly, then faster.

"Jim," the nurse says again, in a louder, even more gravelly voice. "*Jim.*"

"Carla?" I say, but she's gone.

"How are you today?" the nurse says as I follow her. "I'll need to get your weight first. Step up on the scale."

Casting the Net

by Joanne Jagoda

As the January sun fades to gloom, Damon Southeby adjusts his high—powered binoculars, keeping his eye on Anne Donaldson's beat up Honda in the second row of the teacher's parking lot. It's a chilly San Francisco afternoon, and he zips up the expensive leather jacket he picked up on his last trip to Istanbul. His boots are handmade in Italy; his dark brown hair is longish and perfectly cut. Damon curses this uncomfortable rental car cramping his 6'1" frame, not his usual luxury wheels. Because he doesn't want to be noticed, it serves his purpose blending in with the cars parked near the school.

Anne Donaldson, fifth grade social studies teacher, erases the blackboard with a furious swipe. Her students were impossible today, rude and inattentive. She felt like telling them to *shove it* and walk out, but she still needs this job. Her twins were only nine when Paul had his fatal heart attack on the basketball court. She had been a stay—at—home mom until then. Not only did she have to deal with his death, but it was a huge shock discovering he had been gambling online, burned through their savings and had even cashed in his life insurance. She had to find a job providing health benefits. Anne had worked at Cabrillo School before she had the twins and was lucky they had an opening.

She grabs quizzes to correct, opens her closet for her purse and parka, groaning when she glimpses herself in the hanging mirror. Tomorrow she turns fifty, and she's been fretting over this birthday for months. Anne traces lines at the corners of her eyes and fluffs her hair that badly needs a cut.

She sighs and closes the closet but pauses at her desk, picking up the picture of her and Paul, in the heart–shaped frame, on roller skates in Golden Gate Park. She'd loved him from the rainy night they met when she was a junior at CAL working at the information desk at the library. He kept badgering her until she agreed to have coffee with him. They became inseparable and married when he finished Hastings Law School.

Anne locks her door and waves to colleagues in the hall wishing her an early "happy birthday". They're taking her out tomorrow night to Perry's for the usual birthday drink.

She unlocks her Honda, tosses her tote bag in the back, starts the car but doesn't move – pounding her palm on the steering wheel.

Paul damn you. I'm done blaming myself for your heart attack. And I'm done blaming you for your gambling addiction. Enough blame! It's time to move on. This birthday is going to be my fresh start.

Anne's little tantrum is observed by the attractive man with binoculars in the blue Ford hidden in the shadows across from the teacher's parking lot. Damon Southeby did his job thoroughly and has been collecting information on Anne Donaldson and her seventeen year old twins for three weeks – hacking their computers, email and Facebook accounts and breaking in their house through a back window to hide tiny listening devices and cameras. Finding Anne's diary next to her bed was an unexpected gift. *I bet she's venting about her birthday. Good thing women pour their bloody hearts out in their diaries.*

The Donaldson women would be shocked he knows so much about them and their daily routines. Damon considered different scenarios of how to get involved with Anne, but when he saw the girls browsing dating websites for "older" singles he knew just what he needed to do. He created a website catering to over–forty singles. With pop up ads and fake coupons, the twins were soon hooked into his phony website, and they signed up their mother just as he planned.

He parks across the street from her modest split level to watch and listen on his laptop. Tuesdays and Thursdays, the twins get in around five after Robin's volleyball practice and Cassie's orchestra rehearsal.

Anne unloads her groceries on the kitchen counter, opens a bag of pre–washed salad, adds tomatoes, croutons and cucumbers. She pops the marinating chicken into the oven with some potatoes and sets the table. She pours a glass of white wine and says out loud in front of the hall mirror, "Happy 50th Anne Donaldson."

Anne sips her wine wandering to the family photos crowded on the mantle over the fireplace. Her favorite is the four of them in Maui – sunburned and grinning, in front of a huge sand castle on the beach. Cassie, who is Anne's clone, has wild auburn curly hair and Robin, even at ten, was six inches taller and blonde like her dad with a cute sprinkle of freckles. Ever the joker, she was making rabbit ears behind her sister. Raising them as a single parent has been a roller coaster ride. Cassie had a bout of depression and Robin hung with the wrong crowd for a while, but somehow the three of them have made it.

She sees the picture of the girls when they were twelve in Disneyland with their grandparents. She says a silent prayer of thanks for George and Lillian. They adore their only grandchildren, and the twins love spending lazy weekends at their home in Hillsborough, with the big pool and tennis court, where the weather is much warmer than San Francisco.

Without George and Lillian's financial help, she wouldn't have made it. Anne didn't want to tell them about Paul's online gambling but broke down when they hounded her over why he let his insurance lapse. Even though they can be overbearing, they were generous and set up trust funds for the twins to cover the double tuition hit coming up in September. George owns a top secret research facility in the Silicon Valley that he doesn't like to talk about but has made him lots of money.

The girls come in like two cyclones. "Hi Mom," they yell and head upstairs trying to hide a pink cake box. They've become close in the last few years but they went through a stage when they couldn't stand each other.

"Hey kids. How was your day? Dinner in twenty. I made Southwest Chicken."

Robin shouts, "Yum … and don't forget … Donaldson Family Meeting tonight!" Anne created this ritual after Paul died for going over important family business. After dinner, Cassie clears the dishes, and Robin brings in a chocolate fudge cake from Anne's favorite bakery, with six lit candles.

The girls sing, then hand her a large white envelope and say together, "Mom, don't open it yet."

Robin raps on the table. "I'm calling this meeting to order." Anne smiles at her daughter, who has turned into a lanky Gwyneth Paltrow with a purple streak in her blonde hair; eyes outlined in black, wearing torn jeans, acting like a corporate CEO.

Cassie, in a plaid skirt and dark tights, chews her thumbnail, which she does when she's nervous and tosses her curly auburn hair. She clears her throat, "Mom, we're starting college next fall. It's time for you to get out." She nods at her sister like they've rehearsed this.

Robin continues, "We're talking about *dating*. We signed you up on an online dating site for singles over forty." She gives her sister a high five.

Anne takes a big bite of chocolate cake. "Online dating? I don't know. I've heard you have to be so careful and …"

"Mom, come on ... you have to give it a try. Dina's aunt met someone nice online." Robin opens her laptop. "Here's your profile: *Attractive widow, wants to see foreign films, discover neighborhood restaurants, and hike in the Marin headlands.*"

Anne wipes away a tear. *They know me so well and zeroed in on things I haven't done that I used to love. I think I'm ready for this.*

Cassie points to the envelope. "Open it Mom. We decided ... you're lookin' a little 1980's ..."

She holds the gift certificate like it's a proclamation then reads it out loud: "Complete Makeover: haircut, massage and makeup application at *Sheer Pleasure.*" Then she laughs. "Wow kids. That's a swanky salon. How did you get the money for this?"

Robin is exasperated, "Duh ... we robbed Wells Fargo. Mom, give us a little credit. We do have part time jobs."

Outside in his car, Damon Southeby shakes his hand in the air and yells, "yes!" He's been watching this heartwarming scene unfold on his laptop and smirks because his plan is taking shape. He drives off thinking about the expensive dinner he is going to have tonight to celebrate, courtesy of the wealthy employers in the Middle East he'll update in the morning.

Friday, 31st January 2014

I'm so glad

by h. l. nelson

Dear Diary,

Can I call you that? It seems a bit childish, but also awesome! I haven't had a diary since freshman year of high school. Then stepmom read it and that put an end to that. She slept in my bed for two months, because I wrote about how I snuck Andrew Madison in my window. Oops. I remember I would write my name all bubbly, with his last name. Then I crossed it out and put Drew Lufstetter's, when I liked him more. I did not like the name, though. Joan Lufstetter. Ew. What a cat–lady name that would have been.

So, as a New Year's resolution (yes, I know I'm late), I've decided to begin this diary and only write on the 31st. Which means I don't have to write in it every month. (See, I'm smart.) I just need an outlet. And Mom won't be reading this one, thankfully.

I'm so glad Christmas is over. But, of course, Anne is already preparing for this year's party. Let me tell you what happened earlier today.

I let myself into the unlocked front door of Anne's mansion, where we meet for our Palm Valley Moms' Group. I strode past the marble columns and planters of bougainvillea and entered through the solid mahogany door. Anne was in the middle of a story about her "amazing" new artichoke soufflé recipe, though she doesn't cook. Ailsa, her personal chef, was serving truffle finger cakes when I walked in. I would have called Anne on it, but I was in a good mood this morning since Rob made love to me for a full ten minutes before heading to work. Ten minutes? you say. Hey, I'll take what I can get.

Anne was saying, "... have to make sure to whip it just so, or it won't come out perfectly, like mine — Well hello, Joan, love. It's good to see you, even though we've already begun our refreshments. Here, sit, and I'll have Ailsa serve you yours."

She flashed her perfectly polished smile in my direction. I wanted to grab the platter of finger cakes and smash it against that infuriating smile.

Her husband makes more than all our husbands, combined. And she loves to flaunt it all. From her drapes, custom—made and shipped from France, to her bleached asshole. (Drunk one night at a martini bar downtown, she told us all about it.)

Anne is one of those rich, driven moms. In their home gyms with personal trainers. Couture workout gear. Headbands. Running shoes. Constant multi—tasking on PDAs or iPads while completing strict regimens. Stair—stepping. Treadmill. Light weights. Alternated with various classes. Pilates. Spinning. Zumba. Asses hard as rocks. If Anne's husband wants anal one night and she doesn't, there's no way in hell he's getting past those buns of steel. Access. Denied.

She ships her outfits from overseas. On occasion, she slums it up at Burberry, while the rest of the group digs in the trenches at Macy's and Old Navy. Even Anne's three girls are picture—perfect: lush symmetrical features, slender tanned legs, and tight bodies. They're straight—A students, vastly talented at ballet, debate, the mandolin. Seriously. Her youngest won some music scholarship for Berkeley. I secretly hope they all end up pregnant before 18.

Anne isn't as perfect as she seems, though. I snooped in her bathroom cabinets one day and saw a bunch of pill bottles. I mean, we all take pills, but this was ridiculous. Vicodin. Percocet. Valium. Xanax. Adderall. What kind of doctor would prescribe all that? She could be a dealer.

I'm not snooping, I told myself, as I closed the cabinet door, *I'm a friend and I need to know if Anne has a pill problem.*

Ailsa handed me finger cakes and a cherry vodka sour and I sat down and glanced around the room to see who was there. Julie, at the kitchen bar with her nervous looks and smiles. I like Julie. Her problem's her husband. He's an obsessive–compulsive freak. Their house has to be spotless. Everything in all cabinets, including the medicine cabinets, has to be organized to the nth degree: by height, color, and size. It's ridiculous. He probably has a small penis.

Julie's house has five bedrooms and four bathrooms, so she wakes up at 4 A.M. every day and cleans and organizes, placing kitchen, bathroom, powder room items on their respective shelves in precisely the correct places, labels facing outward. Her kids have learned they can treat her like a pushover, always asking her to make extra food, take inane trips to the mall or grocery store, and wash their clothes right before school, with no thanks. It's no wonder she's so nervous. I see her pull strands of her own hair out when she thinks no one is looking. Poor thing.

The only other one there, lounging on Anne's chaise lounge, was Robin the alcoholic. When she drinks, she's fun – the life of the party, bantering, making cocktails, daring us to do outrageous things like run down the street naked while reciting Shakespeare. Otherwise, she's sullen and scathing, making unfunny cracks at everyone. Which I don't really mind, but the other women can't handle her at those times, they become silent and look meaningfully at each other, like, "No, I said something to her last time. Your turn." Luckily, she usually has a drink in her hand. At one of Anne's dinner parties last year, she turned off the music and announced that her magic show was about to begin. When everyone quieted down, she dropped her pants, spread her legs, and tried to give herself a Goldschläger enema in the middle of Anne's living room. My husband and I pulled her out of the room and helped her dress. All of us, except Anne, laughed about it for months. Honestly, I think Robin drinks to fight off loneliness. Her husband travels a lot. Commodities or trade securities. Some bullshit like that. Really boring. I think he cheats on her while traveling. It's a damn shame.

Robin was banging back a whiskey. She likes 'manly' drinks, and she drinks them fast. I'm sure Robin's liver's destroyed. It really doesn't matter. In the ultimate scheme of things, we're all slowly rotting away in our designer 'mom jeans'.

I swear, it seems like we blinked, then we were through our hot years and into MILF and cougar−land, despite desperate attempts to hang onto our youth. Apparently, growing old means you watch your ass slowly spread. But not like a decadent soft cheese. More like an angry oil spill that no one has the time, and few have the money, to clean up. Skin slowly wrinkling and sliding off faces that boyfriends once gazed at for hours. Vaginas, dried and shriveled prunes. Hormones worse than a teenager's. Breasts going down quicker than the Titanic. Hair sprouting where none should ever grow.

In other societies, we would be matriarchs, prized for our wisdom and prowess. In America, we're just dried−up old whores. Only good for chauffeuring around spoiled, drugged− out, and oversexed teens; concocting elaborate dinner parties where we flirt too much and give our neighbor's husband head in the garage; and wear skimpy swimsuits (once we have our stretch marks lasered, tummies tucked, and Brazilians done) while seducing the pool boy.

Being middle−aged in America sucks. You're in−between your "prime" and cookie baking. Your body is falling apart and you still don't know who the fuck you are. It's the new tweens.

At some point, Anne said, "All right, ladies, we need to talk about the Winter Wonderland neighborhood party."

"What do we need to talk about?" Robin spat. Julie chewed her nails at the kitchen bar.

A smile glazed across Anne's face, as if she was speaking to a child, and she answered, "Well, honey, we need to decide whom is to take care of what tasks." Anne uses the word 'whom' even when it isn't correct. "As you know, this is a very important event and if all doesn't go as planned, the whole neighborhood will blame me. You ladies don't want that to happen, right?"

Anne beamed her fake smile around the room. I thought her brilliant, lasered teeth might sear our retinas if we didn't agree. Julie nodded, as if she wanted to shake loose her own teeth.

"OK, at least that's settled. Now, how about if I just assign everyone their tasks. I think it will go more smoothly if we just do that," Anne said.

So there it was. All along, she had wanted to tell us what to do. Such a surprise. So much bullshit. I drowned my groan in my cherry vodka sour. It was going to be a long day.

And it *was* a long day. Quite long. But, I must be off to bed. Maybe a hot bath will help. Talk to you in a few months, diary.

Not−Anne's−Bitch,

Joan

February

Saturday, 1ˢᵗ February 2014

The Chablis and Sushi Miracle

by Guilie Castillo Oriard

Just past ten AM Luis Villalobos walks into the lobby of Ehrlich Fiduciary with a thick binder in one hand and a hazelnut cappuccino in the other. He's already a regular at the Barista place, even though it means a detour. Given this island's appalling lack of choice, good cappuccino – strong, the foam thick enough to chew – is worth any sacrifice. Mornings like today it might warrant arson. Or murder.

In the elevator he takes a grateful sip and squares his shoulders for the mirror. He didn't shave, and his hair is still wet from the shower. At least it's gelled and combed. His shirt is untucked, sleeves rolled to just above the elbow. Still, he looks better than he feels. Between the files and Milena's wine, he slept maybe an hour.

On the third floor he waves at the other die−hards. Wendolyn of course, the head of the LatAm team. She's there every Saturday, even some Sundays. Julissa, her assistant, nods from the printer room. Stepan, Group Legal Counsel, lifts a royal hand from his corner office opposite the hall from Luis's.

"Ciao, bicho."

Luis opens the door wider. "Jesus, Stepan. You experimenting with cryogenics in here?"

Stepan sits back and his chair creaks. "Blasted heat. Every morning I consider suicide. Or a transfer to Luxembourg."

Luis sets the binder on Stepan's desk. "I vote Luxembourg. None of this bullshit there."

"Nowadays? Everyone has US investments. No escape from FATCA."

"But in Luxembourg – anywhere, actually, except here – they make their clients provide proof of tax residency." Luis jiggles the binder, a little tap–dance on the desk.

Stepan looks out at the Caribbean morning glittering outside. "When I started here – I'm talking years, not decades – dude could come in off the street with a driver's license and a suitcase of money, and we'd set up an investment structure for him. Any trust company would."

"The good old days. Right." Luis presses his eyeballs until fireworks bloom under his lids. "Stepan, OECD directives started back in the seventies. How did you people slip under the radar?"

"The whole Caribbean did. How?" Stepan snorts. "Isn't it obvious?"

"Offshore means, or meant, unregulated. Not sloppy. This," Luis makes the binder dance again, "is sloppy. Negligent, even."

"Well, then." Stepan peeks over his wire–rimmed glasses at Luis. "Isn't it lucky Ehrlich has you. Tackle one of these a week, I'd say you're fully booked for the next, oh, five years."

"We don't have five years. Ehrlich or me. The FATCA deadline is April."

"Better get to it, then. Find anything?"

"Bunch of trust deeds, not slapdash enough to be sham, but close. And bank accounts. Everywhere. Ehrlich isn't a signatory in any of them, apparently."

"Pity." Stepan sighs. "I left the evaluation of the other files on your desk. Did Milena say how we'll proceed?"

Luis feels his armpits dampen. "We, uh, didn't go into that. But she'll approve."

"Sure?"

"Why wouldn't she? It's win—win. The client, Ehrlich, the —"

"IRS?"

"Not if there's no US persons involved."

Stepan blinks at him.

"Stepan. Fuck. I thought that was policy here. No US persons as clients."

"Without proof of tax residency, how can I – or anyone – assert that?"

"See no evil?" Luis's stomach is on a wild ride.

Stepan chuckles. "Plausible deniability. Let's get to work, bicho. Make the fiduciary world a better place and all."

Luis thought his stints in Hong Kong, Guernsey, Wall Street – Wall *Street* – would've prepared him for anything. Those big financial centers are paradise. Here, in the cradle of the trust industry, it's just a step up from the abacus. From quills and inkwells, a cowled monk recording transactions in spiky longhand. At least there's computers. With Windows; welcome to the future. While his boots up, Luis swigs the last of his cappuccino and starts on Stepan's report.

Source of wealth declaration says inheritance. But where's the backup? No will, a faded death certificate, copy of a copy, and not notarized. A certification stamp on a corner, a scrawl over it. He turns the page to study it. M. Durant. Milena; it figures.

An hour later, when MD herself – how apropos: her initials also stand for Managing Director – pops into his office, he's turned Stepan's three pages into a twelve—page litigation dossier.

"Good morning, Luigi. Again."

He looks up. "Sorry I left so early. I had to —"

"Don't. I hate excuses." She saunters in on six—inch slingbacks, pointy things with red daisies fragile enough to be made of glass, certainly too fragile to carry Milena's curves. She sits a thigh on the corner of his desk, pushes the to—do tray away, leans over the report. It's on purpose, all of it: the skirt riding up, the twist from the waist so her ass looks rounder and her cleavage shows just enough swell. He knows this, and still that non—discriminating entity between his legs twitches in appreciation. He glances across the hall, but Stepan has his back to them.

"This is wrong, Luigi."

"Sloppy, yeah. Negligent too."

But Milena is giggling. "No, honey. This one," she points to a triangle in the structure diagram, "Almeida N.V. That's the only entity domiciled in Curaçao. All the others aren't. The audit doesn't include them."

"They're part of the client's structure. We need to —"

"No. We disclose what we're required to disclose. We do not volunteer information."

"But —"

She grazes his cheek. "You didn't shave?"

"Milena, listen. FATCA isn't a game. Once Curaçao signed that exchange of information agreement, all fiduciaries operating under a Curaçao license are bound, by law, to provide the declarations —"

"And we will. But the request is for entities domiciled in Curaçao. Until the IRS learns to widen the scope of their requests, we provide only the information they ask for. Not a goddamn byte more. Are we clear?"

The upbraiding stings like a bitch slap. "Yes ma'am."

She puts a palm back on his cheek, ignores the bristle this time. "Don't pout. I'm just training my replacement."

He ignores the impulse to recoil. "Is it official?"

"That I'm leaving next year? I already signed the Singapore contract."

"That I'm your replacement."

Milena's red mouth purses. "Potentially. Is that enough?"

Luis trails a finger over the contour of her knee. "For the moment."

"A threat?" But she's laughing. "If you don't get to be MD you'll – what? Leave?"

"There'd be nothing to stay for."

"You could come to Singapore."

He laughs too. These things are best approached disguised in humor. "As your lapdog? Enticing."

She tweaks his ear, a tad too hard. "Speaking of. How's the monster mongrel?"

No trouble smiling for real this time. "Dog food is bankrupting me."

She turns away, fiddles with his computer, clicking through the open programs. "You should take him to the shelter."

The feel–good lasted all of three seconds. Maybe Milena does it on purpose. "Nah. We're good, Al and I."

Her laughter is sharp, the one she uses with novice account managers. "Does he call you Betty?"

The Paul Simon association never occurred to him. Creatively challenged as he is, he'd planned to call the dog Guy. Then, for reasons he doesn't think about much, a fragment of poetry started looping in his head as he drove to the vet that first time. *Let us go then, you and I / When the evening is spread out against the sky.* One more thing Al can be grateful for. He could've spent the rest of his days answering to Pru. "It's for Prufrock. You know. The Love Song of Albert J."

"Whose song?"

He almost says the lines out loud. Suddenly he doesn't want to share it, another piece of his soul for her to play with. "An old poem. Doesn't matter."

"Isn't poetry wasted on a dog? Seems to me your Pure Frock might be better served recited to me. Over Chablis and sushi on the beach? I have a bottle cooling in the car. You get the sushi?"

If he had a tail, it would be expected to wag. "I've got hours to go here."

"But I just cut today's workload by –" She glances at the structure diagram. "By five. Come on, it's too beautiful a day."

"One condition."

She's already at the door. "No Al, Luigi."

He thinks of the dog's forlorn face at the window, the joy when Luis comes home. But this due diligence project is the key to getting out from under Milena – figuratively and otherwise. "No, no Al. But hear me out on the FATCA thing. You're right about the scope of the IRS request. But Ehrlich can't function, not anymore, without tax residency certificates. For every entity."

Her lacquered fingernails tap against the pressed wood. "Fine. This once. Then you promise to never bring it up again."

"Just – hear me out."

A Chablis and sushi miracle. That's what Luis needs.

La Ronde / Gina and Joey

by Townsend Walker

Joey, it's Gina.

Gina?

Your sister, you smuck.

I got a sister?

Okay, I get the message. It's been a while. But with things, you know how it is.

No, I don't know.

Look, I'm very sorry I haven't called you. I apologize. I should be nicer to my older brother.

I'm starting to hear you, but lighter on the older bit.

So how are you?

Not bad, moving business is good, the economy, house prices up, lot of people decamping to Florida, permanently now. Last two winters have been a bitch – Hurricane Sandy, then the big power outage. Sonia is keeping busy with Mama and her round of doctors. Kids are finally getting good grades. Put them in a school run by nuns. They know how to crack the whip.

Been there; felt it. Hey did you hear? Punxsutawney Phil didn't see his shadow this morning, short winter we're gonna have.

You called to tell me about a groundhog? I don't think so. What do you want from your big brother that your big rich daddy can't give you?

You remember Madge? You went out with her moons ago. When we were at Barnard I fixed you up. The blonde, big brown eyes, built.

Madge? Oh, yeah. I remember Madge.

There something you're not telling me, Joey?

Sounds like she never did either.

What?

There was more than one date; we went out from Christmas til I graduated and left for San Fran.

But she was stuck on some guy from Rome. They'd go off somewhere every weekend. Never let any of us meet him.

Giancarlo Falcone?

How do you know?

That was me.

You? My brother.

All those stories of Latin romance she carried back to the dorm were made up in a tiny room we had in Little Italy; well, some were made up.

You jerk. You're both jerks – my brother and my best friend. I don't believe it.

So ask her.

Look, I called because she needs help.

What kind?

Her husband runs around and –

So?

beats her, loses the kids, believe that? And there's a pre nup.

Where's this going?

She wants to get rid of him.

So why do the two of you need my help getting her a divorce.

Divorce is not the kind of *rid* she's thinking about. She's thinking of a permanent *rid.*

Why doesn't she buy a gun? Not like they're hard to find. Shoot the bastard the next time he goes after her.

So what if he grabs her and the gun is in the other room, huh? Or, you remember that woman in South Carolina? She shot her husband as he came through the door with a bat. She didn't wait for him to hit her with it before she pulled the trigger. She ended up in prison. Some kind of justice that is.

But you're calling me, because?

You used to hang around with Uncle Tony, who used to hang around with people who know about these things.

Whoa. It's been a long time since I've seen Uncle T. We went sideways on a deal couple of years ago. So no. Can't help you there.

Come on, you gotta know somebody.

Why I gotta know somebody?

Joey, Joey, you always know people. Madge is in a real pickle. I saw her day after she got beat up. Make up couldn't cover it up. She limped out of the bar. It was brutal. I cried and cried. I would of done Frank myself if I knew how. Think about it, please.

Hold on a sec. Got another call coming in. Bidding on a big job. Moving the Pru to a new building near the Newark airport.

I'm back.

How's Mama? She better?

Yeah, she's doing fine.

I hope so. The fall certainly didn't help her any.

How long you gonna go on about that? My wife goes out for an hour and Mama picks that time to try to get out of bed and make coffee, something she's never done in her life. When we're here she won't get out of bed unless someone is there by her side. I might fall. I might this. I might that. It wasn't Sonia's fault.

Sure, it was Mama's.

Look, you're not here with Mama. We are. Sometimes you gotta get out of the house. The constant yammering, bitching. You'd think she was little Red Riding Hood: too hot, too cold, too salty, but never ever right.

You telling me about my mother? My mother? All I hear from your dear Sonia ... do you know I get three e-mails a week from her complaining how I don't do enough for my mother, how I don't see her. And that doesn't count those she sends to our sisters and not me. Christ on the cross!

Gina, let's not get into that, huh? Sonia, well you know how she is. It's just when Mama's going off.

Sonia blabs on to Lucy and Carol about what I don't do and then I hear from them about how I'm mistreating our mother. It's like everyone's happy to take the money, but if I'm not there every day I don't get any points. In fact, it means I hate her. Since we moved up to Greenwich it's at least an hour each way and that's if nobody's on the Cross Bronx. When did that ever happen? I get sick, sick to my stomach and it's because of Sonia.

What do you want me to do about it? Tell my wife that she's upsetting my sister. Somehow that is not going to work. But I swear whenever she goes negative, I stick up for you. And that's not easy sometimes. Just ignore her. Delete the emails.

But it hurts, Joey. She's turning the family against me. Any little spark, she's there with a gas can.

Sec. Hey Soni, can you get the door. I'm on the phone ... with Gina ... yeah, I'll tell her. Sonia says hi.

I'll bet.

So Madge?

Did I mention how much she's willing to pay? Fifty big ones.

For that I think I could do some looking around. Guy I used to know, name of Max.

Max Fiori?

No, another Max. Probably still in the business, or knows who is.

160

So you'll let me know.

Yeah, I'll let you know.

And you'll talk to Sonia?

Yeah, I'll talk to Sonia.

So I'll tell Madge Giancarlo is taking care of it.

Yeah, tell her that.

Bye, lover boy.

That was a long time ago.

Five minutes later.

Yo, Gina, so what's this guy's name and what's he look like? Be kind of useful to know.

Name is Franklin Lancaster Cabot III; goes by Frank. Works at Goldman Sachs on West Street, downtown. Six foot three, 200 pounds, perpetually tanned (some gel he uses), curly black hair going gray, beak for a nose, Brooks Brothers dresser, loafers with tassels. And Hermes ties, you know, the silly patterned ones. Outside, Prada Aviators, high end sunglasses, blue tint, all seasons.

Be back. Love ya.

Monday, 3rd February 2014

A Visitor

by Derek Osborne

"Ahoy the boat!"

They're still in Miami, waiting to leave for a month–long shoot on Nantucket. It won't be a pleasant sail this time of year so Max is fine with hanging out while they wait for the contract. The marina's been footing the bill; the little boutiques near the dock have also chipped in. *Gadabout* makes for a great attraction.

"Ahoy the boat," Max hears again. He's been taking more naps these days. It's always pleasant up on deck after the morning rains and before it gets too hot. The bouts of fatigue are getting more frequent so he's been doing any heavy work first thing and then resting after. The tests up in New York went off as planned. It was good to see his daughters. The youngest, Andi, is going to NYU. His sister was there as well, armed with special diets and brochures from other clinics, recommendations for second and third opinions. "Pam," Max had said, "We haven't even gotten the first." But that was his sister.

"Hell–lo–oh?" he hears the person on the dock say again. The voice sounds familiar. It's probably the woman from the photography studio. Max is lounging in the cockpit. It's upholstered in deep green ultra–suede and quite comfortable, his favorite place to nap, and now she's woken him up.

"Come aboard," he says, not bothering to rise. His body is still feeling sluggish, he needs more sleep. Blame it on a Monday.

They ran a new halyard this morning and Eddie had to go up the mast. Hoisting him took its toll. Max closes his eyes again, what's another minute?

"Aren't we the lazy bones."

It's not the photographer. The voice, up close, is unmistakable, the hint of Chilean accent, the studied enunciation of someone who learned English later in life, all of it wrapped in that sexy confidence, the "it" Katherine Hepburn spoke of, as if every word is newly minted just for him. The sound of her voice is spreading a warm, wonderful calm through every discomfort he's feeling, every cell in his body taking a long, deep breath, letting it out with a sigh. He can't help but smile.

"I'm afraid if I open my eyes you won't be there."

"But I am," Rebecca says, "and it wasn't easy coming here."

Something's wrong. Max opens his eyes. She's wearing soft, loose fitting cotton pants and a pale blue tee that somehow manage every curve of her body, her hair tucked under a Yankees cap, dark glasses screaming – *Leave me alone.*

"You never called," she says, pulling off the glasses.

Max wants to laugh. It's a bad habit, imagining conversations three or four lines ahead, life as if it were all some B–Grade movie – a way to avoid, his wife used to say – he starts to sit up.

"No," she says, "don't."

This is not what Max has imagined. True, he never called after the wrap party last month. He'd started to, several times, but he wanted to wait for the tests.

"Becca."

"I told you to call me Becky."

That night at the party he'd called her Becca, it just seemed to fit, the effect had been startling.

"I don't want to call you Becky."

"I can't stand when you call me that …"

Max can't believe what he's seeing. She's crying. It's so adorable he just wants to hold her and let it come. He starts to get up and she takes a step back.

"I mean it, Max ... I mean it. I came here to tell you this isn't going to work. I know, it sounds crazy, we haven't even had the 'It' part of it yet and I'm already playing 'It' out and I know how 'It's' going to end ..."

"That's a lot of 'Its'."

"Don't make jokes."

"I'm sorry."

Another bad habit.

"You don't know," she says, "it's this god damn business. You're surrounded by so many people who want something from you and ... it's lonely, and then this great guy comes along like some fucking life raft and all you want is to never let go and NO!" she says, backing away as Max tries to get up, "I mean it, don't come near me. It's best just to end things now and I can at least imagine what it might have been like to ..."

"To what ..."

"Just please don't get up. I have to ... I have to go."

And before he can she bolts, leaping over the rail and landing on the dock like a cat, like she does on the show, not even bothering with the boarding block. Max is forgetting she does her own stunts.

"Becca," he says.

But she's already down the dock, walking quickly, her arms out wide and stroking back and forth like people do when they exercise. There are others there on the pier, people on the dock, people on their boats. Maybe that's what she wants them to think. She's put the glasses back on.

"Becky," Max calls. She slows but doesn't stop. A hand comes down, low with the palm facing down, let it be for now, she seems to be saying. She doesn't turn.

"We're not done," Max says, but only the boat can hear.

They're far from done. He's watching her now, waiting to see if she'll turn. She's almost out to the parking lot, walking up the long steel ramp.

"Turn around," he says.

She's reached the top.

"Come on, Becca, turn around."

There's this heavy white gate and a chain link fence. They lock it after sunset. She's pushing the gate open, lingering.

"Take your time."

Just then the SAT phone rings. Most of his friends are sailors and they're scattered all over the globe. He looks at the little screen calling out the ID, the latitude and longitude location of the call. "Of course," he says, pushing the TALK button and bringing it up to his ear, "please hold."

"Max, don't hang up…"

It's Pam, his sister. Rebecca has turned around. She can see him there with the phone, and now he can see her digging into one of her pockets and pulling out her own.

"Shit, she thinks I'm calling her."

"What?" his sister says.

"Pam, hold on."

Max is digging out his own cell. He's had Rebecca on speed dial ever since the night of the party. It's already buzzing.

"Hi," he says to the phone.

"You tried to call?"

"Yes, I tried to call."

Now he's holding a phone in each hand, the big SAT phone and the sexy iPhone. His sister is running on but he can't make it out. Pushing the speaker button on the SAT phone, he lifts the iPhone back to his ear.

"Rebecca, let's slow this down."

"What?" his sister says.

"Yes, Max, I agree."

"What's your schedule like?"

There's a pause.

"I'm home the rest of the day."

"Not you, Pam."

"I have to fly out to LA," Rebecca says, "That's why I came down to see you."

"So how 'bout we talk next week?"

"No, we have to talk now. Are you docking the boat again?"

"Who is that?" Rebecca asks.

"My sister, she's on the other phone."

"Who are you talking to?" Pam says.

"My girlfriend," he says to his sister, "We're having our first quarrel."

"Max, you're dating? Oh, that's great. Who is she?"

"Rebecca Vasquez."

"Yeah right."

"Max?" Rebecca says.

"Yes?"

"That felt nice."

He looks down at the face on his phone. He'd taken the photo the night of the party. It's from the side and she's looking down. The camera flashed and she lifted her eyes. "Gotcha," he'd said that night, "Gotcha Becca." That's when he saw the look on her face.

"So we'll talk next week?" Max says.

"No, we have to talk now!"

"God damn it, Pam, shut up for just one minute."

"There's someone else?" Rebecca says.

"No! I didn't mean you."

"I'm teasing."

"Are you talking to me?" his sister says.

He's holding both instruments out in front of him, arm's length, looking from one to the other.

"Pam, you need to wait just a moment, okay?"

Putting the iPhone back to his ear. He's standing now at the stern of the boat, out on the great, wide deck, looking up at her there by the gate.

"Becca?"

Why not? What if the chance never comes? He knows these things; knows how quickly life can come. "Becca ..." he begins.

"Max, don't," she says, cutting him off, hearing it in his voice, "Not over the phone. I want to see your face. I want you to see mine."

He knows she's right. He knows she's going to be right about a lot of things from now on.

"Come back here, now," he says.

"No, there's something I have to do."

"Becca ..."

"Think of me?"

"Are you kidding?"

He watches her put the phone in her pocket. She waves, closing the gate. A red, M650 convertible pulls up. It's Anja, her assistant. Talk about hiding in plain sight. Her car flickers in and out of the masts and the other boats lining the pier, running beside the little white shops. There's traffic out on the boulevard.

"Max," his sister is saying, "Max?"

He picks up the SAT phone.

"Yes, Pam, what is it?"

"I just called to see if you got back the tests."

Tuesday, 4th February 2014

A Precise Science

by Gloria Garfunkel

Bipolar Ralph here. Chloe and I are on the last day of our fabulous ski vacation in Park City Utah. We are both incredibly excited to ski powder instead of the slush and ice they call snow in New England. I spend the nights while she's sleeping perfecting my Quality Assurance Data reports. No room for error there.

"Boy," she says, "I didn't realize Quality Assurance was such a demanding and complicated field. I thought it was just fabricated busywork bullshit full of arbitrary numbers to intimidate employees into thinking they are being watched and empirically measured."

"It's a precise science. You've no idea. It's like being a psych. nurse only for a whole organization." Chloe is a psych. nurse for one unit which I admit is worse.

This morning, Chloe says, "Ralph. I think you're bipolar like my father was. You need to get help before a disaster." Her bipolar father had committed suicide.

"Right," I say. "Me bipolar? I just have energy cycles. Is everyone with energy cycles bipolar?"

"Yes, in fact," she says.

And by the way, I am seeking help and take Lithium and I'm still cycling, though you should have seen me before the Lithium. I just don't want Chloe worrying about me. She's been through enough in her life. She being a psych. nurse, really, we both know I'm not fooling her at all. Besides, I know she's gone through all my pills in the medicine cabinet. Truthfully, I'm on a lot more than just Lithium. That's the big gun, so to speak, the 'Anti−Suicide Pill'.

"I'd really like us to talk about this," she says.

"I'd really like not to," I say. "I'm OK. I'm taking care of myself. Don't worry. I'm not your father. I would never commit suicide. He was much worse. He was Bipolar I and I'm Bipolar II."

She gets very quiet and still. I want to hug her, but I can't. But then I do and we both cry.

"I was twelve when he did it and I just thought if I'd been a better daughter …"

"I know."

Crying is not a good sign. I am headed for a downslide.

Ochre

by John Wentworth Chapin

Esther fidgets. She's used to sitting still in bed; she's been bedridden for two months, her multiply–fractured legs mending from the accident, seven metal pins in both. The sheets aren't as clean as they could be, but at least she is out of the hospital. Sitting still to recover is one thing; sitting for a portrait, however, trying to remain motionless, makes her aware of every square inch of skin, every itch, every regret. The late afternoon light bathes the room in a fickle glow, the color of buttery warmth but cold. Always cold.

"I aim to take a sip of my water, and then I might be ready for a little shut–eye," she says.

He concentrates on the oversized watercolor pad in front of him, daubing greens and mustards, pigments a white boy uses to capture the hues of a light–skinned black woman beset by age and catastrophe. She knows he heard her, because his lips move slightly in response. She takes a sip, tilting the water into her mouth from a tall sports water bottle, resting the bottom against the metal safety bedrail.

"How's the painting coming?" she asks. He still doesn't answer. She wants him to answer, and she considers saying his name to get his attention: *Charles*. That seems too personal, though. He makes a popping sound with his lips which reminds her of her father spitting loose flecks of tobacco from his handrolled cigarettes. The memory firms her resolve. She presses a button on the side of the bed, and with a low hum, the top third of the bed reclines. The late afternoon sun slips from her skin, now illuminating a patch of ochre on a far wall.

"Wait!" he cries.

She's startled by the outburst but keeps her finger on the button. "I need to rest," she says, thinking what a surprising thing the world can be that sitting in bed taxes her to the point of exhaustion.

Charles mutters that he is almost finished, but she is beyond politeness. She agreed to the portrait thinking that the company would be nice. It's worse with him there. The stillness forces her into her own mind, and that's the last place she wants to be. She hasn't been able to listen to music or watch television since the accident, and she's not sure why.

He stares at his painting for a moment, then back at her. He sets down his brush and runs his fingers through his hair, a long, plaintive exhale escaping him. His hair is slightly damp.

The center of each of her fingers is frozen with an implacable chill, and he's sweating.

"It's terrible," he sighs, crossing his arms against his chest.

Ten, twenty, thirty years ago, Esther might have reassured him that it was fine, even without seeing the painting. "Do you want to show it to me?" she asks.

Charles nods. "I do. But my painting teacher said it's not a good idea to show a painting until we're done with it."

"Well, *I'm* done," she says, with finality.

"Do you mind if I use the men's room?" Charles asks.

She's hesitant. *You've become a truly wretched old woman who should up and die when you consider not letting people use your toilet.* She points down the hall and shuts her eyes as he leaves the room.

§

She told at least forty people – police and doctors and lawyers – that she doesn't remember the accident. She told them she was driving down the street and the next thing she knows she's lying in a cold, white room that's so bright it hurts her eyes.

But: she remembers every single moment of driving up onto the sidewalk and plowing down three strangers. Her windshield was sprayed with blood and two bodies, so she couldn't see what she hit when she crashed to a halt, but she remembers the blood spatter and the way a stranger's hand smeared it like a finger painting. She remembers the loud racket of her car's damaged engine clacking and sputtering, then voices screaming and yelling.

It was easier to claim amnesia and blackout. They tested her for brain damage and heart damage. They tested her for drug interactions and drug abuse and alcohol. They did a psychiatric evaluation. They theorized about black ice. They begged her to remember, and she pretended to try.

She couldn't explain what she knew: that she was feeling fine and then suddenly she was doing things she didn't expect to be doing. She didn't want to kill those people, *but she didn't try not to*, either. That's something you don't tell a policeman or a doctor or a lawyer. So she remembers everything, but she doesn't understand any of it. She is beginning to fear that she never will.

Charles holds the unfinished painting out to her, a rough pencil sketch of shapes – bed, head, body – painted in washes of tan and olive. Her vision is not what it used to be, but her first thought is dismay that he swallowed her afternoon yet it looks like he's barely gotten started. Her second thought is that it looks like a seasick gingerbread man.

"What do you think?" he asks.

Esther reaches for her bottle of water and tilts it toward her lips.

"Be honest," he says.

She sips, nodding her head slightly to nudge the liquid through the little nozzle. "How long have you been painting?" she asks.

"You hate it," Charles says.

"I don't like when people put words in my mouth," she snaps.

Charles is chastened. She sees the boy in him, always doing what he's told, and she tucks that away for later.

"This is my first painting," he says. "Outside class, I mean."

He called on her three days earlier, introducing himself as a witness to the accident and explaining that he wanted to paint her because he needed to get over the accident. She didn't understand how a portrait would do that, but in that moment of confusion, she assumed he was a painter. She sees now that his brushes and his little easel are new, and she feels tricked, even though he has done nothing wrong. She imagines more days like today, with the torture that silence and awareness bring.

"I'll be honest with you," she says. "I don't want you to finish it."

After a moment of quiet, Charles says, "I need to do this. I don't know why." When Esther doesn't reply, Charles keeps talking. "I can't get the accident out of my head, so I'm trying new things, like this painting class, and I see your face in the windshield coming at me ... I'm so lucky to be alive. You were driving straight at me but ..."

This perks Esther up. "You saw me driving? Saw me hit them? What did I look like?"

"It was a quick glimpse. You looked straight at the woman you hit, no reaction on your face. Then she was on the

173

windshield and blocked my view. I thought they'd find you slumped over dead from a heart attack or something."

Esther says, "I didn't see you."

"You looked happy!" he says, remembering this now for the first time, surprising himself.

"I wasn't," she shoots back.

Charles stops himself from answering and takes a sharp breath.

Esther looks at him, carefully, seeing him.

Charles sees her, too.

He says, "Why didn't you swerve? You could have missed her."

"I was not in control of my body," Esther says.

"Then who was?"

"I'm not a religious woman."

"Me neither," he replies.

"This is not a ghost story," she says sharply.

Charles nods vigorously, frowning. "I know, I know. But what happened?"

"The answer is that I don't know." She picks at the thin cotton blanket and looks at the watercolor pad as though she hopes to find an answer there in the swaths of paint. "You come back sometime soon and work on that painting," Esther says, "and we'll talk about it."

"Tomorrow?" Charles asks.

"Not tomorrow," she says. "But soon."

Avoidance

by Lynn Beighley

I'm in my robe, my feet are up, and I'm watching that new show with the smart, snarky, gorgeous city woman who is trying to survive in the male–dominated world of bull riding.

In each episode this happens:

Kristen, our heroine, encounters anger and prejudice because she, a woman, chooses to intrude on man's world.

Jed, the enlightened but sexy cowboy who was brought up by his strong, lesbian grandmother, played by Betty White, argues with her about her actions, but with an intense, obvious sexual tension beneath the encounter.

Her supportive gay rodeo clown friend, Zeke, provides comic relief and emotional support, while also expressing how hunky he finds Jed.

In tonight's awful episode, she jumps into the ring to distract a bull before he can maul Zeke. And now Jed is yelling at her, and she's yelling back at him. And suddenly they're kissing. This is the first time they've kissed, and I know it's predictable, but as corny as it is, it gets to me. I'm a sucker for romance, even predictable romance.

And then, of course, there's a commercial. I look down at the notebook on my lap. I open Facebook and get a shock. Sitting on my lap is a picture of my dad in a cherry red Speedo. Dad. Speedo. I close my eyes. My stomach is roiling. My old cat,

Pollock, chooses this moment to leap on the couch and does his best to shove my notebook aside to occupy my lap. Normally I'd shoo him off because he drools and is often gassy, but right now I need a moment to consider what I just saw. I close the machine and put it on the coffee table.

Pollock purrs on my lap while I ponder. There's a picture of my dad in a Speedo on Facebook. Is this that big a deal? Yes, yes it is, I tell myself. But okay, it really isn't.

I reach forward and open the notebook again. He's still there, almost all of him. I cringe. It's not that my dad looks terrible, I guess. But it's far more of his skin than I ever want to see. I want to be the kind of person who is open−minded enough not to care that her dad is nearly naked online. No, I'm lying. What kind of person is that? Not me. Okay.

The last time I saw my dad in a Speedo I was 13 and my friends and I had just finished swimming in our pool in the backyard. He came out wearing a baby−blue Speedo and my friends started giggling and my face felt like it was on fire and I ran inside to complain to my mother. That evening after yet another huge fight, my mother made him agree to never wear a Speedo again.

This sounds bad. My dad's not like that. I mean, he didn't have any skeevy motive in wearing a Speedo around a bunch of little girls. No, he didn't. He just liked Speedos. Likes Speedos, apparently.

It has 23 likes, his photo. And 13 comments. Above it, he's written, "What do U think of this as my profile picture for online dating sites?" He's using online dating sites now? He types "U" instead of "you"?

I open the comments to see what the consensus is. Several older women I don't recognize have posted things like "ooh baby! I wish Henry looked like you" and "sexxaay <3 <3 <3".

I look away, that's all I can take. Now I'm wondering how I can get him to take this picture down without ever having to actually discuss it with him. I can't even imagine bringing it up.

Until they divorced, I was always able to get my mother to get him to not be so ... out there.

Then I think that maybe it's not a big deal. He's lonely, right? I wonder what sort of mature woman will respond to this picture.

I hear a voice I recognize. I look up and there's Bill Plover, my coworker, on my TV in all his Ploverness. It's a commercial for *You Tell Me*, the reality show he's going to be on that begins next month. I'd like to forget about his show, but nearly every day at work someone brings it up because a big component of this show is romance, and the office thinks that awkward Bill loves me.

"It's up to you what happens. Everything from what to wear to who to date. Everything," the voice says, "and they'll have to do it."

My phone rings, and Pollock farts.

Friday, 7th February 2014

Freak's Father

by Andrew Stancek

Yeah, I'm the freak's father. That's what the tabloids call me.

Wingy. That's what they call him. They covered his story from every angle, making him into a monster, a fraud, a savior, and everything in between, and then they move their scavenging tentacles on those around him, so they can sell more papers. I'm not all that interesting, I don't think, but then again I never thought he was all that interesting either.

You know I never saw the least sign of battiness in him when I still lived with him and his mother. He was a kid like any other, not particularly athletic, kind of nerdy, enjoyed chess and stamp collecting more than baseball. Soccer is my game, understandable for someone who spent most of his life in Europe, and I kicked a ball around with him sometimes. He wasn't disgraceful but he tripped over his feet trying to dribble and didn't throw himself on the ground to catch a ball when he was goalie. I always thought he only came out to please me and would have preferred to be inside reading, or whatever. He was relieved when I said we'd go in for a beer and a lemonade. We weren't terribly close, ever. No, it's not tabloid material. I didn't abuse him and he didn't shoot me with an improperly stored weapon. That's what *The National Conspirer* and *Full Moon* would like. But our past holds no smoking gun.

I moved out when he was bed–ridden with Perthes disease. Does that make me a terrible creep? Maybe. He was in traction for almost two years, then the surgery and his life–changing breakthrough, his flying, merging, modern day Icarus, all that. But you know his story, you don't need me to tell you his. I'm talking about myself here. The timing of my leaving home could have been better, sure. Yveta and I hadn't been getting along for years, not fighting much but not having much use for each other either. It was most likely going to end in divorce no matter what. And then he got sick, really sick, our Adam. Maybe in some families that leads to bonding, and patched up conflicts, and the couple lives happily ever after. All I can say is that didn't happen to us. Yveta was more tense, more tired, more preoccupied with him, Adam. I was suddenly walking the dog three times a day and Scruffy was the only one whose tail wagged when he saw me. Then the dog died, ran into traffic, and whether I was there or not made no difference to anybody. I wasn't looking for trouble, looking to leave, but trouble has a way of finding you, even if you're not looking. The dullest, commonest story: my new secretary broke up with her live–in, at a bar after work she listened to my whining and I listened to hers and it seemed life with her would be better than what I had at home. She wasn't even pretty, kinda mousy really, but she was there and for a while she listened. I moved out, shacked up with her, and less than a year later that was over, too. The charm was pretty thin. But I didn't go back to Yveta and Adam, either, saw no point in that. I wasn't going to eat crow for leaving.

You could say this is the first time I ever really apologized. I've cried into my beer and had a pity party lots of times, of course. But apologized to Adam, no, I've never done that. He's famous now, some would say notorious, but that's not the reason for my apology. I don't want anything from him, no money, not even reflected glory.

I'm looking at my life, reconsidering. I was in a car accident, fractured a fibula, a concussion shook me up, maybe knocked some sense into me. Two of my friends died in the last year. It's Friday today and I'd like to go and knock back a few but there's no one whose jokes I haven't heard a hundred times. What do you really have in life? What is it all about? I'd like to have a better relationship with Adam. Maybe I can still share something with him, maybe he wants to know, maybe he cares.

Everybody wants to learn how to fly like he does. I'm glad he stepped back from all the glory a bit, that he's not on the front covers of every magazine any more, on every TV show. He needs to take stock, too, decide what is right, right for humanity but also right for him. This isn't a patent we're talking about, but a human being. All the yelling and screaming, the controversies, the certainties about what he has to do and how. Well, he's the only one who can decide. He doesn't belong to the world or to a government. He is only himself.

Maybe he wants a father back. Maybe we can do things together. Some fathers fly a kite with their sons. We never did that. Maybe we can fly together, spread our wings, father and son.

Talk to me, Adam. Talk to me, son.

I am sorry.

Saturday, 8th February 2014

Consequences Need Action

by Rachel Ambrose

"I don't know, Isa," I say into the phone. It's cradled between my neck and shoulder as I'm washing dishes in the sink, and I've been talking long enough that my shoulder is starting to ache. "I like Charlotte, but she comes in late and she leaves her stuff everywhere and her cat likes to knead his claws on my comforter."

"I told her to get rid of that damn cat," Isa replies, and I can hear the sigh in her voice. "Look, Claire, it's just a few more months. I'll be back after that, and you won't have to pick up her dirty panties anymore." She pauses as I chuckle into the phone. "College roommates don't change, you know."

I quickly hang up after Charlotte walks in the kitchen. She's taller than me, with bright eyes and brown hair that she dyes varying shades of green and blue. She works in a restaurant as a sous chef, so she's gone a lot, which is a great perk as far as I'm concerned. Mondays and Tuesdays are her days off, and sometimes she cooks for us. She doesn't go to the grocery store much, but she brings home food from her restaurant and that's good enough. Tonight she's humming and shimmying around in a slinky black dress. "Where are you off to?" I venture. Sometimes my voice seems like a squeak in my throat.

"Oh, this birthday party for one of my friends at Bubble, I got the night off work specially," she replies. I've heard of

Bubble; it's a champagne bar in the artsy downtown district. "You're welcome to come if you want, the more the merrier." She shoots me a smile that almost cracks on the edges it's so sweet. I consider it for about half a second, and then it occurs to me that I'd have to get out of my sweatpants if I did go.

"I don't like champagne," I say. There's a moment of disappointment in her face, but she hides it quickly. "And I don't know any of your friends, I'd feel awkward."

"They're awesome!" she says. "You should come, even if you don't like champagne. Come on, I bet you have something cute in your closet." She bounces on her heels to my room and I follow her reluctantly. "You won't even have to stay long if you drive yourself!" she says. "We haven't been out on the town as roomies since I moved in." She's wheedling me, and I know I might mess up the subtle and delicate harmony of our roommate–ship if I refuse. I roll my eyes at her black–sequined back, but say, "Yes, okay, I'll come. You can't leave me in the corner with a whiskey and soda, though."

She makes a noise that conveys far more excitement than I think the situation merits. "This'll be so much fun!" She starts going through my closet, but stops abruptly after I clear my throat. "I'll, uh, let you get ready then. Take your time!"

"Sorry," I say. "I just don't like people going through my stuff except for me."

"No, no!" she says, beating a hasty retreat out of my room. "It's cool! Come out when you're ready to go."

I emerge, finally, a torturous twenty minutes later after wrestling myself into a bright blue sheath dress that I'd forgotten I borrowed from a cousin. I run a wet brush through my hair. Makeup's for people who actually give a shit, I decide, as I shuffle through my shoes and remind myself that bunny slippers aren't an acceptable public footwear choice. I settle on some white flats, grab my wallet, and decide that I'm just going to have to suck it up and have a good time. The horror.

We slip into Charlotte's car and head off downtown. The trees are festooned with little yellow lights like the kinds you see at old carnivals and fairs, and the sky is blue like my dress. I tug at it as she puts the radio on scan. "You'll like Blake," she says as we pull up to the parking lot. "He's really sweet, he's a painter and we go back since before college." I just hope that the drinks aren't too expensive.

As we walk in, the dark heat of the bar envelops me and reminds me of being wrapped in a comforter. I can deal with this, I think, as I wave a little to Charlotte's friends as she introduces me. There's Katie and Kevin, a real estate agent couple, and Ralph, a food truck owner, and Jason, a couples therapist. My lowly "administrative assistant" job title seems so sophomoric compared to their polished careers. And finally there's Blake himself, a short dark-haired guy with a smudge of green paint on his nose and hazel eyes. I know I don't get out a lot, but I can't stop staring at him in his black button-up shirt with the sleeves rolled up to the elbows, exposing lightly muscled forearms. He smiles at me and I see his teeth have a gap in front, and I have to swallow down my hard-beating heart. I take a champagne glass from Charlotte and we stand and toast Blake's birthday, and I gulp down the drink and nearly choke on the hidden cherry at the bottom. I try not to make a face at how sweet it is.

"I haven't been out in a while," I find myself joking to Blake. "Even drinks keep trying to kill me." What is this? I don't quip. You can't call me witty. Instant Human: Just Add Champagne? Good to know. I immediately order another, taking care this time to remember about the stealthy fruit.

"I know what you mean," Blake says, nodding and sipping from his glass. "Some days it doesn't seem like I can physically leave the house." Are we secretly the same person? I wonder. We talk about his paintings and how landscapes can capture emotion, and his eyes seem to glow as I drink more (did I mention I haven't had more than a glass of wine in one go in over a year?). I'm on my third glass when Charlotte taps me on the shoulder. "Don't monopolize the birthday boy, honey," she says, grinning, but there's ice behind that warmth. Does she have a thing for Blake? I can't tell. Does Blake have a thing for her? I suddenly feel the need to sit down. Being social is hard work.

We eventually leave and head to a pancake restaurant, where Blake and I manage to make everyone else feel like third, fourth, fifth and sixth wheels, which may set a new world record. Kevin and Katie head out before the food hits the table, and the others sit there poking at their waffles and coffee, reminding me of petulant children. Blake tries to draw the others into our conversation, but no one else quite seems to grasp what we're talking about (what are we talking about?) and I'm having too much fun to care about stepping on toes. We exchange numbers as we're leaving and he makes my insides do a cartwheel when he leans in close and brushes a rough kiss against my cheek. "It was a great birthday, thanks to you," he says, and he smells like woodsmoke and citrus and male and oh boy. I sweep into the car with Charlotte sitting silently beside me and burble, "Man, I am gone," and I don't think to explain which definition of "gone" I mean, because I kind of mean all of them at once.

Sunday, 9th February 2014

Valentine's Lay

by Gill Hoffs

If I don't stick it in, I might leak. He said 'smart casual', so black trousers are fine, but I know from the preference form he left with the agency that tight tops and bared midriffs are what he's hoping for from our girls, so something long and drapey from the 'camel toe coverups' section in my wardrobe is out. I could stick it in my bag beside the candle and matches and hope for the best, trim the string like when I was a stripper and hope a handjob will hold him off, maybe offer my arse, or even call in sick and let Pamela take my role.

But I like my job, I like him. Never mind the loafers and too short trousers; I want to go on this date.

I stick the paper bullet in my bag, down a half−pint of orange juice, and go for a shower then take my tweezers to the topiary heart between my legs, and make sure the edges are tidy. I can feel the orange juice working its magic in my intestines and do some sit−ups to help it along.

Ten minutes later and I'm reading up on Mozart as I shit. Arse it is, then.

I've an hour before my taxi arrives in which to choose a final outfit, do my hair and makeup, and floss my teeth. He likes to lick the ones at the front, so I give them an extra scrub before applying scarlet lipstick then get on with the usual faff of mascara (chocolate), eyeliner (black), eye shadow (bronze), concealer (ivory) and blusher (pink). Hair in plaits, one draping each breast with a long thin black ribbon tied round the end. He likes to watch them tickle my nipples when I go on top, then pull the ribbons free and watch my hair loosen as we fuck. I bet he uses my plaits like reins when he takes me from behind.

I pull on a black satin thong, a present from a grateful client last Valentine's Day, then fiddle with its matching shelf bra, my boobs jiggling as I hook the clasp in place. As with Christmastime, Valentine's Day leaves me with too much red–and–black themed nonsense to sensibly handle at home. So unless the underwear, buttplugs, whips and fine chains are something I can use with a client or for my own entertainment, onto eBay they go. I much prefer whipped cream to whips and chain–stores to chains, but if a client is willing to pay for my exceptional services, so be it. Sean just likes a bit of kinky candle play and for me to show up in exotic underwear, though he fancies himself as the new Marquis de Sade. I reckon Sade is more up his street, though a 'smooth operator' he is *not*.

Stockings, suspenders, trousers, heels, stop for a minute and pet the cat. I miss her when I'm working, though I doubt very much that she gives a shit so long as her auto–feeder works. Now for a top. Something that clings and shows the world if I'm cold or not, something that shows my client there are no cups on a shelf bra, just uplift and easy access for fun.

I decide on a clingy red number and pull it on, the deep V neck allowing me to dress without smudging my makeup, the soft fabric showing off my nipples and plaits and leaving a broad band of skin showing around my waist. Then I sit and read a little more about Mozart until the taxi beeps and I grab my bag and umbrella and head out for my 'date'.

§

We're feeding each other sushi and acting like we're in love when his boss walks past our table and halts in a double-take.

"Sean? Hallo! And this must be ...?"

I smile angelically at the face above the belly hovering so close to my cheek.

"Donald, hi. Good to see you mate. This is Jennifer. Jennifer, Donald, Donald, Jennifer."

I offer my hand but he leans down for a kiss and a look down my top. We mutter about delight and pleasure and I make like I'm shy but push my elbows into my lower ribs, and Sean's boss stares at my cleavage as his crotch alters and his cock pushes against the fly of his jeans.

"Donald, Jennifer's studying the history of classical music. Jen, Donald's team manager at my work."

"Sean's told me so much about you, I'm so glad to finally put a face to the name."

While I feign enthusiasm, Sean fiddles one-handed with the phone hidden under his napkin. It rings out, and he checks the screen, easing his bulk from the booth while saying, "Sorry, it's important I take this, it's the Wiederman account. Donald, would you ...?" and pointing at me.

Donald inclines his head slightly and gestures to Sean to go, then eases himself into the vacant seat. It's a small booth, adequate for two or cosy for three, and he scoots along until his thigh brushes mine under the table.

"I hate to keep you from your wife ..." I murmur, and he holds up a hand to stop me.

"Nonsense. It's a pleasure to take care of you, my dear, a pleasure. I'm here with some golfing buddies, anyway, not my wife."

"Sean told me just the other night what a great boss you are. I'm so pleased to meet you and tell you how grateful I am for taking such an interest in his career."

His eyebrows raise a little at this, and I know it's because he does nothing of the sort.

"Well ... he's a good worker. He deserves it."

I lay a hand on his thigh, not so high up or so far in as to be indecent, lean closer, and say, "Still, I appreciate it." I pull in my lower lip with my teeth and murmur, "Really appreciate it."

The next move has to be his. His eyes flick to the side, checking for Sean who said I'd have five minutes tops before his return. I can smell whisky on his breath and perhaps this skews his judgment, I don't know, but one of his hands moves mine up his thigh to his crotch and the other slips up the side of my top closest to him, invisible to anyone who might be watching in the restaurant. I groan quietly and let my eyelids droop a little, still holding his gaze, while he fingers my nipple and damn near drools.

"Jesus ..." he whispers, and I rub his cock through the over–washed denim. It's small enough to be a hardened bollock.

"I'd like to say ... thank you ... properly ... some time ..."

"What for?"

His nostrils are flaring with each inhalation of breath, and I know I have him.

"For Sean's ... promotion."

"But he ... yes. Sometime soon?"

I nod and lick my lips, grateful to the cosmetics industry for long–lasting lip stains. One last rub and I sit back as if I hear someone approaching, Donald's hand slithering down my side and back to normality, away from my tit. Sean takes his cue and returns from round the corner, where he's been monitoring the situation using the mirror behind the bar.

"Sorry about that, Jen. Thanks for looking after my girl, Donald. You know how it is, I just can't seem to leave my work in the office."

Donald scooches over, stands up to let Sean regain his seat, and claps him on the shoulder with an open hand as he does so.

"Sure, no problem. That's some woman you've got yourself there."

Sean winks at me openly.

"Oh, I know. Enjoy the rest of your night."

"Shall do."

Donald catches my eye as he moves away and I smile at him. He hesitates, turns back, and says, "Oh, and Sean? Come see me in the morning. Pleasure to meet you, Jennifer. Hope I see you again soon."

I nod, saying, "I'm sure you will."

Once Donald is away, Sean raises an eyebrow at me. I nod. We finish our drinks and leave.

I drip candlewax in a heart on his chest, my version of romantic, and let Sean spank me with the single red rose (no thorns, thank goodness) he got me for Valentine's Day before I turn around and lower myself onto his cock. No cramps, no warning signs, so fingers crossed I'll make it home before I end up riding the red wave. Up go his hands to the ribbons, and I rock my hips back and forth for a bit before reaching behind me to tickle his balls.

He grabs my arse to rock me harder, and I use my other hand to play with the candle some more.

"Thanks ... for ... the ... promotion."

I wink at him.

"No problem. Happy Valentine's Lay."

Monday, 10th February 2014

Mister Weatherbee

by Susan Tepper

"God is good, God is great, and we thank him for this food. Amen." I make the sign of the cross.

Because somebody, a gift from God, God the father almighty, has cut a hole in the chain link fence surrounding the school yard. And the hole is in a very good place, a God-like place, behind a clump of thick juniper bushes that stay bushy all the year 'round. "Glory be to God in the highest."

Over the weekend I traded in the Dodge for a Buick LeSabre. Or should I say the Dodge went on the scrap metal heap. This Buick is toast-colored. A bit more roomy than the Dart, which makes for more comfort. It has a good back seat. I've lain there, alone, holding my little darling, this one a small black boy with the most exquisite head of curls. I have held him and held him until we both nearly died from the rapture. I cross myself again. "Jesus, our savior and our light, protect us."

Some druggie cut a hole in the fence to find God, too. God has his ways of coming to us all. He comes to me in the form of so many beautiful boys. God led me to this school yard. I could have taken the main highway to get on the parkway, but that day it was detoured on account of road work. It detoured past the school yard. God knows and protects us all if we follow his path.

Yesterday I practiced going through the hole. Tight but doable. I felt like Alice down the rabbit hole. "Frankly, Alice, women don't do it for me." Girls, either. I don't like their stuff it scares me shitless.

I get out of the Buick, lock the door, and crouch down squeezing through the fence hole. It's a cold, damp day. The ground smells like a fresh dug grave. I think about my mother. *So much blood from you we had to throw away the mattress*, she'd say. Smacking my cheek hard. *Cloudy with no chance of sun*. That's what Mister Weatherbee said on the telly this morning. I gauge my days by Mister Weatherbee.

Wedged in the junipers I can see the boys and not be seen. This is much better than being in the car. I can see my little darlings, yet also hear their sweet chirping voices. I love when they make their little bird sounds and squeals. Once their voices change they are of no interest. I want the smooth cheek like the hand of God. The face with its dark down that will turn to a stiff growth – no thanks. I want my baby chicks cuddly smooth and hairless.

My little darling has a name! A real name, not a made-up one by me. I get the goose bumps! Masia some of the others call him. Masia. Could be Egyptian. Or Ethiopian. He's very dark and beautiful, my Masia. Jesus was a black man, too, despite that the Catholics made him into a blue-eyed blond. I have done my research on Jesus. So fuck the pope and the rest of those Catholic dickhead priests. God exists outside of the church. I am God and one with God.

Masia is a panther boy, the way he moves he needs to be in a warm place where the grass is tall enough to cover his movements, where he can slink and slither and no one will ever find him.

A little girl is smiling at him, handing him something. Candy? Masia puts it in his mouth and smiles back. Can he be so easily bought by a girl?

I shift my position in the junipers noticing the blue–gray berries; debating whether they are edible. None of the other little darlings capture my attention the way Masia has. There is all the time in the world. It's been constructed this way. "At the right hand of God the father almighty."

The teachers are scarce today, and only one teacher aide. Is there a strike and these are the scabs? Scabs, because instead of the usual hovering, watching, this group is yapping among themselves, ignoring the kids, talking on their phones, texting. The kids are not being properly watched or handled. It should be reported. If these are scabs they need to find more responsible scabs. It's a travesty what goes on in this world.

When these filthy scabs finally hustle the little darlings back inside, I slip out through the hole. I think about covering it up. Protection is first in line. I will get a slab of wood and cover up the hole. This way only I can gain entrance and exit. I'll figure out a way to latch it to the chain link fence.

At Home Depot I walk the aisles. It's a miserable place. Reminds me of Desert Storm, those Quonset huts the military constructed. What a freaking fuck up. Some of the nurses tried making me there but I put a fast stop to that. One got pissed and called me Candy. Made no bones about the fact that her nose was out of joint.

In the plywood section, I examine several thicknesses. None of the employees wearing the orange aprons show any interest in helping me. "Hey! Some help here!"

An old guy bordering on seventy comes over finally. "Yeah?"

"I need to board up a hole in a chain link fence."

"Wood isn't your answer," he says. "You trying to keep a dog from running away?"

"Yeah, Grandpa, that's the ticket. My bulldog Hairy Pits keeps escaping the yard."

The guy stares at me under long, bushy gray eyebrows trying to figure out if I'm dicking him.

"So what do you think?"

"You need a fence fixer." He walks off.

I push my tongue around inside my jaw. He could be right. It may not be a plywood operation. I decide to leave things go for the time being. *Chance of rain*, Mister Weatherbee said.

Let God do his work and I'll do mine.

Tuesday, 11th February 2014

Lost and Found

by Jessica McHugh

"Through him, with him, in him, in the unity of the Holy Spirit, all glory and honor is yours, almighty Father, forever and ever."

There was a time when Edward McKenzie's thoughts couldn't stray during the Liturgy of the Eucharist, especially during an event as sacred as a wedding. For years, speaking the ritual's sacred words and hearing his parishioners' passionate replies quickened his heart with joy. Now, he runs on autopilot. It still inspires joy, but he can't deny that it would be tenfold if he could prepare the sacrament with feminine, manicured fingers. He uses the oddity of a Tuesday wedding to justify his distraction, but looking to the young bride and groom, their affection aglow, he can blame no one but himself.

After nearly thirty years of service, Father McKenzie's love in God is not lessened, only his faith in his *right* to serve God. What kind of man can stand in the house of the Lord, the consecrated host at his fingers, and wish, beyond Heaven and Earth, that he were a woman?

A selfish man. A frightened man.

A sinner.

As the bride and groom look up at him in adoration, Edward tries to focus on the task at hand. He lifts the communion paten to his people. Beneath the host, it is freshly polished, shining like the jewelry he's too afraid to wear outside his apartment. The candles are reminders, too. Lit by the altar boys, their scent is similar to his grandmother's perfume, the kind he dabs behind his ears and knees, hoping someone might lean in for a closer sniff. He pours the wine and no longer sees blessed blood. He sees a night of desire, even debauchery, in the chalice, and he aches to scream his truth from the pulpit.

Calm yourself, child. Take a breath and tell Grandma Eleanor what's troubling you.

"No, not here," Edward says, shaking. The chalice tilts in his hand, spilling a drop of wine.

An altar boy sidles up, whispering, "You all right, Father?"

Most of the boys let their hair grow shaggy this time of year, but not Nelson Wade. As usual he's clean−cut, his vestments appropriately pressed for the occasion, and he wears a room−brightening smile that puts most Edward sees to shame.

"Father Edward?"

"Everything's fine, Nelson. Thank you."

More lies in God's house. What has he become? And worse, what will become of him when his wicked life is through? Other people live as they wish without fear of damnation, so part of him believes he could too, but too many evil interpretations from the old days linger in his heart. He wants God to love him no matter his manner of dress or sexual preference, but he grew up believing those desires would earn him a one−way ticket to Hell.

To his parishioners, Edward McKenzie is the mild−mannered minister who lives alone for better religious reflection. He supports the community through charity work, helping to clean up the parks, volunteering at the local soup kitchen, even reading to children at the library, but it isn't a social situation for him.

The reasons are rarely questioned. He thanks God daily for that − and apologizes. God knows his mind and the sinful thoughts filling it. He fears damnation, but fears losing his flock more. He can't imagine remaining their shepherd after revealing he's a wolf in chiffon clothing.

"The Body of Christ," he says to Charlie Kitner, a strapping man who runs the local hardware store.

Charlie whispers, "Amen." When his tongue slides over his bottom lip to catch Christ's love, Edward shivers.

No, he hasn't acted on *every* desire.

The man's lips bend upward. It's as if he knows the glory of the Lord, riveting his soul as the wafer dissolves on his tongue. His pleasure makes Edward's lips do a similar dance – until Sarah Kitner takes her husband's place, her tongue a protruding plank.

Sarah doesn't make Edward's mind wander. The revelation is a knife, especially when he sees how happy communion makes her. Both Kitners. They repeat "Amen" together and clasp hands for their stroll down the aisle. The only time Edward feels that happy is when he's hidden away, his face soft and ivory from his grandmother's makeup, pretending – no, *becoming* – Eleanor. For the Kitners, for the newlywed Barrons and so many of his parishioners, happiness comes easy.

After the service, he cries in the sacristy. Hunched over the desk, his hands clasped in prayer, Edward's tears fall upon the marriage certificate still needing his signature. He dabs it dry with a tissue and signs the paper before setting it aside. They come again, harder.

He's felt post–service sorrow before, but he used to be better at disguising it.

Because you want to tell them the truth. Eleanor crouches beside him and kisses his hand. *Dear child. Would it be so hard?*

He buries his face in his hands, and nods.

Nelson Wade opens the door. Seeing the priest hunched over, his body quaking, he says, "Father, what's wrong? Please don't tell me everything's fine."

Edward wipes away the tears before he turns to him.

"I promise it's nothing you need to worry about," he says. "Is there something I can do for you?"

Nelson holds up a purple tube of lipstick. "Someone left this on one of the pews. I figured I'd drop it in the Lost and Found."

He hands it to Father Edward, who removes the top and spins the lipstick out. It glints under the sacristy fluorescents, too deliciously. He doesn't see Nelson's stare until he rolls down the lipstick. Clearing his throat, Edward slides past Nelson to the jar by the sacristy door. He lifts the lid and drops the lipstick inside. It looks regal atop hair elastics, earrings, and action figures.

"I might know who it belongs to. I can let her know at the next service," Nelson says. "Unless you don't want me to ..."

Edward clamps the jar closed, but his eyes don't leave it. "Is there anything else, Nelson?"

The boy shakes his head and closes the door behind him, but his "unless" stays in the sacristy, hanging over Edward like a sweltering, strangling fog. Certain he's alone, he opens the jar again. With the lipstick's pastoral purple winking at him from the Lost and Found, Edward's happiness comes easy.

Wednesday, 12th February 2014

Supermarket Sweep

by Shane Simmons

"Ihaveanewboyfriend!"

I'm pinned against the shelves where the dusty tinned vegetables and soups sit, and despite the fact that we haven't talked to nor seen each other since last month's heated exchange, Sandra wastes no time getting onto bragging about her new bloke.

"Oh, he's gorgeous! I can't believe how perfect he is for me!"

My attention trails off as I pay more mind to the woman with greasy, tied back hair, bent over at the other end of the aisle, concealed from full view by a circle of screeching blonde girls and a pram. I'm certain she's shoving things in amongst the blankets covering a poor kid in the pram.

"Oh you won't believe this!" Sandra reaches over and takes a bottle of vegetable oil down from the shelf behind me. "My sister called. Can you believe she actually called *me*! And, she was hysterically crying!" she cackles. "She's preggers and he's left her! She doesn't even know where he is!" Sandra bursts into a full on belly laugh and startles a nearby pensioner who wobbles dangerously on her sticks.

She skims over the jars of ready–made pasta sauce and says, "I just told her to fuck off and die," before picking one up and dropping it in her basket. The pensioner sneers before she shuffles away, muttering under her breath.

"He must've realised I was a better fuck than that whore. See, things always turn out for the better!" Sandra states. "Karma will always fuck you up."

She bares me the widest grin before walking ahead but I wonder just whether she should be smiling so soon. I'm certain there's a bit of bad karma coming to bite each one of our sorry arses.

"You'll need to meet my new man and give him your seal of approval! We should all go out for dinner sometime!"

I can't think of a better way to spend a night.

"I would invite you around just now but I'm making a romantic dinner for him coming over!"

I examine the contents of her basket. "Spag bol?" It's all she can really cook.

"What else? So, any signs of *lurve* on your horizon?"

My silence and blank stare give Sandra all the answer she needs.

"*Anyway*, I was thinking, with your love life, or rather lack of, you need to get a job in the hospital with me!"

In the short time I've known Sandra she's met every one of her male interests through that place. It's more a free–for–all dating agency than a job. Maybe it's the horrible, baby–poo green uniforms.

"There are *so* many gays! Nurses, porters! You just tell me your type and I'll keep a look–out!" She leans in and whispers, "There are rumours about a few of the surgeons and specialists too! Just imagine, you could bag yourself a well–paid doctor! I've been trying to get one since I started there!" She winks, but I'm certain nothing she's said is in jest.

I open the fridge and take a pint and pop it in my basket, it's all I really came in for. Sandra's basket is overflowing with tasty goodies, garlic bread, pancakes, a tub of Häagen–Dazs for her and her new bloke. There's the milk and a microwave macaroni cheese in mine. I wonder if she's right. Maybe I need someone to cook for. Or even better still, cook for me.

"Spag bol, white, red or rosé?" she asks, scanning over the bottles on the shelves.

"Oh come on, that's easy. Red with red meat."

"I'm sure there'll be plenty of red meat tonight! Oh, that reminds me, johnnies!" She marches away as I'm left rolling my eyes and shuddering.

When we arrive at the tills there's a crowd of people waiting to be served and a few of them are shouting, "Just give them the stuff so we can go!" The greasy woman is stood with her arms folded shouting, "I dun 'ave nahthin'!" at the man blocking her path. The kids around her are deadly silent and I find myself feeling a little embarrassed for them. Just then the door opens and two uniformed police officers walk in.

"Ooh, look at the policeman! God, he's so tall!" Sandra stretches her neck out for a better view.

"You've got a man to make dinner for tonight, you're not meant to look. And I thought I'd seen that woman nabbing stuff earlier, bet you it's all in the pram."

"I was only pointing him out for your benefit!"

"And I know you can't resist a man in a uniform, Sandra."

The officers take the woman's arm and lead her, the pram and her troupe to the back of the store. The policeman is about 6'6" with striking hazel-coloured eyes, a dimpled chin, and tightly cropped dirty blonde hair underneath his hat. Not that I'm checking him out.

"Shouldn't you go tug him and give him a statement?" Sandra winks away as if she has a twitch.

"I'm not tugging any policemen, besides, they have cameras so just be quiet!" I lightly punch her on the arm.

§

We exit the store to find darkness has fallen.

"Oh for fuck sake, where did the time go? I need to get on with this dinner!"

Sandra strides into the road only a few steps down from the zebra crossing and I find myself following her to the blare of a car horn that just misses me as she reaches the other side.

"So, the three of us, we'll sort out something soon, okay?" she puffs. She doesn't wait for the answer and turning on her heel, heads off down the pavement.

"I can't wait Sandra," I mutter to myself, "I can't bloody wait."

Thursday, 13th February 2014

Kia

by Michelle Elvy

Stevie stands just inside the arched doorway, watching Ellie, sitting in her mother's Kia with her head bowed. It's an impossibly yellow car. No one should have a car that color, thinks Stevie. He watches Ellie as people come up the steps past him, each one saying some small nice thing. He nods silently, keeps his eyes on Ellie. The wind is fierce and her window is shut. She's closed off the world and he's not seen her in a month. He does not like recalling the last time he saw her, yet that's all he thinks about when he thinks of her. He sees her now through the fogged–up window as she wipes the end of her nose and blows hard. He sees her pull the tissue away, look at it, put it back in her lap. He wonders if she'll just sit there all day, blowing her nose on that same small scrap of tissue. He wants to go talk to Ellie. He could at least give her the handkerchief in his pocket that his mother gave him. He has a million things he thinks he might say. He has nothing to say.

He thinks maybe he could go stand next to the car and just being there would be enough to help her open the door and step out. He will give her a new tissue for her runny nose and they will walk up the steps together. He knows how she can't get out of the car and get on with the day. He feels the same way, but his parents helped him through the small moments of the morning – his mom laying out a pressed shirt on the foot of his bed and squeezing his hand as he sat up, feeling small and terrible; his dad glancing at him in the rear–view mirror – *You okay?* – as they parked along one of the neat rows allotted for this occasion. His parents had been there all along, through this whole wretched month. He knew Ellie only had her mom, and her mom was a drunk. Still, she'd driven her daughter here today, in that impossibly yellow car. That was at least something.

"Hey." It's Manny. He must have come from the side entrance, because Stevie's been here at least fifteen minutes, freezing his dick off but unable to move.

"Hey." He's only seen Manny once this past month, when Manny visited him in the hospital. It was a few days after the accident. Stevie'd had to stay a week – for observations, they'd said. Manny stopped in late one night, long after visiting hours. He'd brought a bottle of Jack and sat in the seat near Stevie's bed, not saying anything but repeatedly touching the cut on his head where they'd stitched him up, like maybe he expected to still feel blood. Finally, he asked if Stevie remembered anything. Stevie shook his head. He could not bear to tell his friend that he remembered everything. That he recalled soaring through the air, hurling away from the sounds of crunching metal and the smell of burning rubber. That he was suspended on cottony clouds as the car flipped once, then twice, then maybe a third time, rolling and rolling some more – away from him. That he saw the flames fly up and punch the sky just as he met his Great Grandpa Gus somewhere around the roiling seas of Cape Horn. That he heard the stereo still playing from his dream–cushion until finally those moments passed and all went silent. And that he knew in the moment he hit the frozen cornfield that he was not dead but that someone surely was. How could they not be? No, he did not tell Manny all that. He just shook his head and took the bottle of Jack.

Now they're both standing here on the steps of Our Lady of Sorrows. The whole community's here. Half the school, too. Stevie did not expect to see Manny, but he's glad he's here, even if he doesn't know what to say. He wishes Manny'd just pass a bottle.

Two women come up the steps. The doorway is small and the boys have to turn sideways as the women slide past. "Should have a fuckin' program or something," says Stevie. "You know – to hand out." As soon as he says it, he's sorry. Like there's a program for how this all goes. Like a program will change the stabbing pain they've lived with for a month and the quiet whispers filling the air today. He knows there are programs inside that will walk them all through the next hour but will fail to tell them anything they need to know. He knows the program will mark this day forever, Thursday, February 13, in the year of Our Lord 2014. One month to the day after the crash. He wishes to God he hadn't said that thing about the program because now he worries Manny thinks he's supposed to say something back. He knows Manny's got nothing to say. He knows all eyes are secretly on Manny and Manny's not supposed to be here. He knows Manny's not in the program.

It's cold but Stevie is suddenly sweating. He's not ready for this. How could he be? How could any of them be?

Rick's nowhere to be seen. Stevie's glad because he doesn't want to talk to him, not here, not now. He wishes he were here so Manny would have someone else to talk to. He sees Rick in Trig class every day, but he can't talk to him today.

Who he really wants to talk to is Lucky. Lucky'd know what to say. He'd smile that stupid crooked smile, pass a joint – yeah, even here – and say, *Go on, pussies, get on with it.* He'd laugh at them for being such dicklesses. He'd laugh at them for wearing pressed shirts. He'd stroll out to the lemon–yellow Kia and open the door and pull out a whole box of tissues and wipe his girl's snotty nose and turn around and smile his stupid crooked grin. He'd see all the dopey people and say *Fuck this* and hijack the Kia and drive off into a yellowy cottony haze. He'd say *What're you waitin' for?* so Manny and Stevie would hop in the back seat and they'd drive to the South River where Lucky'd climb out of the car and strip down to his Jockeys and jump – *Geronimo!* – into the freezing river, just to show them he had more balls than any of them, and come up spluttering *Fuuuuuck* and grinning again, all goosebumpy and shrivelled. He'd sit in the car drying out with the heat and stereo blasting and tell them all they're losers for not jumping in, too. He'd look back at Manny and Stevie, wonder why he's driving and not Manny, wonder for a moment why they are in Ellie's mom's car but then shrug and glance around again, saying, "Hey, where's Rick?"

He'd do all those things, and more. He'd graduate next year and go to University of Maryland, get a degree in biology and eventually become a high school teacher and soccer coach. He'd still light up with Stevie and the boys – they'd pass a bottle of Jack around on a Thursday night after poker, get a little stoned, and reminisce about what bad–asses they were back in the day. He'd be a great soccer coach – he already coaches the Brave Bears in town, because no one else will. He's a stoner, sure, but he's a stoner who can outrun anyone on the soccer field and average two goals a game all season. He's actually quite something, Lucky is.

"Have you been inside?" asks Stevie.

"Yeah," says Manny.

There is a long pause until Manny finally says, "He's all laid out neat. Dressed in a suit like a pussy."

Stevie sees Ellie pull down the visor and put on lipstick. He knows he should go to her and help her out of the car, help her take that first step. He knows her mother is nowhere to be found, and he feels deep in his gut that no one should have to emerge from that impossibly fucked up cheerful yellow car and step toward the darkness inside.

A celebration of life, it will say on the program.

Yeah. Fuck.

He moves to go down the steps when Manny reaches out and grabs his forearm. He thinks Manny's going to say something but instead a sob breaks forth from a place he's never seen or heard before. Manny says loudly, "Fuckin' Lucky … he was supposed to live! He was supposed to … *wake up!*" Stevie is aware of all eyes on them, here on the threshold of Our Lady of Sorrows. "He was supposed to wake up, man!" Manny says again.

Stevie feels the weight of Manny collapse onto him. He's holding him and shivering. He puts both arms around his bulky frame and realises that no one has done this in a month for Manny. No one. He feels the weight of metal and fire and rubber and burning hell in Manny's heaving shoulders. He holds his friend.

He sees Ellie open the door of her mother's yellow Kia and step out. There's a snotty wadded tissue in her hand and she walks toward them, alone.

The Thaw

by Len Kuntz

On the second Friday in February, a raucous thaw begins. Ruptures of ice, one after the other, crack like cannons, echoing in the snow−encrusted treetops. The lake is no better than a defenseless animal under attack, as slabs explode and drop into her dark belly.

Rosie ambles into the kitchen, nosing my hand to be petted, and behind her, Virginia, the woman whose home I've been staying at the last month.

"Sounds like torpedoes," she says. "I'll bet it's something to see."

Virginia taps the edge of the counter, feeling her way toward the coffee pot, retrieving a cup from the cupboard, and filling it precisely to the brim.

"What's it look like out there?"

"Destruction," I say, "but kind of beautiful, in an angry sort of way."

"Beautiful and angry. How wonderful. More coffee?" she asks holding up the pot.

"I'm good."

The night I arrived at Virginia's house, after a five hour trek across the frozen lake, she answered her door and welcomed me in without any hesitation, as if I was a relative instead of a complete stranger. Later I learned that she was widowed, childless and lonely. I hadn't expected to stay this long, but fell into a comfortable pattern of laziness. Other than once on the phone with my wife, I haven't spoken to anyone but Virginia and her Labrador, Rosie.

"Now that the weather's turning, I suppose you'll be going soon," Virginia says. Her housecoat has flapped open and I can see the gleaming outline of one of her bare breasts. She's just past sixty, yet fit for her age, hardly wrinkled except for a smattering of crow's feet. Despite her being blind, I feel sleazy for staring and take Rosie's snout in my hands.

"Yeah. Maybe this afternoon."

When I told my wife I wasn't at our house, she said good, because she'd moved in with her boss. She said I should be on the lookout for divorce papers in the mail. She said marrying me was the worst thing that's ever happened in her life, which is some kind of dagger considering she was sexually assaulted by her father for years as a child.

As if channeling my thoughts, Virginia says, "So your marriage, it's over then?"

I remember the few nights we made love, when my wife's fingernails pierced the skin of my neck, nothing kinky or erotic about it, just her disdain of me being verified.

"Over and done," I say, realizing for once what a release it is to be finally free.

"Relationships are quite a challenge."

"But you were married for thirty years."

"Yes, and most of the time I was miserable. If David hadn't died, I think I would have ended up killing him."

"Why stay then, in a bad marriage?"

Virginia points to her eyes, wide as they always are. "I'm pretty independent, but being blind is a tricky thing to negotiate all alone."

I stayed in my marriage because my identity was all wrapped up in being Jess's husband, her a successful bond broker, me a failed alcoholic.

"Would you happen to have a drink handy?" I ask.

"Water?"

"Something harder."

Virginia's eyebrows arch. She likes the idea. "Well, why not, it's noon somewhere. There are a few bottles in the shelf above the fridge."

I haven't had a drop of alcohol in five years, not since the car accident, then losing my job and not having the confidence or wherewithal to get a new one. I thought that being sober would center me, that I'd discover my true, authentic self as they say in AA, but I only felt more lost, empty and soulless.

I make us screwdrivers, mine mostly vodka. The first taste is like seeing old yearbook photos. I don't know what I'm doing, but I'm enjoying the missile of heat that slakes along my nerves, making my senses electric. I have another and another. As if I'm leafing through a magazine, I start to count my past mishaps and failures, picturing them in my mind, bloody and glossy.

I don't even realize that Virginia has gotten up and is standing behind me until I feel her hands on my shoulders. "You've gotten quiet all of a sudden."

When she leans forward, her breasts are squeezed over my head like earmuffs, warm and plush.

She whispers in my ear, "Before you go, do you think you could do me a favor?"

Rosie's asleep on her mat. My glass is empty. Outside the ice sounds like steel beams breaking.

"It's been a very, very long time for me," Virginia says, kissing my head. "And after all, it is Valentine's Day."

I put my hands over hers, ready to push them off. Instead I grip Virginia's fingers, stand and walk with her toward the bedroom.

Saturday, 15th February 2014

Second Inning

by Michael Webb

I see her as I enter the clubhouse. Spring training is now big business, even during the pitchers and catchers portion, so it doesn't surprise me to see press on hand. She's wearing a thin, gauzy, lime—colored dress, appropriate in the Florida heat, but too thin for the chill of the locker room. She walks towards me, smiling.

"Mark Hamilton?" she says cheerfully.

"Y—yes," I say. "I didn't expect to be recognized so soon."

"Hi! I'm Jen from Comcast. I covered you in Chicago. Well, I was an intern then. But I was there." I think about that year in Chicago for a moment, the long climb into the playoffs, followed by the abrupt exit.

"How about that," seems like the only thing to say. There are a few other pitchers and clubhouse attendants scattered around the room, everyone suddenly intent on their shoes.

"It's so nice to see a familiar face," she says. She focuses on me, her television eyes wide and fluttering. "I have to come up with six items for the website every day," she continues, "and I just don't know how I'm going to do that."

"I'm sure you'll manage," I say.

"You were always such a gentleman then," she says, standing a bit closer. "Do you think you can give me a hand with that?"

"Well," I say. "You were in Chicago, you've been around the game. You know the drill."

"It's just that I don't know any of these guys much. Would you mind if I come to you for quotes when I'm stuck?"

"Of course," I say. "As long as you don't mind the usual predigested crap."

She smiles, a brilliant sunrise that shows why she has a job on television. "Oh, I don't think they even care. As long as I fill space."

"Well, I can fulfill your BS quota, for sure. I've played long enough, I know all the clichés. You've probably heard them all, too."

"Oh yes," she says, chuckling, tucking a long strand of hair back into place. "I could probably write them without you. You just want to fit in, do your job, and as long as you execute, you'll help put the team in position to win. All that 'one game at a time' stuff Kevin Costner says on the bus in *Bull Durham*."

I smile back. "That's it, exactly."

"Seriously, though. Can I count on you?" She shifts her weight from hip to hip, pulling her dress tight across her taut abdomen.

"Sure," I say. "I'm not going to rat anyone out. But I'll help you fill space. That's no problem."

"Thanks," she says. "They want you to do everything now. Radio, web, TV, podcast. Plus all new content for every platform. It is such a strain. And like I said, I don't know anybody here yet. Plus you're not like some of these idiots." She looks down at her toes, brilliant and scarlet against the red and gray carpet.

"Well, just ask my wife about that."

She laughs. "No, no. I mean, some of the players, you know."

"Animals? Well, you know I'm not like that."

"Yeah," she says. "That's why I appreciate it so much. It's nice to have a friend. I'm new in town too."

A notion trickles up from my subconscious. "Hey, do you think maybe …" I begin.

I hear the sound of footsteps in the tunnel, followed by John "Tex" Holman, the multimillionaire kid closer consuming most of the attention and oxygen in the few days the team has spent together so far, all spiked hair and braggadocio. A print reporter with a beard follows along beside him, nodding and smiling like a courtier to a prince. In an instant, my new friend turns, walking towards the tumult. I watch her walk, suddenly hip−twitchingly alluring and seductive.

"Hey, Tex!" she says as she walks, her voice an octave higher, leaving me to bend low and untie my shoes.

Sunday, 16th February 2014

A Visit from Mother

by James Claffey

Over the river the Bird pedals, the brittle sound of rubber on macadam as he makes his way home. The beam from his lamp yellows a narrow strip ahead of the bicycle, the rainclouds blocking out the moonlight. In the fields on either side of the road plastic—covered hayrolls stand as silent monuments, the only sound the rain pattering on plastic. Far to the right the Bird eyes the humped mound of the fairy fort.

As a boy his classmates once tied him with rope and left him there on a dark Halloween night. By the time the Bird extricated himself from the knots, the screech owls were calling to one another, and muffled drumbeats seeped from beneath the ground. He ran home in tears, the jeers and cruelty of his classmates stored in his memory for another day.

He thumbs the Rosary ring on his right hand, repeating the Hail Mary's and Our Father's falling behind him on the road as he pedals townwards. On the final downhill approach to town he sings the Hail Holy Queen in full voice as he freewheels across the bridge to the corner, where he dismounts, blesses himself, and unfastens his pants' legs from the bicycle clips. He could, he knows, cycle the route blindfold, the number of times he's traveled that road in the past, but if a squirrel, or a cat, or dog crossed his path, he'd be smashed to bits if he crashed.

In the house all is quiet and he moseys about the kitchen for a bit of supper. He puts a match to the cooker and sets the kettle on the hob. Bread and cheese, both a bit hardened about the edges, but beggars can't be choosers, he thinks as he spreads a pat of yellow butter on the loaf. In the mirror above the dresser he catches sight of his reflection and even though he's not the handsomest of men, he at least has all his hair, not like that hoor, Maurice McGettigan, bald as the Dome of St. Peter's. Swarthy, too. Might be black Irish, a touch of the Spaniard about him, by all accounts. Didn't someone tell him Maurice slept well past midday most mornings? Siesta, they call it over there, he thinks. Bloody laziness, more like.

The Bird wedges a bit of bread and cheese in his mouth and chews diligently until the kettle whistles and he fills the teapot to the brim. After commiserating with himself over the French girl's not showing up at the Sunday *seisiun*, he distracts himself with a look at the Sunday crossword puzzle. He licks the tip of the pencil, tasting the familiar lead flavor, the same taste from all those years ago at the local secondary school. Back then the inkwells in the desks were little ceramic pots, and the students would spend hours soaking spitballs in ink and flicking them at one another with their rulers and setsquares.

After flicking the light switch off, the Bird mounts the stairs and in his bedroom undresses and lies on top of the sheets naked. He thinks of the beautiful Melodie, her smile, the twinkle in her eye as she played the reels. Charm, that's what she has, he decides. And the next time he sees her, well, he's going to go through his mammy's necklaces and pick out the finest one to present her with. Ladies like jewelry, that's what his daddy had told him often. Treat them like precious stones, and you'll be all right, he'd told his son. The Bird wonders if his daddy ever listened to his own advice. Many's the time he'd arrive home from school to the pair of them going at it hammer and tongs.

He stares at the picture of Christ on the wall. The Sacred Heart of Jesus, indeed. He should have taken it off the wall when the pair of them had died, but instead he'd transplanted it from their bedroom wall to where it now hangs. He shifts positions so he can avoid Jesus's eyes searching his face and soon is asleep on top of the covers. When he wakes, it's to a loud thump nearby and an odd moaning sound. Chilled from the night air, his arms and legs are covered in goose bumps, so he pulls trousers and shirt on and takes the small statue of St. Anthony by the head for protection.

The landing is in darkness and only the moonlight coming through the window allows the Bird to find his way without stumbling. He grips the doorknob to his parents' bedroom in his free hand and turns the knob. Inside, the room is quiet, but a rocking noise comes from the wardrobe.

"Come out, you hoor!" he shouts, raising St. Anthony above his head, ready to crown whoever's in the wardrobe. The door rattles. The Bird takes a step backward. The door creaks and his ginger-haired mother opens the closet door, wearing a knit wool cap and a pair of angel wings. As she holds both arms out as if to cradle her son, he crawls up against the bedstead and forces himself not to look at her naked, fat body. It's one thing to behold your own mother in "that" way, but to see her appear out of your own closet, clad in a wool beanie, all done up like a seagull gone awry, is too much to bear. "Oh dear Jesus," the Bird exclaims when she hops on the end of the bed and jumps up and down as if the mattress were her own personal trampoline. "Go away. You're only a figment of my poor imagination, aren't you?" A cloud of lint and dust rises from the bed and he begs her again, "Arrah, would you let me alone, Mammy. Isn't enough you tortured me when you were alive."

"Puritan," she hisses, flapping the angel wings and stirring up more lint, or perhaps dust from the wings. "You'll have to make me go away," she says.

The Bird slides off the bed and swings the statue of St. Anthony in wide circles. "I'll take the head off you if you don't leave me be." He brings the saint down on the bed with a dull thump and sends his mother fluttering for the lightshade. A wingtip touches the bulb and the smell of burning flares his nostrils. His mother lands by the closet door and when he looks across at her, a strange orange glow fills the inside of the closet, and with one hop, his mother disappears into the floorboards.

"Jesus Mary and Joseph," he says, searching the wardrobe for signs of his mother's ghost, or whatever he just witnessed, "I'll give up the drop for a year if you never darken my doorstep." The silence in the room is too much for him to bear, and he returns the statue to the other room, goes over to the small, walnut bedside table and turns the transistor to Radio 2. A loathsome punk band, the Radiators from Space, is playing and in disgust he presses the off button.

Under the covers, he fidgets and turns, sleep refusing his call. The creak of a floorboard has him on his feet, gravitating towards the statue once more. When he treads on the landing carpet the creak sounds again and he tiptoes towards the staircase. Down to the hall he goes, statue gripped in both hands as if it'll protect him from whatever apparition he might encounter.

The house is empty and he drags a chair out from the kitchen table and sits in the center of the room until the day lightens outside and the first birdsong comes. He thinks of his mother, his dear old mother, transformed into some hideous winged creature, and the tears run down his cheeks. At this moment he understands the house is no better than a tomb, and he might as well have been buried alive when his parents died.

Live For

by Gwendolyn Joyce Mintz

They've agreed to meet. Same place, same time, but Mora and Diane get to Kelly's Bar & Grill late. They follow the hostess to the booth where Aaron waits for them.

He is not alone.

Mora gives a quick once—over to the two men sitting to Aaron's left. One is early twenties, she figures. Wears thick—lensed glasses and has a scruffy mop of brown hair on his head as well as face and chin.

The other is older, late twenties, she's sure. She can't get a good look at him because he's staring into the near—empty drink in his hand. Mora notes, however, that he is beginning to lose his hair on top.

Aaron smiles at the young women. "Hail, hail," he says, "the gang is finally all here."

Mora lifts a brow.

The scruffy guy moves in, toward Aaron, but the other guy stands.

"I like the end," he tells Diane.

Mora peels her coat off before easing into the curved wooden seating next to Aaron. Giving him a brief hug, she whispers, "Why are you wearing glasses, who are these people and are you drunk?"

Aaron touches the rim of the black metal–framed glasses and grins. "I slept in my contacts, eyes are a mess." He picks up the beer bottle before him and brings it to his lips. After a drink, he points the bottle at the man sitting next to him. "This is Phil and that guy," he adds, shifting the bottle to the man next to Diane, "is Vincent. I met them on an internet forum."

"On dying," Phil says.

"But they have been cleared for membership," Aaron declares, setting the beer bottle down with a slight thud. "You wanna die, this is the place to be."

"Vincent," Diane says. "Kind of apropos." She unbuttons her jacket and shrugs it off.

"What is?" Mora asks.

Running her fingers down her hair falling on both sides of her face, Diane hooks the blonde strands behind her ears. "That song," she replies. "The one about van Gogh."

"Hmm," Aaron murmurs. He hums a few bars of *Vincent (Starry, Starry Night)*. "This is to those with no hope inside," he says. He raises the bottle in the air for a moment then presses it to his lips, finishing the beer off. Placing it on the table, he leans toward Mora and whispers, "And, yes, I am drunk."

She glares.

"What?" he asks.

"You tell me," she replies.

The server arrives with the water for Mora and Diane and to take their drink order. Diane wants a margarita on the rocks. Mora simply shakes her head 'no.'

When the server leaves, Aaron tells Mora. "We ordered nachos."

Mora raises her brow and exhales. She looks across the table and wonders why Phil's left hand remains out of sight.

Aaron addresses Phil and Vincent. "As president de facto of The Suicide Club, I invite you to fully introduce yourself and your story, while I get another beer." He waves down their server – Lindsey – as she is leaving a nearby table.

"Something else?" she asks.

"You don't need another drink," Mora tells Aaron.

"Since you are *not* my girlfriend, you don't get to tell me what I need."

His words, the bitter and sharp tone, smack her head back in surprise.

Aaron's apology is immediate. "I'm drunk," he says.

"Given that confession, I'll bring you water," the server tells Aaron. She scoops up the beer bottle as well as Vincent's glass, and departs.

Diane stares across the table at Mora, who's looking back at her.

What the hell? Mora mouths.

Vincent is sifting through the near—empty bowl of popcorn. He picks out the last few popped kernels, tosses them into his mouth.

Aaron leans his head back and watches the ceiling.

Phil says, "This is an interesting idea." With his right hand, he adjusts his glasses.

Mora wonders how many times as a child he heard the words: "coke bottles."

Diane turns to him. "The club?"

He nods. "On the forum, when people talk about committing suicide, others try and talk 'em out of it."

Vincent grunts. "Or they ask why you're on the computer and not doing the deed."

A smile comes to Aaron's face as he lowers his head and faces the group. "They like doers not talkers."

"But we're gonna talk *in order to do*, right? I mean, the point to this is to support each other so that we do kill ourselves," Diane says.

"Why would you want to kill yourself – you're so pretty."

Diane shakes her head. She lifts the glass of water to her lips and drinks 'til it's empty. She sets the glass on the table and spins it with her two hands.

"Pretty people kill themselves all the time. Models. Actresses," Mora tells Phil, in answer to his comment. "She's not looking for a why; we're here for the how and when." She leans back, crosses her arms in front of her. Then she says, "Let's go get a cigarette." An invitation meant only for Diane.

She nods. Scoops up her jacket and they leave.

"You said they were cool."

Aaron assures Vincent they – Mora and Diane – are. "We're just off tonight." He sighs. "This is a bust."

Phil and Vincent agree.

It takes Mora more than one try to get the cigarette lit.

Diane paces before her. "Aaron's weird tonight."

Mora nods as she takes a long drag. Though she doesn't tell Diane, she knows that he drinks to excess only when he's emotionally hurting.

"And those guys he brought with him."

"Why would you want to kill yourself – you're so pretty," Mora mimics.

Diane grins. "Maybe he thinks only ugly people should die."

Mora grunts. "What does that say about his self–image?"

Diane shakes her head at her friend's comment. "That is so wrong."

Mora shrugs and finishes her cigarette.

"We staying?" Diane asks.

Mora's curls tremble as she shakes her head in haste. "I say we blow this joint."

When the women return, Aaron says, "We're gonna call this."

"Not a problem," Mora replies. She scoops up some cheese–covered tortilla chips from the plate.

"I want my drink," Diane says, picking up the glass that has come, along with the nachos, in her absence. She stands, sipping at it.

Vince and Aaron scoot out of the booth.

Phil's left hand is on the table.

Mora notes a deformity as he moves to get up as well. She wonders about his story but is in no mood to stay and find out.

Aaron pulls out his wallet and throws some bills on the table. "This is on me."

"Give me your keys, Aaron."

"What?"

"Keys." Mora holds her hand up and flicks her wrist as if she were working the ignition.

Aaron stares at her for a moment then he drops them in her upturned hand.

"I'll let you kill yourself," she tells him, "but you're not bringing anyone on the road into this."

They don't talk on the drive to Aaron's apartment. But there, he and Mora sit outside on the step by the front door, waiting for Diane, who was following them, to arrive.

Though Mora has mittens, her arms wrapped tight around her body and her pink knit scarf coiled around her neck, Aaron can feel her shivering.

"If you're too cold, we can go inside."

"Nope." She folds at the waist, crosses her arms on her knees and lays her head down. "What was your problem tonight?"

"You."

Mora springs up. "What?"

Aaron doesn't turn from her questioning and accusing stare. "Friday was the 14th. It was very unlucky for me."

"What?" Mora tilts her head. "I didn't know you were superstitious; but it's the 13th that isn't lucky. Last Friday was —" Her eyes widen.

"Yeah, Valentine's Day. And I wanted to spend it with you."

Mora turns away. She sighs a heavy breath.

"That was on my list of things I wanted to do before I died. I like you, Mora. I always have."

"Diane should show up right now. As if on cue."

"Please," Aaron reaches out for her hand. "Just listen to me."

Mora nods.

Aaron opens his mouth but says nothing. He starts again then shakes his head.

"We tried already; we don't work, remember?"

Aaron nods. "I just wanted to be with you." He turns his attention to the road. "You wouldn't stay the night."

Her answer is immediate. "No." Still Mora leans toward him. When he faces her again, she presses her mouth against his. After a minute or so, she pulls away slightly, and tells him, "Don't say something dumb or corny like that was to die for."

Aaron shakes his head. He promises not to.

Diane arrives.

Aaron pulls Mora to him, buries his face in the nest of her dark curls.

"I have to go," she whispers.

He nods. Releasing her, watching her trot down the walk to the car, he wants to tell her if he didn't have other plans, it — she — would certainly be something to live for.

Living Dead

by Stephen V. Ramey

Doctor D is a fortyish woman with short, dark hair and wide hips. She doesn't smile often, but she's pleasant enough. I see her for a checkup every couple years, and then we part ways. It's like the mating ritual of a nomadic cat, or *Star Trek* Spock. Yes, I know that show. That's where I learned that people have specific roles, and the captain always gets the girl.

I never wanted to "get the girl". I wanted to find someone who would love me for me, hold their own in discussions of right and wrong, and inspire me to become a better man. Anne was that person, and she found me. It was a story about lima beans and self—hatred that did the trick. "I glimpsed your soul in that story," she told me years later. "I knew you were the one."

The door swings open, and in steps Dr. D. I like the way her eyes flare at first contact. It's like watching an ember settle. Her real name is D'Onosto or something. A young man trails her. He's wearing scrubs like the nurse who took my vitals earlier.

"Scott will be assisting today," Dr. D says. I nod to him, and he sort—of—nods back. He must be new.

"How have you been feeling?" Dr. D says. She takes my hands and moves the joints around.

"No complaints," I say.

We go through the ritual, Dr. D methodically probing glands, thumping knees, listening to my heart and lungs.

"How are you tolerating the cholesterol pills?" she says.

"I quit taking them. Free samples are fine – thanks for that – but I can't afford a hundred bucks a month."

She frowns like a concerned mother. "You can't just go on and off those pills, Stephen. There are risks."

"Anne has me on Niacin," I say.

"Make sure it's time–release." Dr. D glances at a chart. "Your blood pressure was one–thirty over ninety. That's borderline high." She scribbles something. "I'm going to have Scott draw blood. I want to check for sugar since your father had diabetes, and cholesterol, of course. And I want to do a PSA to establish a baseline for you." She nods to Scott. Hands trembling ever so slightly, he tourniquets my upper arm and arranges vials as if he's familiar with the process. I look away. It hurts worse if I watch the needle go in.

A pinch. I wince, and look back as blood surges into the first vial. I feel a splash of guilt. Why is my blood so anxious to escape? Scott rotates to a second vial, then a third. He caps and labels the samples while Dr. D pulls on rubber gloves.

"I need to examine your testicles," she says.

Oh God, I think, *I forgot this part.* With stoic precision, I hop down from the table and unbutton my fly. Pants accordion down to my knees. I pull down my briefs.

Dr. D squats. I feel embarrassed. What about all that hair, the gray and the brown and the messy tufts? *Pubic defoliation, pro or con?* I think. The practiced intensity of Dr. D's expression stops me asking her. She doesn't enjoy this either. *Let it go.*

She squeezes my balls, slides my foreskin up and back, and stands. We do not make eye contact.

I reach to pull up my pants.

"One more thing." She lubricates her gloved finger.

"Do we have to?"

"No," Dr. D says. "But we should. I need to see if your prostrate is enlarged. You're of an age, as they say."

"I'm not having problems," I say. *Other than the sudden urges to pee, difficulty initiating a stream. And my erections leave a lot to be desired.*

"Lean onto the table," she says. "I'll be quick."

My eyes seek out Scott, but he's having none of it. *You're on your own, dude.*

I wince as Dr. D wriggles her finger up my butt. I feel cold all over. Memory flashes of Rose lifting my hand to her cheek. It's ludicrous. This is not even remotely the same.

Anne and I walk downtown for a late lunch to celebrate my checkup. She's always on the lookout for opportunities to reward good behavior. That I didn't find an excuse to duck out of the physical she scheduled for me months ago, qualifies.

The day is cold, but sunny. I haven't worn gloves, and my coat is only partway zipped. *Winter's losing its grip*, I hope.

"How's The Fountain sound?" Anne says as we stroll the northeast facet of The Diamond. The Diamond is a roundabout, only the lanes form angles rather than a circle, and it's bisected by the busiest highway in town. The effect is of triangular islands divided by a short stretch of highway with stop–lighted intersections. A statue depicts a Civil War soldier on one side of Highway 18, a fountain burbles on the other.

We cross the street to a hole–in–the wall cafe with a drooping, rusted awning and battered sign. The Fountain is a mainstay in New Castle, but has fallen out of favor in recent years (decades?). When we first moved here, I poked around on Google, and found this review: *Pleasant little place to sit and work quietly or relax over a cup o' joe. Betty the waitress is still here after 61 years of "how ya doin', honey" hospitality.*

And that is exactly right.

Bells jingle as I swing the door open. I smell grilled lamb. The dining area is deceptively deep, as are all the stores in these old buildings. A lunch counter stretches along one wall, fronting a polished soda fountain. Vintage signs hang everywhere: *Coca-Cola, Orange Fezz, Barq's*. Through a serving window at the back, I see the owner, a seventy-something Greek man, perched on a stool overlooking the grill. He's reading a newspaper.

Anne and I slide into opposite sides of a booth. The springs are shot, and duct tape covers several tears in the green vinyl. Still, there's a cozy comfort here, the sense of visiting a more innocent time.

Betty brings laminated menus. "Hi, honey, how're you doing today?"

"Fine," Anne and I say together. At 84 years young, and with her hair piled high, Betty reminds me of the Bride of Frankenstein, in a good way. Hers is the human face, the gentleness that Frankenstein's monster could never master.

"What can I get yinz to drink?" she says with a friendly smile. I think of Anne's father taking out his bridge because it doesn't fit his mouth.

My order for *Coke* gets translated to *Pepsi*, then, "Sorry, hun, I just sold the last one. Is diet okay?"

Anne orders iced tea, and Betty shuffles off. I watch her lug a pitcher to a group of white-mustachioed men at a table in the back. One man laughs, and the grating sound bounces around the room until it is exhausted of emotion. For an instant, I'm in a Hollywood scene, a dusty restaurant inhabited by the living dead. Nostalgia crumbles. The Fountain is not so much a pleasant reliving of the past, as a pointless denial of the truth that all things die.

My phone buzzes, and I startle. Anne looks over the edge of her menu. There's a list of daily specials pinned to the front. I can't remember what day it is.

Another buzz. I take the phone from my pocket. It's Doctor D's office. Panic flutters and subsides.

"I better take this outside," I say. Reception is spotty in these brick buildings. "Order my usual."

Anne frowns. "You don't have a usual. We've only eaten here a couple times."

"Then order whatever you think *should* be my usual." I slide from the booth and hurry outside, phone pressed to my ear.

"Yes?"

"Stephen? This is Doctor D'Orenzio. I have the results from your blood work. A couple of things concern me."

"Oh?" Cold sweeps into me. I zip my coat.

"I felt a couple nodes in your prostate," she says, "and your PSA is 8.5."

"Is that bad?"

"It's not good." She sighs. "It may be nothing, Stephen, I don't mean to worry you. But I want you to see a specialist."

How much is this going to cost? is my first thought, not, *OMG, Cancer!*

"I can recommend several good people," Doctor D says. "That's one benefit of living in a geriatric city."

I can't help seeing my father in his final days, blood splattering from his lips, that horrid grasping fear in his eyes. I can't help seeing myself in that bed, Anne at my side. She looks determined. She looks sad.

I'm the reason you're destitute, I think. *I'm the reason you could never be content.*

"No," I hear as if from a distance, then firmer, "No."

"What do you mean?" Dr. D says.

"No specialist," I say. I snap the phone shut before she can continue. *This is where it ends*, I think. *This is where I die.* The idea is not as frightening as I want it to be.

Wednesday, 19th February 2014

Nesting

by Gay Degani

A warm February morning, Sybil on her porch, wearing one of the silk robes she ordered from the internet. She sips sugared coffee and studies her bunions, her swollen ankles, the varicose veins tracing up her calves, all the while keeping an ear out for the blue jay. She's filled the crystal candy bowl on the table next to her with sunflower seeds, a peanut or two. It's been a month now since wind stormed the Old Road at 90 mph, knocking down trees, severing electrical wires, turning the neighborhood into a disaster area, a month since Jamie and the kids climbed into their dilapidated old car and disappeared, a month since Sybil last saw the jay.

Most of her property, the group of five small rental houses facing a courtyard, has been cleaned up by tenants pitching in with rakes and wheelbarrows, but the front bungalow where Jamie lived is still buried beneath thick heavy limbs and red–tagged as uninhabitable. As for the blue jay, with his smart–aleck chirp and curious nature, he too lost his nest when the giant oak tumbled.

"Morning, Beautiful," Ian calls from the porch of bungalow #2. He's the newest resident in Sybil's domain, a thirty–two–year–old man whose mother, a real estate agent, employs him to sit on her open houses, hire cheap labor to "polish" her listings, and flirt with female clients. She also pays his rent, one of the

228

many parental "trends" that causes Sybil to wonder what the world is coming to.

"You're up early," she says. "Want some coffee?"

"I'd love some." He's already striding over on long legs, his lanky body awkward in a dark blue suit, light blue shirt, pink tie, his eyes cobalt, his grin charming. "Any word from your insurance company yet?"

Sybil grabs a paper napkin and dusts off the other rattan chair. "They're taking care of it, though I haven't seen any money yet."

"They've set up a loan center somewhere over at city hall for storm damage. Dress in that hot yellow dress of yours and they'll whip out their checkbooks."

"I've owned this place free and clear for forty years, Ian Shane, and I'm not about to go into debt now. Let me get you that coffee." She heads inside, thinking, why'd I invite him over? She never did learn to keep her distance from tenants. You'd think by now. Probably the blue suit. She's missing the jay. That's it, but talking to the bird is a lot more fun than talking to Ian Shane.

She returns with a small thermal pot, another cup, and a plate of chocolate biscotti on a tray, and the man's face lights up. He thinks he's got her now.

"You know, Sybil, you're sitting on a gold mine here."

"You want to start digging?"

"Funny, but I'm serious. Don't you want to be done with this headache?" He gestures at the property, the fallen tree sprawled across the front bungalow, the stop sign on the corner bent like a flex straw, the telephone pole braced by 4x8s, not yet replaced. "With all the redevelopment going on around here, I can find you a buyer in no time and put you in a nice condo downtown, one of those penthouse lofts with stainless steel appliances where you wouldn't have to do anything."

"Stainless steel appliances," she says with derision. "You want Splenda or real sugar?"

"Black, thank you. You brew better than Starbucks. Come on, Sybil. Think about it. Walking distance to the movies, restaurants, Target. I know you love Target."

What a con artist! She sips her coffee. Doesn't tell him she's been thinking about selling. Started thinking about it since he first brought it up the day after the windstorm, but she's owned the bungalows on the Old Road since 1971 when her grandfather passed away and she moved in, letting that grease monkey "what's—his—name" come with her. Memories should be enough to keep her here, the lovers who paraded in and out of her little house over the years, the tenants who brought her turkeys for Christmas, champagne at New Years, took her to lunch on her birthday, but it's Jamie, she admits now, packing up her kids and taking off without so much as a good—bye, that gives her pause. If she left, she wouldn't be here when they came back. If they come back.

Where had Jamie gone? She missed smart little Lily. The boyness of Collin. At least when Jamie's husband knocked on Sybil's door the day after the storm, she could answer honestly that she didn't know where they were. Had he found her? Sybil didn't even know whether or not Jamie wanted to be found. Jamie'd never confided in her. Never said if Sean was abusive. Sybil didn't think he was, at least not physically. He was selfish, thoughtless, maybe even dishonest, and it seemed that Jamie had simply had enough because she took off without anything. When Sybil and the tenants did the initial clean—up, they'd found her packed suitcase crushed under the tree.

Ian's still talking. "Sybil?"

"Sorry. What'd you say?"

"There's a great place over on Central. Nice view. I could pick up the keys and take you over this morning if you want. Pool, clubhouse, exercise room. Keep that great shape of yours."

"Do you even have your license yet?" She catches him glancing at her neck. Thinks, he's wondering how long I've got before I keel over.

"You want to get out in front of this, Syb."

Syb? *Really?*

"Once everyone on the Old Road decides to sell, you won't get as good a price. My mother says your neighbors are listing their house."

"Which one?" It's her turn to stare, bits of cookie in the corners of his mouth.

"The Treacher mansion next door. They're going to tear it down and put a hotel."

"Never happen."

"They want to bring tourists into the neighborhood like the old days. Put in some cute little shops. Revitalize the creek, that sort of thing."

"Sounds like the perfect time to stay put, not sell." She grins hard, but tugs the two sides of her robe together at the neck, as if clouds have hidden the morning sun. "Aren't you going to be late for work?"

He shrugs. Stretches his legs, sticking his feet between the horizontal bars of the porch railing, his hands behind his head as if he's got nothing better to do than chat up the landlady. Oh right. Today, she thinks, I'm his work. His mother is behind this.

When Ian finally pulls himself to his feet, he thanks her for breakfast and waves good−bye. Adds as he turns the corner toward the carport, "Your blue jay come back yet?"

"No, but he will."

"It's a wild bird. He could be anywhere by now."

"Not so wild, really."

The Follow—Up

by Sally—Anne Macomber

To: Milton Flaxmill, Red Cow Publishing
From: Trudy Polaris
Date: February 20, 2014 10:03 a.m.
Re: Great News

Hi Milton,

Just following up my email from last month, where I sacked you as the publisher of my book *Nuclear Fission in the Pyrénées*. I've thought about it since then and have decided to give you the benefit of the doubt: perhaps the two accents on *Pyrénées* just fell off.

Did you get my email with the explicit instructions for extra spacing for note—makers in the 'academic' edition? If not, I will resend, so please let me know.

I will be offline for a few days as I fly to Europe tomorrow but I will be online again once we settle in to our Tyrolean hideaway.

Glad to have you back on board!

Trudy Polaris

Well, actually

by Mandy Nicol

Celeste watches me fill the dishwasher and I know she's dying to ask me something. Or tell me something. But more likely ask me something. She's driven two hours on a scorcher with a three year—old and Celeste never visits. She prefers to summon. Yes, she must want something all right. So I enjoy myself and place the dishes carefully, with precision, one at a time, even the forks. I think I can hear her teeth grinding.

Mum's in the lounge room reading a dog—eared copy of *Green Eggs and Ham* to her youngest grandchild. The Little Soldier She So Rarely Sees, as she calls him.

I set the dishwasher a—sloshing and sit down at the dining table opposite Celeste. "So what's up?" I ask.

She scowls, "Why should something be up?"

"Okay then, what do you want?"

She smiles, "Well, actually I do have a favour to ask. You know Scott's little sister Angela? She's getting married."

"Oh. That's nice."

"Yes. And I sort of told her that you'd make her dress. I hope you don't mind."

"Why would I mind? It's what I do. I'm hardly going to mind you drumming up business for me. When's the wedding?" Celeste is biting her bottom lip so I add, "And what aren't you telling me?"

233

"The wedding's in September so you've got oodles of time. Umm, the thing is, I said you'd do it for nothing."

"Oh. Really?"

Celeste wriggles forward in her seat and plonks her elbows on the table. She is preparing to launch one of her rehearsed and inarguable arguments. I'm too tired so rather than subject myself I say, "Well, I suppose she is family."

Celeste smiles. Cat with the cream and the mouse. "She's hoping you can show her some patterns and samples next weekend," she says.

"That should be okay."

"But you'll have to come to Melbourne because she can't drive."

I scan her face to see if she's joking. She isn't. "Sorry," I say, "That's asking too much."

"Well, actually I told her you would."

"You what?"

"Don't look at me like that, I've thought it all through. You can bring Mum down, drop her off at our place, and pick her up on the way back. It'll only take you an extra twenty minutes or so. And Mum will love it. It will get her out of the house, she'll get to see all the kids, spend some quality time with them." Celeste lowers her voice, "You know how much she misses her grandchildren. It would be a nice thing for you to do for her, Nadia."

Well, actually ...

I bite my bottom lip. Hard.

Worry

by Margaret Bingel

Sleep is the brain's way of recharging, and in a coma the patient's mind has an opportunity to dream. At St Jude's Hospital a graduate student monitors a select group's brain waves. She's researching how active the brain is while in a coma versus a vegetative state as part of her thesis, and she had told Nora Billingsly her theory that Nora's son Ned is probably dreaming while in his coma.

"Can he hear?" Nora remembers asking the student.

"Most assuredly," the student had smiled at her. "He can most likely hear everything you say to him. Of course, it's just a theory …"

Nora can't remember the rest, but she holds on to that theory as she reaches to hold Ned's hand while visiting him at St. Jude's coma ward. Sitting down, she squints at him, squeezing his hand a little, and says, "Morning, Boy."

Nora remembers the phone call she got from the hospital a month ago, the paramedic asking for "Mrs. Billingsly," as if she is married. Only telemarketers ever call her that, and this did not sound like a telemarketer.

"Your son's been in an accident," the paramedic had said. "He's here at St. Jude's."

Time stopped for Nora. My son, she had thought at the time, but that can't be. That won't be him when I get there, she kept thinking while grabbing her coat, walking out the door, leaving her routine of chores and home. It won't be him at all.

She looks into her son's face, and moves her free hand over to his left eye, and opens the eyelid. "Anybody home?" His pupil doesn't dilate. She lets it drop, disappointed. Nora releases her grip on his hand and pulls out a book. She reads to him because she doesn't want him to be bored in his dreams. While she's reading, she's aware of the nurse who comes in to check his vitals, a short, skinny woman who has ashen hair she keeps in one long braid. The nurse marks her clipboard and bustles out of the room, saying nothing.

Nora reads until her throat is dry, and then she knows it's time to leave. She remembers reading somewhere that being close to family helps, but she doesn't know if that's really true. She comes in every Saturday, to read for an hour, but it has been about a month now. How much longer does he need me, she wonders.

Where was I when he needed me to hold his hand?

But her Boy is a Man now, and has been for a while, and he needed to live on his own. She holds her breath, and lets it all out in one, big gust. She lays the bookmark down on the page, and slowly closes the book shut, careful not to crease the pages.

"Goodbye, Boy," she whispers. She rises to her feet, and closing the door behind her, walks out on another Saturday.

Building a Sunday

by Darryl Price

This day, the again of it, that broke my heart with the piano heavy hammer, that buried me underwater like a bomb from a different world, another century, that froze the sky in place, solid like a dream that once was a summer, this day that went up and up and never came back down, stuck like a fish head between the avalanche of stars, this day that lost my name forever among the sad—eyed lint in its pockets, that walked to the edge of the world without me and fell over into nothing, this day behooves me, that created a fatal fracture on the surface of the sun on the bed we shared and seared my skull onto my face like an ancient bamboo tapped in tattoo, this day you took and hid away from me in your wisdom, that I'm always looking for in the middle of the night, this day with its strange overcoat balled up on my sofa, how can I ever name you properly, how am I supposed to live in your absence, now that my being is hollow in your shape, now that my words pour themselves on the floor and must be swept up and thrown away, now that every object contains the same emptiness as before, this day that started something but never finished, this day of ultimate sentencing, this day that disappeared without warning, that became my ghost, that took the place of my regular ghost, that appears in the window between a breeze and some moonlight like someone smoking alone in a cramped attic, this day that now sits on a shelf like a cat made of rope, dangling, dangling, waiting for the unseen fire to begin, for the grand awakening of feeling? This awful day. This amazing, dull thing. This precious, lost ball that started it all.

White Rabbit

by Teresa Burns Gunther

Nine days ago

Stella does her business out back then starts digging at the fence. I poke my head over. The neighbors are making a racket. Joyce is watering. "What's going on?"

"Oh! Crikey, Rachel!" Joyce says, eyes wide, a hand clapped to her cavernous cleavage. "You startled me."

"What's all the noise?"

"We're going to raise rabbits!" Joyce says.

"Why?" I envision being overrun, like the Brits. "Will you eat them?"

She purses her lips. "Well, Larry's talking rubbish about stew," she says with a jerk of her head at her string bean husband. "Says, since we can't eat our egg–laying chooks we may as well eat rabbits for all the money we're spending."

"Sensible," I say. Stella growls. Joyce steps back, wide–eyed, like Stella will fly over. Joyce is not a dog person.

"Having your coffee?" Larry asks the obvious question and joins us.

I raise my cup. "Stella heard the noise and woke me," I say, not to put too fine a point on it.

"Oh, sorry about that. We have to get this finished. We're going away next weekend – my nephew's graduation." He beams like it has something to do with him.

Stella barks. She's not crazy about men; who can blame her? Joyce clucks and scurries off, she has it out for my dog.

Two days ago

I'm exhausted from a week of working on my People Skills, #1 of my 2014 Resolutions. My job depends upon it. My face is stiff from smiling. I'd figured I could move on to Resolution #2 – Patience in February, but People Skills are a tough nut to crack.

I refill my coffee and step out on my back porch to enjoy the winter sun on a San Francisco morning. Stella's a blur, shaking something in her mouth, something brown. She's a beauty, a natural hunter, so at first I'm afraid it's Mrs. Franklin's cat. I pull my robe tight and race down my steps, slippery with leftover fog. "Stella, drop it!" She does and looks up, expecting praise for having killed a cat. But it's not a cat. It's a rabbit, stiff, matted and caked with dirt.

"Bad girl, Stella," I say, raising my hand to her. *Hey,* her expression says. *I'll share.* It's a bad habit, raising my hand when I'm upset. I'd never hit her. She's my family now. It's just a reflex I learned from my dad.

I brush the critter off and tell myself *it* snuck into *my* yard. Larry and Joyce's blinds are drawn. Good, still out of town. I don't see the kid who garden–sits, which apparently involves pilfering fruit and smoking dope in their hammock.

I walk the fence and find the hole – big enough for Stella, who sits, poised for play, tail fanning the dirt. "Oh Stella." She cocks her head. I consider sliding the rabbit back through the hole, but they'd know. It wouldn't take much more for Joyce to sick the SPCA on my Stella.

I try to remember when they're coming home. "Come on girl." I wrap the bunny in an old towel, relieved it doesn't stink. I could leave it outside; maybe a hawk would take it. I could tell

Joyce I saw it happen, I'm thinking this is brilliant until she wants to know how a hawk got the warren open. I leave it on the washing machine and close the door.

It's still early. Newspapers dot each driveway. I go out for my paper, grab Larry and Joyce's and slip into their side yard. If anyone asks I'm all about "Neighborhood Watch," though I wouldn't be caught dead at the meetings.

I pass their gardening supplies, composting bins – all neat and orderly. I've never accepted an invitation to their parties, so I've never seen the fruits of their noisy labors. Paths wind through flowerbeds filled with citrus and what look like upside down onions, herbs, tipis of fava beans, large leafy kales and colorful chards. I'm in Oz. Bird houses hang throughout the yard; their singing drives my Stella crazy. The *not for eating chooks* are making a ruckus. Fricking Garden of Eden. My yard's a hump of juniper and calla lilies around a concrete slab.

I'm hoping a little face will stare out from the rabbit house, but the door's ajar, the cage empty. I wonder how Stella got it open. She is brilliant!

Fortunately, I'm the only neighbor who can see into their yard. I find the hole. If Joyce found it she'd want Stella's head on a platter.

I find a shovel and refill the hole, a plan forming as I work. I drape an overzealous vine across the dirt and stand back. It looks wild. They'll never know Stella came calling.

Coming out of their yard I bump into the guy three doors down. "Christ!" I say. "You scared the hell out of me." He's decked out in skintight leggings. Nice bod.

He pulls his ear buds out. "What?" He looks from me to Joyce and Larry's house, back to me, confused.

"They're away," I say with a sweep of my hand I slide quick it into my pocket to hide the dirt. "Just taking their papers in."

He smiles.

"Out for your run?" My hand flies up to slap his butt, urge him to get going, until I catch myself and feign a stretch.

"20 miles today," he crows. "Marathon's next week." His smile tells me to be impressed.

"Good for you." I shove my fist in the air. Freak!

"See ya." He waves, sticks his ear—buds in, and sets off.

Stella is howling outside the laundry room when I return. I take the rabbit upstairs, fill the bath and add bubbles. I'm relieved there's no blood. Probably had a heart attack from the shock of Stella's teeth. The bath water turns brown and the rabbit is white. The eyes are filmed over. I can't close them. I dry it with my hair dryer. The fur is so soft. Stella whines at the door.

Not wanting to risk another neighbor run—in, I scramble over the fence and put the rabbit in the cage, on her side, like she's sleeping and close the door. Back on my side I fill what's left of the hole Stella made, press old bricks into the dirt and drag a pot of desiccated geraniums to set on top.

Today

I wake to the smell of coffee I cleverly set the night before. It's not until I step outside for the paper that I remember. Larry stands on the sidewalk cradling his paper, staring into space.

"Oh, hiya Rachel." He's always nice, even though we've had "differences". Joyce is another matter.

"Good trip?"

"Very nice," he says.

"I took your papers around back for you." He doesn't respond. "Everything okay?" My heart's cranking up my heater.

His face creases. "Well, it's weird …"

"Yeah?" My mind races for the explanations I've devised.

"The weirdest thing happened," he said.

"What?" Oh shit.

"We got a rabbit."

"Oh?" I say.

"A little rabbit, Ophelia." He shakes his head.

"What happened?"

"Thing is, she died last week," he said. "We only had her a few days. Joyce was beside herself. Ophelia must have eaten poison in the garden."

"She died?" I asked. "Poison? Isn't that dangerous." I'm pissed and start to say that if Stella had actually eaten it, she'd have been killed but catch myself.

"Yes," he said. "But here's the thing. We buried her before we left, but when I go out this morning —" his eyes go wide, "she's in her cage, just like new."

"Alive?" I ask, hoping for a miracle.

"No." His voice is sad. "I can't make sense of it." He looks back at the house. "Joyce was so upset." His face softens. "The woman has a heart of gold."

I let that slide by. "What did you do?"

"I reburied it. I didn't tell Joyce."

"That's probably wise." I wait for the relief to settle in, but all I feel is deflated.

"Yes. It would freak her out."

I'm surprised to find myself so close, my hand on his shoulder. "Sounds like you did the right thing."

His sorrowful face opens into a snaggle—toothed smile. Then he hugs me! "Thank you, Rachel. You're very kind."

"Me?" It occurs to me to ask to get it in writing, show my boss. But I don't say a word; I have a little lump in my throat.

"Well … I think that's my phone. Better run."

He's still standing there, smiling at me, the nice Rachel he thinks I am, when I close the door.

Tuesday, 25th February 2014

Morgana Malone and the Case of the Blushing Bride

by Matt Potter

"Oh, God!" Seventeen eyes dart in Zebadie's direction. Looking at me as she lowers her head on the reception desk in exasperation, she breathes out and says, "I soooooo miss porn."

I look over the beige laminate counter into the waiting area. Mr Rubinstein, he of eye no. 17 and an eye patch, bobs up in his chair. I smile and nod, like it's every day the receptionist in a therapy practice admits to working as an adult entertainer in the so−recent past.

"Something caught in her throat," I say, as Mr Rubinstein's eyebrows and eye patch lower. "A bit of déjà vu, I think."

Zebadie − whose neon−blonde like−nylon hair is in thrown−together pigtails today − peers up at me, eyes glistening. "You know what kept me doing porn?" she says. "It wasn't the sex or the practical jokes or the catering, Morgana." And she sniffles at the thought. "It was the conversation. There was always a lot of great conversations happening on the set." A tear appears in the corner of her eye. (Just one.) She sighs, sits up, and reaching under the counter, pulls out a scrapbook with *Wedding Plans* sprayed in Bedazzled jewels on the cover. She opens it and the plastic gems smack the desktop. "That's what first attracted me to Grigor," she says, "his level of conversation. That" − she licks her finger and rifles through to the next page – "and his Porsche."

(It's only my second day here and already I have my favourite patients. "I luff your racink schtripe," Mr Rubinstein said to me earlier, when he walked in, nodding at the grey–brown regrowth yawning through the orange on my head. "They make you go fasta." Smiling under his eyepatch, his toupée undulated on his head like a motley possum caught in the air conditioning draught.)

"The only real downsides to a life in porn are laxatives and plastic surgery," Zebadie says. "And no paid holidays. But it's the kind of job that travels and no one judges you by how fake your orgasms sound because they're all fake. So it's kind of like a level playing field. You store up the real orgasms for the real players. I mean, you have to draw the line *somewhere*."

Zebadie flicks through her wedding planner. She's not really looking at the pages, but sits mesmerized by the colour and movement as each page flicks past at breakneck speed, her wrists working up and down and showing no sign of tiring.

"So I guess porn is paying for your trousseau," I say.

"Well, for my first marriage, it did." And then she touches my forearm with her hand, all blue–eyed wonder. "Don't tell Grigor, though," she whispers. "He still thinks he's the first one."

I look at the push–up bra holding her three and a half boob jobs and the coffee dripolator tan and the scorched hair –

"After my re–birthing," she cuts in, her voice grave and knowing, "of course. Re–birthing means you're also a virgin again." She covers her mouth with her hand, and burps. "Although I want to know if I can get my money back on that one: every morning when I wake up the first thing I smell is placenta. And I don't care what anyone says: that's just not normal."

A door opens and out steps Barry, Grigor's brother and partner in this psychiatry practice, and of course, my ex–

brother—in—law. His hand under her elbow, Barry ushers out an older woman dressed in a black boiler suit, a red pillbox hat perched on her curly grey bob. "Susan will help you with your next appointment," he says.

Boiler suit looks at him, eyebrows quizzical.

"I mean Morgana," Barry says. "Sorry, *Morgana* will help you. *Morgana* will help you with your next appointment."

Sometimes I forget my real name is — was — Susan. And sometimes I forget Barry still calls me the name he first knew me by, when I first met him, when Grigor and I were first married.

Right hand on the mouse as the cursor rolls across the computer screen, I — the new office junior, though I *am* "up—managing" as Grigor told me — focus on looking important: back straight, jaw set, eyes steady.

"Tuesday the 4th at 11.00am," I ask, my eyes on the screen. Though it's not really a question. I type in her name, my hands clunky on the keyboard: *clunk clunk clunk.*

"Tuesday the 4th at 11.00am," Zebadie the office senior (she who's being "up—managed") repeats, large appointment book now open on the desk, her hand curving across the page as she carves the paper with her curly—curly cursive: *scr—a—tch ... scr—a—tch ... scr—a—tch.*

I click an icon on the screen and a printer spews out a green appointment slip. Reaching across, I tear it off the printer and hand it to boiler suit lady, who slips it inside her boiler suit breast pocket.

I don't know if Tuesday the 4th at 11.00am is good or bad. That's not what I'm paid to do, Grigor tells me, I'm here to work the new computer system and keep Zebadie on track and attend therapy sessions with Grigor when he thinks I need them, so there's some semi—déjà vu for me too.

Boiler suit lady is not even out through the door before Zebadie says, a little too loud, "Didn't you fuck him in the backseat of his Porsche?"

"Who?" I ask. "Which Porsche?"

"Barry."

"Well," I say, my voice low and directed towards the counter top, "it was Grigor's Porsche. But I *thought* it was Barry."

Zebadie's eyes bulge. "But they're not even identical."

"I know. But Grigor and I ... it was a very messy evening and I had a cold and I couldn't smell."

Zebadie shakes her head and smirks, like she's just discovered the Theory of Relativity while I can't even count to ten. She slaps the large appointment book shut, pushes it aside, then reaches for her wedding planner again. It opens on three long fabric swatches, pale purple ribbons stuck to the page with clear sticky tape.

"Lilac, mauve or lavender," Zebadie says. "It's so hard choosing the right colour for my bridesmaids." She pushes the scrapbook in front of me. "What do you think?"

I look at the fabric swatches again, shiny and pale purple and I can't decide which is lilac and which is mauve and which is lavender. I set my face in an interested look: eyebrows raised and eyes wide. "Choose the one that's easiest to spell."

Looking up, I see Grigor poking his head around the door. "Morgana?"

He cups his hand over the receiver but his voice draws me in — tones so even and measured and demanding to be listened to — so I hear every syllable like I'm sitting on his lap.

"I want it perfect for the wedding," he says. "My fiancée is giving it to me for a wedding gift. I want to remove this flaring" — he brushes his nostrils with his free hand — "and I want a more aquiline line. This bump" — now he touches just below the bridge of his nose — "is ruining an otherwise perfect profile."

Actually sitting on the black leather armchair — titanium frame, tight across the seat: elegant but unyielding — I cross my knees and my right ankle starts twitching like a metronome. I read the nameplate on the desk: Grigor Smiroveich™. When we married he was Grigor Smith. Before that he was Greg Smith. Now he's a trademarked Russian.

He drops the receiver back into its cradle and opens the file marked *Morgana Malone* on his desk.

"You know what would be the perfect wedding gift," he says, closing my file again. And as he looks up, his eyes mist over. "Oh, I don't know if I dare."

He looks at his hands on the desk, strokes his nose again, and opens his mouth to speak. Then stops. Is he blushing?

"Your face is red, Grigor."

Grigor coughs. "It's just a bit of pre—surgery swelling," he says. "Marrying a former adult entertainer drives my need to improve my looks."

He opens my file again then snaps it shut.

"You know what would be the perfect wedding gift?" he says again, now looking straight at me.

A penis extension? I want to say.

"Something that will mean just as much to Zebadie as it will to me."

A penis extension? I want to say.

"We'd really like you to be Zebadie's matron of honour on our wedding day."

I think that's the day I'm having my penis extension, I want to say.

"Barry's going to be best man," he adds.

My jaw flaps in mid—air but nothing comes out of my mouth. So it's lucky the 'phone rings and Grigor picks it up.

Zebadie's telephone voice, shrill and nasal and garbled, pierces through the plastic.

"Yes," he says, "she's smiling and looking very pleased." And then he looks over at me. "Lavender, mauve or lilac?" Grigor asks. "Zebadie wants to know."

"Lavender," I say, presuming it's the right answer. But when I picture myself standing at the altar and taking Zebadie's bouquet of wild cherries and spinifex from her re-virginated hand, I can only see myself in pale violet.

Dylan, A Love Story

by Gary Percesepe

My ex calls. It's about the dog of the family. Dylan is dying, she explains. There are decisions to make.

I met Savannah when I was nineteen, married at twenty-one. We divorced, after more than thirty years. I'd had an affair. She'd waited till near the end to have hers. In between we'd reared two children in the company of canines.

Dylan is a white standard poodle. If he makes it through the long Ohio winter, he will be fourteen years old in April.

Having seen us through the end of a marriage, Dylan's time is near.

His eyes are dull. His hearing is failing. He falls a lot, and is incontinent. Worse, Savannah says he appears to be in pain, with hip dysplasia, lower back trouble, and a spindly hind leg he can't use.

Shortly after we met, Savannah showed me a picture of Sandy, a cocker spaniel she'd taught to balance on a seesaw. Sandy holds a Lucky Strike cigarette between her teeth.

A newspaper photographer snapped the picture at her grandfather's house, where she'd gone to live after her alcoholic father abandoned her. Maybe her grandfather thought the picture would cheer her up. It was taken just before dark, in the gloaming.

Savannah's mouth is set in a straight line. Her pale blue eyes are fixed on Sandy; she concentrates on staying balanced. The picture was taken shortly after her mother died of cancer, at forty. Savannah was eight.

It is the same expression she had in one of our wedding photos, I later realized.

We met in college. Our courtship was a series of contests, to prove how much I loved her. I passed every test. She called me her knight, come to the rescue. At nineteen, I liked hearing that. I was sure I could make her happy.

But six years into our marriage I had an affair. The marriage survived, but Cupid's arrow had festered, an arrow too deep to be driven through and impossible to pull out. I agonized over things that could not be fixed, and understood that, from some things, there is no rescue. In the last two years of our marriage, she had an affair with a guy from high school she'd reconnected with on Facebook.

When I asked her to marry me, Savannah asked one thing: that I never abandon her. We lasted across four decades. Dylan is the last dog we had together.

On the phone Savannah explains that she can no longer carry Dylan up the long winding staircase to her bedroom, and down again in the early morning, for fear of falling herself.

My new landlord won't allow dogs.

Euthanizing him may the best thing, Savannah thinks. "He was always your dog," she says. "But he's been such a comfort to me here. I really appreciate you letting him stay with me. But since you moved out he's been giving up."

She asks if I want to come see Dylan. I tell her I'll be right over.

I cut the engine, and look at my former home. All fourteen rooms hold holiday candles. An Italianate villa, with emphatic eaves supported by corbels, a low slung roof, and six brick chimneys for Santa to choose from, the house is guarded by an antique wrought iron fence and a tall hedge. The neighborhood is scarred by high poverty and failing schools. We were urban pioneers when we moved here in 1997.

A year after we moved in, I contacted a breeder I admired in San Luis Obispo. I stressed that I wanted a male. She described a white charmer, borderline show quality but perfect as a pet, with an even temperament but plenty of attitude. How much? I asked. A thousand, plus the plane ticket from California. I told her to ship him to Dayton, Ohio as soon as possible.

Dylan took the redeye. He arrived the next morning, pristine, a study in elegance. His coat was gleaming white, with flashing black eyes and nose; his top knot and tail fluffed, he sported a puppy cut that made him look like a lion. His shipping crate was unsoiled. He stood squarely on four big feet and smiled that killer smile, his pink tongue set between razor sharp puppy teeth, his short wiry tail banging against the bars of the crate.

I carried the crate into the kitchen. Grabbing a camera, I sprung him loose. He walked free like a movie star hitting his mark, facing the flashing paparazzi, the tiled kitchen floor his red carpet. He followed me like – well, like a dog. I took one step forward, he took one step forward. I took one step back, he took one step back. I reached down to hug him, pulling him into my chest. His hair smelled of California shampoo, and his nose was wet against my cheek. He was the size of a Miniature Schnauzer, but those big feet promised growth. By his first birthday he would stand twenty four inches at the shoulder and weigh over fifty pounds.

I think about that day often, Dylan in the kitchen. We were inseparable, Peter Pan sewed to his shadow.

Dylan was not our first standard poodle. When I was a graduate student in Saint Louis we purchased a large white male. Amour was on hand to welcome Sammy's birth. Janelle was three. Soon after, I was offered a teaching position at a small liberal arts college. We moved to a twelve acre spread in the Ohio countryside. Off his leash at last, Amour chased our horses, and terrorized the barn cats and peacocks. I walked the property with him, showing him the road and trying to find a common language, the language of no, danger, stop.

One morning I walked toward the road to check the mail. Amour flashed by, a white blur chasing a cat. I screamed, "Stop!" but it was too late. Brakes squealed, then a dull thud. Amour walked away, and I took heart. He staggered to me, then collapsed at my feet, dead. The driver cried apologies, but I waved him off without a word. I carried Amour's broken body to the house, dug a hole, gathered Savannah and the kids. We shared favorite memories, said a prayer.

More pets would die. The road was a cruel presence. We had an Australian Shepherd with bright blue eyes. I found him dead by the door one day, a note attached to his collar. One day a pack of wild dogs savaged our rabbit hutch. Janelle came tearing through the house, screaming, "Dad, quick!" I grabbed my rifle and shot one of the dogs as he lunged at my throat. He fell in a heap, a bullet in his head. The others ran off, but the bunnies were dead.

Jesse was our second standard poodle. Savannah named him after Jesse James, because he was a thief. When one of the kids was missing a stuffed animal or a mate to a sock, we learned to check Jesse's dog run. At dinner one night he walked off with a sixteen–ounce porterhouse steak. Shimmering black, he was a bit undersized, but had personality to spare. He babysat the kids. They'd feed him popcorn by the fireplace, and he helped with their homework, listening to nightly complaints about math.

Jesse got cancer in his thirteenth year. By then, Janelle was in college, Sammy in ninth grade. We assembled again and said goodbye to our thieving friend.

The kids were gone when Dylan came to live with us. He was the first dog Savannah and I had to ourselves. A snowstorm hit just after his first Christmas in Ohio. A newspaper photographer snapped a picture of Dylan leaping and twisting in the air on the snowy street. The next morning, Dylan was splashed across the front page, with the caption, "Blowin' in the Wind."

I sometimes think that Dylan was an ambassador. Everywhere he went he made friends. I am convinced he kept Savannah and I together when our marriage ran out of steam. He was our baby. We stayed together for the sake of the child? Maybe. Or maybe we just loved the way he stayed present with us during days of unbearable loneliness in the house, our love dying as embers in the fireplace. He'd pad up to me and nuzzle his head in my lap, then go to Savannah and do the same, allowing us to transfer to him the affection we still had for each other but were somehow unable to express. Never once did that dog disappoint us. He was a conduit of unconditional love.

Last month I took Dylan to get clipped. Savannah had gone to see her Facebook boyfriend, and I had custody for a month. I had met a woman in New York City who knocked me out. Neither of us is ready for "a relationship." The barriers seem insurmountable. Pari's going through a difficult divorce, I'm considerably older, and we live in different states. We joke about how "it's *so* not us." But having her in my life, however complicated, has been a comfort

Coming out of the clip joint, walking to my open convertible, I tried to explain the situation to Dylan. He listened without judgment, as always. Blow dried and pampered, he sat upright in the passenger seat. He smiled at his parking lot admirers who clustered and pointed, oohed and ahhed. He really was a movie star.

I knock at the back door. Savannah opens it, and lets me in. Dylan comes right up to me and buries his muzzle between my legs. I kneel to the floor and hold on to him. I say my goodbyes. Then I get to my feet and tell Savannah I'm grateful for the care she's given Dylan, and will support her decision. She snaps one last picture of the two of us. I'm wearing a ski hat and sunglasses to hide my tears. Naturally, the picture is taken in the kitchen.

Waking Up Samford Again

by Nathaniel Tower

Samford wakes up to the sight of a decent–looking woman snoozing at his side. Her face is almost pressed against his and the warm breath rhythmically blowing into his nostrils makes him cringe and smile. It makes him feel like a human, for all the good and bad that comes with such a feeling.

Staring at her, not moving, he tries to recall the evening that led him here. This isn't a routine for Samford. It has been a month since he's had this, at least he thinks, and he has no idea how long it had been before that sexual incident, if ever.

He stares at the woman until he starts to remember something. An involuntary flutter of her eyelids sparks his memory, and his eyes squeeze shut so last night's movie can play in his mind.

"My name is Samford," he had said to the woman at the bar. He had no idea why he was in the bar, or even what the bar was called or if he had come alone or somehow with someone else. But he knew he was sitting at the bar with a woman who looked good enough to talk to – especially with drinks – and maybe even good enough to take home.

The woman's head whipped back in surprise, her drink nearly toppling over. "Your name is *Samford?*"

"What?" he had asked.

She settled back on her stool and fingered the rim of her glass. "Oh, nothing. It's just weird because Samford is an unusual name, but I know I've met a Samford before."

Samford shrugged. "I supposed it is a bit of a rarity. I could always be normal and just go by Sam."

"My name is Sarah." She smiled. He had no idea why either of them were at a bar on a Wednesday night. In the present, he has no idea why she is in his bed on a Thursday morning.

Samford recognized the name, but not in the way his had registered with her. Every woman was named Sarah. Or Sara. Or some other variation. He was sure he had slept with many Sarahs before, but he couldn't remember any specific sexual encounters or any specific women named Sarah. The only woman he could remember at all was that crazy scientist—cloning lady he had run away from a month ago. One day shy of a month, that was. This month—long drought embarrassed him, although he supposed it didn't matter since no one knew. He hadn't found any friends since his strange discovery. His only source of human contact was at the grocery store and the occasional run in with a neighbor at his apartment. Of course, he wasn't exactly sure it was his apartment, but it matched the address on the license in his wallet, and no one had bothered him about living there. He had yet to find any clues about his life in the confines of the small space, but at least it was a place to sleep and a place to bring girls named Sarah.

Samford opens his eyes and looks at Sarah again. The drought is over. The twenty—seventh is apparently his lucky day. He recalls the orgasm and how great it had felt. It almost made him not worry about whether or not he's a real person. He couldn't shake the feeling entirely though. If he's just a clone, was he anything more than a dildo attached to a moving body? Could he impregnate Sarah if he hadn't been the product of pregnancy himself? At least not directly.

Samford is snapped out of his orgasmic recollection by something brushing against his penis. He opens his eyes and sees

Sarah sitting up, her right foot caressing his member, trying to get her toes wrapped around it. He becomes rock hard even though the sight of her feet disgusts him. Her toes are too stubby for her long, slender feet, and he thinks he sees more than one corn. He grimaces, but this only makes his dick harder.

"Do you like that?" she asks.

He lets out a soft moan. He doesn't want to like it, but he can't help it. Perhaps he has been programmed this way. He shakes his head. He refuses to accept that he is just a programmed body.

She wedges the shaft between her toes, and squeezes as if trying to crack a nut. Samford yelps. She giggles.

Sarah releases the vice grip of her toes and crawls up to Samford. "So, what's it like?"

"What's what like?" He hopes she doesn't mean the footjob she's trying to give him. He doesn't want to admit how amazing it felt.

"Having sex with a clone, silly." She smiles and shoves her breasts in his face. "Can you even tell these aren't real?"

"You're a clone?" He cups her breasts with both hands and pushes her body away. The flesh feels real to him, but what does he know.

"Of course I am. Didn't you see the serial number on the inside of my anus?"

He breathes in. His lips curl in disgust and his stomach churns at the imaginary smell of shit and butt sweat. "How would I have seen that?"

"You spent plenty of time down there last night." She plops the breasts in his face again. "So, do they feel real?"

He pushes the breasts away again. "Do all clones have a serial number in their anus?"

"I don't know. I just know that's where mine is. I know all clones have one, unless they are illegals."

"Illegals?"

"Yeah. You know, unauthorized."

He stares at her, trying to make her read his thoughts.

"Do you want to see the serial number again?" she asks. This isn't what he had been thinking at all.

"I have a better idea. Why don't you look at my anus?"

Her eyebrows arch. "You mean you might be a clone?"

"I really don't know."

"Then let's have a look."

He flips over with her help and spreads open his cheeks. He can't tell what she's doing back there, but it feels weird. Not necessarily in a bad way though. His penis hardens against the mattress.

"Do you see anything?"

"Hmmm. I do see a little something."

"What is it?"

She pulls her hands away and his cheeks snap shut.

"Nothing."

"What do you mean nothing? You said you saw something."

"I thought I did, but I guess it wasn't. Look, I have to go. Right now."

He tries to turn over and grab her, but she's on her way out before he can even roll to his side. He watches her cloned ass jiggle its way through the door and down the hallway, and wonders why they didn't tighten that a bit in the cloning process.

Still naked, he stands and grabs Sarah's abandoned purse from the bedside. Opening it, he pulls out a brochure. He gapes at the sight of the familiar text and images. The brochure slips from his hand and flutters to the carpet, just as he collapses to his knees.

Friday, 28th February 2014

The Bite

by Kimberlee Smith

Today is two weeks since my and Dean's second wedding anniversary. Every day since he and my mum Maybell brought our baby Etheline Margaret home from the hospital, Dean's been out in the garden just before dawn and again as dusk draws near with Maggie, as he likes to call her, fused to one hip while he wrangles the watering hose with the opposite hand, making sure to soak the roots and electric–green leaf sprouts on the jacaranda saplings he planted as a Christmas present for me. Our home was one of the last to be sold in the new development. The lawn was bare dirt; the grass laid by the builder had long since scorched, dried up, and blown away. Dean set quick smart to rolling out new sod and planting the jacaranda.

The sun is climbing; the sky is a mix of pink and blue fairy floss. Dean forces the trigger on the hose down with such a tight grasp it's like he's shooting a gun. He sprays too hard. The jacarandas tremble. Leaves that haven't had a chance to fully develop flutter off their boughs like butterflies with busted wings. His eyes are red from smoke, liquor, and sleeplessness.

He throws the hose to the ground and, with his free hand, grabs up a fistful of fallen leaves, and aims to toss them into the ravine behind the house. They fall softly, spinning through the air, and some whorl right into his face even though the air is still as a soldier.

And the whole time he cries. Rumbling with stifled tears. The baby is soothed by the rhythmic motion of his gulping breath and becomes drowsy as he rocks toe to heel, like a hobbyhorse. He is trying real hard to hold his shit together.

He and my mum take turns keeping the baby in their rooms, alternating nightly, so they are able to each catch up on lost sleep. Neither one of them suspected they'd end up sharing the mothering duties, and they were ill−prepared. Dean figured I'd do it, and certainly Mum would lend a hand, but not doing it full time at her age. She's only 48 but those 48 years have been long, hard ones.

When it is Dean's night to take care of the baby, as it was last night, he gives in to exhaustion and lets her suck away on a bottle of formula until she's sucking on nothing but air. He tosses and turns; sleep doesn't come easy to him these days. He's become a worrier.

Maggie fusses because she's got a belly overfull of formula and air. He pops a dummy in her mouth and she sucks like heck until that poor little angel chucks up the curdled formula. When will he learn it's worth the time it takes to burp her? The book I bought him on being an expectant father collected dust in the magazine rack whenever he went in the loo to take a crap.

I have the perverse pleasure of watching him sit on the toilet and speed read what he should have been learning all along. Sometimes my husband can be a real fool. You should know that I'm gone. Never had a chance to hold my baby, never got to meet her. It's not that I'm being blameful – but fact of the matter is, it *was* Dean's fault.

The bite. It came just a couple weeks before the baby was due. Hottest summer any of us could recall, but it was the first one I lived anywhere with air conditioning. Not the kind that blows all through the house in vents, but the kind that mounts in a window: an electric box that plugs in to keep one particular room cool. Dean bought them for every room except the spare bedroom where he keeps his snakes. He's an exotic reptile dealer and having the snakes living *with* us was a new arrangement since we moved from the Bonnie Doon Mobile Estate Park down on the chapped lips of Lake Eildon in Victoria, which if you ask me is pretty much the intersection of Absolutely Nowhere and Oh, Well. We made the big move to be closer to Kingsford Smith Airport in Sydney, where all of the stock was moved in to and out from.

I didn't mind his business when he kept it out of the house and his partner, Junior Volpe, kept the snakes at some storage facility in Eastern Creek. They took turns tending to their investment, but when Dean starting bringing in big cash by brokering the deals – being the brains behind the business – Junior put the pressure on Dean to take some of the load off him. Junior's in his late 50s and doesn't have the same energy he used to when he and Dean's daddy were in business together. Fair enough.

Dean bought the house – paid for it outright, in cash – and decorated it without any help. You can tell. There's a black leather sectional sofa with two recliner chairs built−in; it's roomy enough to seat eight people. But we never had so many people in our home at once and I imagine they *never* will. He bought the sofa just because he could. Swallows up the whole damn room, just about. And it's the biggest lounge room I've ever been in.

He bought two waterbeds, one for him and me and one for Maybell, and satin sheets to go with. He has room for a couple dozen terrariums to keep his stock, which includes Taipans, Death Adders, good old American Rattlers, etc, etc, depending. Understanding the laws of supply and demand, you see.

Dean even has room to grow their food. Little white mice. Hundreds of them. Those, he keeps them in the garage in the same kind of glass boxes he keeps the snakes in. You'd think there's no business for snake dealers in Australia, as a continent we have a plentiful supply of dangerous wildlife, but Aussies like to keep exotic snakes not found here; overseas, they like the badass reputation of the snakes that are native to our country.

Every buyer wants what's hard to get. Human nature. The craziest part of the business is the exporting. The guys who do that for a living, working under Dean and Junior, risk their lives every time they transport those snakes on flights that are at least half a day or night long. Ironically not one of the smugglers has been fatally bitten yet. I'm the one who succumbed to death by snakebite because I cohabitated with them. In a very short while we got used to them being around all the time. That was the big mistake.

That singular day, the sun stretched over the Blue Mountains, casting shadows the color of tobacco spit on the houses in our development. The asphalt streets were so hot they turned spongy and soft, sticking to children's bicycle wheels like chewing gum, causing them to flip and fall over while the neighbourhood dogs furiously licked the tar that burned the pads of their paws.

There was a colossal dust storm on the M4 where an 18-wheel truck jackknifed and closed the motorway down in both directions for two days. Bushfires ripped across the Southern Highlands and charred every type of animal life: sulphur-crested cockatoos and rainbow-hued lorikeets fell from the skies, wings singed. Wombats perished from smoke inhalation as they hunkered deeper down into their burrows. Eucalyptus trees became burning bushes baring skeletons of koalas, with babies never having a chance to peer outside their mums' pouches. Only the platypuses survived unscathed, but of course they're cranky and sneaky as all get out, so when their bogs were invaded by immolating creatures they were miserable beyond usual. Armageddon seemed to be upon us all.

It was my third trimester of pregnancy. I grew heavy and swollen. It was impossible for me to lower myself down on the waterbed mattress that wiggled like jelly and forget about those slippery satin sheets. No matter how concerted my efforts, every time I lowered myself onto the bed I sunk so deep my tailbone smacked the base. Whenever I tried to roll out of the bed, I'd get a stitch in my side. I was peeing a bunch of times every night so it became exercise too rigorous. As newlyweds we whispered often about how fun it would be to roll around on a waterbed. Of course that was until we owned one. Like many experiences you don't realize are overrated until you have them, sleeping on a waterbed ranks right up there.

In the last few weeks of my life, I took to sleeping downstairs on the leather sectional sofa that was nice and stiff. If Dean hadn't bought waterbeds, or a new house big enough to keep those snakes – especially the pair of Coral snakes that he had to hold onto a few extra days longer than usual for a client who was tending to business in Southeast Asia (I don't ever ask what kind of business his customers are tied into) and kept a dominatrix den next to his wine cellar – then I would still be there today with him, raising our daughter with the beautiful name we chose together. Mum picked Etheline. Dean was in shock and could not protest. He's wrong about being alone now; I'm there with him. He just doesn't have the sensitivity to my presence.

§

This morning Maybell is taking Etheline Margaret for a stroll in her pram around the neighborhood before it gets too hot for them to leave the house. Even though there's a shade attachment to the pram, little Etheline's eyes are watery slits. Today I notice they've changed from the grayish–blue color many fair–skinned babies are born with to deep amber, like a rich lager. I'm trying not to think about how serpent–like they are, yet they're the most beautiful eyes I've ever seen.

Maybell notices. Dean notices. They don't say a word about it. Dean is spending hours threading together twenty rattles from the snakes he traded, captured, bought and sold. These particular ones are Sidewinders, Western Diamondbacks, and Baja rattlers imported from North America. It's all he can think to do to make something good out of something so bad.

Back to the day of the bite, the extreme heat caused the earth below us to move. Tectonic plates expanded, shifted, and quaked. The temblor that hit us was only a 1.6 magnitude on the Richter scale, but it was enough to knock out the electrical power for a couple hours. We were all dead asleep, but the snakes felt it coming well before the earthquake hit. Their terrariums were stacked up on snap–together plastic shelving Dean put together himself, and he might have done a better job of it. I stumbled down the hall to the loo, bracing myself against the walls from the lounge where I slept, through the kitchen, and then approached the reptile den on my way to pee. The air was dark as squid ink and if I had tried to see my hand in front of my face, I would have smacked myself in the nose.

That's when I felt a rolling squish under my foot and right after a fierce plunge of razor–sharp fangs into the meat of my calf. It was so clean it didn't hurt at first, but then the snake dug in again and again. Then the pain stole my breath. I fell to the floor and tried to scream, but I could not get one sound out. The whole episode lasted about five minutes, I reckon. Then that was it.

The thud of my body against the floor is what must've woken Dean. The power flickered back on and I watched him – from right above his shoulders – race down the staircase to find me splayed out like a busted doll, snakes writhing all around. I saw it all like I was watching a movie. I was gone.

Etheline Margaret took a long afternoon nap while Dean finished up making her rattle toy. Maybell is back in the kitchen putting frozen meat pies in the oven for tea and is drinking lemon squash with a splash of gin. Her fifth of the day. Dean has sweet Maggie in his arms and they lock eyes. He knows there's serpent in her now. She looks at him so wisely, like she's a thousand years old. And I believe she is. He takes the rattle and slides it over her plump little fist and before he can blink she slips one of those nubbed spires – one from a Sidewinder – between her lips, suckles on it, and smiles up at him.

March

Saturday, 1ˢᵗ March 2014

Dive

by Guilie Castillo Oriard

Under the palapa roof of the school's terrace, the dive instructor with ridiculously sun–bleached curls brings the briefing to its merciful end. Luis Villalobos swallows a caustic cheer. He'd be in a better mood if he'd stopped at Barista for a cappuccino, but there was barely time to shower before Wendolyn showed up.

He sneaks a look at her. Like the other two diver wannabes at the picnic table, she's hanging on each of the instructor's words, simpering like a groupie.

The instructor – Jan from Amsterdam, which rhymes pronounced the Dutch way, the stress on the *dam*, the short *a* – rubs his hands in a bad imitation of a wicked witch. "Let's check if you've been paying attention. What's the first rule of diving?"

"Keep blowing bubbles!"

Luis's knee jiggles under the table impatiently. He – Wendolyn, too – should be at the office. Milena seems pleased with the results of the FATCA project so far, but she expected nothing. She had to be wrestled in, and now she's broadcasting each success to the Ehrlich mothership in Singapore as if it was all her initiative. She won't be so eager to claim credit a month from now, when Ehrlich's credibility is in shreds before the US Treasury.

No. A month from now it'll all be on Luis.

But it's Carnaval. The halls of Ehrlich Fiduciary stand deserted. His FATCA task force is otherwise engaged: teener parade, children's parade, main parade, costumes, rehearsals. He laughed at first, until Marco from HR sat him down and explained about this most sacrosanct of Curaçao celebrations. And so, exasperated, he let Wendolyn rope him into being her buddy today. *Buddy.* Next he'll be best *pals* with Jan from Amsterdam.

"All right!" Mr. Amster*dam* claps once and gets up, nods at the six—foot—eight dive master on the terrace steps. "Guillaume will get you your gear."

"You excited?" Wendolyn brushes his arm as they fall behind the giant Guillaume. Her judicious flirting is still subtle enough to be ignorable. Luis hopes, somewhat ruefully, it stays that way.

The other two novices, an American couple on their honeymoon – Who takes a diving course on a *honeymoon?* – save Luis from lying. "We're excited," the girl says, and tugs on her child—husband's arm. "Aren't we, Robbie?"

"Stoked, man." Robbie grins at Luis. "You?"

Luis rolls out a smile, more charity than irony. "Totally stoked."

"Hey Luis?" Jan pronounces it Louise. An improvement; usually he gets Loo—is. "Hold up a sec. You look a little out of it. You okay?"

An honorable exit. But Wendolyn's still within earshot, so he says, "Yeah. No, I'm fine. Just – late night."

Jan looks him over, nods. "Drank a lot?"

"Ten, twelve beers." He had eight.

Jan flips through the medical histories on his clipboard. "You smoke, huh? But no cardio history, no back problems, no regular headaches. Except for now?"

Luis obliges with a chuckle.

"You in good shape? Physically?"

Luis shrugs, nods.

"Fifty push-ups, soldier."

"Seriously?" Hope rises. He'll never make it past five.

Jan chucks him on the shoulder. "Nah. But I want you close to me, understand? Your eyes, on me, all the time."

"Actually —" Luis lowers his voice even though Wendolyn has disappeared into the equipment room. "I'm not feeling so hot. Maybe it's best if I —"

"No chickening out, man. It's just an intro dive. You'll be fine."

Guillaume is waiting, holds up a pair of boots. "You are 11, yes? Try these booties."

Booties?

The rest of the equipment comes with grown-up names. Wetsuit — XL, because the L felt like medieval testicular torture. Buoyancy control device — BC in divespeak — that hinders everything, protects nothing. The dive master tugs at three of the hundred straps on the vest-like thing and decrees, "It fits." Flippers — more straps. Mask — another strap.

So that's that. Luis is expected to survive underwater in boots, a wetsuit that — regardless of what size the tag says — still feels too tight, and an inflatable lifesaver that requires more assistance than Marie Antoinette's corsets. As a plot twist, Guillaume tucks four two-kilo metal blocks into the thing's pockets.

"Guillaume will assemble your gear today." Jan stands over the giant kneeling on the sand in front of six tanks, each a tad smaller than the dive master's thighs. "Intro courtesy only. If you sign up for the course, you'll learn how to do it yourselves next time."

No next time for Luis, and for that he feels immense gratitude.

Short-lived. "Luis." Jan is crooking a finger at him. "Over here."

Guillaume holds up a tank with Luis's BC strapped to it. Jan parts the snarl of nylon and velcro to reveal an armhole of sorts.

277

He adjusts and clasps and clicks Luis into place. "How does that feel?"

Luis wriggles his shoulders. "Like a straitjacket."

Jan snorts. "Pussy. Guillaume?"

The giant lets go of the tank. The vest tightens against Luis's shoulders and stomach. "Ooof. No, it's good." He hates that he sounds so strained.

The walk down the beach to the surf, all twenty steps, is a purgatory of awkwardness. The wetsuit is hot. The tank bumps the back of his legs. His feet feel clumsy in the boots. The harness velcroed at his waist makes a ripping noise with every breath. The rubber hoses spouting from the regulator, aptly nicknamed octopus, tangle his arms. One hooks up to the BC. Another ends in a gauge with numbers in the thousands that mean nothing to Luis. Two other hoses, one yellow, one black, end in mouthpieces. Jan folds the yellow into one of the myriad BC pockets. Luis fishes behind him for the black one, studies the mouthpiece, turns away from the happy crowd. He hopes it's been cleaned properly. It tastes rubbery. He breathes in, gets nothing.

"Tank is not yet open." Guillaume pats his shoulder, fumbles behind Luis's head. "Oh–kay. Try now again?"

Luis takes a tentative pull, gets a loud life–support sucking sound. And air! Funny–tasting. Dry. Drier than normal, at least. He will never again take that lovely, effortless provision of oxygen for granted.

He's not cut out for this. The only reason he doesn't call it quits is because he's certain he'll never be able to get out of this torture chamber people call diving gear on his own. He's equally certain Jan and Guillaume will be happy to set him free – once they've shown the Three Enthusiasts the marvels of life underwater.

Ocean, finally. The water feels so good on his skin, sautéed in sweat beneath the wetsuit. He dunks his head, soaks off the grumpiness. Taste of salt on his lips. Sound of baby waves kissing the beach. Photoshopped blue of this ocean.

"Inflate your BCs," Jan says somewhere to the left. "Luis! Where you going, man?"

Luis has drifted on the current. He floats back to where the others are standing in waist–deep water, on his back to keep the tank's nozzle from poking a hole at the base of his skull.

Jan takes hold of his vest and drags him into position between Guillaume and him. "Remember our deal? With me. All the time." He gropes at the hose on Luis's shoulder. Again the life–support whoosh but somewhat muted. "How does that feel?"

Like the hand of King Kong crushing his ribs. Panic subsides when Luis realizes he now floats without effort. "Good. Yeah."

Jan readjusts straps, checks the gauge, fiddles with the tank, hands Luis the black mouthpiece. "Check your air. Can you breathe?"

Whooooosh. Luis sounds like Darth Vader. Probably looks like him, too. Hard to talk with that thing in your mouth. Luis gives Jan a thumbs–up.

Jan rolls his eyes. "That means up. Get your signals straight."

Right. They covered hand signals in the briefing. Luis makes a circle of thumb and forefinger, the universal OK sign.

"Good boy. All right, everyone over here, please. We're going to do some drills underwater, get you comfortable, then we'll head out to the reef. Okay?"

The Enthusiast Chorus holds up comically identical finger circles. "Okay!"

Forty minutes later, six heads bob back up onto the surface. Six faint splashes. The whoosh of six BCs inflating. The pop of six regulator mouthpieces being spit out. Six faces marked raccoon–

style from the masks. And the eyes, the telltale eyes: four pairs brimming with the high of boundaries breached.

Luis wriggles his jaw, winces. He must've been clenching that mouthpiece too hard.

Jan is looking at him. Is that a glint of pride in his eye?

Head still full of the great blue below, the thrill of weightlessness (even though Jan had to add four more kilos to convince this lily—livered, oxygen—addicted body to sink), a feeling of having returned, the prodigal child, to a primeval state of grace, Luis grins. Already in love with the pain in his jaw.

"When can we do this again?"

Sunday, 2nd March 2014

La Ronde / Joey and Annie

by Townsend Walker

Joey drives into the parking lot of Comfort Suites, there, off Route 21, looking for Annie's green Mini. A tradition, short–lived (two months), for Annie to go to the motel, check in, park her car in front of their room, change into something comfortable (she's been raiding Victoria's Secret), wait for him.

He opens the door. He sees Annie, a cat stretched across the bed, blonde hair fanned out on the maroon spread, giving him a what–are–you–standing–there–for look with her eyebrows, uncurling her legs, sitting up to lure him with the full effect of her latest bit of flimsy red lace. He doesn't see the Everyman motel room, its green shag rug, molded wood particle furniture (always in white–beige, sometimes mottled), wide screen TV, or popcorn ceiling.

The magnet force of the lingerie and what is barely hidden pull Joey across the room.

"Can I unwrap my present now."

"Only if you untie the bows carefully."

An hour later.

"That was nice," she says.

"We should do it more often." As soon as the platitude slips out, he knows better.

"That's what I keep telling you. Two afternoons a week is not enough. How serious are you about us?"

"Serious enough to drive fifty miles in the snow telling Sonia and the kids that I had to take some papers to my accountant."

Facing Sonia's wrath for leaving the family on a Sunday afternoon. *What? Your accountant doesn't work during the week? And in this snow? Get a new one.*

"I brought those receipts you asked for."

Joey stretches his arm out from under the covers to open his briefcase and fumbles for the files he brought.

"Not here, you idiot."

The files move from his hand to her hand to her nightstand and will be forgotten when they leave the room.

Annie is, in fact, the accountant for Joey's moving business; has been for some months, since she moved from Los Angeles, transferred by PricewaterhouseCoopers to the Newark office. Joey's friend Max recommended her. *A great accountant, a great rack. Enjoy.*

Yes, a great accountant: nailed everything he'd hidden in the books (Sonia's car, kids' schools, trip to Bermuda) first time through the accounts. Then told him how he was going to come clean with it costing him a dime more in taxes.

On the second count of the recommendation: they'd both been invited to a New Year's Eve party, sparks ignited during a casual dance, dampened by Sonia's presence of course, but two days later Annie called, suggested lunch at the Hilton. Dessert followed in Room 634.

Joey thinks he needs to stop this fling with Annie; thinks about it when he drives home after being with her; the kids crash into him with hugs when he opens the door; when he's with Mamma and Papa (married fifty years); with Sonia making love (Annie's eagerness to get to bed, Sonia's reluctance; Annie moves, Sonia responds): he isn't going to screw up the kids with a messy divorce, which he knows it would be.

He props himself up on his elbow. Even with smeared lipstick, Annie's mouth beckons. It's change—the—subject time, Joey tells himself.

"Hey, somebody asked me about Max the other day. You see him recently, know how I can get in touch? We were close, but last couple of months I haven't seen him around."

Joey tells Annie about this friend of his sister Gina (leaves out the part about his college affair with Madge) who is looking to get her husband offed because he is beating the shit out of her. Looking for a hit man and this Madge doesn't run in those circles. Paying good, mid five figures, could go higher.

"Why doesn't she go to the cops?"

"This guy is rich as Croesus, but she'd end up with squat—all and miserable for years having to deal with him and custody arrangements."

"So you're asking your accountant, partner track at a Big Four firm, to find a hit man? Not really my line of work."

"All I need is to get in touch with Max."

She stretches her legs, rolls on top of him and sits up.

"I do other things in my spare time. Show me *your* hit man routine."

An hour later.

"Jeezus, look at the time. Sonia is going to have a cow."

"Not for me to delay you, lover boy, but what do you want me to tell Max if I run across him?"

Joey gives her the info he got from his sister Gina. Guy's name is Franklin Lancaster Cabot III; goes by Frank. Works at Goldman Sachs on West Street, downtown. Six foot three, 200 pounds, pasty complexion, curly black hair going gray, beak for a nose, Brooks Brothers dresser, loafers with tassels. And Hermes ties, the silly patterned ones. Outside, Prada Aviators, high—end sunglasses, blue tint, even in a March snow storm.

"We need to talk before you go."

Joey has his pants up to his knees.

"What about?"

She kneels on the bed and wraps the red lace around her.

"What I asked you before. Where do you see us going?"

Joey's trying for a little obliviousness by focusing on zipping up his pants.

"I don't know, honey. I enjoy being with you. I know that. No one's ever been as good as you." *Maybe Madge,* hoping the thought doesn't show.

Annie puts her hands on his shoulders and leans her forehead into his.

"Listen carefully, you are going to think about us and on Thursday you will give me your decision: me or her." Unsaid, his business is on the line too.

Joey calls Gina on the way back from the motel, tells her he's made a contact for Madge. Gina asks who; Joey won't say, Gina asks how Frank was described; Joey goes though the litany, suddenly throws the phone on the other side of the car as a screech comes through the speaker, "Not pasty, not pasty, tanned, tanned, go back and tell them tanned!"

Joey figures: *whatever.*

Monday, 3rd March 2014

The Moment

by Derek Osborne

They made it as far as Annapolis before Max went in for the first round of chemo. Pancreatic carcinoma, locally advanced, too late to operate, a drawback from being in such good shape, the body masks the problem in borrowing strength from other organs, other systems, by the time you think something's wrong the cancer has moved in for good.

He's been there a week, Sloan–Kettering in Manhattan. His room faces the East River and he's got a great view of Hell Gate, that narrow part of the channel behind the UN where tugs and barges pass one another while battling six knots of current. There's always something to watch, always some mayhem but mostly he sleeps, pukes and sleeps. Pam, his sister, comes every day; Andi, his youngest daughter, a student at NYU, comes with her iPad and shows him the film she's been editing for class.

He and Rebecca talk every night. She left that morning down in Miami but called before boarding the plane. She's out in LA doing a season's worth of *Miami Blue* interiors. She'll be getting a break the end of the month and coming back out. Max hasn't told her yet; Eddie's been sworn upon pain of death. Max and Rebecca are having a blast, telling each other their childhood stories, how she got started in television, what it was like to move from Chile to Miami at age nine. Max talks mostly about the boat, his glory days in school, he's never talked to anyone about the war, and for obvious reasons, he avoids his wife's battle with her own cancer. He's told Rebecca the basics but that's about it. He'd much rather listen. They're like a couple of teenagers, even playing the game of who'll hang up first, who gets the last goodbye. She has no idea how her voice affects him, but he can't go down that road. They've both made a promise not to go near what Max began on the boat. If one of them even gets close the other changes the subject. When they hang up Max lulls himself to sleep in the echoes of her words, watching the boats on the river, the red and green navigational lights moving below in the dark. At night, on the ward, things grow quiet. Every so often the rattle of carts and shuffle of rubber-soled shoes come racing down the hall. Sometimes, in the morning, the room where they went is empty, no flowers or knick-knacks along the window, the white board erased, the bed too neat.

Max does not dwell, for him it's another Monday and he's getting out tomorrow. He'll be able to continue the therapy at home. He hasn't told them home is a ninety foot ketch tied up in Annapolis, that home will be sailing next week to Nantucket. Max is still in the initial stages. Like everyone else he's Googled the graph and seen the survival rates. He's doing what all good sailors do in a storm – he's clearing the decks, battening down, watching the sky and the radar – he knows the boat, knows the odds, knows that God is coming but God has come before and he's always survived. Why should this be different?

The SAT phone rings. It's not his sister; she's been using the room phone ever since he yelled about spending two dollars a minute just because it's convenient. He gets up from his chair by the window, rolls the little blue robot back to the night stand and checks the phone's screen. It's coming from somewhere in Kansas. It's also coming from an altitude of forty-two thousand feet. He's so used to that number reading zero, sea-level, he notices immediately.

"Hello?" he says, pressing the big red button.

"Hi, it's me."

Max lets the voice sink in. "You're in Kansas?"

"How did you know? Maybe. I'm on the CBS jet."

"Really?" he says.

"We'll be in DC around seven."

"Really?"

"I don't need to be back on set till Thursday so I hitched a ride."

"You celebrities," Max says, teasing, "Just hop on the jet whenever you like."

She's laughing. He closes his eyes, sitting there on the edge of the bed. One of the nurses has come in to check. He's pretty sure the robot tells them whenever he moves; like *Gadabout's* GPS, it sounds an alarm whenever the anchor is dragging.

"You're still in Annapolis, right?" Rebecca says.

"You got on a plane without checking?"

"I had Anja call Eddie."

"And what did Eddie say?"

"He said you were somewhere in town."

"I'm in New York."

"Oh no?"

"Up here on business."

"Oh no?"

Max is doing some quick calculations. He's already had the coaching concerning his discharge. All he needs is the meds and paraphernalia. He can call Doctor Bloom and get them now.

"It's okay," he says, "I'll drive down tonight after dinner."

That should allow enough time. It's only a four-hour drive but he might need to stop and rest – or puke.

"You're sure it's okay?"

He's imagining her there on the boat, curled up on the sofa in the salon. It was designed to be more of a library, complete with a tiled hearth and freestanding furniture. The dining table, usually center in most big yachts, is offset to starboard and gives the illusion of two separate rooms, each with a six foot skylight above, Herreshoff interior, raised panels painted off–white, all of it trimmed in cherry.

"Max?" she says when he doesn't answer, "I just did it. I heard the suits were going and barely had time to pack."

"It couldn't be more perfect."

"Oh Max."

It just comes, for both of them, they never know when.

"No tears, Becca, we can finally be together."

All this time, months, and they haven't even kissed. The nurse sees his face and whispers she'll be back. Max is thinking on his feet now, trying to work things out.

"Eddie's going to pick you up. If you're wheels down at seven you'll get back to the boat around nine. You should miss most of rush hour. If I make my excuses and leave dinner early I'll be able to get there by midnight, unless I hit traffic on the Jersey Turnpike, they're doing construction all up and down … Becca, you listening?"

"Who are you having dinner with?"

Max can be fast on his feet.

"One of your competitors."

"Bastard," she says, "Which one?"

"I shouldn't say."

"I'll get it out of you."

The flirting is so much fun. Everything else disappears.

"Now say goodbye and hang up," she says.

"You first."

"One of the guys wants to use the phone. They're having a conference call."

"They can do that?"

"It's a G5."

"Of course it's a G5."

"See you soon."

Out on the river a bright yellow tug is pushing a line of blue barges. The barges are filled with stone, deep in the water, pushing a huge white wave. Coming the other direction is a forty–foot sloop, a small yacht taking advantage of the tide, probably traveling ten knots and everyone hanging on for dear life as the boat pitches and yaws in the steep chop. The tug is at full throttle, black smoke shooting from its angled twin stacks, kicking a good–sized wake that only grows larger when fighting the current. A ten–foot face has formed, a regular surf as the sailboat bellies down in the trough. They climb the face, see–saw the crest, crash down the backside flipping up into the air, all of them landing again in a jumble of red foul weather gear and confusion of lines. The sails rattle. The guy at the wheel sees they've made it and raises both hands in triumph. The others join in. The tug sounds its horn. Max can just hear it through the glass. *They're having the time of their lives*, he's thinking. He looks down at the dull gray screen of the phone. In little black letters up in the right hand corner it reads, STANDBY.

He looks around the room, the clean white walls, the molded plastic furniture, the white board telling him who he is, who is his nurse, the room and telephone number. It's Monday, March 3rd.

"Come on, Pam," he says, "Where's that call when I need it?"

Tuesday, 4th March 2014

The Crash

by Gloria Garfunkel

Depressed Ralph here. I started crying constantly on Valentine's Day and haven't stopped since. I'm in a Depression Coma, can't get out of bed, have taken a sick leave. Have nothing to say except that I am a big fucking failure who can't even keep New Year's Resolutions.

I am malfunctioning on so many different levels at once. No one at work knows I'm bipolar and I want to keep it that way. I lost a job telling everyone I was bipolar once, believing it was just like revealing I was gay and they couldn't discriminate. People freaked. I've heard of other horror stories like mine of people telling colleagues leading to firing under all sorts of false pretenses, calling normal behaviors "symptoms". Admitting you are bipolar is admitting you are unreliable and impulsive with poor judgment and distorted thinking no matter how excellent you are at your job. No, I would never tell a soul. And believe me, it's not paranoia. The Americans with Disabilities Act is totally hopeless when it comes to standing up for Bipolar Disorder. Only geniuses and actresses get tolerated for being bipolar. It's even cool for them.

Chloe doesn't work where I do. Seeing me in a more subdued state of mind changed Chloe's view of me and she's decided to stick around. She thinks my cycling mood swings are like her father's and it is her job to save my life.

Wait until she witnesses my Mixed Mood Episode, when I have manic energy while feeling horribly depressed, irritable and angry with racing paranoid thoughts. If that doesn't scare her off, nothing will. I can feel it coming on.

Wednesday, 5th March 2014

Azure

by John Wentworth Chapin

Charles wishes he wasn't angry, but he is: angry at India, angry at the yoga center, angry at himself. He is angry at Esther, who talked him into coming here. As he prepares to add to the angry list, the woman in a sari next to him loudly vacuums a bolus of snot from her sinuses, then hocks it into her mouth. She turns her back to Charles and fusses with the bus window, sliding it open enough to spit out the window. She daubs at her mouth with the end of the sari draped over her shoulder.

Charles tugs the signal wire, catapulting himself away from the woman and toward the front of the bus, which stops almost immediately. Charles sees the deep blue ribbon of ocean beckoning beyond the same string of derelict buildings he has seen everywhere, and he steps off the bus. When he was meditating in this oppressive swampy heat just an hour ago, he had to put aside any thoughts of sweat, to ignore the heat and the flies and the smell of the people around him and just *sit*. They told him to cultivate awareness: *thoughts are just thoughts – push them aside.* Thoughts are one thing, but a numbness in your asscheeks and a mosquito in your ear is another.

Instead of feeling a wave of relief, he is immediately aware of all the misfortunes his impulsiveness could invite: lost, robbed, sold into white slavery. He ditched his yoga–meditation–vegan retreat. He ditched his bus. He has a useless iPhone, a useful wallet, a passport, a handful of foreign coins he can't easily count, and a girlishly tiny knapsack holding underwear, soap, a condom, phone charger, and a toothbrush. He's only a couple of miles south of Chennai, an easy walk; he can see the lump of taller buildings at the city center, a long strip of beach connecting him and the city.

He runs toward the beach. The sun pounds on him, but the ocean is *right there*, so he keeps running. When he stops at the pounding blue waves, he doesn't dare leave his things on the beach for the hordes to pilfer. He empties his pockets into the knapsack and wades waist deep into the ocean, holding flip-flops and sack and shirt above his head. Despite the balancing act, the water cools him.

"I don't do well with discomfort," Charles said, frowning at the yoga retreat website they looked at on his iPad.

Esther read the screen in silence. Yoga and meditation sounded too much like religion for her peace of mind. She wanted answers, not hocus-pocus.

"I guess I mean more like with *challenges* or *difficulty*," he said. "If your life is easy and then it is suddenly hard, it's still *hard*, you know?"

The old woman still stared at him, reclined in her mechanical hospital bed set up in her dining room.

"You're judging me," he said.

"I don't see why you need *my* sympathy to get through *your* life," she said, snapping the words.

"I don't know why you think telling you my problems is looking for sympathy," he answered. He was fully aware that she lost the ability to walk and possibly even her mind in a car accident a couple of months earlier, an accident – which she caused and he witnessed – that killed three people. But *still*.

"I have far better things to do than tiptoe around your attitude. Why don't you just go ahead and go to the meditation retreat? What's the worst that could happen?" Esther said, tiredness front and center.

He answered, "I have been reading a lot of women's confessional memoirs lately. I guess the worst is that I won't find what I am looking for."

"You won't know if it was a good or bad decision until you go. If you don't go, you will never know."

Charles realized that she just made the decision for him. "What does the other side of the world have that I can't find in Baltimore?" he asked.

Esther brushed from her forehead a strand of gray hair lighter than her dark skin. "Go find out," she said.

Charles is wrong about the beach. It doesn't go all the way to the city center. A barrier of blue cuts across the sand, the mouth of a lagoon or river. He considers trying to cross it, but his phone could get wet or he could be eaten by crocodiles. He doesn't know if there are crocodiles, but since he can see a bridge not too far inland, it doesn't seem worth it.

He walks a few blocks away from the beach, searching for a road to the bridge. He comes across a temple with garishly bright sculpted columns of gods and fruit and animals. A throng gathers outside: old and young, saris and jeans, t—shirts and suits. Most of them have marks on their foreheads, either carefully drawn dots or smudges of color. He should join them, abandon himself to the masses, but he is too pissy right now for noise and people. It's hot. It stinks. He can't.

He walks until he finds a major thoroughfare and follows it north, pleased with himself when he discovers the exact bridge he saw from the beach. Halfway across the bridge, he stops to survey the beach, the river/lagoon, the city ahead of him. He catches his breath. *I have good instincts.*

That brings him to two hours earlier, when he was sitting in meditation for the second full day, increasingly agitated that he wanted to shut off his mind, but he couldn't. Flies and awful heat and stench assaulted him and he couldn't bear the feeling of his own fingertips touching his own thumbs in meditation, but that was camouflage. In the misery of silence, on the other side of the world, he couldn't escape his only thought: *you are wasting your life and the clock is ticking and you have nothing to show for it.*

But here I am! he shouted at the void. *Doing this!*

The void did not respond but the accusation echoed. *You are wasting your life.*

He spies a flash of bright blue along the water's edge, a strange bird. When he squints, a peacock comes into focus. Are there wild peacocks? He doesn't know the answer, and he can't look it up on his phone. The peacock disappears behind tall, dark brush, returning Charles to himself on the bridge.

He doesn't quite know what to do with himself. The five days before his flight were to be filled with meditation and pathfinding. Now he's suspended between sky and water with two possible paths.

He continues north, sweat–soaked. The walk is good for him, although suddenly it is very crowded on the street. He thinks it's time now to find a cab or a hotel but the crush of bodies around him becomes greater, another throng of people swept up in religious fervor. This is what he wants: ecstasy and spectacle, animal sacrifice and widow–burning and fire–walking. This is why he has come to India, after all. Isn't it?

Charles walks with the crowd, now spilling into the road and stopping traffic. They move like floodwaters around trucks and cars. Time has ended, the world around the crowd frozen as the throng surges on toward its ecstatic finale.

The crowd comes to the foot of a soaring white building. The people behind press up into the mayhem, some funneling through the open doors of the building, some people streaming out, fresh dark marks on their foreheads. *Yes*, thinks Charles, surrendering himself. *I'm ready for it.* He closes his eyes as the crowd carries him forward: feeling, hearing, smelling. Inside the building, he breathes incense and hears familiar music, prompting him to look more carefully around.

He's in a church, a soaring white cathedral, in a line of people streaming up to the altar where they receive a quick daub of gray ash on their foreheads from a priest. There are only two white men in the place: Charles and a blue-robed Saint Thomas statue.

He has come all the way around the world to a goddamned Catholic church. Charles turns and crashes back through the surging crowd, out the door, down the steps, and onto the street. At the edge of the crowd, he pauses to catch his breath. "Fuck!" he exclaims, half out of breath with frustration.

A man about his age, skin darker than the ash on his forehead, catches Charles's eye. "Friend," the man calls, "what are you giving up for Lent?"

"Religion," Charles replies, standing straight. He walks north to the city under the hot, blue sky.

Thursday, 6th March 2014

Punch Drunk

by Lynn Beighley

Best night on tevee, right? Thast what they say whoever they are. Excuse my wine glass has somehowb ecome emptied.

Better. and I just pullled the phone cord out from the wall because pieople won't quit calling and calling because ITS FRiCKING LUV WEEEK/

I mean on that realty show with Bulldozer Plover its all about the love. love week can bite me.

My dad is here. Its he's cool about me drinking, he thinks i'm a riot. I am so so ANGRY and Im also really scared okay? wht is bill going to say in a minute, I don't think I want to watch. But I cant not.

Dad's got pollock on his lap and is petting her and shes all happy and he's all happy and the only one in the entire wolrd who's not happy is me. I've got my chat cliet open on my lap, I mean on my computer on my lap. Not close to as nice as having a cat one wons lap, but okay. ON the othere end of my chat is Seamus.

Seamus: You think America will make him propose to you? I can't imagine anything more romantic!

Me: bite me

Seamus: Maybe you can have the ceremony during the final show of the season! It'll be perfect, America and call in and tell you both how to answer to I DO. Oh oh OH and

Me: fuck u

Seamus: there'll be a cliffhanger, where America chooses if you get to use birth control on your honeymoon to wherever they vote for you to go (I'm thinking Disneyworld, so romantical!), or if you'll have America's FIRST CROWDSOURCED BABY! That's a WHOLE NEW SERIES.

Seamus is a giants dickhole. I strat to pound out a very obsene reply but Dad's leanig over and trying tosee my screen so I close it. and show's on. FUCK

Ther's a teaser part with Bill. He looks okay, they cleaned him up preetty good for this but still, meh.

"Next we hear from Bill with his love question for you this week," greasy announcr guy says. I hate the host guy even though he's farking hot. Afater all this is over i'm going to get bill to interoduce me to him

So Bill. It's been a few weeks since YOU TELL ME strted and so far Bills spiffed up his wardrobe and gotten a lot less annoyiong at work all because of the way America answered the poll questions for him. Iand he's so funny because he says he has to do what America tells him to do because it wouldn't be right otherwise. So whem AMERICA told him to him to go all GQ and the show bouth him the clothes and stuff he did it. Look, I'm not a fan of trends whatever but he looks so much better without the crap he used to wear.

"Was that him? He looks really sharp." my dad asks during the cialis commercial.

"I'm going to update my Match Dot Com profile photograph, do you think he would help me buy an outfit for it? Oh, and I need to refill my Cialis."

swear to god my dad's a freak and I'm ready to scream but instead I get more wine wine because bill because FUCKING LOVE WEEK . at least I trya to but things are spinny so i sit down

and Bill

Bill: Yes, Mark, there is a particular young lady I have had my eye on for some time. She seems as though we would be quite compatible. However, there's the difficulty of her being my coworker to overcome, so I 'haven't made my move' as some people say. As well as, he pauses, her tendency to laugh inappropriately. She has a terrible sense of humor.

WHAT DO YOU MEAN TERRIBLE YOU WEASLEASS I yell and my dad says OW as Pollock sinks her claws in his leg in frigth. And it hits me

coworker fuck fuck fuck fuck fuck fuck I zone out and don't really here waht else he says. he mand mark go back and fortht. I hear GINGER nad I start cussing out loud until my dad puts hims arm around me amd pull sme close. I love my dad even if he's a dating freak and smells like old spice and onions.

And my atteniot returns to hthe teevee when I hear

Smarmy Mark: I'd say it's time we let America decide. AMERICA, HERE ARE YOUR OPTIONS:

A) BILL GETS TO GO OUT WITH A DREAM DATE YOU, AMERICA, CHOOSES FOR HIM !

B) BILL ASKS OUT HIS GINGER–HAIRED COWORKER WITH THE LOUSY SENSE OF HUMOR!

C) BILL'S LOVE LIFE GOES NOWHERE THIS WEEK

we won't know the answer for almost an hour and I'm sleep

It's morning and I'm on my couch in the clothes from last night and oh my god does my head hurt. I'm covered with a blanket and a note from my dad is pinned to it. Before I open it, I feel my cell phone vibrate and I slowly pull it from my pocket.

"I hear there are treatments for impaired humor tolerances," says Seamus. "I'd say Billyboy pegged you right off. You signed off just as I was on a roll, Ginger."

"Not so loud," I say. "I committed suicide by alcohol poisoning last night, be a little bit respectful of the dearly departed." It's already after 9, crap. Must hurry.

"So what are you wearing?"

"Um, excuse me?"

"For your big day. You've got to look pretty for the cameras, Red."

Dear AMERICA, bite me.

Friday, 7th March 2014

After the Flood

by Andrew Stancek

The problem is language. I am extraordinary with feelings, with observation, with picking up nuances of emotion between people. I am even better with birds now. I sense the slightest reverberation, too fine for a human instrument to calibrate, like a sound perfectly audible to dogs but nonexistent for humans, like a whale song ... No. That's all wrong. But it shows what I'm trying to get across. Words don't work. Language is inadequate. I know what I am saying because I have merged, I have communed and I have done it without the slightest recourse to language.

Professor Langeweile is the most interesting of the hundreds of people who have quizzed me since the revelation. He is quite enlightened, I think, and he truly wants to know, not to get an advancement, a promotion or something, but for himself, in order to understand. He has spent time in India, I think he said, and studied their mystics, and the Christian ones, and he says that is really what he sees in me. He is still stuck dealing with language, and is quite rational and that holds him back, but his questions are of a different sort. He is humble and gets excited when suddenly he sees something, or is explaining about Hildegard of Bingen or someone like that, a real professor, and then catches himself and laughs and says, "Well, of course you know that." Sometimes I do and sometimes I don't but I nod and we laugh together. The music of the spheres. Mystics. The thing is that I am not a mystic; I'm not seeing the face of God or anything of the sort. I merge but it's not a religious experience, or maybe you could say it is one of a different kind, a communion of sorts. Yeah, there is that problem with language again.

I won't try to explain to you how I do it. Nobody has ever learned to ride a bike by following instructions on paper. It's an action, not a theory. If you think you can sign up and in just eight easy lessons at a low low price of just, you too can, well, you are on the wrong channel. Being, not doing.

This is about birds. They know, they take off, they have the instinct, an inborn, inbred something. Maybe we used to have it too and just bred it out, or suppressed it or something. I'm not a scientist, a geneticist, any more than I am the fraud that so many would like me to be. I have gone beyond, mastered, allowed myself the freedom to go beyond the suppression.

It's so much easier not to talk. I just do.

Watch. I stretch them out.

Look. Yes. Up here, way up here. My weight does not matter.

Sometimes after the grilling and all the nonsense I put up with, I get away and soar. I clear my mind of everything and there is nothing but flight, movement, being one with the air, with moisture in the air, with sunshine. I am becoming more attuned to the differentiations in the air itself, not just velocity and pressure but the very molecules of moisture and air.

Maybe it was something like this for Noah, after the waters receded and he was no longer listening to squawks and breathing flatulence inside the ark, and after constantly wondering *will I really get through this no matter what He said, and soon they'll start dying off, and eating each other and if only I had a tiny little space, only for myself to stretch, to only hear myself,* and then yes, and there was hope, and he began thinking yes, I will see land again, and sometimes, just sometimes I feel what he felt, I can stretch out and not feel and smell anyone else in the world, it is just air, moisture, sunshine, me. I brush the tops of the trees and I want to break off a twig, to carry it somewhere to say, "Look, there is land, there is hope, there is growth and life," but then I don't. It is best not to break off anything living. I don't have to prove. It is enough that I know.

I have pains occasionally, sensations, twinges. With birds suddenly a top flyer will hold a wing a little askew and is less aggressive at the feeder. Then sometimes he comes back good as new, but sometimes you don't see him anymore. A black crow covers my mind with a wing and I don't breathe. Maybe it's not *can't* but it certainly is *don't*. My heart is weighed down by a smell of an unremitting wet emptiness. I've never belonged anywhere but now sense this will be short. Professor Langeweile says the mystics talk of a great light. I'd welcome a great light but it might be a great darkness on the horizon. No, it's not a physical ailment; I don't want a CAT scan or a pill. It's not depression.

Noah was trapped on that ark. A regret came, too, after the initial relief that unlike those who had not opened up, he was still standing and breathing. But because he was a favoured one, for him it was *Behold, a dove came back to him in the evening and in her mouth was a freshly plucked olive leaf.* No doves at my feeders, not a single olive leaf.

As I was saying, the problem is language. I've merged, moved to a new realm. But that means no one can help sort it out. I have a body, a mind and more. I'm still exploring. I'm on my own.

Saturday, 8th March 2014

That Awkward Moment

by Rachel Ambrose

I can't help but bite my nails when I hear Charlotte coming down the hall. She's been grumpy and quick–tempered ever since Blake and I started dating, and I've been trying to avoid her since my ability to Deal With Shit has absolutely flatlined (not that it ever had much of a pulse to begin with). But I've resolved to be in a good mood today. Blake and I are meeting by the river to have a picnic lunch, and I've bought a new dress, and I want another girl's opinion on how it looks.

"Charlotte?" I call bravely out into the hall. She opens her bedroom door and stands there, nose wrinkled like I'm secretly keeping a rat with diarrhea in here. "What do you think of this?" I ask, spinning slowly to show off the dress. It's a fit and flare in a pretty peach color with white lace around the neckline and the hem, and I'm planning on wearing a little white sweater on top.

She shrugs. "It's fine. You know you're a day late on your half of the rent check, right? It was due yesterday."

I'd actually forgotten in the excitement of choosing brie or camembert to bring with me on the picnic. "I'll write you that check tonight," I say, blushing despite myself. Blake's really gone to my head, I think dizzily. He's taken me out on six dates so far and all of them have been amazing and thoughtful. I'd think he was gay if he wasn't trying to get his hands down my pants at every opportunity. Today I thought to wear a dress to make that mission easier. His thoughtfulness is rubbing off on me.

Charlotte shakes her head. "Honestly, if I hadn't reminded you, you wouldn't have had any clue at all, would you?"

"I'm sorry!" I say. "It's just that things have been a bit of a whirlwind lately, you know, with Blake and all."

"Yeah," she replies, shaking her head. "Blake's a real gentleman, knows how to treat a girl right." She forces this out through gritted teeth, and her hands are visibly shaking.

It's then that I realize that she's been into Blake this entire time and never said anything. How could I have missed this fact? I feel like an idiot. "I'm sorry," I say again, but now I say it slower and softer, lingering over my remorse.

"Whatever," she says. "I'll be in my room, Claire, and I'd appreciate it if you could just slip that check under my door when you get the chance, after you're done being swept off your feet all afternoon." She slinks away and slams her door, and I stand there for a minute, feeling the cold chill of her departure. I grab a bottle of wine from Charlotte's wine rack in the living room, grab my purse and tiptoe out the front door. Now that I've stolen her man, I may as well keep going and steal her wine, too.

Sunday, 9th March 2014

Rory's Glory

by Gill Hoffs

I hum a theme tune I can't quite remember as I wait for the elevator, and remind myself to tell Jenny at the agency the flavoured condoms they gave me last week made my crotch smell like bubblegum. I'd even checked my pubes in case my client had forgotten to take his Juicy Fruit out before going down on me. I'd made it look like I was playing with myself, which made our 'date' pass faster than it usually does – another note to self: do NOT pretend to do that with clients who have problems with stamina.

Today I'm booked for a spring wedding, a posh one. The client's ex is marrying some nob with a title, so I've travelled through the night in the back of a limo, ready for a preparatory breakfast and champagne with Rory, my jilted host.

The lift arrives with the soft ping of a hidden bell, and I appreciate the plush pink carpet and wood panelling inside it, push 7, and listen to the hum of the machinery transporting me upwards, then stride through its open doors and along the corridor towards room 721. Lilies, minus their staining stamens, are arranged in an alcove opposite his door, and I revel in the opulence of my surroundings. Fresh flowers, Howson sketches in gilt frames on the wall – I'm particularly impressed by the Bosnian sketches – and carpet so thick my feet sink centimetres with every step. It's worth taking on a job so far away if it means luxury like this.

He opens the door and catches me sniffing the flowers' peppery perfume. I smile, straighten, hold his slender body close then let him carry my hatbox and overnight bag in. Then I strip.

After an hour of sucking, licking, fucking, and flicking, we're done. My lips have swollen nicely – why bother with collagen when a lengthy blowjob does the trick? – and Rory's lost the strained look on his face. Some of the lines are gone from the freckled skin round his eyes, long-lashed eyes the purply-blue of a five pound note. He runs me a bath, and kisses the nape of my neck as I clip my hair up to keep its straightened length free of suds. I don't have to fake the shiver he provokes.

I can tell he's not used to being a client instead of a lover, running me a bath, putting a towel to heat on the radiator for when I get out, asking if I'd like a cup of tea and a biscuit while I'm in there. It's nice. He's nice. So nice that when he calls me by my work-name I almost correct him with my real one.

We dress slowly, him in a grey morning suit complete with top hat and tails and platinum cufflinks in the shape of sea-turtles, both of which I have to wiggle through the silk shirt, and me in a summery mint-green frock and pale aquamarine leather boots. My hat's a monster, a giant creation of cream and blue and green with tiny silk hydrangeas and seed pearls swirled round with lace and a brim as wide as the rings of Saturn. No undies, but a thick velvety wrap to match the dress and I'm done. Well, I think I'm done, but then Rory says, "Hold still a sec," and fastens a single chain round my neck. I turn a little to look in the mirror by the door, to see what's pulling it down, and it's a pearl. Not a typical white one, either, but a purply-green rainbow one on a platinum chain.

"Thank you. It's beautiful."

I mean it.

"It suits you."

Dammit, I blush.

The bride is so happy. Her father walks her down the aisle, with a similar grin, and I can feel Rory's thigh tense beside mine and rub it to soothe him, but he slips his hand into mine and squeezes instead. I would lean my head on his shoulder, but the bastard hat's too big. The minister breezes through the service with a smile and barely a pause at the "speak now or forever hold their peace" bit, though Rory's hand clutches mine as if he might just stand up and offer an objection for the hell of it, or rather, for the hell of witnessing a woman he once – still? – loved marrying the man of her dreams.

When they kiss he surprises me by cupping my chin and turning to kiss me. Not a 'So there!' kiss for the benefit of those around us, either. A gentle smooch, just lips, as if I was her and he was her husband. As if we were in love.

We fling confetti in the churchyard, some landing on the couple, some on the daffodils and hyacinths bordering the path to the waiting horse and carriage. I notice the bride looking for Rory amongst the crowd, glancing at his face and tipping her head slightly as if to check he is alright. His arm is warm and welcome round my waist and from the corner of my eye I can see him smiling and nodding back. The photographer flashes the grey from the sky, over and over as if this is a horrible nightclub with only a strobe to perk up the party. She poses with her husband and innumerable lineups of relatives, squalling children, and friends, then passes through the medieval archway. Pause – flash flash flash – step up to the carriage – flash flash flash – helped up to her seat – flash flash flash – sit watching husband climb in – flash flash flash – snuggle together – flash flash flash – wave goodbye – flash flash flash. And … gone.

We shake hands with people in suits and their female companions, murmur variations on "The bride looked divine!" and edge towards the vintage double–deckers parked far away from naked trees and defecating pigeons in the gravel carpark. I stumble on the gravel, and Rory takes my arm to help. Even when we get to the bus, he doesn't let go. We're the first there, and instead of just sitting anywhere he leads me up the narrow stairs to the top deck, then gestures with his free hand to the front row.

"After you."

I haven't sat like this since I was a child. The view is terrific: weathered gravestones, clusters of daffodils, and the vivid blue of muscari stand out between ancient yew trees and neat stone paths winding through the shadow at the back of the church.

"She seemed very happy."

He nods, smiles a little, private smile.

"She is. They make a good couple."

"There's just us here. Would you like me to do anything to help … pass the time?" I want to say 'make you feel better' but I don't want him to know I can tell he's struggling despite the smiles. He's very good at looking happy when he isn't. I wonder if it's a natural gift or due to a depressing amount of practice.

"Yes." He takes my hat off, smoothes down the strands this inevitably ruffles, then instead of guiding my head down to his crotch puts his arm round my shoulders and pulls me into his side for a hug. "Thanks. I know this is just work for you, but I'm still glad you're here."

I lean right in, enjoying his lack of aftershave and the solid warmth of his body. I can't remember the last time a hug was just a hug.

I want to say that sometimes it isn't just work.

Sometimes I get paid for things or people I quite enjoy doing anyway. The money's a bonus that pays the bills and keeps me focussed on the future.

But I saw how he looked at the bride.

So I stick to "Me too," and keep my heart closed. At least for today.

Swoon

by Susan Tepper

I name this one Swoon. In the cupboard a jar of apricot jam that's down to the dregs. I pry open the lid. "Swoon will like this," I say, placing the sticky jar on the floor near my futon. When he doesn't come out right away, I start feeling jumpy. My arms start itching. What if something happened to the sleek white rat? Maybe the others, ordinary brown, were jealous of the silky albino hair. Maybe they castrated Swoon.

Lying down on the futon, I touch my balls carefully. That time in Bellevue – the first shock treatment. I woke up to some orderly squeezing my balls. Now I shake them to be sure they're still attached. Worrying about Swoon which starts me hiccupping. I get up to open the window then slam it shut. A TV doc said sudden loud noise can stop the hiccups. Not this time. Still no sign of the Kingly white rat; though some others, the regulars, huddle around the jam jar.

The boys at the brick elementary school, the new one I found the next town over – those little darlings, they would like Swoon. Those boys, they'll come out of hiding. One by one or in pairs. In their miniature GAP clothes just like the daddies wear. All I need to do is open the car door and in they'll climb. For Swoon. They'll get off the freaking jungle gym and all that other kiddie crap the schools install to keep them busy. Distracted. Too busy to notice a man in a car who watches their every movement. Loving them. Each of them. Whole lines of little darlings. My boys.

In an hour, when the recess starts, I'll be parked near the fence. Waiting with Swoon.

Shady Grace

by Jessica McHugh

Not a day passes that Edward McKenzie doesn't wish his mother, Betty, had died in the accident instead of Grandma Eleanor. She shouldn't have been driving anyway. Eleanor had offered to take the wheel, but as usual, his mother lashed out when her functionality was questioned. Betty McKenzie had screamed, jerked the wheel, gone mad at the wrong moment.

She'd also been the least harmed by the collision and shed the fewest tears over its result. Her lack of guilt made Edward hate her even more when she forced him to hear her confession. The vodka on her breath was louder than her regret, but he had to give her God's forgiveness. To this day, his own has never been offered.

His disgust at Betty isn't helped by the fact that she still lives in town, or that he visits the most abusive resident of Shady Grace Nursing Home every Tuesday. These visits are his penance. For one day a week, he takes the abuse so someone else doesn't have to.

"Hello, Betty."

His mother's head bobs, but she doesn't turn from the window. He sets a chair beside her and sits, touching her shoulder, but her gaze is fixed on the bare branches outside.

"How are you feeling today, Mom?"

"Eighty-seven in a shithole. Give me some room for Christ's sake. You're practically on top of me," she says, exhaling a cloud of liquor.

In spite of Shady Grace's no-alcohol policy, Edward isn't surprised. He doesn't know how her sour tongue sweet-talks the nurses out of searching her room, but after a lifetime with the woman, he suspects fear is involved.

As a child, Edward often pretended Betty was just some loud, mean dog who passed out on their couch or threw up on the dining room table. He also used the soft, sweet-smelling things in his grandmother's apartment for distraction. Wrapped in chiffon, he couldn't hear his mom's slurred insults or the ridicule from townspeople about the "drunk woman who killed her own mother."

But it doesn't work anymore. Even dressed as a man, Edward hears his fears blast from those in town. "Just look at his mother," he thinks they whisper. "Are you surprised he turned out to be a freak?"

Edward opens the top drawer of Betty's bureau. Beneath the clutter of letters and hairpins he finds a bottle of cheap rum. He takes it out and her head turns. Her eighty year-old body looks like a papier-mâché skeleton, but alcohol abuse has left a fatty shell sagging on her skull.

"Put the bottle back," she barks, her liquor-lard shaking.

"You're going to kill yourself with this stuff," Edward says, tucking the bottle into his jacket pocket.

"I've been hearing that since I was eleven. I guess it's not a very aggressive killer, huh?" she replies. "Or were you referring to my soul, *Father?*"

"Your soul is a lost cause, I'm afraid."

"You may be a priest, but I don't think you're anyone to judge on unsalvageable souls. Yours is the most perverted I've ever seen," Betty says. "You should thank your lucky stars no one but me knows how perverted."

Edward sighs. "I don't have any lucky stars anymore."

She sings a snide "boo hoo" and stands to face him. "You think I ever had any? With a pious mother and a freak for a son? What did I have to be thankful for, or be proud of?"

"I'm not going to apologize to you for anything."

"Why should you? You're no more to blame for your trip−ups than a retard on roller skates."

"Mom, that's horrible."

"Well, I'm a horrible person, aren't I? A lost cause?" she asks, her arms flapping like an injured bird. "You can drown your misery in your grandmother's perfume, why can't I drown mine in liquor?"

"You don't know anything about my misery, Betty. You never did."

"I think I know a bit," she says, grabbing her cane. Although she leans on it with each step, it isn't used for walking. No, not Mother's cane.

It taps the floor, a portentous metronome to pain, but Edward glares at Betty, unafraid. Her chins quiver in amusement before the cane rises. Betty's slower these days, but her arm hasn't lost its snap. Her cane strikes his thigh, but he doesn't give her the satisfaction of flinching. As the fiery stripe burns down his leg, Edwards clenches his jaw and swallows his pain. In the past, he might have run. He might have cried out or cursed at her, but none of those things ever made him feel better, and none ever taught her a lesson.

He lifts his chin, latches onto Betty's cane, and wrenches it from her hand. She scoffs, but there's shock behind the derision – for Edward, too. The shock turns to pride when he throws the cane to the floor and his mother backs away.

"Where's the rest?" he asks.

"I don't know what you mean."

He looks into the drawer, rifling the contents for more bottles. He doesn't find any, but something familiar catches his eye.

He removes the picture, his heart racing. The boy in the photo smiles, which means he hasn't been broken yet. He's still strong. All things are still possible. And with possibility at the helm, a strong child can change the world.

Betty slams the drawer closed, smashing Edward's fingers. Growling through the pain, he drops the photo to the floor. His mother kicks it under the bureau, hiding the strong child from the world again, and pulls a flask from her robe. After a smirking swig, she drops the flask in her pocket.

"Don't think a memento or two means anything," she says. "There's a lot of trash around here."

He walks to the door, whispering, "I know that, Mother." Massaging his throbbing hand, he feels small again — until he plucks her cane from the floor. If she doesn't need it to walk, she doesn't need it at all.

Edward McKenzie hooks the cane on his arm and closes the door on his mother, wishing it were closing forever. He says, "See you next Tuesday," but before the door shuts, he hopes the last thing Betty hears is the sound of him breaking her cane in half.

Wednesday, 12th March 2014

Rotted Leaves, Wilted Flowers

by Shane Simmons

Our heads hang silently as we brush aside rotted leaves and wilted flowers with our bare hands to reveal the two plaques. I peel the polythene wrap from a bunch of flowers I'd picked up on the way and arrange them into the empty pots at the side. "That looks nice," she comments.

The muddied plastic bags around our shoes rustle against the soggy grass as we stand back and I look at the engravings. I read the words to myself, over and over. Aunt Patricia sobs quietly. Should I have been doing the same? I gently pat her back, we say nothing.

Back at the cemetery path we untie the bags and place them in the bin. From the boot of her car, Aunt Patricia lifts a large, tartan picnic basket. "I know it's a little chilly, but I thought it would be nice to have something here." We sit down on a nearby bench. She pulls forth a flask of hot tea, perfectly quartered salmon and cream cheese sandwiches, and even a small Tupperware box of biscuits. There's nothing to break the silence except the birds and our own conversation.

"You don't look like you've been eating!" she scorns.

"I have, just all the wrong things and at the wrong times."

She sighs. "And how's work?"

"Oh, it's going well enough. How's Uncle John doing?"

"Looking forward to retirement, but they seem to want to keep him on as long as they can. It's a shame you won't be able to stay for dinner."

"I only managed to get a half—day off, we're on a tight deadline to get the image archive started online."

She pours more tea into the plastic cup in my hand and asks, "Do you miss them?"

I rub my curled fingers past my closed lips, only knowing that I should say, "Yes."

"I have a little something for you in the car. You will let me drop you off at your work when we're done here?"

"But aunty, it's such a long ..."

She tuts and shakes her head before she shushes me. "I insist, it'll be nice."

A spot of drizzle lands just on my cheek. "We'd better pack this all up soon, those clouds look ominous."

My phone vibrates against my thigh, I'd left it on silent since the cemetery.

"Hey hun," I hear her voicemail, "I know it's a hard day for you, hope you're OK. Say 'hello' to your lovely aunt and uncle, call me later if you like."

"Who's that?" Aunt Patricia asks.

"It's Sandra," I say, slipping my phone back into my pocket, "she says hello. I don't think she's drunk, as yet." Aunt Patricia guffaws. I don't think she'll soon forget Sandra, who tagged along with me for my Boxing Day visit, drank far too much mulled punch, crushed a bed of winter pansies when she fell on them before violently throwing up into a box hedge. It took a fair while to hose that multi—coloured mess away.

"So, aside from boisterous Sandra, have you met anyone, someone special?" Aunt Patricia enquires from the steering

318

wheel. "Just, I want you to know that if there is anyone, anyone at all, they're as welcome to visit as you are."

She of course means well, so I give a simple "Thank you" in response. But there is no one.

As she drives us towards the city, Classical FM plays second fiddle to the hiss of tyres against damp tarmac. The roads become harder to see through waves of lashing rain. The traffic slows to a crawl along the A20. But it's good to spend some more time with her.

Eventually, we pull up outside of my work. Aunt Patricia leans over to open the glove compartment, she takes out a bag and hands it to me.

"I found this photo. It was taken when your mum and dad first started dating. I had a copy framed for you."

I unwrap the white tissue paper to find a pair of faces staring back at me from inside a silver filigree frame. They're young, at ease, and dare I say, happy. They're strangers to me. I look at it, a beautiful, beaming woman resting her head upon the shoulder of the handsome, youthful man next to her. I don't recognise them.

"It was taken at Margate. It was a gorgeous summer's day, a Sunday if I remember right. All four of us jumped on a train together and went to the coast. It was so busy. I can recall it like yesterday." Her voice crackles and as I turn to look at her I see her eyes are fogged over.

"Thank you aunty, it's a lovely picture." I fold the tissue paper back over the frame and lean across to give her a hug. "I promise to come over sooner, perhaps this weekend?" But the words muffle against her shoulder.

She whispers into my ear, "Please don't forget them." When she pulls away from my hug, I see her eyes are now red and as swollen as a riverbank about to burst.

"I'd better get going," I say. "Thank you so much for the lift, tell Uncle John I was asking after him. I'll call tonight to make sure you got home safely."

319

I clamber out of the car, and quickly disappear into the building. The bag in my hand trembling, I stop dead in the foyer to take slow, deep breaths. I wipe my eyes clear. I'm grateful there's no one around.

Somehow, she must've known I had almost forgotten them.

Canary

by Michelle Elvy

Stevie's riding his bicycle. It's early March and it's snowing. He hasn't ridden much this year. He only pulled it last week from its musty place in the garage, leaning against the old ping pong table no one uses any more. He used to ride it everywhere – every day after school, every weekend. All over the roads of South County, getting lost in the dark narrow spaces that curved and bent in unexpected ways. He could ride those roads blindfolded. He knew every single moss–covered bank and every single turn.

But February was unusually cold, and January – well, January was lost. And last summer he only rode it once. Most days last summer, he was with Manny, Rick, and Lucky. He'd known Manny since they were eight, when Manny's family had moved in two doors down. Rick lived closer to town, so they didn't see him as often, but Rick was tedious anyway, even if he was Manny's cousin. Lucky, on the other hand, became a permanent fixture in their lives in sixth grade – the coolest kid by far, without even knowing it, which is what made him so cool – and he and Manny and Stevie were near inseparable ever since. They moved from collecting Pokemon to playing Mindcraft together as their tastes morphed over the years. Why they started jacking cars was something they couldn't explain; it was outrageous – a challenge and a thrill. And no one expected it from them, so they got away with it. Stevie's got a knack for breaking into cars, you could say. But it's all harmless fun – they'd take a short joyride then ditch the car, sometimes only two streets from where they jacked it. It is in fact the only dysfunctional thing about Stevie, really, his only vice. He doesn't drink and he doesn't get stoned with Lucky and Rick. Stevie's a good student, a good son.

Now he's riding down Claret Street, back behind the old post office, not entirely sure where he's going. It just feels good, with the snow falling lightly on his face, with his fingers gripping the handlebars in the morning chill.

Up ahead he sees a small girl on the side of the road. As he gets closer he sees she has no coat. Wait, no: she's wearing her pajamas. He slows and he sees that she's barefoot. Her long hair is hanging over her face, her bangs covering her eyes. She's just standing there. Her pajamas have small cats on them – cats chasing mice. When he stops in front of her she looks up and he sees it's Sylvie, Ellie's little sister. She's easily a half–mile from home, just standing there on the road, with her head down.

"Sylvie?"

No answer. Not a muscle moves.

"Sylvie? Are you alright?"

"I lost my bird."

"Your bird?"

"His name is Yellow Bird. Like Big Bird."

"Where'd you lose him?"

"Out here. He flew out the window and I followed him."

"Did you find him?"

"No."

"Do you want a ride home?"

"No. I have to keep looking."

Stevie shifts on his seat. He's not sure what to do, but he's pretty sure he ought to find a way to get Sylvie home.

"You want me to help you look?"

"Yes."

"Alright. So let's walk back the way you came, and we'll look out for him as we go. Sometimes birds fly back to their homes, you know." He doesn't think this is true, but it seems like a good thing to say.

"I don't think that's true, but OK," says Sylvie.

Stevie hops off his bike and they start walking back toward Sylvie's road. They are both pretty wet now; it's just warm enough to make the snow melt as it floats down to earth. It will all turn to ice tonight but for now it's just slushy. There are puddles in the potholes and Stevie guides Sylvie away each time they get near one. She's maybe four or five, he can't tell. She's barefoot and wet from the falling snow and he's worried more about her fingers and toes than her bird. "What are all those stickers for?" asks Sylvie, pointing to the frame of Stevie's bike. He tells her about some of them – one from Vermont, one from Maine, one from Illinois. Many, many stickers. All from different family trips.

"I like the bear," says Sylvie. "And the smiling sun." California. And the sunshine state. Both very far from here.

Stevie's had the Schwinn since he was twelve. It's old-fashioned, sure – not a BMX, not an offroad machine – but it's the bike his dad got him for Christmas that year – *just like my old bike*, his dad said – and he likes it for that reason alone. All around him his friends have rebelled more and more: Lucky in a constant cloud of weed, Manny practically dropping out of school. But besides stealing an occasional Honda hatchback, Stevie is still a contented part of society and his family. He tolerates his little brother more than is warranted, and he likes his parents. He feels he's a bit too bland, but it's a terrible truth he can't help. He's just not a bad boy.

When they turn onto Sylvie's road – the old gravel road – they avoid the big pothole at the edge and move more toward the center. And there, lying only a few feet away, Stevie sees a small brownish pile with sticky feathers and a sad pale yellow showing through the wet mass, like little bits of hay. Stevie keeps walking. A mild panic grips him and he wants to run. He hopes that his body and his bike are blocking the view just enough so Sylvie does not see. But just as they are almost past the pothole and moving on toward Sylvie's driveway – which he can see up ahead, only a few more houses down the street – a truck turns into the road behind them, and Sylvie pivots to see it. She waves at the driver, her neighbor, then somehow catches the yellow smudge out of the corner of her eye, and Stevie knows there's no avoiding it. He braces himself for inevitable wailing. He feels certain Sylvie will need to be carried the rest of the way and he briefly wonders how he'll carry her and his bike and the dead bird.

Instead, Sylvie takes his hand and says, "Look. There's Yellow Bird. In the big puddle."

"I see him." The only thing Stevie can think to say.

"I have to help him out."

"Yeah."

"You have to help me."

"Yeah."

Stevie rests his bike on the side of the road and digs in his backpack and finds a blue–checkered handkerchief. He pulls it out, smooths a used crinkly corner on his knee, and hands it to Sylvie.

"Here."

Sylvie takes the handkerchief from him and blows her nose loudly. Then she steps toward the large pothole and reaches out toward Yellow Bird. She can't quite reach him, though, and Stevie thinks she may fall forward and into the puddle. He steps quickly to her side, kneels in the gravel beside her. He scoops up the dirty mess in his hands. He looks at Sylvie, who has now spread the hanky in her palms. She's holding them out with an expectant look. For a moment, Stevie almost laughs at the scene – this unlikely calm child with her outstretched hands, caring for a bird so quietly while the cat and mouse scream around in maddening circles all over her now soaking wet pajamas, her bare toes poking out red with cold and her nose running steadily down to her upper lip. He places the bird in her palms and watches as she gingerly folds the corners of the hanky over her bird.

"You're gonna help me bury him, aren't you." It's not really a question.

They stand. Stevie pulls his bike up by the handlebars and they walk down the road together toward Sylvie's house. He's thinking about this brave girl with the crazy cat pajamas and it suddenly dawns on him that he has not thought about Ellie once during this whole episode – Ellie who almost incessantly rattles his thoughts; Ellie who has not seen him in a month, not since Lucky's funeral; Ellie who he's sure is as lost as he is; Ellie who may not even know he exists anymore. And now he's walking toward her house.

His throat feels a hard lump.

"Come on," says the cat–mouse–bird girl. "Yellow Bird will need a good funeral. With songs. Do you sing? Ellie will sing."

Now he has a new image of Ellie: Ellie, who sings.

Trail's End

by Len Kuntz

It's noon on a Friday and already the liquor store is packed.

I ask a man wearing a hunter's tartan shirt, "What's the deal? Why's it so busy?"

He looks at me, then walks away without a word, as if I've offended him, as if I'm foul−smelling.

The clerk at the counter wears a turban. He seems annoyed but has beautiful skin, shiny, too, the color of maple syrup.

My cart is filled with five gallons of gin and loads of tonic. When I ask if they sell limes, Turban Head flares his nostrils and says, "This isn't a grocery store."

I feel like punching him. I feel like strangling him with his turban and watching that pretty skin of his turn blue, then purple, but there's a woman in line behind me whose Chihuahua keeps trying to hump my leg.

"Really, lady? Can't you get your damn dog fixed?"

"Fix yourself," she says, not doing anything about the filthy mongrel.

When Turban Head flashes me a grin, I flip him off.

My next stop is a convenience store where I buy cigarettes. I haven't smoked since high school. I open the pack and light up as soon as I exit the place. It's the same as if I've shoved a blow torch down my throat and no matter how subtly I inhale, I end up hacking.

Around the corner, on the curb by a dumpster, two teenagers are singing a Dylan song, *Blowin' in the Wind*, the guy strumming a guitar.

They notice me but don't say anything. The girl is blonde and pale and her partner has dreadlocks coiled all over his head like hydras made out of yarn.

When they're finished, the girl asks if they can hitch a ride. I tell them I'm not going their way. They ask how I know. I say because I don't know where I'm going. The guy says, "That's cool. We're just floating, too."

"My car's loaded with stuff."

The guy tugs at his shirt. "Look at us, man, we're skinny."

They are. A pair of ragamuffins.

"All right," I say. "If you can fit, you're in."

I've got the gin on the front seat. The trunk and back seat are loaded with shit I don't really remember buying, and I only took it because I'm never going back to the lake house again.

"See?"

"No sweat, man," the guy says. He lifts up the sacks of gin, sits down, pats his lap and has his girl sit on him.

"I think that's maybe illegal," I say.

"Lighten up," the guy says. "I'm Buddy. This is Lana."

They keep singing in the car, going through Dylan's early protest catalog. I've been driving for half an hour when I remember the guy's guitar. "Where is it?" I ask.

"Left it," Buddy says.

"You left it back there?"

"It wasn't mine anyway, plus it's a piece of crap."

Near Seattle, a torrent begins, but they don't stop singing. Now it's *Hurricane*.

I wonder how they know such old songs. I wonder where their parents are and what the hell they're doing, but I don't ask because learning too much about people has only caused me trouble. But it feels good to have company, even if they're more strange than strangers.

It's night by the time I reach the Idaho border and I'm beat, so I pull over at Trail's End Motor Lodge.

Buddy says, "Hey, man, you mind if we crash with you? Just for tonight. We'll sleep on the floor."

When I tell them that sounds like a bad idea, Buddy pulls out a blunt as large as a cigar. "We could party," he says.

In the room, I go through half a gallon of gin like it's a scorching day and I'm drinking lemonade. Buddy and Lana are blitzed, sitting with their backs against the wall. Buddy keeps tracing patterns on Lana's face, then marveling over his designs, as if his fingertips are leaving paint, which has me thinking their pot must be laced with something.

He tells her she's beautiful. He compares her to springtime, a wild fawn. He goes on and on. Lana stares back at him, her eyes wet. She unbuttons his shirt, helps him off with his jeans.

"Hey," I say. "No way."

Lana pulls her ratty sweater off. She's braless. In the time it takes me to polish off my glass, she's naked and they're both entwined, rubbing as if trying to light a fire with their flesh. I think about throwing a bottle against the wall to make them snap out of it. I think about Virginia and how different it felt with her, me wanting nothing than to please her.

I watch Buddy and Lana writhe and slide. I listen to them whimper and whisper. I tell myself this is just a movie I'm watching, that I'm merely a spectator, that all this is as right as rain.

Saturday, 15th March 2014

Third Inning

by Michael Webb

The tumblers of thought click into place as I walk across the diamond in the Florida sun, sweating pleasantly while the crowd buzzes around me. The events of the previous inning, a long home run from our second baseman Juan Mihares followed by a fastball right between the threes on the back of the uniform of our right fielder 'Sliding' Billy Hamilton, suddenly spelled it all out for me. I have to hit somebody, and the first man up in the fourth, Marlon Starling, is, in baseball's peculiar calculus, the equivalent player.

It is one of the rules. When they get one of yours, you get one of theirs. It's Sean Connery logic, from his speech on the bridge in the film *The Untouchables*. "That's the Chicago Way!" Efficient and brutal, it is the way pitchers, long isolated because of our peculiar work schedules and fragility like hothouse flowers, prove we are part of the team, by stepping up and defending our mates the only way we can, an equal and opposite fastball in the ribs.

Hitting batters is rude in the extended casual attitudes of the spring. Results don't matter, a sudden run of success or paralyzing failure greeted with the same casual bromide, "it's just spring training." Plunking, or dusting, or flipping someone, or throwing what they called a purpose pitch, is something you reserve for the more serious combat of the regular season, when jobs and careers and the agate type that determine our value for all time is determined.

It was determined before the game that the fourth inning is mine, for good or ill, so I just headed out without being told anything. I'm confident my spot on the team is secure, but just like everyone else, I have to get my work in, and a quick inning will no doubt raise my stock in the minds of my new bosses, which can't hurt. But the reality of the situation has suddenly come to me. I think about Charlie Brown, and I feel a stab of stomach pain.

I'm at the mound, Hector Cruz, our catcher, already there with the baseball.

"OK, 1 for heat, 2 for slide, 3 for change?" he says in thick, accented English. We have spoken a few times, but I have thrown only a couple of times to the man who will receive the majority of my deliveries this year.

"Yup," I say.

"We flipping this fucker?"

I put my glove to my lips, a pointless gesture intended to thwart HD−watching lip readers. I hate throwing at anyone. It is against my nature, and everyone who does this for a living knows the names, the unwary or unlucky who were hit in the head or the face, ending a career, or back in 1920, the life of Cleveland's Ray Chapman. In such a precise matter, where fractions of inches change destinies in fractions of seconds, a mistake, though unlucky, is not far from the minds of anyone.

I think about my new teammates, wary in a workplace where friends are shipped to Toronto or San Diego or Columbus without another word. I feel their eyes on me. Does this guy have any balls? Will he defend me if I'm the one who gets whacked? Will positive feelings toward me help an outfielder dive for a dying quail? Will it coax a walk to extend a rally and get back a run for me?

I think about baseball, its codes and traditions, and of Starling, staring at me from the on−deck circle, having done nothing but share a uniform with someone who could have simply made a dumb mistake under the sweaty light in God's waiting room. I don't want to hurt him. I don't want to hurt anyone. I think I remember reading that Starling is a new father, a baby boy born over the winter, according to the note on ESPN.com.

But I have a family to feed too. I have new teammates whose doubts I have to soothe. There are rules, and I'm their prisoner. I take the ball from Cruz' enormous mitt.

"Yup," I say.

Sunday, 16th March 2014

Petals and Perfume

by James Claffey

The twenty chickens sell at market for a not too shabby profit, given the amount of feed the Bird had invested in that winter. A bitter, miserable time, too, it was. The nights short as burned candles on saucers, the rain never less than drizzling down for weeks at a time. The money burns a hole in the Bird's pocket, so he steps in to Quinn the Haberdasher's.

"D'you have a pair of those fancy slippers with the fleece lining?" he asks, patting his oil–slick hair down.

"Grand day to you too, Bird," Quinn replies. "Are you looking for the ones from Australia?" He slips behind a shelled curtain and returns with an opened shoebox.

"No, no. Not those ones. The ones with the curled up toes. Like feckin' genies wear, you know?"

"We don't have the like. Sure, won't you take these anyway? They're your size and all."

"I'd rather get a new frying pan, instead, thanks all the same." And out the door he marches, coat whipping in the wind, his face lashed by the stingers of rain pelting down from the dark sky. Instead of more shopping he steps into the arcade and plugs a few coins in the slot machine. He has a terrible love for the one–armed bandits, and imagines a holiday to Las Vegas one day, to Caesar's Palace. He hears they have doormen with white gloves, and moving statues. It'd be powerful fun to play the machines there, he thinks. Maybe he'll do a bit of partying while he's at it.

Across from him, the Hanlon boy rides a pinball machine, his crotch banging the front of it, a high−pitched whine coming from the screen when he sets the steel ball on its journey. The lad would be better served doing his bloody homework if he was worth his salt, the Bird thinks. Cherries aligned and jingled coins fall into the tin tray. It's turning out to be some day.

In Lowery's Pub the bell above the door clangs and Ned Lowery nods. "Greetings and salutations!"

The Bird orders a Guinness and Powers and stands Ned a drink.

"Your health," Ned says, raising the glass.

"Slainte." He drains the warm Guinness in one go, imagining there'll be nothing but bloody Budweiser beer in Las Vegas. Behind the bar a calendar for Russian Vodka a good two months off the mark, the young lass all skin and lipstick in a skimpy Santa Claus outfit, a white stole across her bare breasts.

"She's hot on her leather," the Bird remarks, knocking on the bar to signal time for another.

"She's a grand sight, and make no mistake. Look at those plump lips, and isn't it a shame we've no young ones like her in this town?"

At the far end of the counter a woman wrapped in a dull shawl worries her toenails with silver clippers, the occasional click causing the Bird to flinch, afraid the shards will land in his drink. She has a visible sadness to her, and he recognizes her as one of the travelers from the crossroads on the Navan Road, the ones he passes every week on the way to market. His cheeks flush when she catches him staring, but she shoots him a gap−toothed smile, and digs the dirt from under a big toe.

He drains the whiskey and raps the bar with his knuckles in farewell. With a bit of luck the tinkers will be gone by summer and he'll be off in America on the pig's back.

§

On the Dublin road the Bird tacks into the wind and his bicycle creaks along as the land–locked seagulls caw caw caw overhead. As he's freewheeling around the curve of the road toward home, a battered VW Camper van overtakes him, horn tooting, and a waving hand raised. The van pulls to the curb and the Bird sees it's the French woman from Hogan's bar. The one with the flute.

"Bird! How are you? Very windy, no?" She smiles, her hair ablow in the breeze.

"Ah, it's yourself. Nice to see you again." The Bird clears his throat and fiddles with the bell on the handlebar. "Fresh day, isn't it?"

"What is it about you Irishmen and the weather?" she asks, a hand smoothing down her grey hair. "Is it the only subject you are comfortable having an opinion about?"

"No, no. We'll talk the hind legs off a donkey if you give us a chance," he replies.

"Let us take the chance and drink some tea, then," Melodie says, and points at the small café across the road. "Shall we take tea over there?"

"Well, now. If you don't mind, I'd be happier if we took tea around the corner at my house, it that's all right with you?" The Bird dismounts his bike in anticipation and when she nods, he pushes the black Raleigh onto the footpath.

He puts the key in the latch and pushes the door inward, wheeling the bike into the hall and resting it on a long, white painted radiator. She follows him along the hallway, shutting the door behind her. The place is lit by bare electric bulbs, no shades over any of the lights, and wallpaper that curls from the walls.

"Sit down, now," he says, offering her the one empty chair at the kitchen table. The others are piled with newspapers and cardboard boxes.

"Are you moving out?" Melodie asks.

"Ah, no. It's the parents' bits and pieces. They both died in the last while and I'm getting through their belongings."

The whistling kettle startles Melodie and she says something in French, but the Bird only smiles and thinks how wonderful the strange words sound in her soft voice. Scald the pot. Three heaped spoons of black tea. Jug of milk from the fridge. The Bird takes a packet of Marietta biscuits from the cupboard and fans them in a semi−circle on a plate.

In silence they sit, the ticking of the clock punctuating the sips of tea, the crunch of biscuit, and when the Bird tries to say something he chokes on a crumb, his face reddening. Melodie slaps him on the back with the palm of her hand. He rises, the chair rattling to the floor, and coughs violently, a spatter of wet crumbs spraying the air. Melodie rights the chair and rubs the Bird's back, her hand gentle and comforting to him.

"You must think I'm an awful eejit," he says, sitting back down and finally catching his breath.

"Oh, no. You are a nice man. This happens to me too sometimes." Melodie smiles at him over her raised teacup.

"Would you like to see the rest of the house?" he asks, rising from his chair and gesturing towards the hallway.

"Oui, I mean, yes, of course."

He walks behind her to the front room, her dress flowery, reds, greens, yellows, a meadow of movement, a sea of memory. He closes his eyes, imagining the skin beneath the cotton, the softness. All he hears though is his mother's voice admonishing him to get a hold of himself, and why on earth would a woman like this French harlot ever see anything in him.

"Shut up!" He claps a hand to his mouth, and says, "Sorry. I was talking to my mother."

"But, she is dead. No?" Melodie stops at the door to the front room.

"Yes, but I hear her voice in my head."

The French woman smiles, reaches for the Bird's hands, parts the flowers of her dress and engulfs him in a cascade of petals and perfume.

Monday, 17th March 2014

The Lucky Ones

by Gwendolyn Joyce Mintz

It's St. Paddy's Day and, being restaurant workers, Mora and Aaron can't get the night off. Aaron makes Mora promise to make Diane promise that she'll show up for the March meeting of "The Suicide Club."

"The guys are so new," he tells Mora about Phil and Vincent. "I don't want them to think we don't care about their pending deaths."

So Diane shows.

Kelly's, the bar and grill where they've been meeting, is hopping. Full of revelers dressed in green, conversations spiced with a touch of brogue.

Diane waits at the hostess podium, her arms crossed tight. She's aware of the dulling sensation building inside.

The hostess appears. "Booth or the table?"

Diane shakes her head. "You know, I think I'll wait for the others and see what they want." She takes a seat on the bench by the door.

At the appointed time, Vincent walks through the door, followed by Phil with the left leg he seems to drag along.

Diane pops up and approaches them before the hostess can. "It's really crowded in here," she says. "And loud." She raises her voice for emphasis.

Vincent looks around. "Not meeting then?"

"We can go somewhere else," she says.

Vincent glances at Phil who shrugs.

Diane takes it as a 'yes' and she leads them to the door.

"Another time?" the hostess asks.

Diane looks back over her shoulder. "Yeah, sure," she says.

They opt for a diner. A booth. Diane on one side, Vincent and Phil on the other.

"So, you couldn't take all their happiness?"

Diane looks up from her coffee cup at Vincent. It only takes a moment for her to register what he meant. "They're not happy; they're *drunk*." She holds his gaze until he looks away. Shaking her head slightly, she turns her attention back to her cup. She wants to tell him that they're the lucky ones; that the closer they get to death, the closer they are to what matters.

"So what exactly do we do at these meetings?" Phil asks, cutting into her thoughts.

"We really haven't done anything yet," she replies. "I think we're just gonna have a place to go talk."

"I still can't believe you want to kill yourself," he continues.

Diane's smile is wry. "Well, if I could find someone to do it for me ..." She sips at the coffee. Lowering the cup, she asks; "So what's your story?"

Phil lifts his useless left hand. "Cerebral palsy. So tired of living with it."

"Tired. That's what this singer said in her suicide note. She was tired."

Vince jumps into the conversation. "And your method will be?"

"Pills. This time," Diane shares, "I'm opting for pills. Just like Marilyn Monroe."

Phil agrees that's how he'll go. "It's not like I could tie a rope or something."

They all chuckle.

"For me," Vincent says when their laughter subsides, "it's gonna be a bang."

Something inside tells Diane to keep quiet but she can't. "I don't buy what people say about suicide being selfish, well it is if you're leaving children behind and if you shot yourself. That's pretty selfish."

Vincent scowls.

"You leave a mess that someone else has to clean up. How is that fair?"

"Exactly," Phil chimes in. "I've always thought Hemingway was a jerk for making his wife find him that way."

Vincent glares at Phil. Turning back, he lifts his glass to his lips and finishes off his soda. He sets it down and says, "You're both full of shit."

Phil laughs.

Diane looks across the table though Vincent is now busy reading the copy on the placemat.

She's gonna tell Mora to tell Aaron that they need some kind of rules if they're going to keep meeting.

Diane thought she was going to like Vincent. Now she's having spiteful thoughts about him. She plans, now, to cut this evening short before her feelings escalate. After all, they're meeting to work out killing themselves, not each other.

The Comedian

by Stephen V. Ramey

I'm in the produce section of the supermarket closest to our house. Anne needs green peppers for tonight's dinner. It's only noon, but I couldn't stand being in the house any longer. When I get stuck on writing a scene, I soon find myself feeling the cancer inside, pushing at my rectum, spreading through my blood like dandelion fluff.

Staccato laughter draws my attention. Jimmy Magerko is holding court near the cantaloupe bins, a half–dozen shoppers arrayed in a semi–circle. I should be surprised, but nothing surprises me where Jimmy is concerned.

"Don't get me wrong," he's saying. "I love my honey, but really? Another stray? You can't drop a crumb in our house without starting a catfight. I told her she could take in another one the day she lets me have a threesome." He dons his go–to expression, part smug defiance, part innocent kid caught with one hand in the cookie jar. "The new cat's name is Fluffy." Polite laughter. "And, yeah, I got my *ménage a trois*. I have the claw marks to prove it." Louder laughter and an actual guffaw.

A uniformed man approaches him. "I'm sorry, sir, but you'll need to move along. No solicitation."

Jimmy's eyes flash, a striking effect when combined with his hawkish profile and sleek silver hair. "Do I look like I'm soliciting? Did I tell these good people that I'm appearing this weekend at Benefields?" He does a deadpan to an elderly woman hunched over her shopping card. "That's in the Mill Street building, darling. They have a ramp." I wince, but the woman only chuckles. Jimmy is always saying that comedy is an equal opportunity offender, and everyone is the butt of one joke or another.

The shoppers disperse, leaving the uniformed man to confront Jimmy. Jimmy hands him a cantaloupe, and walks toward me.

"What did you think?" he says.

"I only heard the last joke," I say. "It was good."

"Thanks. It's always best to include a kernel of truth."

"Which part, the cat or the threesome?"

Jimmy winks. "Does a magician give away his tricks?"

I look around. "Where's Rose? I thought she was recording your routines for a webcast."

"She is. I'm just testing new material for my pop–up at Lowe's tonight. Come on over if you have time. I hear they sell tomatoes in case I bomb. Well, tomato plants."

"I don't think we can make it," I say. "Anne has a meeting after dinner."

"Come without her. Do you need a ride?"

"No," I say. Sadness wells up suddenly. "I'm ... I need some alone time, you know?"

"Sure," Jimmy says. "There will be other gigs." He touches my forearm. "Did you get your results back, is that what's bugging you?" The intensity of that gaze serves his comedy well, but makes friendship a little dodgy at times. I feel as if I'm being sized up for a meal.

"Not good," I say. I didn't see a specialist, but Dr. D did convince me to come in for a follow–up exam. More blood work, a CAT scan, and the diagnosis is clearer. I have growths in my lower GI, a suspicious spot on my liver. It doesn't look good for the good guy.

"What's next?" Jimmy says.

"Nothing," I say. "I'm done with doctors."

"I don't get you, man, you're going to stand by and let that shit eat you up? What about Anne? Don't you care what happens to her?"

"Of course I do. That's one reason I'm doing this, Jimmy. I don't want to put her in the poor house."

"You have insurance. I heard Anne tell Rose."

"Yeah, but it's only bronze. High deductable, high out of pocket. A week in the hospital, and our savings will be gone."

"That's bullshit," Jimmy says. "What are you really afraid of?"

"I'm not afraid. It's ..." I pick up an orange and rotate it in my hands. "I'm working on a book. I haven't told Anne yet because, well, because the last three books didn't get finished, but this is the one. I know it."

"Good for you," Jimmy says.

"If I start treatment, that'll be the end. I watched my dad go through surgery, radiation, chemo. Once you begin, it takes over your life. I can't afford that now."

Jimmy gives a sour look. "Seems to me that if you watched your dad die, you ought to be a little less enthusiastic about following that same road."

The security guy interrupts, still holding the cantaloupe. "You need to move along, sir." He nudges Jimmy. Jimmy nudges back. Several bunches of bananas fall. The uniformed guy scrambles to pick them up.

Jimmy grabs my arm, and guides me to the next aisle. Bags of potatoes and onions surround us. I think of the earth they were pulled from, my father's grave.

"I don't want to die, Jimmy, I don't. There's only two things I've ever really wanted, to play professional baseball – took me seventeen years to figure out that was a pipe dream – and to write a book that matters, you know, like Tolkien or Salinger, something that leaves a mark."

"How about *Dianetics*?" Jimmy snorts. "That shit is so fucked up it's definitely going to leave a mark."

"I'm serious, Jimmy."

"And I'm not? Look, here's the thing – and, by the way, I'm a little disappointed that getting laid didn't make your top two goals, or having a great comedic friend for that matter – but this is the thing: we don't always get what we want, Stephen. Life is struggle, man. Take me, for example. Some nights the audience is so dead it would make Brad Pitt nervous. Do I give up? Hell, no, I dig deeper next time."

"Yeah, well writing a novel is not the same thing."

The security guy shows up again. He looks determined this time, steely eyes, mouth set, hand hovering by his hip as if he's about to draw from a nonexistent holster. "You need to take it outside, gentlemen."

"Don't say anything to Rose," I say. "Anne talks to Rose at least twice a week."

Jimmy laughs. "Yeah, I'm going to start lying to my fourth wife, it worked so well for the first three."

"Sir –"

"Yeah, yeah," Jimmy says, brushing the security guy aside.

"I mean it, Jimmy. Anne can't find out. Not yet. She'll ... I don't know what she'll do. She trusts me, you know? We tell each other everything."

"Then tell her this," Jimmy says. "I know a bit about slippery slopes." He glances at the security guy, who is fumbling with a hand–held radio. "Try the green button, buddy."

Static sounds. The guy grins, triumphant.

"Okay, okay," Jimmy says. "I'm going." He walks briskly toward the exit. The security guy hangs back as if debating whether to kick me out too.

"Don't worry," I say. "Comedy's not contagious." I stroll to the chiller to pick a pack of peppers.

§

Anne is sitting at the kitchen table eating a salad when I walk through the back door. A half-dozen bottles of dressing are arranged before her. She has a habit of getting them all out even when she's eating alone. I usually end up putting them away. I shouldn't resent that – she's the one bringing home a paycheck these days – but I can't help myself. Why six, when you'll only use one?

"Would you like some green pepper?" I say, thrusting the plastic shopping bag forward.

She slides a cell phone across the table. My gut goes cold. I check my pocket. Yep, it's mine. Anne doesn't like it when I forget to take my phone with me. How will she reach me in an emergency?

"Sorry." I set the bag on the counter. "I guess I forgot."

"You have a voicemail," she says.

"Oh?"

"Doctor D'Orenzio."

Oh. "I wonder why –"

"She scheduled an appointment for you with Dr. Matta a week from Friday."

Damn. I smile sheepishly. "Yeah, I forgot to tell you. She wants me –"

"I Googled him," Anne says. "He's an oncologist."

"Yeah," I say, thoughts spinning. "It's, I'm, yeah, I'm writing a book. Survival rates for cancer. Dr. D –"

"Don't even bother making something up," Anne says. "You're a terrible liar." Her eyes gleam.

"No, really, I'm wri –"

"I could understand you hiding an affair," she says, "but *this*? Christ, Stephen, will I never get through to you? I'm your fucking wife! You don't have to hide behind your walls any more. You promised me, you ... promised."

345

"I know," I mumble. I promised to tear down the walls between us that had frustrated her so thoroughly before we married. *No secrets, Stephen. We'll build a bridge, we'll fight for each other.* "I'm sorry."

Her face suddenly balls up. She shoves her plate away, stands, and runs out of the room. I feel powerless as the plate balances on the table's edge like a roller coaster car reaching the top of a hill ... then topples. Salad splashes the floor, leaves glistening with oil.

I watch, open—mouthed, unable to articulate my thoughts. My feelings are clear enough, though. Guilt. Regret. If only I had acted faster, I might have stopped it all.

Father and Son

by Gay Degani

As the sun's orange glow streaks his window, Gus German watches the last few minutes of the TV news, Gracie alert at his feet, tail whisking across the shag carpet. He ignores the dog because he's learned that making any movement or comment at this time of day will send the animal into paroxysms of impatience. When the perky blonde newscaster finally signs off, the old man clicks off the TV and grins at his mutt. "You ready for your walk?"

The path down to the creek is steep, so the old man and the dog take their time, Gracie burying her muzzle in every clump of weeds, every pile of dirt. Boy Scouts have spent hours of community service cleaning up the mess from the January windstorm, all except for the huge eucalyptus that fell over Gus' favorite path. Each afternoon he and Gracie hope that when they reach that point, the tree will have been removed and they can go into the little clearing where the city recedes behind rustling shrubs, where chittering squirrels and afternoon parrots provide the only sounds. Gus longs for his Iowa roots, the serenity that comes from acres of endless corn around a stand of cedars, the burble of a stream.

He stops at the fallen eucalyptus, his closed mouth moving in silent frustration. What did he expect? Mounds of debris still wait for city pick–up at curbs along the Old Road.

Gus tugs on Gracie's leash and ambles toward the path edging the flood channel. Years before, the Army Corp of Engineers had built a dam in Homestead Canyon, lined the meager stream bed with cement and enclosed it with chain link fencing. He wished they'd let it be. Sybil, his landlady up at the bungalows, claims she played in the creek when she was a girl. Remembers catching trout. Trout! How wonderful, he thinks, if there was trout.

"Dad?" Mars tramps down the path after Gus, grinning.

The old man mutters to himself, "And now, my day is ruined," as he continues to plod along the chain−link fence.

"I knew I'd find you here. Hey Gracie, you dog."

"What'd you want, Mars?"

"Thought we'd go out to dinner, you know, since it's your birthday."

"I don't like missing *Wheel of Fortune*." Gus stops. "Besides, why do I wanna go out and eat somebody else's food?"

"For the fun of it?"

"Fun is saying, 'Time waits for no man' before some doofus shouts it out on TV. Oh never mind. I got a couple of boxes of mac and cheese. If you wanna eat, let's eat." He yanks on the dog's leash, and Gracie trips on her short feet as they turn back, heading home.

He feels Mars' eyes boring into his back. In the old days Mars was the one who stomped off, and the old man wouldn't see him for days. And for a second, Gus imagines his boy at fourteen, kicked out of school, and packing a grocery bag with jeans and t−shirts. Gus had let him go then. He'd let him go now, but when he reaches the street, there's Mars trudging up the path after him.

Inside the bungalow, Gus fills a saucepan with water and puts it on the stove to boil. Mars opens the fridge and brings out a bottle of wine. He grabs two mismatched glasses from the cupboard, one with a stem, one without, pours the Sauvignon blanc, and hands the stemless one to Gus who feels the familiar irritation he always feels when his son is around for more than ten minutes.

"I got a job," says Mars.

"What kind of job?" Good, thinks Gus. Don't want you moving back here.

"You know Ian, that guy next door?"

"The shiny penny? You're gonna work for him?"

"His mother. She has people working for her, you know, when she's got a house to sell. She wants me to run one of her crews, cleaning up yards, painting, moving furniture. They clean 'em up now. Stage 'em, she says."

"Well, don't go walking off with anything. One stint in jail is enough. Thank heaven your mother never lived to see that."

Mars stares at him, clinching his teeth, his body stiff and awkward, just like when he was a boy. "Why do you think I'll never change?"

Gus knows his son is trying, but change is impossible. No, that's not right. Change is unlikely. Whatever Gus's own faults were when he was young, they've magnified with age – impatience, severity, and intolerance. Yes, that too – but he's too old and too tired to make himself change. Mars won't be any different.

Mars says, "You want me to go? I'll go."

"No I don't want you to go." Gus' arm comes up fast to wave off the idea, and Mars flinches. That flinch. The surge of annoyance shooting through Gus requires all his willpower not to turn wave into blow. Mars the man stands his ground where Mars the boy would have thrown himself to the ground. The old man shakes himself, turns quickly to the pan on the stove, lifts the lid and breathes in steam. It takes him a couple moments, frowning at the few tiny bubbles forming around the sides, to regain control. If he'd only said yes to Mars' dinner invitation to go out to eat, they would've been polite. They've always been okay in public, and maybe they'd already be seated at some Mexican restaurant, the waitress scribbling down their order.

The food would come out pronto and they'd eat, both of them keeping their mouths full, and they'd be paying the bill in a half hour or so. Mars would drop him back home and Gus would tell him "don't bother coming in" and off the kid would go. But none of that is possible now. He should've known.

Mars moves around the kitchen, finally settling against the counter, drinking his wine, blocking the two packages of Mac and Cheese. He clears his throat, says, "Did Sybil ever hear from that woman with the two kids?"

"Not that she's ever said." He nudges Mars aside to get to the boxes. Rips off their cardboard tops.

"Where'd she take off to?"

"I don't know. Back to her mother, I guess."

"I think Sybil said she didn't have a mother."

"Then why're you asking me?"

"I'm just making conversation."

Gus lifts the lid of the water again, but it's still not boiling. Spots his own glass of wine, takes a long deep drink, thinks happy damn birthday to me.

There's an awkward silence, then Mars asks, "Her husband ever show up?"

"What're all these questions? You got a thing for her?"

"No. No. Just curious. Seems like she had a tough go of it is all."

"He showed up, asked where his wife was, and when nobody knew, he left to look for her."

"Okay, sorry. I just thought it was strange the way she took off without saying good-bye to anyone."

Gus checks the water. Almost there. Good enough. He dumps in both packs of noodles and stirs it.

"So Dad," says Mars, his voice a little sly. "What'll you do when Sybil sells the bungalows?"

"She'll never sell."

"Mrs. Shane is pretty certain she will. She says she'll help you find a better place, same rent."

"I don't wanna move." Gus glances at the clock over the stove. Too early for *Wheel*.

"But what if you have to?"

"What are you getting at, Mars?"

Mars holds up his hands, palms out. "Just saying, Dad, that Mrs. Shane doesn't want anyone to feel displaced."

"Displaced?"

"That's what she said. She wants to be fair. Which is why I'm giving you a heads up. Since she's my boss, you have an in: *me*. My birthday present to you."

"You're my 'in'? For what?"

"Whatever you want. A new place, a better place. Maybe closer to downtown."

"What about the other tenants?"

"She's happy to help them too. She wants everything to go smooth as silk."

Gus gives his son a hard look, turns away, back to the water and the macaroni boiling over and hissing on the stove. "I bet she does."

Thursday, 20th March 2014

Schöne Grüße aus Tirol

by Sally–Anne Macomber

To: Milton Flaxmill, Red Cow Publishing
From: Trudy Polaris
Date: March 20, 2014 10:03 a.m.
Re: Nuclear Fission in the Pyrénées

Liebe Milton,

Greetings from Tirol (or Tyrol)!

How's the editing proceeding with *Nuclear Fission in the Pyrénées*? I'm glad it has such a methodical and tireless editor working on it. I raise *ein Stein Bier* to you!

BTW I was thinking, maybe you might want some assistance, just to speed the editing up a little, because it's taking a little longer than it would normally, probably because summer has hit you early and that red pen can get a little slippy and slidey all over the page.

Once the cows are milked here in our Tyrolean hideaway each morning and I slap them on the rump and put them back in their stalls, I spend the rest of the day twiddling my thumbs, really, and I'd just as soon spend it on something intellectual and hands–on.

I wouldn't even charge you the regular fee.

The spring flowers will soon be here and it's a magical time, so the cowherds tell me in their fractured English. And the fresh mountain air will put hair on your chest too, as a Tyrolean saying goes.

And there's a synergy here with the *cows* outside and you working for Red *Cow* Publishing.

The maître−d' at the Gasthof Traube in Hopfgarten im Brixental asked after you just last night and is looking forward to showing you the town. (He mentioned you'd met once at a Rotary convention in New Guadalcanal.) A local tourist guide says the Traube's a great place 'where you can try meals such as schnitzel, strudel or noodles'. And the town 'also has a renowned church with a wonderful ceiling'. So there's a lot to do here when you down your red editing pen.

The nearest airport is Langkampfen Airport in Kufstein, which is only 30 minutes drive away but there are quite a few heliports which are a bit closer. So there are loads of ways you can get here. Maybe even the local bus would drop you off.

Just let me know the best address to send your ticket to. Or would it be better to download one and email it? Whatever's easiest.

Looking forward to seeing you and getting down to work on the book. I always enjoy being part of a team!

Auf Wiedersehen!

Trudy

Friday, 21st March 2014

Candles

by Mandy Nicol

I'm trying on dresses, deciding what to wear to Tom and Ellie's wedding tomorrow.

I get a lot of wedding invitations. Months of intimate contact seem to compel a bride to invite the lonely little dressmaker.

Usually I decline.

I wish I had declined this one.

Mum told me I'd be mad to go so of course I sent an acceptance straight away. She thought I was mad to make Ellie's dress, too.

Mum thinks I still hold a candle for Tom.

Tom would have thought he was doing a good thing, suggesting Ellie get me to make her dress. Good for my business, he'd have thought, without considering the awkwardness. We had both wanted to stay mates, hadn't we?

I had expected to get at least one chance to stab Ellie with a dressmaking pin. Turned out she's a sweet, uncomplicated girl who I can't help but like. I can see how she turned footloose Tom into marriageable Tom.

I take off my green dress, the emerald green that mirrors my eyes, according to Tom. I'll wear the boring beige instead.

Dreaming

by Margaret Bingel

Ned is dreaming about the dogs again. Purple and floppy−eared beagles bounding through fields of pure plaid, with a pale clock bleeding from the sky, melting with the solid blocks of ice Ned thinks are clouds. He watches the dogs while they yip and yelp, sniffing each others' asses and then, recognizing their smell, as they sit on the grass, or at least what Ned is pretty sure is grass.

Ned doesn't know he's been dreaming any of this. For the past two months, he thinks he has been awake. Everything makes sense to him in this place: animals outside, the sun in the sky, even himself barefoot. Ned is at peace, and in no rush to leave.

I love it here, he thinks. Why would I ever leave?

The ice shatters with every hour of the sun−clock, always cracking but never hailing down and hurting Ned or the dogs. But it isn't the threat of death or lack of pain that puts Ned's mind at ease: the hands on the clock don't move. Time Stands Still.

Ned sits down, running his hand over the tartan grass. The fact it is plaid does not bother him, mostly because he's tired from wearing tight shoes all day and needs to take a load off his feet. Breathing in the smell of rosemary and forget−me−nots, he focuses on the dogs.

As he watches the beagles, now panting on their purple backs, their bright yellow eyes drooping in their faces just like the sun dripping in the sky, their chests rise and fall so slowly, like they are as unperturbed by the lack of time as he is. Maybe I should be like that too, Ned thinks, opening his tuxedo jacket and loosening his bow—tie. Maybe I should be more like a dog.

Maybe I should get a dog instead of a gun.

Ned's hand grabs a clump of grass. Why do I want a gun? When did I get a gun?

I never got a gun, he remembers. I never made it to the store.

Suddenly, the clock hands move, at first like paddling through pudding, then faster, like snakes in sand rippling the sky. Faster and faster the clock moves time forward and all of Ned's memories return to him. Ned remembers walking out the door, and seeing two beautiful women, then tripping over ice and then

. . .

Ned tries to remember what happens next, but all he sees is emptiness. He focuses on the beagles and they are breathing faster now, in quick gasps, and their colors change to a royal purple, then ashes—of—rose, then anemic pink. Their eyes, now closed, move rapidly under their eyelids, until one of them, the fatter of the two, opens its eyes and looks Ned right in his.

I fell down and hit my head, remembers Ned.

Nora grabs her son's hand and says, "Bye, Boy." She feels a squeeze back. She grabs his other hand and, feeling her son's grip, "Ned," she whispers, her voice choking with tears. She shakes her head.

"Boy, wake up."

Ned opens his eyes and, unfocused, stares at the hospital ceiling.

Sunday, 23rd March 2014

Big Words

by Darryl Price

This day does not deserve its own paragraph.

So I wonder what makes a tree such a good companion when you're out walking alone in the universe?

At least clouds keep their distance.

I wish I could shrink myself down to the size of a blade of grass.

Then nobody could find me.

No one is looking for me that I know of.

But inside the tall blades I'd be like buried alive.

Her enormous green eyes were hazel just like some kind of spin art.

I hate green sometimes, well right now I do I think.

But not really.

What's the point of hating a color?

Hate is useless.

Pretty useless.

The only useful thing is air.

Air and sunshine make a good combination.

I want to go home.

I have no idea where that is.

Instead of shrinking I've enlarged to the size of a house, I'm towering like a tree myself.

I'm standing on top of the earth.

I'm floating off into outer space.

I am my own rocketship.

The heels of my sneakers are spitting plumes of real fire.

I know there's something I'm not supposed to care about any more, but I can't remember what it is.

It hurts too much.

Oh yeah.

This stupid day.

The wind makes more of a pissed off noise than me.

Cars are big dumb animals chasing each other.

I think I think too much.

Another Man

by Teresa Burns Gunther

A moth, wings wide, rests in the globe of the ceiling light. A quitter. Rachel, on her back in her closet, resolves to clean it. The crisp sleeves of blouses and jackets point down at her from their hangers. Normally cleaning gives her satisfaction, but today she's stalled out. Her father is coming.

March is the month she'd set aside on New Year's Eve to purge her house and life of the old and unwanted. It's already March 24th, only seven days left. Her father, Peter Stoddart, theater director – or *theatre* as he insists on misspelling – is a tall, heavy man, handsome in a square–jawed and exuberant way. Life on his planet is an endless E–ticket ride and Rachel knows he sees her as the sorry slob who opted to do the sweeping up.

"The IRS?" he'd asked, incredulous when she'd finished her joint law degree and masters in taxation. "You have gifts. You could have been a concert pianist."

She drums her fingers into the floor regretting taking the day off. It's a busy time at work at the IRS – April 15th is 22 days away. Her phone buzzes with a calendar alert: *Dad. 30 minutes.*

She scrambles up, alarmed. How could it be 11:00? She is not a woman who loses track of time or leaves things unfinished. She is never late. Hurrying to the shower, Rachel nearly trips over Stella, who is used to Rachel's bursts of business and lays on the floor, her lovely head on her paws.

During college, her father questioned her about her degree in math, claiming it boring work for narrow minds. "I like numbers," she'd explained. Numbers are constant, no drama, they embody fidelity. She wonders if there could be another father–daughter combo as mismatched as hers. She's always imagined she'd marry a man who might meet her father head on, bowl him over. But life so far has diverged from her plans for finding a suitable man.

Her father phoned the week before to say he was flying into "Frisco" on the 24th and wanted to see her. She kicks herself for failing to deflect him; she's usually good at putting people off, without even trying. She quickly dries her hair then brushes her teeth, steps 4 and 5 in her morning 10–step–rise–and–shine routine. Her phone buzzes again. *Dad. 15 minutes.*

She settles on a pair of pressed jeans, a turtleneck and scarf that aren't trying too hard, simply making an effort. After slipping into boots she dashes through her apartment, lining up couch cushions, picking a twist of lint off the floor. The large old–fashioned school clock on the wall ticks the remaining 240 seconds, 239, 238 ... She turns the radio to the A's pregame show; the standings and stats fill the room, relaxing her.

He's late. Six minutes. She sits on her leather sofa and stares out at the fog–shrouded skyline. Eleven minutes. Stella curls on her bed watching. "He's coming," Rachel tells her. "And you have my permission to bite."

When her doorbell buzzes she jumps. Stella leaps from her bed, barking as she races to the door. "Good girl!" Rachel smooths Stella's fur standing stiff along her spine. Through the fisheye Rachel is surprised to see an old man, bald. It takes her a moment to recognize her father. She grips Stella's collar and opens the door.

"Rachel!" His arms open wide. Stella growls. He steps back. "Jesus. It that a wolf?"

"Yes," she tells her father though Stella's really a mix of Alsatian, Shepherd and Ridgeback. "This is my father, Stella. I guess he doesn't approve of you, either."

His jeans need pressing; his leather jacket is as worn as his face.

"Do you want to come in?"

"Do you think it's safe?" he asks in his stage voice.

Rachel opens the door wide and orders Stella to bed. Her father stands in the hall, his suitcase beside him. The light from the window is not kind to him.

"You don't look so good," she tells him. "What happened to your hair?"

"Okay." His smile wavers. "Thanks for that." His eyes survey her spotless, symmetrical living room. "Nice place," he says. "How long have you been here?"

"Five years. So nice of you to drop by."

"C'mon, Rach." He drops his chin and gives her an impish smile that works on most women. "Let's have a nice visit." Stella growls and he eyes her warily. "Maybe we could go out for lunch."

"I had a large breakfast," Rachel says, annoyed at her heart's racing betrayal. "Stella and I took a long run."

"Okay. How about a short walk and a quick drink?" He grins, hands in his pockets, like life is easy.

Rachel looks at her watch and raises her brows, though a scotch is tempting. He seems shorter, his middle wider, as if life has pressed down on him, hard. She suggests the coffee house on the corner.

As they walk Peter fills the air with his hands and his chatter about his new season, offering her tickets, inviting her to New York. He greets the neighbors: the cadaverous marathon man from down the street, and the Aussies next door who look surprised that Rachel is related to such a friendly, exuberant man.

§

The windows of Kaffeine's are steamy from the crowd and hot coffee. Her father rubs his hands together and asks, "So, are the numbers behaving at the IRS?"

"What do you want?" she asks, a mug of black coffee cupped in her hands.

He stirs cream then one, two, three large teaspoons of sugar into his coffee.

She looks pointedly at the belly bulge above his belt. "That explains a lot."

"Rachel. Could you try, for once, to give me a break?" He shakes his head.

"Okay. What do you want?" Rachel asks again.

"To see you."

"And?"

He sits back in his chair and studies her. "You really look great," he says.

Rachel waits.

"I thought I might stay for a little while, spend some time together. Just us two."

"We two."

He closes his eyes for a moment. "I have a month before the new season gets underway and ..."

Is he suggesting he stay with her? Rachel hasn't had a roommate since her first semester in college. Before he gets to his punch line: another new wife, short on cash, she says, "My landlord won't allow it."

He looks confused. "I thought you owned your place."

"I do. I'm the landlord and the CC&Rs clearly state: no multiple tenancies."

"Is that why you don't marry?"

She considers this, hating to be reminded. "Let's say it's not on my bucket list."

"Is that my fault, too?"

She pushes her coffee away; it's lukewarm and she likes it hot. "I do best on my own."

A waiter appears, disrupting the awkward silence. She shivers at his mutilated earlobes stretched wide with a metal wheel. He tops up their cups and deposits a large chocolate croissant before Peter. Rachel cringes; she hates excess. Her mother indulged him everything, doting and adoring, always his riveted audience, something he must have found irresistible, at first. Now her beautiful mother is in a facility, high-quality care for the demented, and still believes Peter is her husband.

"Do you ever see her?"

"Your mother? I try," he says, the corners of his mouth turn down.

"Do you need money, Peter?" He wants to be called Dad, but she told him years before that "Dad" was a nickname reserved for men who parent.

"No! Of course not, I just want to spend time with my little girl."

Her mother withered after he left them. Rachel was six. Her mother never went to college, had never been told she could be someone else, someone great. At least Peter had given Rachel that.

"Aren't you old for a midlife crisis?" she asks. He's 64. His shoulders drop and for once she regrets the zinger. She avoids his eye. She is so much better with numbers.

He turns at the sound of an ambulance, siren screeching, closing in. His eyes follow the blurred red lights across the steamy windows and in that moment his face, naked of manufactured élan, reveals him. He's lonely! She'd never imagined it possible; his life has always been crowded, standing room only.

He takes a bite of his croissant. His hunger is unbearable to watch.

Tuesday, 25th March 2014

Morgana Malone and the Mystery of the Opium Den

by Matt Potter

Mary Agnes flicks crust from the edge of her mouth with her finger and sits back into the armchair. Tucking in her triple chin, she looks at me and says, "Doesn't she, Morgana?"

In the mirror, I see tears welling in Zebadie's eyes.

(Zebadie's ex–co–star Virginella Vox pulled out last week, due to a Botox overdose, so I'm the lone bridesmaid now.)

Zebadie, blonde nest piled on her head, stands in front of the three–way mirror looking at her own reflection. Poured into a sateen wedding gown that's somehow off–the–shoulder *and* plunging to her navel, it also has a giant hood that I think, in its more gymnastic moments, might double as a train.

A tear rolls down Zebadie's cheek. She turns to look at Mary Agnes, her little teeth flashing, and Mary Agnes looks at me so Zebadie looks at me and then looks back at Mary Agnes. I don't know who to look at, so I stare in the mirror, at the widening grey–and–brown strip showing through my dyed–orange hair.

"Like I said," and fingers drumming on the worn velvet armrest Mary Agnes repeats her pronouncement: "You look like a whore."

I catch Zebadie's eyes again in the mirror. Her shoulders sag, and she looks like a helpless bunny – Playboy bunny; rabbit–

caught—in—the—headlights bunny; victim of someone's cruel joke bunny – so I pipe up: "You mean professionally or do you mean personally?"

"All I said is," Zebadie whispers, the fabric flowers she holds in her hand – the *test bouquet* as the bridal shop assistant told us – jiggling as she shakes, "my right side is better so when we're standing at the altar thing I want to have my right side closer to the cameras and the audience."

There's no denying it, with her three and a half boob jobs, Zebadie's right side certainly creates a larger impression.

Mary Agnes raises an eyebrow.

"This is *my* wedding, Mum, may I remind you," Zebadie says.

Mary Agnes pulls herself up in her seat. Her chins wobble in time with the flowers shaking in Zebadie's hands. "I didn't come here to be insulted, Melissa," – Melissa is Zebadie's real name – "especially when I'm doing you a favour." Mary Agnes slumps back into the chair. "I don't care which side anyone sees as long as it's covered up!"

Zebadie throws the test bouquet on the floor at her mother's feet. The flowers lie squashed and faded, but actually, look quasi—tasteful against Mary Agnes's red diamante—studded wedgies with velvet bows across the toes.

"I should have gone bowling instead," Mary Agnes continues, now waving her flabby arms and jabbing the air with her index finger, like a rapper. "It's the inter—zonal finals for the late Tuesday afternoon Mini—League. But no, you're getting married – again. So I'm helping you choose a wedding dress – again. Looking at you dressed like a slut – again again again!"

I cross my knees and put a finger on my lips, wetting the tip with my tongue. With wobbling chins and heaving bosoms and snapping nerves I can't help but think of Grigor's new nose job and what if Grigor has the same good side as Zebadie? Will they both want their right side to the camera? How will he kiss the bride? When I married Grigor thirteen years ago we had the ceremony in my mother's garden and he kissed me on the mouth afterwards and no one cared about profiles but if they both have the same best side, what will he do after the 'You may now kiss the bride' speech? Kiss her on the back of her head?

And then – I don't know why I say this, but it just flies out of my mouth: "Define *whore?*"

Like I'm the arbiter of all things whorish.

"If you'd loaned me the money I would have been able to get the left one done at the same time, Mum," Zebadie continues, like I'm not in the room. She's sniffing now, four layers of false eyelashes glistening in the yellow bride–to–be light.

I put my hand over my mouth and swallow a yawn.

"And it would have been a tax deduction so I would have paid you back when I got my tax return!" Zebadie says. "So it would have been a win–win–win situation all round," and she points to her mother and then to herself and then to her own left breast.

Reflected in the mirrors, a door opens and a woman of about thirty – tall, long brown hair slicked down and pulled together at the nape of her neck – steps into the bridal sanctum. "Ho–ow's it going?" she asks as our heads snap to watch her. And before there's time for any reply, she looks snivelling Zebadie up and down and says, "Oo–oh! You look gor–orgeous!" The muscles in her face shift upward and her mouth curves into a smile and her voice bounces around the room, but the way her words stretch out isn't convincing: her eyes are wide but their light is extinct.

"You look tired," I say to her in the reflection. She pulls some of the dress fabric away from Zebadie's thigh and, shoulders slumping as she cranes to look, lets it fall. She must have done this thousands of times, I think, to make it look so ... spontaneous.

As she pulls more of the dress fabric away from Zebadie's thigh, like she's prepping Zebadie for a fashion shoot or a cakestand, I see her name badge. *Kylie Jay's World of Dream Weddings*, it says, in sparkly silver, and below that, *Hi, I'm Conradine*. But the sparkly silver is scratched, like it was caught on the bottom of her shoe as she walked across cement.

Conradine folds her arms under her breasts, and looks Zebadie up and down again, this time like she's a mannequin in a ... I don't know, a porn bridal shoot.

Zebadie turns to look in the mirror. She flicks out the bottom – or the crown – of the draping hood, and looks at her own bottom in the reflection.

"It's exci−i−ting, isn't it?" Conradine says, watching Zebadie in the mirror looking at her bottom. And as we watch her, Conradine unfolds her arms, laces her fingers together, locks her elbows, and stretching her palms outward, cracks her knuckles. "Ste−epping off into the re−est of your li−ife."

"Stepping in front of a runaway train!" says Mary Agnes.

"Grigor owns a Porsche, Mum!" Zebadie snaps. Like she's saying, *Grigor's developed the patent for world peace, Mum*. Or, *Grigor really loves me for the person I am inside*.

"Hmmm," says Mary Agnes, and shifts her flobbing arms on the worn velvet. We wait for the rest of her retort, but her lips are pursed.

"So, do you thi−ink you'll take it?" Conradine pipes up. "Because it looks one hu−undred percent stu−unning on you, you have ju−u−ust the fi−igure for it."

I watch Conradine's jaw extend and snap to get around those vowels. Maybe talking like that stops her from growing completely bored.

Zebadie shakes her head, and looks downcast at the hem gracing the floor. "I was really looking for something more 50's," she sniffs, the fussy customer again. "A bit more velour. A bit more glam. A bit more shinier. And I don't like the hood."

"We can always take the hood off," says Conradine.

"No, I want it bigger," Zebadie says.

"Were hoods that big in the 50's?" I ask. (I don't know why I do this, the conversation draws me in and words fly out of my mouth.) Now all eyes are on me. "I mean, big as in popular."

"Oh ye—es," says Conradine. "It was the e—e—era of the hood. The hood was derigeu—eu—eur in the 50's. It was only later that pe—eople stopped wea—earing them. When I think hoo—oods I always think 50's. Hoo—oods. Fi—if—ties. Fi—if—ties. Hoo—oods. Hoo—oods. Fi—if—ties. Fi—if—ties. Hoo—oods."

I take it back. I don't think she's staving off boredom with her elongated vowels and snapping jaw. I think she's on laudunum.

The sun blazes deep in the western sky and we're standing by the kerb waiting for Grigor to screech up in his Porsche and drive us all to dinner at a new seafood restaurant right on the wharf at Port Adelaide called *Scabs*. ("I've cancelled all my patients," he told us, as he helped us into a taxi earlier this afternoon. "I can't solve people's deep psychological problems *and* escort them to and from the reception desk at the same time.")

Conradine stands around the corner, foot flat against the brick wall behind her, smoking a cigarette. Her shoulders are relaxed and her eyes are steady. Maybe it's just serving customers inside *Kylie Jay's World of Dream Weddings* that makes her sound like she works inside a centrifuge.

I turn to look at the rush hour traffic. I don't know how we'll all fit in Grigor's Porsche. I remember from the time I mistakenly fucked Grigor inside it, there's not a lot of room in the back seat of a Porsche. The jaws of life would have a hard time extracting anyone from that thing.

Though if Grigor skids into the *Scabs* car park and the Porsche spins off the wharf and we all crash into the water, I plan to grab on to Zebadie's right airbag and not let go. That should keep me afloat 'til the Water Rescue Squad arrives.

Shot

by Gary Percesepe

This happened in Saint Louis. I was a graduate student, and a regular at a half dozen bars. I managed to fail my language examination in German, then French, a language I had studied since seventh grade. By this time I was meeting students after class in bars. The students were female, Catholic, and underage. I made $550 a month as a Teaching Assistant. Rent was $225. Jobs in my field were non-existent. What I did next is that I fucked one of my students, then fucked another.

The first girl was named Ann and the second one I don't remember.

Ann was trying to stop smoking. She sang along to the radio in my rusted Triumph Spitfire. It was winter and I had the top up and the heater blasting. She wore a tartan skirt with a kilt pin and red knee socks. The skirt rode high up her waist and she twitched and sang off key. She was drunk and I was well on the way. Her hair was dark and shiny and she wore one pink barrette, which kept slipping out of her hair.

In class, she tracked my movements. She sat in the second row, just to my right. I smoked in class, which was illegal even for the Jesuits, and came to class half lit after three beers and whiskey shots at Humphrey's bar. Ann liked that I smoked, and teased me about the way I held a cigarette like a joint. Word was out among the undergraduates about my teaching. Student evaluations were among the best in the department, and my classes always closed early. Ann told her parents that she was staying overnight with a friend in West County. From the SLU Library, she called a friend in Ballwin to make sure she had cover. Then she took my hand and walked me out of the library and into my car. She was nineteen with good ID. She set the radio to a station I never used.

We made our way to Rollo, Missouri, where we hooked up with a few of her friends who attended engineering school. Ann made me stop at a grocery store in town where she bought a toothbrush and toothpaste. She told me she hated brushing her teeth with her fingers after a night out. She pulled me into a long sloppy kiss when we stalled in the checkout line. Her small breasts pressed against my chest. She jammed her hand into the back pockets of my Levis and held on.

We got back in the Triumph and drove to a dive bar. Kicking aside some empty longnecks, I jumped the accelerator. Ann lit another cigarette.

Tom Petty and the Heartbreakers wailed *American Girl.* Her friends looked at me, hard. Ann said, "He's a great teacher." I wanted to smile. She looked over and said, "You're a bad guy, you know that?"

We ended up at some guy's house. There was a single bed and we fell into it. I pawed at her. She pushed my hands away and said, "Mmmm, later, I'm sleepy." Ann was too drunk to fuck, so I watched her sleep for two hours. Her small chest rose and fell.

I lit a cigarette and checked my watch. The watch was a high school graduation present, with hands that glowed in the dark. Ann's eyes were shuttered black buttons. She hadn't removed her makeup or brushed her teeth. I parted her lips with my finger and ran it along her teeth until she sucked it. She moaned and turned over. Her pale arms sprawled behind her like a baby seal. Her body took little space on the bed. I felt like a giant. The kilt pin was still fastened to her pretty skirt. I peeled off her knee socks, one at a time and placed them carefully on the hardwood floor. The bed had a small patchwork quilt. I pulled the quilt up over her hips.

After the second hour I pulled the quilt off. I pushed her skirt aside and looked at her plump white thigh. She was small but finely calibrated in that way petite women have, that can drive you crazy if you let it; everything made to scale but fully operational. Her thighs narrowed into runner's calves. I kissed the back of her knees, traced her tendons with my tongue and got as far as her feet, which had red lint between the warm toes.

Ann got up to pee. I watched her go and then she was back. She criss—crossed her arms to remove her sweater. Off came the black bra. The palest nipples, I could barely see them. Her doll's eyes were sightless. I liked how the black bra looked against her white skin, but then the bra was off and tossed to the floor with the socks. She left the skirt on, but reached down with two fingers and twisted her panties aside. "Have at it," she said.

The next night I was at Tom's Bar & Grill. Stephanie wasn't a student. She explained that she was an event coordinator. I bought cocaine from a guy I knew at the bar and told Stephanie. Her sweater smelled of cigarette smoke and White Shoulders perfume. She was working this event, she said, but we'd get together later. I nodded. Stephanie was five ten in strappy heels with long straight hair, a blonde, and her voice was whiskey and soda. Some guy saw the way she looked at me and said, "Sure, her shit don't stink." I turned away toward the wall. Where I watched her in the big mirror Tom had mounted above the bar. The liquor bottles stood like soldiers. Stephanie caught me looking and smiled. Her teeth were white and even and she was tan under all that blonde. She was pretty and slightly used, and I mouthed at her into the mirror, "Sure, I'll see you later."

But I did the rest of my drugs and then poppers and my nerves were jangling and time sped and then slowed, and I nursed a pint and grew tired of waiting for her. Just before leaving I saw her come out of the bathroom, her heels off and slung over her shoulder. She still had a full eight inches over Ann. I told her I couldn't wait for her anymore. She said, "You seem angry," and I said, "No, not angry, just tired of waiting." I left her there and went out to my car.

I went back a week later, and the week after that, and she wasn't there. I asked Tom whatever happened to Stephanie? The leggy blonde with the voice? Tom looked at me (I was a regular) and said, "Stephanie? I don't know any Stephanie, sorry."

Ann struggled to write an analytic paper on Descartes' *Meditations on First Philosophy*. She couldn't understand the Pakistani guy in the writing help room, so she climbed three flights to my dingy office. I sat with her under blinking fluorescent lights, diagramming sentences. Multiple choice threw her, too. Ditto Venn diagrams and Aristotelian logic. We took a cigarette break and walked into the weak Saint Louis sunlight down by the river. She told me she had had twelve years of Catholic school and attended mass until she was sixteen. Then one Sunday, standing in line for communion, she saw a girl her age wearing a T-shirt that said "I love my pussy." Then that was that.

Oh, I liked her.

These were years I counted as lost. Soon I would be married, though I couldn't have known it at the time. Waking up, married, I would think I heard someone crying, then rush through the house, remembering. Outside, bright moonlight on concrete.

I held on and finished my dissertation but there were still no jobs in my field. The teaching continued for a while. I gave up trying to find Stephanie. It was as if she never existed.

There were other students, none I liked as well as Ann. But she was right, I was a bad guy.

The day Reagan got shot I was at Tom's, drinking. The bar exploded in applause. Dan Rather was on the CBS news, remembering dead presidents. Dealy Plaza. This was a bar where guys handed over their paychecks, fifty cent beers the norm. The TAs would huddle together and try not to make eye contact with the regulars. When Dan Rather announced that the president was going to be OK, the bar groaned. One guy threw beer at the TV. A fight broke out. I left the bar and called Ann at her parent's house in Ballwin, but she wasn't home.

Someone once told me, or maybe it was a poet, that marrying is like throwing a baby up in the air, the baby happy and gurgling, and then throwing it higher till it hits the ceiling, jarring the bulb loose, and it goes out as the baby starts down.

I tried to find Ann on the Internet, which led me to idiotic sites like "My Life," which is a joke in itself, right? All I could come up with was her name, her age, and her city. She hadn't moved. I could have paid money to discover more. She'd be twice as old as the girls I see now, in bars, and yeah, in class. More than twice as old.

It'd been late March, all those years ago, when I made that trip to Rollo with Ann in my Triumph. Now it's March again, the month I managed to finish my dissertation, the year after I had Ann in class. I received my doctoral hood the following May. I saw Ann walking to class one day, before I left St. Louis for good, and nodded to her, but she didn't know me, or pretended not to. I taught Maimonides in those days, *The Consolation of Philosophy*, but there didn't seem to be any. Women were my consolation, but even then, every day that passed seemed an assault on a flimsy castle.

There is a time after what comes after one is young, and this is that time. There is a time after that, and I'm headed to it, unsteadily. You tell yourself it will get better, and that joy is aligning yourself with what is most real, and the moments of self—soothing arrive when you say don't cry, I'll get you something better. And you hope for whatever hope is for.

I gave Ann a "B" in my course and that's a pity, really, because she tried so hard.

Samford gets a rectal exam

by Nathaniel Tower

Samford is waiting in the office of the proctologist. He is nervous, not because he doesn't want to be anally probed (he doesn't want it, but that's not why he's nervous), but because he's worried that this proctologist is some sort of government spy. He is fairly certain that everyone is a government spy.

Samford has been fornicating with his clone–friend Sarah almost every day for a month. After the first shag, she didn't return for a few days, but she eventually had to get her purse back. Samford never bothered asking about the brochure. He put it in the nightstand underneath the condoms, which he doesn't need to use because she apparently can't be impregnated. Sarah is one of the non–fertile clones, a sort of test specimen. There are several government agencies searching for her, but somehow they can't find her even though she does absolutely nothing to hide herself. Samford is afraid that his apartment is bugged, that one day several government agents will storm inside his house and arrest him for harboring a terrorist clone. They'll throw him in jail forever and perform evil tests on him. In spite of these fears, he still lets Sarah screw his brains out every night. Her moans are the only thing that comforts him, the only thing that makes him feel like a real human. He knows the irony of it all.

Samford thinks of all this as he flips through a copy of *People*. The issue mentions nothing of the clones. Sarah has told him that at least one-quarter of the population now consists of clones, just like her. Well, better than her, she says. Not likely, thinks Samford. He knows without doubt that he is in love with her. Every piece of her is perfect, including her scrumptious ass, which now has far less jiggle in it thanks to the hours and hours of sex. He is glad she is incapable of procreating and that he never has to worry about the menstruation that plagues so many couples. Sarah never has mood swings, and she's always ready to fuck.

Samford is flipping a page in *People* when a nurse calls his name. They are ready to see him. He stands and tosses the *People* on the chair. The nurse gives him a *you-fucking-slob-now-I-have-to-pick-that-up* glance. Samford ignores her annoyance and starts thinking about the pain in the ass he is about to get. It's the first time he's thought about it. He's had this date, March 27th, circled on his calendar for over two weeks, and he's just now realizing what exactly is about to happen. It shouldn't be too bad, since Sarah spreads his cheeks open and shines her phone into his hole every night. "I just can't get a good enough look," she always says.

Samford is taken to Room 3C. He doesn't know why it is labeled as such. He sees no 2C and no 3B. There is no reason to have a 3C. The room is far too cold and his skin looks speckled in the unnatural light. He doesn't criticize the light for being unnatural. He may be unnatural himself. He's hoping the proctologist can shed some light on this.

A nurse comes in and takes his blood pressure. 120 over 70. "Is that normal for you?" she asks. Samford says he thinks so, although he isn't sure when his blood pressure was last checked.

"You must have a very healthy lifestyle," she says before leaving.

He doesn't stop her to tell her that all he does is sit around his house, eating chili mac and reading about government clone conspiracies while waiting for Sarah to come home and fuck him. He has no idea what Sarah does all day, but he is sure it is much more productive than what he does. Maybe she even does something that pays the bills. It doesn't really matter to him. As long as each day ends with sex. Although he often worries that he might be a clone, sometimes he is convinced that he must not be because of how horny he is. Even with the nightly fornications, sometimes amounting up to four or five orgasms, he still finds himself jerking off three or four times a day, often to the website www.clonedbitches.com, which is the only porn site he has ever subscribed to. The bitches are furious with their sex, but he doesn't find them as sexy as Sarah. If she ever agreed to do a video with him, he'd stop watching these crappy videos. At least that's what he tells himself.

Samford also finds at least five hours a day for couch napping, often with videos from the Cloned Bitches website streaming on his TV. Sometimes, he wakes up and wonders who pays for his internet. He hasn't paid for anything for as long as he can remember.

The door smacks open against the wall and the doctor barges in. Samford wonders why he doesn't knock first. Then he realizes it doesn't matter. This man is about to be in his ass anyway.

"So how can I help you today?" the doctor says. Samford wonders if the doctor just sticks his finger up butts all day. Surely he must do something else during the eight hours he spends at the office, minus the hour for lunch and the other hours when he sits in his office doing nothing.

"I need a rectal exam."

"Of course you do. That's all you people ever want."

Samford wonders if the doctor is trying to be funny. Maybe this is an icebreaker, a way of getting to know each other before the intimate deed.

"Can we just get this over with?" Samford asks.

"Fine. Drop your pants and bend over on the table."

Samford has seen many Cloned Bitches in this same position. He knows just what to do. He thinks about propping up a leg to give the doctor deeper penetration.

Samford hears the glove snap and the squirt from the bottle of lubricant. He wonders if it's the same type Sarah sometimes rubs on his dick when she wants him to stick it in her ass. He also wonders if she ever poops and how all the wiping would affect the serial number.

"You may feel some slight discomfort," the doctor says, but the finger is in Samford's butt before he can even prepare for the discomfort. It actually isn't uncomfortable at all. It only lasts a few seconds before the finger is out and the glove snaps off.

"Looks fine," the doctor says. "You can pull up now."

"That's it? Don't you want to look up there?"

"Are you fucking serious? What are you, one of those fetish weirdos?"

Samford turns around, but he doesn't pull his pants up. His cock and balls are just hanging there, shriveling up in the cold while he tries to muster the strength to make them look not embarrassing.

"Doc, I need you to look. I think there might be something in there?"

"Don't tell me you are one of those homosexuals who shoves things up your butt. I had these two queers who came in once and –"

"I'm not gay," Samford says. He finds the doctor's speech mildly offensive, but he doesn't blame the doctor. He understands that someone who shoves his hand up butts all day has to do something to reaffirm his love for vaginas.

The doctor frowns, like he's apologizing for his comments. "I didn't mean anything by it. Gay guys are okay."

"Can you please just look? I just want to know if there's anything in there."

Samford thinks about winking, to give the doctor a hint about the serial number. Surely a doctor who touches butts all day knows about this. Samford can't be the only one.

"Okay, I'll have a look. Get back into position."

The doctor opens a drawer and Samford hears him fumble with some tools. Then the snapping glove. Then the squirting lubricant. The doctor doesn't mention the discomfort he may feel this time. As the cold metal shaft slides up his butt and spreads him open, Samford can think only of Sarah and how she has taken a liking to playing with his butthole for a few minutes at the end of each round of sex. A flicker of an erection comes and goes, and then the tool is removed and Samford's butt is back to normal. The glove snaps off.

"Well?" Samford asks as he turns his head, still leaning over the table.

The doctor shakes his head hard. "I didn't see anything. Nothing at all." Then he rushes out of the room without giving Samford a chance to ask anything. Samford's heart starts racing. He knows something is up. The doctor must've seen a serial number up there and is off to report him. He pulls on his pants and bolts out of 3C. He hurries past the receptionist's desk and rushes through the waiting room. On his way out of the building, he starts calling Sarah to tell her what he's done. Then he decides to hang up. He doesn't want to risk losing out on sex tonight.

Friday, 28th March 2014

Reunion

by Kimberlee Smith

My husband Dean hasn't seen me in months, but I get a feeling he will today. Ever since the snakebite, I've developed a constant but slowly intensifying extra sensitivity, a perception as to what might occur in the world. This is something new to me, just since I've been gone. When I mean gone, I mean dead.

Dean's headed out today on a trip with his business partner, Junior Volpe, in that little rusted−out tin can Junior owns and pilots. It's a single−prop Cessna that's older than he is − and that's over half a century of hard living. Junior flies the two of them around the country to "attend to their transactions," as Dean says, in an attempt to sound professionally legitimate in a business that's anything but. What they do is buy and sell deadly snakes on the black market. What they do is illegal. Here in Australia where only native species are legally allowed to exist, it's against the law to keep them as pets.

That goes back to a hard lesson learned when cane toads were imported from Hawaii in the 1930s to deal with the cane beetle bugs eating up all the sugar cane crops. As luck and the Darwinian theory of evolution would have it, the cane toad thrived. And so did the cane beetle. So importing any new species of reptile into Australia was outlawed. There's that little bit of history for you. I learned it all from Dean.

Even though he didn't finish school, he only went up until Year 11, he knows a lot. He has that raw smartness that even some people who go through years of university do not.

What Dean and Junior specialize in are deadly and beautiful snakes. Colorful or killers. What I particularly don't approve of is their brokering endangered species. I observed a little while ago one of their smugglers bringing a stunning and supremely rare San Francisco garter snake back from the United States. The snake's brilliant coloration and striped pattern make it look like a psychedelic rainbow.

The courier had that poor snake sewn up in between two pieces of leather like it was in a sleeping bag and he wore it as a belt to get it from Los Angeles to Sydney. He traveled about eighteen hours with a live animal strung through his belt loops. That particular breed is on the U.S. endangered species list, which makes owning one so desirable, which also means it costs a lot of money. Something like $30,000. That particular type of snake isn't venomous; can't do a thing to you but give you a set of silly little puncture wounds. So it's the perfect creature for a coward to show off.

Dean and Junior have a handful of runners like the guy I just told you about who I never met but I get to know them now like I'm looking through a one-way mirror. Dean and Junior handle all the business within Australia on their own; their employees take the riskier, long-haul international trips.

I know it seems odd there's a thriving underground business in buying and selling exotic snakes, especially in a country known for an abundance of dangerous species, but sure as I'm *here* and you're *there*, it's a fact. Take my word for it, because I've experienced it firsthand. It provided us with a really nice lifestyle. But boy did we pay a price for that.

§

I never met Dean's clients in my life. But ever since that coral snake made a picnic out of my leg and injected enough venom with its fixed fangs to stop my heart for good, I've been privy to much more about who he deals with than I got to know when I was alive. I don't harbor any ill will against the snake, it wasn't doing anything but what nature told it to do. But Dean could have been more careful in keeping them.

With regard to the business end and the people he dealt with, I know Dean was trying to protect me, because the less you know about that kind of business, the better off you are. Now I see who he meets up with, and it's a good thing he never brought them around our home or family. All kinds of shady folks.

There's a man with a skinny little moustache and a jumble of tattoos spreading all down his arms and back, mostly of naked ladies and skulls. He never, ever wears a shirt, but always has on his trucker hat with a cartoon of a bulldog smoking a cigar on it. He's a drug manufacturer, for a living. Cooks up methamphetamine and uses a good amount of it, too. I've watched him smoke it, snort it, and even shoot it between his rotten toes.

Dean has a suspicion but doesn't inquire about the man's business. So now that I can, I followed him back to his house all the way out in Mudgee, and the little building he tells people is a granny flat in the wild bush out back is a filthy drug-cooking factory that looks like it's guaranteed to blow up any second. His littlies are wandering around outside in soiled nappies while their mum screams at them for reasons I can't discern. I wanted to snatch them away, clean them up, tell them they're perfect and not to listen to anyone telling them anything different. It breaks my heart that I saw it all going on and was powerless to do anything about it. Those children are doomed.

Then there's the rotten excuse for a human being who owns a brothel in Parramatta and has his own sisters working as prostitutes. It's not against the law, but that doesn't mean it's right, either. That scum has no qualms with collecting money from his sisters getting banged by married men on their lunch hours, during happy hour, all day and all night long.

The big shot who Dean held onto the pair of coral snakes for has a dominatrix den hidden next to his wine cellar. He keeps the snakes in fancy boxes lining the walls of his pervert palace. He's the man who now owns the snake that bit me. He lives in Rose Bay. Has a mansion on the waterfront with a rock pool and a lovely antique sailboat that once raced in the America's Cup. He's married and his and the wife's children have gone off to university, so now it's just the two of them. His wife travels out of town a lot with her mates for something they call *spa weekends.* They play tennis and get massages and have their nails done. I understand why the wife leaves every so often, given his sexual proclivities that she wants absolutely nothing to do with.

From what I can glean, he brought it up once – waving around a pair of fishnet hose and a ball gag – and that was that. Poor woman fainted cold, hit the floor and got a big old bump on her head. Neither ever brought it up again. The wife's in what you'd say is a classic state of denial. Her absences give him plenty of time to entertain at home. Dean hates that man. He handed off the corals as soon as the man returned from a business trip and never told him what happened to me or with the snakes.

Even though the clients I've found out about come from every conceivable background and lifestyle, what they have in common is the urge to be perceived as badass motherfuckers. They're nothing but weak and insecure. But business is business and Dean has a family to support.

§

A month before baby Etheline was born, Dean spent an afternoon threading together over twenty rattles from snakes he traded, captured, bought, and sold. His is a word−of−mouth business that built steady and fast. Dean has a solid reputation. I'm not saying good, I'm not saying bad. He always delivers the goods he promises his clients.

He wasn't scared of shit until I got bit. And it's not the snakes he's afraid of; it's about his whole world changing in a flash. *His* whole world.

The rattles he fashioned together as the gift for our little girl were from snakes that died in transit or were returned to him because the owners did not have one iota of knowledge how to care for their strange new pets, so the serpents often ended up dying due to overfeeding or lack of or overexposure to heat or light. Dean learned after years of watching his father run a pet shop that specialized in reptiles and birds. He ran the snake business on the side.

People interested in keeping exotic animals are know−it−all tough guys who feel compelled to act as if they know what they're doing and are in control at all times. Dean explains to them like it's a technicality – like he's a carnie regurgitating safety rules for riding a carousel – but he sells fanged, venomous, strangulating snakes with printed out instructions that go something like this: "Feed live rodents but only as directed per your specific breed. Provide fresh, clean water. Keep terrarium locked at all times, except when feeding or cleaning. Maintain a stable temperature consistent with the needs of your particular reptile." Mostly they fuck up.

Dean is unique in his business, like a reputable dog breeder. If something goes wrong, he will take that creature back, dead or alive.

§

I follow Dean mostly. I rarely leave his or our baby's side. When I look down on Etheline, I swear she smiles up at me. I've tried to make contact with Dean, too, but he's been entirely unaware of my presence. Today I'm going to try a little harder.

I'm getting used to my place here in the afterworld. People use the term *afterlife* to describe where I'm at, but let me tell you there's no life here. When it's your time and you arrive, you'll see. It's lonely. There's no one else, just me so far. No angels, no long–lost relatives. I thought maybe I might meet up with my grandmum but no luck yet. I do keep hoping.

I can see Dean, my mum Maybell, and our baby girl who was born right as I died. Baby Etheline was taken from my womb by an emergency C–section. That was the strangest thing, hovering above in spirit watching my own daughter enter the world not five minutes after pronouncing me deceased. Everyone was crying. Even the nurses and the doctors. Terrible tears of pain and some of joy for the baby's survival.

Dean and Maybell take care of the little one, and they do a pretty good job. They trade off, like in shifts. But when one isn't watching the baby, they're drinking hard. Dean likes his beer more than ever; he's up to a six–pack a day when he isn't watching the baby. Maybell splashes gin in her lemon squash. She started that up right after the funeral to numb herself, and she hasn't stopped. Sometimes she puts in more than just a splash. And sometimes she starts at brekkie. They're both just having a hard time coping. I can see that.

§

Dean and Junior are scheduled to make a few different stops on today's trip, which includes a number of stops and is also their biggest day of business ever. They're in Junior's plane, flying out of a mowed down field behind Junior's ranch in Dubbo. They cram four rubber bins filled with snakes into a plane that barely fits two men comfortably. Dean holds an empty metal cash box between his feet. First stop, one bin goes. Cash fills the box. Takeoff. Somewhere outside Adelaide. They've got about half a dozen stops to make at legitimate private airstrips to refuel. Their last stop is outside Perth, and it's windy as hell. They land hard and Dean hits his head, but not bad enough to do anything more than his rubbing it and making some joke. All the snakes are sold, and the moneybox is heavy with bills.

I haven't yet tried to get Dean's attention. I've been waiting for the right moment. But I have been along on the entire journey. Junior all of a sudden pulls a bottle of vodka out from under his seat and takes a long swig. Then he throws that on the floor while the plane is bouncing around in some really wild wind. Dean is drenched in sweat. It's dripping down his temples and his hair is soaked and his shirt is soaked and it's stuck to his chest.

There's a mountain range and a wind farm with about five turbines spinning like crazy a few miles away, but instead of diverting the plane around them, Junior pulls a gun out of his vest and cracks Dean across the face.

Now it's time for me to show up. I take Dean's head in my arms and instead of feeling like a vapor when I've tried to touch him before, he feels solid against me. There's a warm stream of blood dribbling from his ear. His brain is bleeding. He's shaking and the color drains from his face. I put my lips against his cheek and tell him I'm there. His heart races, jolts, and he whispers my name. Over and over. Because I'm finally able to connect with him, neither of us is paying any attention to anything else.

I feel something horrific coming on. Worse than anything before. My energy is on Junior, and he's strapped on a parachute and clutching the moneybox. He hollers in a raspy, evil voice, *fuck you! fuck you!* then punches his window out and dives out of the plane.

Dean is screaming he doesn't know how to fly and I can't do a thing physically to help. But I've been watching Junior fly this thing today and I'm stunned that apparently Dean never paid a lick of attention to how to take over if something were to happen to Junior. He is utterly clueless. Kept his focus on the snake crates, always.

I tell him to hold the yoke with both hands, keep it still and straight. He *can* maneuver the plane around the turbines. I'm doing my damnedest to encourage him, but I am *terrified.* For him, not for me. I tell him to bank around the wind farm, to slowly pull up on the yoke and that will tip the nose down, but he has to do it gradually. The plane will descend steadily under his control. He grips the yoke like he's choking it and his knuckles go white. This mighty windstorm throws the plane every which way, and now it's nose diving. And that's it.

There's an explosion. Fire and metal in a roiling ball of burned flesh and fuel and then nothing identifiable remains. Only smoke, ash, and charred metal.

Off in the distance I see Junior. His parachute knotted up into a blade of the wind turbine's rotor, and he's spinning around, impaled on a blade, like a skewered rag doll. Soon he's shredded into oblivion. Maybell will see it on the news tonight. She will know who it is even before the dead are identified.

The emergency crew can't recover any remains until the gale subsides, because one thing about a turbine is that it stops and goes with the wind. There is no way to control it.

Dean asks me where we are. And all I can communicate is *Together.*

Saturday, 29th March 2014

Winter Weight

by Vanessa Weibler Paris

The Lunch Ladies are crabby today. Even crabbier than usual, since it's the end of the fiscal quarter, which means a mandatory Saturday at work.

The Lunch Ladies are all stabbing their salads. Linda's on her second plastic fork after breaking two tines off the first. Darlene moves her Tupperware a few inches with every forceful pierce. A pink-tinged piece of iceberg, accidentally ejected by someone, plays small sad centerpiece on the round grey laminate.

I'm eating a salad, too. I try to get bites from dish to mouth without them seeing the details: the shreds of cheese, the seeds, the bacon, the beans. The protein. The calories. Anything that might help. My hand, holding the fork, is almost like a flesh-colored fork itself. At my latest doctor's appointment, I got on the scale facing away from the numbers. *Don't tell me,* I wanted to beg the nurse. But I didn't. And she didn't. I heard her inhale sharply after the numbers settled. And then she asked me to please follow her to the exam room.

The Lunch Ladies' meals are watery and insubstantial, pale greens of lettuce and celery and cucumber stuck together with sweet sticky fat-free dressings.

"Celery has negative calories," remarks Barbara, as she does at least once each week. "It takes more energy to chew and digest celery than what's even in it."

It's the same every year. On January 2nd, they all come in with New Year's Resolutions. For a month or so, everything's very cheerful and optimistic and gung–ho. By the end of March, no one's lost much – if any – weight, they're all hungry and tired, and spring break is looming.

I know what comes next: When summer arrives, they've all given up, and resolutions are replaced with the promise of backyard BBQs, burgers and beers.

"We'll start over in the fall," someone will announce, and the rest will agree. And then fall becomes winter, and winter brings holidays, and then it's January 2nd again.

"So does lettuce," adds Dar. "Negative calories. You can practically lose ounces by eating a whole head, if you do it all at once."

At the far table, everyone bursts into laughter, and then a quick hiss hushes them back to whispers. It's the Young Professionals. The ones with bigger cubicles and better titles. The ones with perfect bodies in fitted workwear and shoes that click as they walk. No sad homemade salads for them; it's all takeout. Sushis and schnitzels and souvlakis. Exotic things from fancy food trucks.

At 29, I should be a Young Professional. Instead, I'm the one man among the Lunch Ladies, none under 50. We wear soft–soled comfort shoes that pad slowly through the halls. We all wear oversized clothes – cheap, because we'll save up to buy the real ones soon … once we get to a better size. Once I gain weight, once they lose. Once I look normal. If.

"Don't eat too much," a blonde named Laynie sings out as the Young Professionals stroll by. "Remember there's birthday cake for Brad this afternoon."

We continue crunching until they're gone.

"Goddammit," Linda mutters.

"Goddamn cake," adds Dar, through her teeth.

"Wasn't your birthday last month?" Barbara asks, after a few silent minutes have passed. "Wasn't it, Jim?"

"Not really," I say. "It was the 29th. And there was no 29th."

All my life, I've gotten the question: *Oh, you're a Leap Day baby! How interesting! When do you celebrate? The 28th, or the 1st?*

Whichever is more convenient, I always say, smiling. But that's not true. If it's not a Leap Year, I don't celebrate at all. It doesn't seem right to make myself the center of attention. To make the rest of them look at me, smiling. Pretending to be pleased rather than repulsed.

"We still could've gotten you cake," Linda says, after a pause. She's licking the last bits of sugary dressing from her fork, now down to three tines.

"That's okay," I say. "I don't really like cake anyway."

The Blind Date

by Joanne Jagoda

Anne has the twins drop her off a half hour early for her blind date. She can't stay home another minute. Her stomach has been doing flip–flops all day. Robin is her smartass best on the drive to the restaurant. She shakes her finger at her mother.

"Now Mom, be sure to keep your curfew, no kissing on the first date and call if you're going to be late."

Anne acts like she's annoyed but smiles as she closes the car door. "Very funny. Bye." The twins drove her crazy all day, bubbling over with excitement.

Anne strides in to the grand lobby of the elegant Fairmont Hotel, her head held high, confident she looks good. The lobby is carpeted in a deep burgundy, with mahogany walls, dark green velvet chairs and paisley sofas.

They didn't let up last month until she agreed to try the on–line website they found. Anne looked at different profiles but one stood out, … *retired patent attorney, likes fine dining in San Francisco, wine tasting in the Napa Valley, hiking and traveling.*

When she got up her courage to respond, 'Eric' emailed her back. She was hesitant at first but gave him her phone number. He was charming when he asked her to dinner.

"Anne, let's try *Jupiter,* in the Fairmont lobby. The chef was just awarded two Michelin stars."

"That sounds perfect, Eric." Anne doesn't know one chef from another because Paul was a meat and potatoes guy, and they mostly went to chains.

She finds a velvet armchair hidden by a lush areca palm where she can discreetly watch the front of the restaurant. Well–dressed couples glide by. Hipsters in sport coats and blue jeans and attractive young women in boots, tights and short skirts sit in the lobby sipping cocktails and checking iPhones. Anne picks at her cuticles. *Why does it look so easy for them? I can't remember what it's like to have fun.*

The girls had given her a gift certificate for a makeover for her birthday. She loved her massage, the haircut and sassy red highlights. A makeup artist made her hazel eyes pop, and with blush and plum lipstick, she walked out a new woman. Robin and Cassie went through her closet tossing the baggy clothes, anything black or gray, which was half her stuff. They took her shopping and helped her pick some snazzy new clothes and selected her outfit for tonight; an elegant fitted black pencil skirt with a pretty off white, lacy blouse, a killer belt and high heeled sandals. Early this morning, she went for a manicure and pedicure, bright red. Anne didn't recognize herself in the hall mirror.

Hiding behind greenery, she is as self–conscious as a thirteen–year old going on her first date. Drips of sweat roll down her back. *Great ... I'll have a damp spot on my blouse.* Anne glances at her watch. *He's late. OK ... just three minutes.* The three minutes turn to twenty. She checks her cell but no message. After a half hour, Anne curses under her breath. *I can't believe he stood me up. Maybe he was in an accident. I'm getting a drink.*

She waits another fifteen minutes, then heads to the lobby bar, gets up on a leather stool, figures, *what the hell*, and orders a *Cosmo*. She sips the strong drink but when she checks out couples at small tables laughing and talking, a lump in her throat makes it hard to swallow. In all her fantasies about tonight, she never imagined that her date wouldn't show. He was so friendly, asking her questions about her job and the girls.

Damon Southeby, who has been stalking Anne for the last few months, arrived earlier at the Fairmont and sat in the lobby where he could watch for her. He was surprised she looks so hot – compact and sexy, with a trendy cut and a fetching sprinkle of freckles … much better than she looked two months ago when she was depressed about her fiftieth birthday, as he knew from reading her diary. Damon created 'Eric' for his phony on-line website. Even Eric's voice was distorted with a voice synthesizer. A few keystrokes and Eric Baxter, attorney, existed in the virtual world. A few keystrokes tonight and he'll disappear just as fast.

Ah, so devious, so brilliant. Damon knows he's a cruel bastard but little Anne is part of a much bigger scheme that will net him a huge payday. He watches her expression change from hopeful to glum. Now she's sitting in the bar and he quickly approaches her when an empty seat opens next to her.

"Miss, is this stool taken?"

Anne doesn't answer until she realizes that the gorgeous tall hunk with messy brown hair to his collar, a smile like Robert Redford, and the cutest English accent is speaking to her.

"Uh, no." He takes the empty seat and orders a beer.

"This is a grand hotel," he says turning to her.

"Yes, it is one of the oldest in San Francisco."

"Are you from here?"

Anne can't believe he's talking to her and she blushes because he's checking her out down to her red painted toenails. "No, I was born in Sacramento but I've lived in the Bay Area for years. I take it you're not from here."

"I guess my accent is a giveaway. I'm from a village near London. *David Lewis.* Nice to meet you."

"Hello, I'm uh Anne." She won't tell him her last name no matter how good-looking he is.

"I just moved here four months ago to open the San Francisco branch of my business. We have branches all over the world. Here's my card."

Anne takes his card. *Digital Maneuvers – David Lewis, CEO*, she reads, and places it on the bar.

He grins his best Redford smile. "Miss ... uh, is it 'miss?'"

Her smile is strained. "I'm a widow."

"Ah, well I'm so terribly sorry." Damon gives her a sympathetic look. He says in a quiet voice, "I guess we have that in common. I'm a widower myself."

Anne doesn't know what to say. Then David/Damon stands up.

"Uh, Miss Anne, I have a business meeting now and you might find this forward, but perhaps if you would like to show me some of the sights of this fine city you could call me. You have my card."

David gives a little salute and leaves Anne staring. She gets off the stool shaky from the Cosmo, not quite believing what just happened.

She totters through the lobby on her high–heeled sandals, tempted to take them off and walk barefoot. She asks the bellman to get her a cab.

The cab driver checks her out in the back seat. "Where to Miss?"

She laughs, "Just home. Where else would a slightly drunk fifty–year old mother of teenagers go?" She is silent as the cab speeds from Nob Hill to her home in the Sunset district, the skyscrapers of downtown passing in a blur.

When she opens the door she hears the girls upstairs laughing and playing Maroon Five. Anne calls out, "Rob, Cass, I'm home." Slipping off her sandals, Anne looks at her fancy toes. *What a crazy night.*

The girls hear her and come down the stairs. Cassie blurts, "Mom, you're home already? Was he a *dweeb?*"

Anne opens the Frig door and pulls out cold pizza. She shakes her head. "He didn't show. And never called. I assume he didn't call here either."

"Oh Mom," they say in unison, and Cassie goes to hug her.

Anne puts down the pizza and gives Cassie a squeeze.

"What an *asshole*, Mom."

"Robin do you have to use that language?"

"Well he is and I'm pissed. Mom you looked hot tonight. How could he stand you up?"

"It's really OK. Tonight was a dry run. I promise I'm not giving up. But I did meet some cute guy at the bar from London. He gave me his card … but I'll probably never call him. 'Night kids. I'm getting a headache."

Anne feels badly for the girls who were as excited about tonight as she was. She drags herself upstairs and closes the door to her room. When she takes off her cute new clothes, she lets them fall in a heap on the carpet and puts on her old sweats. She doesn't want to feel sorry for herself. She's done with that.

Across the street sitting in his nondescript Ford, Damon Southeby *or Daniel Lewis* has followed her home. He takes a long sip from a bottle of water watching the lights flicker on in her upstairs bedroom window. He sees her shadow. *There is something sweet and innocent about you Anne Donaldson, and you're very attractive. I'm going to enjoy the perks of this assignment.*

Monday, 31st March 2014

Rinse and Repeat

by h. l. nelson

Dear Diary,

This is how I feel lately:

> *6:02 A.M.: Alarm blares. Abruptly wake. Hit alarm so husband can sleep longer. Stifle urge to hit husband instead. Jump out of bed. Shower. Blow—dry hair. Apply makeup. Put on mom costume. Walk down hall to kids' rooms. Wake them for school. Same thing, Monday through Friday, August through May. Rinse and repeat. This is your life on motherhood.*

Yes, I wrote that. I may have a knack for writing, who knows? What I do know, and hate to admit, is that I never really wanted children. Fuck, I wrote it. I know that sounds terrible. I feel terrible writing it. And this is a really heavy subject for 7:30 on a Monday morning. But, I realized recently it's the truth and I need to admit it to someone or something.

I just want to paint. I'm not one of those women who needs children to fill a void within themselves. The women who, when their kids leave home, wander aimlessly from morning until night, unable to concentrate, work on their hobbies, or keep up with their friendships. While the kids are still at home, they are shells, trying to fill their own voids with ballet, oboe lessons, Kids' Art for Charity events, living vicariously until the day those kids leave. It's sad.

Like all days, this morning I strode into my teens' rooms in turn, exactly 30 minutes after waking, and attempted to gently pat them awake. Dr. Sears suggested this less stressful method. Why I still give a fuck about what Dr. Sears says, I have no idea.

Truth be told, some mornings I feel like slapping the kids awake. Ugh, I'm a terrible mom. But sometimes I despise the little brats. They're typical spoiled, suburban teens who take me and everything they have for granted. Like what happened with Kendra earlier. I suppose it's my own fault. Somewhere deep down, I'm sure I must love being a mom, but I had no idea it would be so hard.

So this morning, Kendra texted me while I was cooking breakfast. The text read: "Cn u gt hollister hoodie frm clset. In shwr." Honestly, I wasn't sure that was even English. Of course, Kendra was in her room when she texted, not the shower. But I still retrieved it for her. It's no wonder they're spoiled. Oh, and I don't even want to write about Kurt. I think he might be doing drugs, but I haven't caught him yet. I ransacked his room and nothing. I still think he's hiding something. Sigh.

You know, I clearly remember being pregnant, like it was yesterday. My ideas about it at first were set by the myth that it's 'a beautiful, life−changing event' and that pregnant women are 'glowing bastions of health'. My pregnancies were indeed life−changing events. I was sick every day. Not just mild nausea, mind you. Daily wracking, heaving vomiting. I lost forty of the fifty pounds I'd gained. Doctor Bailey feared for Kurt's life.

Once we made it through the hellacious pregnancy and Kurt was a newborn, I realized that having a new baby is like giving your number to a drunken stranger in a bar. Both will bug you incessantly at 2 A.M. until you pick up. And will alternate between crying and nursing their drinks all night long. Some say the parent thing gets easier. But as kids age it just gets more complicated. Young girls get periods and cry a lot in the bathroom. Young boys get awkward and also spend a lot of time in the bathroom. Complicated.

As the kids grew up, I vacillated between parenting and self–help books, hoping to get a handle on how the hell to do it better. During upswings, it was the parenting books. Always a new method. Unparenting. You know, the parenting method that suggests it's okay to leave kids in their Superman underwear for days at a time, to let them eat M&M's all day while watching SpongeBob. Unconditional Parenting. This one suggests you shouldn't get angry with your child, that you must remain calm and in control, even if he, demon that he is, is flushing his sister's head in the dirty toilet. Hypnosis Parenting. This one offers no suggestions for situations such as your dog bounding in on one of your hypnosis sessions and your son barking for weeks afterward. It's all bullshit.

On downswings, which happened right after finishing a parenting book, I was on to the self–help ones. *The Secret. Who Moved My Cheese? Awaken the Giant Within.* Books by Dr. Phil. When I read *The Secret*, I meditated for two weeks, envisioned myself as an amazing, loving parent with adoring children and all of the answers. I even wrote out an affirmation and tacked it to my wall. Every morning, I awoke to 'I am the best mom' and started to feel like it was true. Then Kurt told us he had gotten his girlfriend Shelly pregnant and Kendra ran away from home, both in the same week. I was beside myself with guilt and worry. We took care of Kurt's problem, found Kendra and put her in therapy, and I burned that fucking book in the fireplace. Bullshit, bullshit, bullshit.

Sometimes I read romance novels, just for a break. When I was a kid, I swore I would never read those damn things like my stepmom did. I had hated Danielle Steele and loved Stephen King. How things change when we age. We crave sweet, brain–deadening escape.

I've been a SAHM for years, but I dress as if I have a "real" job, as they say. In case anyone reads this and doesn't know, SAHM isn't short for anything kinky. Unfortunately. Stay–At–Home Mom. No wonder someone made it an acronym. It sounds boring. Every time I say it when someone asks what I 'do,' I almost yawn. Even the words "stay–at–home" can't stand alone. They need hyphens between to keep them from falling over in boredom.

"Mom," however, doesn't need any hyphens. It stands alone. Just like I do, since my husband works long lawyer's hours. In this house, "mom" is also synonymous with "slave". I laughed until I cried when I read author Lauren Kessler's blog post: "Being an American mother means you prescribe to this axiom: I am available, at your beck and call, 24/7. Don't even think about what else I might have on my plate or who I am as a person in addition to being your mother. I have no life other than to serve you."

These days I feel less ballsy than my namesake, Joan of Arc. In my younger years, I was more like Joan Jett, going to rock concerts, smoking weed, and sliding myself into leather outfits. The only rock concerts I see now are the ones I drop Kurt off at. Weed, sure – in the backyard. They are always getting into my vegetable garden. Leather outfits – not unless Kendra wants to die young.

Brandon and I haven't done anything kinky with leather in a while. Hell, these days I'm afraid to make a mess on our leather sofa – such a far cry from sex–crazed, twenty–something me. There wasn't an unmessed leather couch in my wake.

I don't think, the way this is going, that I'll put much in this diary like, 'Today, dear diary, I tried a new soufflé and it was just divine. Brandon and the kids delicately ate it all and asked for more. Being the amazing housewife and mother that I am, I had made another and brandished it from the kitchen to a flurry of applause from my loving family.' Fuck. That.

Maybe I'm not cut out for this housewife and mom thing. Maybe I was never meant to have kids. Maybe I should have a large, city studio / apartment with my art up everywhere and a new lover every week. Maybe I should be fucking on large canvasses, covered in paint, with said lovers. Their skin and mine blending colors in never−before−imagined shades, these paintings selling for tens of thousands each. Right. Instead, the food stains on the countertops and on my housewife sweats are blending in never−before−imagined hues, and it's my job to clean it all up. On that happy note, I'm out.

Before I go feel sorry for myself some more, I do have some questions for you. I want to know what happened to my youth? Where did it run off to when I wasn't looking?

And my dreams. I see them so clearly, as if I'm staring at them through bulletproof glass that I will never penetrate. Kurt and Kendra, I love them so much, but, god help me, I always wanted more. And now that I have so much time to myself in the house, I just can't do it. I can't muster the energy and will within myself to pick up a paintbrush, daub on some paint, and go for it. What the fuck is wrong with me? Maybe the moms' group can help. Yeah. I'll call Julie and Robin.

Anne can go fuck herself.

Joan Not−a−Famous−Painter Colderman

Authors

Rachel Ambrose is a twenty–something fiction writer from Connecticut. Her favorite season is winter, she enjoys well–made Manhattans, and she loves Southern fiction. Her work has appeared in *Crack the Spine*, *Exiles Literary Magazine*, and *The Colton Review*. She is currently at work on her second novel and blogs at http://victorywhiskeyjuliet.tumblr.com.

Lynn Beighley is a fiction writer stuck in a technical book writer's body. Her stories often involve deeply flawed characters and the unsatisfying meshing of the virtual and actual world. She has an MFA in Creative Writing and currently has 16 books published.

Margaret Bingel is just a writer, living in Manchester, New Hampshire. She spends her time working at her father's beer store, art modeling, and writing (when she can). She doesn't have a website or a blog yet, but who knows, maybe she'll have one in the future.

Guilie Castillo Oriard is a Mexican writer currently exiled in the island of Curaçao. She misses Mexican food and Mexican *amabilidad*, but the laissez–faire attitude and the beaches of the Caribbean are fair exchange. Plus, the bounty of cultural diversity inspires great culture—clash fiction. Guilie is currently revising and editing her first novel. Her short stories have appeared in *Fiction 365*, *Lady Ink Magazine* and *Pure Slush*. She blogs at http://guilie—castillo—oriard.blogspot.com.

John Wentworth Chapin lives and writes in Baltimore, where he is too frequently starting Project B before finishing Project A. John writes non—fiction as well as fiction. Find him on the web at http://johnwentworthchapin.com.

James Claffey hails from County Westmeath, Ireland, and lives on an avocado ranch in Carpinteria, CA with his family. He is the author of a collection of short fiction, *Blood a Cold Blue*. His website can be found at http://jamesclaffey.com.

Gay Degani has published online and in print including *The Best of Every Day Fiction* editions and her own collection, *Pomegranate Stories*. She is the founder—editor emeritus of EDF's *Flash Fiction Chronicles*, a staff editor at *Smokelong Quarterly*, and blogs at http://wordsinplace.blogspot.com where a list of her work can be found. She's had two stories nominated for Pushcart consideration and won the eleventh Annual Glass Woman Prize for her flash piece, *Something about L.A.*

Michelle Elvy is an editor and writer who has meandered from the shores of the Chesapeake to New Zealand's Bay of Islands. Michelle has published poetry, short stories and non—fiction about travel, faraway places, food, motorcycling, slow travel, the kindness of strangers and raising children in unusual places for numerous literary journals and magazines in the US, Canada, Australasia, the UK and Europe. She edits at *Flash Frontier: An Adventure in Short Fiction* and *Blue Five Notebook*. She can also be found regularly at *Awkword Paper Cut*. More about manuscript assessment and Michelle's take on editing and writing can be found at http://michelleelvy.com.

Gloria Garfunkel is a psychologist and writer with a Ph.D. from Harvard University in Psychology and Social Relations. A former psychotherapist, she has published many stories in literary journals and anthologies.

Teresa Burns Gunther has had fiction and nonfiction appear in numerous literary journals and most recently in *Northwind Magazine*, *Bookslut* and *Best New Writing 2012*. Teresa is the Editor of *The Lakeside*, an online literary magazine, and she founded Lakeshore Writers Workshop in Oakland, California where she leads creative writing workshops and classes and works one–on–one with writers. You can find links to her work at http://www.teresaburnsgunther.com/.

Gill Hoffs lives with her family and an ever–dwindling supply of Nutella in the North of England. Find Gill on Facebook or as @gillhoffs on twitter, email her a dirty joke at gillhoffs@hotmail.co.uk, or leave a clean comment at http://gillhoffs.wordpress.com/. *Wild: a collection* is out now from *Pure Slush Books*. Her non–fiction book *The Sinking of RMS Tayleur: the Lost Story of the Victorian Titanic* is out now from *Pen & Sword*. Feel free to send her chocolate.

Joanne Jagoda of Oakland, California, took an inspiring writing workshop after retiring in 2009, and launched on a long–postponed creative writing journey. Since discovering her passion for writing, she has worked non–stop on short stories, poetry and non–fiction. Her work has appeared in a number of e–zines and print anthologies, including *Pure Slush* and *Idea Gems Magazine*, and she was a poet of the month for a Jewish news weekly in Northern California. When not taking writing and poetry classes, Joanne enjoys being a writer–coach for ninth graders, Zumba, and visiting her three grandchildren in Jerusalem.

Len Kuntz is a writer from Washington State and an editor at the online literary magazine *Metazen*. His work appears widely in print and online. Find him at http://lenkuntz.blogspot.com.

Sally–Anne Macomber was born and raised in Toronto, Canada, and studied journalism at Concordia University in Montreal. Her work on high fashion and the demise of haute couture has appeared in various online and print publications in both Europe and North America. She turned to writing flash fiction in 2010, and hasn't looked back.

Jessica McHugh is an author of speculative fiction that spans the genre from horror and alternate history to epic fantasy. A member of the Horror Writers Association and a 2013 Pulp Ark nominee, she has devoted herself to novels, short stories, poetry, and playwriting. Jessica has had thirteen books published in five years, including the bestselling *Rabbits in the Garden*, *The Sky: The World* and the gritty coming–of–age thriller, *PINS*. More info on her speculations and publications can be found at http://www.jessicamchughbooks.com.

Gwendolyn Joyce Mintz is a fiction writer and aspiring photographer. Her work has appeared in various online and print publications. In other incarnations, Mintz is a writing instructor, a teddy bear maker and somebody's grandmother.

h. l. nelson is Founding Editor/Executive Director of *Cease, Cows* lit mag and a former sidewalk mannequin. Pub credits: *PANK*, *Hobart*, *Connotation Press*, *Metazen*, *Drunk Monkeys*, *Red Fez*, *Bartleby Snopes*. She's also editing an anthology which includes stories by Aimee Bender, Roxane Gay, Lindsay Hunter and other fierce women writers. Her MFA is currently kicking her ass. Tell her what you're wearing: heather@hlnelson.com.

Mandy Nicol grew up in Melbourne, Australia and made a tree change to country Victoria in the mid–nineties – the decade, not her age. She has various animals including a flockette of pet sheep that are thankful for her vegaquarian habits. She writes short stories and loves flash fiction. *Pure Slush* is the first venue to publish her work.

Derek Osborne lives in eastern Pennsylvania. His work has appeared in *Boston Literary Magazine, Bartleby Snopes, Literary Orphans, The Linnet's Wings, Pure Slush* and many others. To read more visit http://gertrudesflat.blogspot.com, or email him at derekosborne1@gmail.com.

Vanessa Weibler Paris lives in Erie, Pa., with a guy, a girl, a boy, a bunny rabbit and a dog. She writes things both real (for work) and pretend (for fun). Her favorite things include hot peppers, bad puns, small–world stories, and tales with a twist at the end.

Gary Percesepe is Associate Editor at *New World Writing* (formerly *Mississippi Review*) and a Contributor at *The Nervous Breakdown*. Author of four books in philosophy, Percesepe's poetry, fiction, essays, and interviews have appeared in *Story Quarterly, N + 1, Salon, Mississippi Review, The Millions, Brevity, PANK, Metazen, The Brooklyner,* and other places. His collection of short stories, *Why I Did the Grocery Girl,* is forthcoming from Aqueous Books. His poetry collection *falling* and his flash fiction collection *itch* were published by *Pure Slush Books* in late 2013. He has taught at Saint Louis University, Wittenberg University, and University of Dayton. He lives in Buffalo, New York.

Matt Potter is an Australian–born writer who keeps a part of his psyche in Berlin. Matt has been published in various places online, and he is, rather amazingly, also the founding editor of

Pure Slush. You can find more of his work at his website: http://mattcpotter.webs.com/.

Darryl Price was born in Kentucky and educated at Thomas More College. A founding member of L. Jack Roth's Yellow Pages Poets, he has published dozens of chapbooks, and his poems have appeared in many journals. He currently edits *Olentangy Review* with his wife Melissa.

Stephen V. Ramey is an American author from New Castle, Pennsylvania. His work has appeared in many places, including *The Doctor TJ Eckleburg Review*, *The Journal of Compressed Creative Arts*, and *A Capella Zoo*. *Glass Animals*, his first collection of (very) short fiction is available from *Pure Slush Books*. Find him and more of his work at his website: http://www.stephenvramey.com.

Shane Simmons is a self–confessed coffee shop writer who believes that regardless of quality, each paragraph penned should be rewarded with sweet treats (cake, muffins, Belgian waffles, etc). London–born, he ran away to Glasgow ten years ago. Since then he has expanded his waistline and he now blogs at http://scribblingsimmons.wordpress.com/.

Kimberlee Smith is a writer whose poetry, essays, fiction, and creative nonfiction have been published in numerous literary journals and anthologies. She was awarded a residency to the Jentel Arts Program in 2013. She lives with her two daughters, two dogs, three cats, two rabbits, and nine chooks on her farm in rural Connecticut. She received her MA in English from the University of Sydney, a certificate in the Creative Writing Program through UCLA, and her BA in Journalism from the University of Southern California. She is enrolled currently in post–graduate studies at Columbia University in New York. She can do a headstand on a trampoline, kill a chook, and make hard cider from the apples in her orchard.

Andrew Stancek was born in Bratislava and saw Russian tanks occupying his homeland. His dreams of circuses and ice cream, flying and lion–taming, miracle and romance have appeared recently in print in *LA Review, Windsor Review* and *New Sun Rising: Stories for Japan*. Among the many online publications featuring his work are *Every Day Fiction, Gemini Magazine* (Flash Fiction Contest Grand Prize Winner), *fwriction, r.kv.r.y. quarterly literary journal, Tin House, Flash Fiction Chronicles, The Linnet's Wings, Connotation Press, THIS Literary Magazine, LA Review, Windsor Review, Thrice Fiction Magazine, New Sun Rising,* and *Pure Slush*.

Susan Tepper is the author of four published books of fiction and a chapbook of poetry. Her most recent title *The Merrill Diaries (Pure Slush Books,* July 2013) is a Novel in Stories that follow a young woman's adventures in love and lust on two continents, spanning a decade. Tepper has received nine Pushcart nominations, and one for the Pulitzer Prize in fiction. You can visit her website here: http://www.susantepper.com.

Nathaniel Tower lives in the Twin Cities with his wife and daughter. After teaching high school English for nine years, he decided to pursue a career in writing / publishing / editing. His fiction has appeared in over two hundred online and print journals. His first collection of fiction, *Nagging Wives, Foolish Husbands,* was released in 2013 through *Martian Lit*. Nathaniel is the founding and managing editor of *Bartleby Snopes Literary Magazine and Press*. Find out more about Nathaniel at http://nathanieltower.wordpress.com.

Townsend Walker lives in San Francisco. His stories have been published in over fifty literary journals and included in seven anthologies. One story won the SLO NightWriters story contest. Two were nominated for the PEN / O. Henry Award. Four were performed at the New Short Fiction Series in Hollywood. He is associate editor at *Grey Sparrow Journal*. During a career in finance he published three books, on foreign exchange, derivatives and portfolio management. Educated at Georgetown, NYU and Stanford, find his website at http://www.townsendwalker.com.

Michael Webb is continually surprised anyone is interested in what he has to say, and he blogs occasionally at http://innocentsaccidentshints.blogspot.com.

Other 2014 compendiums
from Pure Slush

April May June 2014 July Aug Sept 2014 Oct Nov Dec 2014
ISBN: 978−1−925101−46−1   ISBN: 978−1−925101−47−8   ISBN: 978−1−925101−48−5

For the complete catalogue of
fiction and non−fiction
print books and eBooks
visit the Pure Slush Store at
http://pureslush.webs.com/store.htm